The Mystery Q

Fergus Hume

Alpha Editions

This edition published in 2024

ISBN : 9789361474989

Design and Setting By
Alpha Editions
www.alphaedis.com
Email - info@alphaedis.com

As per information held with us this book is in Public Domain.
This book is a reproduction of an important historical work. Alpha Editions uses the best technology to reproduce historical work in the same manner it was first published to preserve its original nature. Any marks or number seen are left intentionally to preserve its true form.

Contents

CHAPTER I .... - 1 -
CHAPTER II .... - 10 -
CHAPTER III .... - 19 -
CHAPTER IV .... - 29 -
CHAPTER V .... - 38 -
CHAPTER VI .... - 47 -
CHAPTER VII .... - 56 -
CHAPTER VIII .... - 66 -
CHAPTER IX .... - 75 -
CHAPTER X .... - 84 -
CHAPTER XI .... - 93 -
CHAPTER XII .... - 102 -
CHAPTER XIII .... - 111 -
CHAPTER XIV .... - 121 -
CHAPTER XV .... - 130 -
CHAPTER XVI .... - 139 -
CHAPTER XVII .... - 148 -
CHAPTER XVIII .... - 157 -
CHAPTER XIX .... - 166 -
CHAPTER XX .... - 176 -
CHAPTER XXI .... - 186 -

CHAPTER I

A STRANGE VISITOR

"A penny for your thoughts, dad," cried Lillian, suppressing a school-girl desire to throw one of the nuts on her plate at her father and rouse him from his brown study.

Sir Charles Moon looked up with a start, and drew his bushy gray eye-brows together. "Some people would give more than that to know them, my dear."

"What sort of people?" asked the young man who sat beside Lillian, industriously cracking nuts for her consumption.

"Dangerous people," replied Sir Charles grimly, "very dangerous, Dan."

Mrs. Bolstreath, fat, fair, and fifty, Lillian's paid companion and chaperon, leaned back complacently. She had enjoyed an excellent dinner: she was beautifully dressed: and shortly she would witness the newest musical comedy; three very good reasons for her amiable expression. "All people are dangerous to millionaires," she remarked, pointing the compliment at her employer, "since all people enjoy life with wealth, and wish to get the millionaire's money honestly or dishonestly."

"The people you mention have failed to get mine, Mrs. Bolstreath," was the millionaire's dry response.

"Of course I speak generally and not of any particular person, Sir Charles."

"I am aware of it," he answered, nodding and showed a tendency to relapse into his meditation, but that his daughter raised her price for confession.

"A sixpence for your thoughts, dad, a shilling--ten shillings--then one pound, you insatiable person."

"My kingdom for an explicit statement," murmured Dan, laying aside the crackers. "Lillian, my child, you must not eat any more nuts or you will be having indigestion."

"I believe dad has indigestion already."

"Some people will have it very badly before I am done with them," said Sir Charles, not echoing his daughter's laughter; then, to prevent further questions being asked, he addressed himself to the young man. "How are things going with you, Halliday?"

When Sir Charles asked questions thus stiffly, Dan knew that he was not too well pleased, and guessed the reason, which had to do with Lillian, and with Lillian's friendly attitude towards a swain not overburdened with money--to wit, his very own self--who replied diplomatically. "Things are going up with me, sir, if you mean aeroplanes."

"Frivolous! Frivolous!" muttered the big man seriously, "as a well-educated young man who wants money, you should aim at higher things."

"He aims at the sun," said Lillian gaily, "how much higher do you expect him to aim, dad?"

"Aiming at the sun is he?" said Moon heavily, "h'm! he'll be like that classical chap who flew too high and came to smash."

"Do you mean Icarus or Phaeton, Sir Charles?" asked Mrs. Bolstreath, who, having been a governess, prided herself upon exceptional knowledge.

"I don't know which of the two, perhaps one, perhaps both. But he flew in an aeroplane like Dan here, and came to grief."

"Oh!" Lillian turned distinctly pale. "I hope, Dan, you won't come to grief."

Before the guest could reply, Sir Charles reassured his daughter. "Naught was never in danger," he said, still grim and unsmiling, "don't trouble, Lillian, my dear. Dan won't come to grief in that way, although he may in another."

Lillian opened her blue eyes and stared while young Halliday grew crimson and fiddled with the nut-shells. "I don't know what you mean, dad?" said the girl after a puzzled pause.

"I think Dan does," rejoined her father, rising and pushing back his chair slowly. He looked at his watch, "Seven-thirty; you have plenty of time to see your play, which does not begin until nine," he added, walking towards the door. "Mrs. Bolstreath, I should like to speak with you."

"But, dad----"

"My dear Lillian, I have no time to wait. There is an important appointment at nine o'clock here, and afterwards I must go to the House. Go and enjoy yourself, but don't"--here his stern gray eyes rested on Dan's bent head in a significant way--"don't be foolish. Mrs. Bolstreath," he beckoned, and left the room.

"Oh!" sighed the chaperon-governess-companion, for she was all three, a kind of modern Cerebus, guarding the millionaire's child. "I thought it would come to this!" and she also looked significantly at Halliday before she vanished to join her employer.

Lillian stared at the closed door through which both her father and Mrs. Bolstreath had passed, and then looked at Dan, sitting somewhat disconsolately at the disordered dinner-table. She was a delicately pretty girl of a fair, fragile type, not yet twenty years of age, and resembled a shepherdess of Dresden china in her dainty perfection. With her pale golden hair, and rose-leaf complexion, arrayed in a simple white silk frock with snowy pearls round her slender neck, she looked like a wraith of faint mist. At least Dan fancifully thought so, as he stole a glance at her frail beauty, or perhaps she was more like a silver-point drawing, exquisitely fine. But whatever image love might find to express her loveliness, Dan knew in his hot passion that she was the one girl in the world for him. Lillian Halliday was a much better name for her than Lillian Moon.

Dan himself was tall and slim, dark and virile, with a clear-cut, clean-shaven face suggestive of strength and activity. His bronzed complexion showed an open-air life, while the eagle look in his dark eyes was that new vast-distance expression rapidly being acquired by those who devote themselves to aviation. No one could deny Dan's good looks or clean life, or daring nature, and he was all that a girl could desire in the way of a fairy prince. But fathers do not approve of fairy princes unless they come laden with jewels and gold. To bring such to Lillian was rather like taking coals to Newcastle since her father was so wealthy; but much desires more, and Sir Charles wanted a rich son-in-law. Dan could not supply this particular adjective, and therefore--as he would have put it in the newest slang of the newest profession--was out of the fly. Not that he intended to be, in spite of Sir Charles, since love can laugh at stern fathers as easily as at bolts and bars. And all this time Lillian stared at the door, and then at Dan, and then at her plate, putting two and two together. But in spite of her feminine intuition, she could not make four, and turned to her lover--for that Dan was, and a declared lover too--for an explanation. "What does dad mean?" Dan raised his handsome head and laughed as grimly as Sir Charles had done earlier. "He means that I shan't be asked to dinner any more."

"Why? You have done nothing."

"No; but I intend to do something."

"What's that?" Dan glanced at the closed door and seeing that there was no immediate chance of butler or footmen entering took her in his arms. "Marry you," he whispered between two kisses. "There's no intention about that," pouted the girl; "we have settled that ever so long ago."

"So your father suspects, and for that reason he is warning Mrs. Bolstreath."

"Warning the dragon," said Miss Moon, who used the term quite in an affectionate way, "why, the dragon is on our side."

"I daresay your father guesses as much. For that reason I'll stake my life that he is telling her at this moment she must never let us be together alone after this evening. After all, my dear, I don't see why you should look at me in such a puzzled way. You know well enough that Sir Charles wants you to marry Curberry."

"Marry Lord Curberry," cried Lillian, her pale skin coloring to a deep rose hue; "why I told dad I wouldn't do that." "Did you tell dad that you loved me?"

"No. There's no need to," said the girl promptly. Dan coughed drily. "I quite agree with you," he said rising, "there's no need to, since every time I look at you, I give myself away. But you surely understand, darling, that as I haven't a title and I haven't money, I can't have you. Hothouse grapes are for the rich and not for a poor devil like me."

"You might find a prettier simile," laughed Lillian, not at all discomposed, although she now thoroughly understood the meaning of her father's abrupt departure with Mrs. Bolstreath. Then she rose and took Dan by the lapels of his coat, upon which he promptly linked her to himself by placing both arms round her waist. "Dearest," she said earnestly, "I shall marry you and you only. We have been brought up more or less together, and we have always loved one another. Dad was your guardian: you have three hundred a year of your own, and if we marry dad can give us plenty, and----"

"I know all that," interrupted Halliday, placing her arms round his neck, "and it is just because Sir Charles knows also, that he will never consent to our marriage. I knew what was in the wind weeks ago, darling heart, and every day I have been expecting what has occurred to-night. For that reason, I have come here as often as possible and have arranged for you and the dragon to go to the theatre to-night. But, believe me, Lillian, it will be for the last time. To-morrow I shall receive a note saying that I am to stay away from Lord Curberry's bride."

"I'm not his bride and I never shall be," stamped Lillian, and the tears came into her pretty eyes, whereupon Dan, as a loyal lover, wiped them away with his pocket-handkerchief tenderly, "and--and--" she faltered. "And--and--" he mocked, knowing her requirements, which led him to console her with a long and lingering kiss. "Oh!" he sighed and Lillian, nestling in his arms, echoed the sigh. The moment of perfect understanding and perfect love held them until the sudden opening of the door placed Dan on one side of the table and Lillian on the other. "It won't do, my dears," said the new-comer, who was none other than Mrs. Bolstreath, flaming with wrath, but not, as the lovers found later, at them. "I know quite well that Dan hasn't wasted his time in this league-divided wooing."

"We thought that one of the servants----" began the young man, when Mrs. Bolstreath interrupted. "Well, and am I not one of the servants? Sir Charles has reminded me of the fact three times with the information that I am not worth my salt, much less the good table he keeps."

"Oh! Bolly dear," and Lillian ran to the stout chaperon to embrace her with many kisses, "was dad nasty?"

"He wasn't agreeable," assented Mrs. Bolstreath, fanning herself with her handkerchief, for the interview had heated her. "You can't expect him to be, my sweet, when his daughter loves a pauper." "Thank you," murmured Dan bowing, "but don't you think it is time we went to the theatre, Bolly dear."

"You must not be so familiar, young man," said the chaperon, broadly smiling at the dark handsome face. "Sir Charles wants Lillian to marry----"

"Then I shan't!" Lillian stamped again, "I hate Lord Curberry." "And you love Dan!"

"Don't be so familiar, young woman," said Halliday, in a joking way, "unless you are on our side, that is."

"If I were not on your side," rejoined Mrs. Bolstreath, majestically, "I should be the very dragon Lillian calls me. After all, Dan, you *are* poor."

"Poor, but honest."

"Worse and worse. Honest people never grow rich. And then you have such a dangerous profession, taking people flying trips in those aeroplanes. One never can be sure if you will be home to supper. I'm sure Lillian would not care to marry a husband who was uncertain about being home for supper."

"I'll marry Dan," said Lillian, and embraced Dan, who returned the embrace. "Children! Children!" Mrs. Bolstreath raised her hands in horror, "think of what you are doing. The servants may be in at any moment. Come to the drawing-room and have coffee. The motor-car is waiting and --hush, separate, separate," cried the chaperon, "someone is coming!" She spoke truly, for the lovers had just time to fly asunder when Sir Charles's secretary entered swiftly. He was a lean, tall, haggard-looking young fellow of thirty with a pallid complexion and scanty light hair. A thin moustache half concealed a weak mouth, and he blinked his eyes in a nervous manner when he bowed to the ladies and excused his presence. "Sir Charles left his spectacles here," he said in a soft and rather unsteady voice, "he sent me for them and----" he had glided to the other side of the table by this time--"oh, here they are. The motor-car waits, Miss Moon."

"Where is my father?" asked Lillian irrelevantly. "Tell me, Mr. Penn."

"In the library, Miss Moon," said the secretary glibly, "but he cannot see any one just now--not even you, Miss Moon."

"Why not?"

"He is waiting to interview an official from Scotland Yard--a Mr. Durwin on important business."

"You see," murmured Dan to Lillian in an undertone, "your father intends to lock me up for daring to love you." Miss Moon took no notice. "What is the business?" she asked sharply. "Indeed, I don't know, Miss Moon. It is strictly private. Sir Charles has related nothing to me. And if you will excuse me--if you don't mind--these spectacles are wanted and----" he babbled himself out of the room, while Mrs. Bolstreath turned on her charge. "You don't mean to say, you foolish child, that you were going to see your father about 'this'!" she indicated Halliday. "I don't care about being called a 'this'!" said Dan, stiffly. Neither lady noticed the protest. "I want to make it clear to my father as soon as possible, that I shall marry Dan and no one else," declared Lillian, pursing up her pretty mouth obstinately. "Then take him at the right moment," retorted Mrs. Bolstreath crossly, for the late interview had tried even her amiable temper. "Just now he is seething with indignation that an aviator should dare to raise his eyes to you."

"Aviators generally look down," said Dan flippantly; "am I to be allowed to take you and Lillian to the theatre this evening?"

"Yes. Although Sir Charles mentioned that you would do better to spend your money on other things than mere frivolity." "Oh!" said Halliday with a shrug, "as to that, this particular frivolity is costing me nothing. I got the box from Freddy Laurance, who is on that very up-to-date newspaper *The Moment* as a reporter. I have dined at my future father-in-law's expense, and now I go in his motor-car without paying for the trip. I don't see that my pleasures could cost me less. Even Sir Charles must be satisfied with such strict economy."

"Sir Charles will be satisfied with nothing save a promise for you to go away and leave Lillian alone," said Mrs. Bolstreath, sadly, "he has no feeling of romance such as makes me foolish enough to encourage a pauper."

"You called me that before," said Dan, coolly, "well, there's no getting over facts. I am a pauper, but I love Lillian."

"And I--" began Lillian, advancing, only to be waved back and prevented from speaking further by Mrs. Bolstreath. "Don't make love before my very eyes," she said crossly, "after all I am paid to keep you two apart, and--and--well, there's no time for coffee, so we had better finish the discussion in the car. There is plenty of time between Hampstead and the Strand to allow of a long argument. And remember, Dan," Mrs. Bolstreath turned at the door to shake her finger, "this is your last chance of uninterrupted conversation with Lillian."

"Let us make honey while the flowers bloom," whispered Halliday, poetically, and stole a final and hasty kiss before he led the girl after the amiable dragon, who had already left the room. The lovers found her talking to a poorly-dressed and rather stout female clothed in rusty mourning, who looked the picture of decent but respectable poverty. The entrance door stood open, and the waiting motor-car could be seen at the steps, while the footman stood near Mrs. Bolstreath, watching her chatting to the stranger and wearing an injured expression. It seemed that the decent woman wished to see Sir Charles, and the footman had refused her admission since his master was not to be disturbed. The woman--she called herself Mrs. Brown and was extremely tearful--had therefore appealed to the dragon, who was explaining that she could do nothing. "Oh, but I am sure you can get Sir Charles Moon to see me, my lady," wailed Mrs. Brown with a dingy handkerchief to her red eyes, "my son has been lost overboard off one of those steamers Sir Charles owns, and I want to ask him to give me some money. My son was my only support, and now I am starving." Lillian knew that her father owned a number of tramp steamers, which picked up cargoes all over the world, and saw no reason why the woman should not have the interview since her son had been drowned while in Moon's service. The hour was certainly awkward, since Sir Charles had an appointment before he went down to the House. But a starving woman and a sorrowful woman required some consideration so she stepped forward hastily and touched Mrs. Brown's rusty cloak. "I shall ask my father to see you," she said quickly, "wait here!" and without consulting Mrs. Bolstreath she went impulsively to her father's study, while Mrs. Brown dabbed her eyes with her handkerchief and called down blessings on her young head. Dan believed the story of the lost son, but doubted the tale of starvation as Mrs. Brown looked too stout to have been without food for any length of time. He looked hard at her face, which was more wrinkled than a fat woman's should be; although such lines might be ascribed to grief. She wept profusely and was so overcome with sorrow that she let down a ragged veil when she saw Dan's eager gaze. The young gentleman, she observed, could not understand a mother's feelings, or he would not make a show of her by inquisitorial glances. The remark was somewhat irrelevant, and the action of letting down the veil unnecessary, but much might be pardoned to a woman so obviously afflicted. Dan was about to excuse his inquiring looks, when Lillian danced back with the joyful information that her father would see Mrs. Brown for a few minutes if she went in at once. "And I have asked him to help you," said the girl, patting the tearful woman's shoulder, as she passed to the motor-car. "Oh! it's past eight o'clock. Dan, we'll never be in time."

"The musical comedy doesn't begin until nine," Halliday assured her, and in a few minutes the three of them were comfortably seated in the luxurious car, which whirled at break-neck speed towards the Strand. Of course Lillian and Dan took every advantage of the opportunity, seeing that Mrs. Bolstreath was sympathetic enough to close her eyes to their philanderings. They talked all the way to the Curtain Theatre; they talked all through the musical comedy; and talked all the way back to the house at Hampstead. Mrs. Bolstreath, knowing that the young couple would not have another opportunity for uninterrupted love-making, and being entirely in favor of the match, attended to the stage and left them to whisper unreproved. She did not see why Dan, whom Lillian had loved since the pair had played together as children, should be set aside in favor of a dry-as-dust barrister, even though he had lately come into a fortune and a title. "But, of course," said Mrs. Bolstreath between the facts, "if you could only invent a perfect flying-machine, they would make you a duke or something and give you a large income. Then you could marry."

"What are you talking about, Bolly darling?" asked Lillian, much puzzled, as she could not be supposed to know what was going on inside her friend's head. "About you and Dan, dear. He has no money and----"

"I shall make heaps and heaps of money," said Dan, sturdily; "aviation is full of paying possibilities, and the nation that first obtains command of the air will rule the world. I'm no fool!"

"You're a commoner," snapped Mrs. Bolstreath quickly, "and unless, as I said, you are made a duke for inventing a perfect aeroplane, Lord Curberry is certainly a better match for Lillian."

"He's as dull as tombs," said Miss Moon with her pretty nose in the air. "You can't expect to have everything, my dear child."

"I can expect to have Dan," retorted Lillian decidedly, whereat Dan whispered sweet words and squeezed his darling's gloved hand. "Well," said Mrs. Bolstreath, as the curtain rose on the second act, "I'll do my best to help you since I believe in young love and true love. Hush, children, people are looking! Attend to the stage." Dan and Lillian did their best to follow her advice and sat demurely in their stalls side by side, watching the heroine flirt in a duet with the hero, both giving vent to their feelings in a lively musical number. But they really took little interest in "The Happy Bachelor!" as the piece was called, in spite of the pretty girls and the charming music and the artistic dresses and the picturesque scenery. They were together and that was all they cared about, and although a dark cloud of parental opposition hovered over them, they were not yet enveloped in its gloom. And after all, since Mrs. Bolstreath was strongly prejudiced in their favor, Lillian hoped that she might induce Sir Charles to change his mind as regards Lord

Curberry. He loved his daughter dearly and would not like to see her unhappy, as she certainly would be if compelled to marry any one but Dan. Lillian said this to Mrs. Bolstreath and to Dan several times on the way home, and they entirely agreed with her. "Although I haven't much influence with Sir Charles," Mrs. Bolstreath warned them, "and he is fond of having his own way."

"He always does what I ask," said Lillian confidently. "Why, although he was so busy this evening he saw Mrs. Brown when I pleaded for her."

"He couldn't resist you," whispered Dan fondly, "no one could." Mrs. Bolstreath argued this point, saying that Lillian was Sir Charles's daughter, and fathers could not be expected to feel like lovers. She also mentioned that she was jeopardizing her situation by advocating the match, which was certainly a bad one from a financial point of view, and would be turned out of doors as an old romantic fool. The lovers assured her she was the most sensible of women and that if she was turned out of doors they would take her in to the cottage where they proposed to reside like two turtle doves. Then came laughter and kisses and the feeling that the world was not such a bad place after all. It was a very merry trio that alighted at the door of Moon's great Hampstead mansion. Then came a shock, the worse for being wholly unexpected. At the door the three were met by Marcus Penn, who was Moon's secretary. He looked leaner and more haggard than ever, and his general attitude was that of the bearer of evil news. Dan and Lillian and Mrs. Bolstreath stared at him in amazement. "You may as well know the worst at once, Miss Moon," said Penn, his lips quivering with nervousness, "your father is dead. He has been murdered."

CHAPTER II

A COMPLETE MYSTERY

It was Mrs. Bolstreath who carried Lillian upstairs in her stout arms, for when Penn made his brusque announcement the girl fainted straight away, which was very natural considering the horror of the information. Dan remained behind to tell the secretary that he was several kinds of fool, since no one but a superfine ass would blurt out so terrible a story to a delicate girl. Not that Penn had told his story, for Lillian had become unconscious the moment her bewildered brain grasped that the father she had left a few hours earlier in good health and spirits was now a corpse. But he told it to Dan, and mentioned that Mr. Durwin was in the library wherein the death had taken place. "Mr. Durwin? Who is Mr. Durwin?" asked Dan trying to collect his senses, which had been scattered by the dreadful news. "An official from Scotland Yard; I told you so after dinner," said Penn in an injured tone, "he came to see Sir Charles by appointment at nine o'clock and found him a corpse."

"Sir Charles was alive when we left shortly after eight," remarked Dan sharply; "at a quarter-past eight to be precise. What took place in the meantime?"

"Obviously the violent death of Sir Charles," faltered the secretary. "What evidence have you to show that he died by violence?" asked Halliday. "Mr. Durwin called in a doctor, and he says that Sir Charles had been poisoned," blurted out Penn uneasily. "I believe that woman--Mrs. Brown she called herself--poisoned him. She left the house at a quarter to nine, so the footman says, for he let her out, and----"

"It is impossible that a complete stranger should poison Sir Charles," interrupted Dan impatiently, "she would not have the chance."

"She was alone with Sir Charles for thirty minutes, more or less," said Penn tartly; "she had every chance and she took it."

"But how could she induce Sir Charles to drink poison?"

"She didn't induce him to drink anything. The doctor says that the scratch at the back of the dead man's neck----"

"Here!" Dan roughly pushed the secretary aside, becoming impatient of the scrappy way in which he detailed what had happened. "Let me go to the library for myself and see what has happened. Sir Charles can't be dead."

"It's twelve o'clock now," retorted Penn stepping aside, "and he's been dead quite three hours, as the doctor will tell you." Before the man finished his sentence, Dan, scarcely grasping the situation, so rapidly had it evolved, ran through the hall, towards the back of the spacious house, where the library was situated. He dashed into the large and luxuriously furnished room and collided with a police officer, who promptly took him by the shoulder. There were three other men in the room, who turned from the corpse at which they were looking, when they heard the noise of Halliday's abrupt entrance. The foremost man, and the one who spoke first, was short and stout and arrayed in uniform, with cold gray eyes, and a hard mouth. "What's this--what's this?" he demanded in a raucous voice. "Who are you?"

"My name is Halliday," said Dan hurriedly. "I am engaged to Miss Moon and we have just returned from the theatre to hear--to hear----" He caught sight of Moon's body seated in the desk-chair and drooping limply over the table. "Oh, it is true, then! He is dead. Good heavens! who murdered him?"

"How do you know that Sir Charles has been murdered?" asked the officer sternly. "Mr. Penn, the secretary, told me just now in the hall," said Dan, shaking himself free of the policeman. "He blurted it out like a fool, and Miss Moon has fainted. Mrs. Bolstreath has taken her upstairs. But how did it come about? Who found the body, and----"

"I found the body," interrupted one of the other men, who was tall and calm-faced, with a bald head and a heavy iron-gray moustache, perfectly clothed in fashionable evening-dress, and somewhat imperious in his manner of speaking. "I had an appointment with Sir Charles at nine o'clock and came here to find him, as you now see him"--he waved his hand toward the desk--"the doctor will tell you how he died."

"By poison," said the third man, who was dark, young, unobtrusive and retiring in manner. "You see this deep scratch on the back of the neck. In that way the poison was administered. I take it that Sir Charles was bending over his desk and the person who committed the crime scratched him with some very sharp instrument impregnated with poison."

"Mrs. Brown!" gasped Dan, staring at the heavy, swollen body of his late guardian, whom he had dined with in perfect health. The three men glanced at one another as he said the name, and even the policeman on guard at the door looked interested. The individual in uniform spoke with his cold eyes on Dan's agitated face. "What do you know of Mrs. Brown, Mr. Halliday?" he demanded abruptly. "Don't you know that a woman of that name called here?"

"Yes. The secretary, Mr. Penn, told us that Miss Moon induced her father to see a certain Mrs. Brown, who claimed that her son had been drowned while working on one of the steamers owned by Sir Charles. You saw her also, I believe?"

"I was in the hall when Miss Moon went to induce her father to see the poor woman. That was about a quarter-past eight o'clock."

"And Mrs. Brown--as we have found from inquiry--left the house at a quarter to nine. Do you think she is guilty?"

"I can't say. Didn't the footman see the body--that is if Mrs. Brown committed the crime--when he came to show her out? Sir Charles would naturally ring his bell when the interview was over, and the footman would come to conduct her to the door."

"Sir Charles never rang his bell!" said the officer, drily. "Mrs. Brown passed through the entrance hall at a quarter to nine o'clock, and mentioned to the footman--quite unnecessarily, I think--that Sir Charles had given her money. He let her out of the house. Naturally, the footman not hearing any bell did not enter this room, nor--so far as any one else is concerned--did a single person. Only when Mr. Durwin----"

"I came at nine o'clock," interrupted the baldheaded man imperiously, "to keep my appointment. The footman told Mr. Penn, who took me to Sir Charles. He knocked but there was no answer, so he opened the door and we saw this." He again waved his hands towards the body. "Does Mr. Penn know nothing?" asked Halliday, doubtfully. "No," answered the other. "Inspector Tenson has questioned him carefully in my presence. Mr. Penn says that he brought Sir Charles his spectacles from the dining-room before you left for the theatre with the two ladies, and then was sent to his own room by his employer to write the usual letters. He remained there until nine o'clock when he was called out to receive me, and we know that Mr. Penn speaks truly, for the typewriting girl who was typing Sir Charles's letters to Mr. Penn's dictation, says that he did not leave the room all the time. "May I look at the body?" asked Dan approaching the desk, and, on receiving an affirmative reply from Durwin, bent over the dead. The corpse was much swollen, the face indeed being greatly bloated, while the deep scratch on the nape of the neck looked venomous and angry. Yet it was a slight wound to bring about so great a catastrophe, and the poison must have been very deadly and swift; deadly because apparently Sir Charles had no time to move before it did its work, and swift because he could not even have called for assistance, which he surely would have done had he been able to keep his senses. Dan mentioned this to the watchful doctor, who nodded. "I can't say for certain," he remarked cautiously, "but I fancy that snake-poison has been used. That will be seen to, when the post-mortem is made."

"And this fly?" Halliday pointed to an insect which was just behind the left ear of the dead man. "Fly!" echoed Inspector Tenson in surprise, and hastily advancing to look. "A fly in November. Impossible! Yet it is a fly, and dead. If not," he swept the neck of the corpse with his curved hand, "it would get away. H'm! Now I wonder what this means? Get me a magnifying glass." There was not much difficulty in procuring one, as such an article lay on the desk itself, being used, no doubt, by Sir Charles to aid his failing sight when he examined important documents. Tenson inspected the fly and removed it--took it to a near electric light and examined it. Then he came back and examined the place behind the left ear whence he had removed it. "It's been gummed on," he declared in surprise--a surprise which was also visible in the faces of the other men; "you can see the glistening spot on the skin, and the fly's legs are sticky." He balanced the fly on his little finger as he spoke. "I am sure they are sticky, although it is hard to say with such a small insect. However," he carefully put away the fly in a silver matchbox, "we'll have this examined under a more powerful glass. You are all witnesses, gentlemen, that a fly was found near the wound which caused Sir Charles Moon's death."

"And the scent? What about the scent?" Dan sniffed as he spoke and then bent his nose to the dead man. "It seems to come from his clothes."

"Scent!" echoed Durwin sharply and sniffed. "Yes, I observed that scent. But I did not take any notice of it."

"Nor did I," said the doctor. "I noticed it also."

"And I," followed on the Inspector, "and why should we take notice of it, Mr. Halliday? Many men use scent."

"Sir Charles never did," said Dan emphatically, "he hated scents of all kinds even when women used them. He certainly would never have used them himself. I'll swear to that."

"Then this scent assumes importance." Durwin sniffed again, and held his aquiline nose high. "It is fainter now. But I smelt it very strongly when I first came in and looked at the body. A strange perfume it is." The three men tried to realize the peculiar odor of the scent, and became aware that it was rich and heavy and sickly, and somewhat drowsy in its suggestion. "A kind of thing to render a man sleepy," said Dan, musingly. "Or insensible," said Inspector Tenson hastily, and put his nose to the dead man's chin and mouth. He shook his head as he straightened himself. "I fancied from your observation, Mr. Halliday, that the scent might have been used as a kind of chloroform, but there's no smell about the face. It comes from the clothes," he sniffed again, "yes, it certainly comes from the clothes. Did you smell this scent on Mrs. Brown?" he demanded suddenly. "No, I did not," admitted Halliday promptly, "otherwise I should certainly have noted it. I have a keen sense of smell. Mrs. Bolstreath and Lil--I mean Miss Moon--might have noticed it, however." At that moment, as if in answer to her name, the door opened suddenly and Lillian brushed past the policeman in a headlong entrance into the library. Her fair hair was in disorder, her face was bloodless, and her eyes were staring and wild. Behind her came Mrs. Bolstreath hurriedly, evidently trying to restrain her. But the girl would not be restrained, and rushed forward scattering the small group round the dead, to fling herself on the body. "Oh, father, father!" she sobbed, burying her face on the shoulder of her dearly-loved parent. "How awful it is. Oh, my heart will break. How shall I ever get over it. Father! father! father!" She wept and wailed so violently that the four men were touched by her great grief. Both Mr. Durwin and Inspector Tenson had daughters of their own, while the young doctor was engaged. They could feel for her thoroughly, and no one made any attempt to remove her from the body until Mrs. Bolstreath stepped forward. "Lillian, darling. Lillian, my child," she said soothingly, and tried to lead the poor girl away. But Lillian only clung closer to her beloved dead. "No! No! Let me alone. I can't leave him. Poor, dear father--oh, I shall die!"

"Dear," said Mrs. Bolstreath, raising her firmly but kindly, "your father is not there but in Heaven! Only the clay remains."

"It is all I have. And father was so good, so kind,--oh, who can have killed him in this cruel way?" She looked round with streaming eyes. "We think that a Mrs. Brown--" began the Inspector, only to be answered by a loud cry from the distraught girl. "Mrs. Brown! Then I have killed father! I have killed him! I persuaded him to see the woman, because she was in trouble. And she killed him--oh, the wretch--the--the--oh--oh! What had I done to her that she should rob me of my dear, kind father?" and she cried bitterly in her old friend's tender arms. "Had you ever seen Mrs. Brown before?" asked Durwin in his imperious voice, although he lowered it in deference to her grief. Lillian winced at the harsh sound. "No, No! I never saw her before. How could I have seen her before. She said that her son had been drowned, and that she was poor. I asked father to help her, and he told me he would. It's my fault that she saw my father and now"--her voice leaped an octave--"he's dead. Oh--oh! my father--my father!" and she tried to break from Mrs. Bolstreath's arms to fling herself on the dead once more. "Lillian darling, don't cry," said Dan, placing his hand on her shoulder. "You have not lost the dearest and best of fathers!" she sobbed violently. "Your loss is my loss," said Halliday in a voice of pain, "but we must be brave, both you and I." He associated himself with her so as to calm her grief. "It's not your fault that your dear father is dead."

"I persuaded him to see Mrs. Brown. And she--she--she----"

"We can't say if this woman is guilty, as yet," said Durwin hastily, "so do not blame yourself, Miss Moon. But did you smell any scent on this Mrs. Brown?" Lillian looked at him vacantly and shook her head. Then she burst once more into hard and painful sobbing, trying again to embrace the dead man. "Don't ask her any questions, sir," said Halliday, in a low voice to Mr. Durwin, "you see she is not in a fit state to reply. Lillian," he raised her up from her knees and gently but firmly detached her arms from the dead. "My darling, your father is past all earthly aid. We can do nothing but avenge him. Go with Mrs. Bolstreath and lie down. We must be firm."

"Firm! Firm!--and father dead!" wailed Lillian. "Oh, what a wretch that Mrs. Brown must be to kill him. Kill her, Dan--oh, make her suffer. My good, kind father, who--who--oh"--she flung herself on Dan's neck--"take me away; take me away!" and her lover promptly carried her to the door. Mrs. Bolstreath, who had been talking hurriedly to Inspector Tenson, came after the pair and took the girl from Dan. "She must lie down and have a sleeping-draught," she said softly. "If the doctor will come----" The doctor was only too glad to come. He was a young man beginning to practise medicine in the neighborhood, and had been hurriedly summoned in default of an older physician. The chance of gaining a new and wealthy patient was too good to lose, so he quickly followed Mrs. Bolstreath as she led the half-unconscious girl up the stairs. Dan closed the door and returned to the Inspector and the official from Scotland Yard. The former was speaking. "Mrs. Bolstreath did not smell any perfume on Mrs. Brown," he was saying, "and ladies are very quick to notice such things. Miss Moon also shook her head."

"I don't think Miss Moon was in a state of mind to understand what you were saying, Mr. Inspector," said Halliday, drily. "However, I am quite sure from my own observation that Mrs. Brown did not use the perfume. I would have noticed it at once, for I spotted it the moment I examined the body."

"So did I," said Durwin once more; "but I thought Sir Charles might have used it. You say he did not, therefore the scent is a clue." "It does not lead to the indictment of Mrs. Brown, however, sir," said Tenson thoughtfully, "since she had no perfume of that sort about her. But she must have killed Sir Charles, for she was the last person who saw him alive."

"She may come forward and exonerate herself," suggested Dan after a pause, "or she may have left her address with Sir Charles."

"I have glanced through the papers on the desk and can find no address," was the Inspector's reply; "yet, if she gave it to him, it would be there." Durwin meditated, then looked up. "As she was the mother of the man in Sir Charles's employment who was drowned," he said in his harsh voice, and now very official in his manner, "in the offices of the company who own the steamers--Sir Charles was a director and chief shareholder, I understand from his secretary, Mr. Penn--will be found the drowned man's address, which will be that of his mother."

"But I can't see what motive Mrs. Brown had to murder Sir Charles," remarked Dan in a puzzled tone. "We'll learn the motive when we find Mrs. Brown," said Tenson, who had made a note of Durwin's suggestion. "Many people think they have grievances against the rich, and we know that the late Sir Charles was a millionaire. He doubtless had enemies--dangerous enemies."

"Dangerous!" The word recalled to Dan what Moon had said at the dinner-table when Lillian had playfully offered him a penny for his thoughts. "Sir Charles at dinner said something about dangerous people."

"What did he say?" asked the Inspector and again opened his note-book. Dan reported the conversation, which was not very satisfactory as Moon had only spoken generally. Tenson noted down the few remarks, but did not appear to think them important. Durwin, however, was struck by what had been said. "Sir Charles asked me here to explain about a certain gang he believed was in existence," he remarked. "What's that, sir?" asked the Inspector alertly. "Did he tell you anything?"

"Of course he didn't. How could he when he was dead when I arrived," retorted Durwin with a frown. "He simply said that he wished to see me in my official capacity about some gang, but gave me no details. Those were to be left until I called here. He preferred to see me here instead of at my office for reasons which he declared he would state when we met in this room."

"Then you think that a gang----"

"Mr. Inspector," interrupted Durwin, stiffly, "I have told you all that was said by the deceased. Whether the gang is dangerous, or what the members do, or where they are, I cannot say. Have you examined those windows?" he asked suddenly, pointing to three French-windows at the side of the room. "Yes," said Tenson promptly, "as soon as I entered the apartment I did so. They are all locked."

"And if they were not, no one would enter there," put in Dan quickly. "Outside is a walled garden, and the wall is very high with broken bottles on top. I suppose, Mr. Durwin, you are thinking that some one may have come in to kill Sir Charles between the time of Mrs. Brown's departure and your coming?"

"Yes," assented the other sharply, "if the perfume is a clue, Mrs. Brown must be innocent. Penn, as we know from the statement of the typewriter girl, was in his room all the time, and the servants have fully accounted for themselves.

We examined them all--the Inspector and I did, that is--when you were at the theatre," he waved his hand with a shrug. "Who can say who is guilty?"

"Well," said Tenson, snapping the elastic band round his note-book and putting it into his pocket, "we have the evidence of the fly and of the perfume."

"What do you think about the fly?" asked Dan, staring. "I don't know what to think. It is an artificial fly, exquisitely made and has been gummed on the dead man's neck behind the left ear. The assassin must have placed it there, since a man would scarcely do such a silly thing himself. Why, it was placed there I can't say, any more than I can guess why Sir Charles was murdered, or who murdered him. The affair is a complete mystery, as you must admit." Before the inquest and after the inquest, more people than the three men who had held the discussion in the presence of the dead, admitted that the affair was a mystery. In fact the evidence at the inquest only plunged the matter into deeper gloom. Tenson, acting on Durwin's advice, sought the office of the tramp-steamer company--The Universal Carrier Line--in which the late Sir Charles was chief shareholder and director, to learn without any difficulty the whereabouts of Mrs. Brown, the mother of the drowned man. She proved to be an entirely different person to the woman who had given the name on the fatal night, being lean instead of stout, comparatively young instead of old, and rather handsome in an elderly way in place of being wrinkled and worn with grief. She declared that she had never been near Moon's house on the night of the murder, or on any other night. Mrs. Bolstreath, Lillian, the footman, and Dan all swore that she was not the Mrs. Brown who had sought the interview with Sir Charles. Therefore it was argued by every one that Mrs. Brown, taking a false name and telling a false story, must have come to see Moon with the deliberate intention of murdering him. Search was made for her, but she could not be found. From the moment she passed out of the front door she had vanished, and although a description was published of her appearance, and a reward was offered for her apprehension no one came forward to claim it. Guilty or innocent, she was invisible. Inspector Tenson did not speak at the inquest of the gang about which Sir Charles had intended to converse with Mr. Durwin, as it did not seem to have any bearing on the case. Also, as Durwin suggested, if it had any bearing it was best to keep the matter quiet until more evidence was forthcoming to show that such a gang--whatever its business was--existed. Then the strange episode of the fly was suppressed for the same reason. Privately, Tenson informed Dan that he would not be surprised to learn that there was a gang of murderers in existence whose sign-manual was a fly, real or artificial, and instanced another gang, which had been broken up some years previously, who always impressed the figure of a purple fern on their victim. But the whole idea, said Tenson, was so vague that he thought it best to suppress the fact of the artificial fly on the dead man's neck. "If there's anything in it," finished the Inspector, "there's sure to be other murders committed, and the fly placed on the victim. We'll wait and see, and if a second case occurs we'll be sure that such a gang exists and will collar the beasts. Best to say nothing, Mr. Halliday." So he said nothing, and Dan said nothing, and Durwin, who approved of the necessary secrecy, held his tongue. Of course there was a lot of talk and many theories as to who had murdered the millionaire, and why he had been murdered in so ingenious a manner. The postmortem examination proved that Moon had died of snake-poison administered through the scratch on the neck, and the circumstantial evidence at the inquest went to show that he must have been taken unawares, while bending over his desk. Some people thought that Mrs. Brown was innocent because of the absence of the perfume; others declared she must be guilty on account of her false name and false story, and the fact that Moon was found dead a quarter of an hour after she left the house. No doubt the circumstantial evidence was very strong, but it could not be said positively that the woman was guilty, even though she did not appear to defend her character. So the jury thought, for they brought in the only possible verdict twelve good and lawful men could bring in: "Wilful murder against some person or persons unknown," and there the matter ended for sheer want of further evidence. The affair was a mystery and a mystery it remained. "And will until the Day of Judgment!" said Tenson, finally.

CHAPTER III

DUTY BEFORE PLEASURE

The year ended sadly for Lillian, since she had lost her father, her lover, and her home; gaining instead the doubtful companionship of a paternal uncle, who stepped into the position of guardian. The girl, although she did not know it at the time, was leaving a pleasant flowery lane to turn into a flinty high road, arched by a dismal sky. It is true that she still possessed Mrs. Bolstreath to comfort her, but the loss of Dan could scarcely be compensated by the attentions of the chaperon. Not that Halliday was altogether lost; but he had been pushed out of her life by Sir John Moon, who approved as little of this suitor as the late baronet had done. "You see, my dear child," he exclaimed to Lillian, immediately after the New Year and when things were more restful, "as your guardian and uncle, I have to see that you make a good match." "What is marriage without love?" queried Miss Moon scornfully. "Love!" Sir John shrugged his elegant shoulders and sneered. "Love is all very well, but a title is better. I say nothing about money, as you have any amount of that useful article. Now, Lord Curberry----"

"I detest Lord Curberry, and I shan't marry Lord Curberry," interrupted Lillian, frowning, and her mind held a picture of the lean, ascetic peer with the cruel, grey eyes. As a barrister, Curberry was no doubt admirable; as a nobleman, he filled his new position very well; but she could not see him as a lover, try as she might. Not that she did try, for under no conditions and under no pressure did she intend to become his wife. "Your father wished you to marry Lord Curberry," hinted Uncle John softly. "My father wished me to be happy," cried Lillian hotly, "and I can't be happy unless I marry Dan."

"That aviator man! Pooh! He has nothing to give you."

"He gives himself, and that is all I want."

"I see. Love in a cottage and----" Lillian interrupted again. "There's no need for love in a cottage. I have plenty of money; you said as much yourself, Uncle John."

"My dear," said the new baronet gravely, "from what I saw of young Halliday he is too proud a man to live on his wife. And you would not respect him if he did. I think better of you than that, my child."

"Dan has his profession."

"H'm! And a dangerous one at that. Besides, he doesn't make much money."

"He will though. Dan is a genius; he has all kinds of ideas about flying machines, and some day he will conquer the air." "Meantime, you will be growing old waiting for him."

"Not at all," Lillian assured him. "I shall be with him, helping all I can."

"You won't with my consent," cried her uncle, heatedly. "Then I shall do without your consent. I shan't give up Dan."

"In that case," sighed Sir John, rising to show that the interview was ended--and certainly it had ended in a clash of wills--"there is nothing for me to do but to make young Halliday give you up."

"He'll never do that," said Miss Moon, pausing at the door with a fluttering heart, for her uncle spoke very decidedly. "Oh, I think so," replied Moon, with the air of a man sure of his ground. "He has, I am sure, some notion of honor."

"It isn't honorable to give up a woman."

"It isn't honorable to live on a woman." The two antagonists glared at one another, and a silence ensued. Neither would give way, and neither would compromise in any way. Lillian wanted Dan as her husband, a post Sir John did not intend the young man to fill. But he saw plainly enough that harsh measures would drive Lillian to desperation, and he did not yet know sufficient of Halliday to be sure that he would not grasp at a rich wife. Sir John believed that men were like himself, and would do anything--honorable, or, at a pinch, dishonorable--to secure a life of ease and comfort. However, as he swiftly reflected, Halliday was young, and probably would be wax in the hands of a clever man, such as Moon considered himself to be. It would be best to see him and control the boy's mind by appealing to his decency--so Sir John put it. "Very good, my dear," he said, when he reached this point, "matters are at a dead-lock between us. I suggest that you let me interview Halliday."

"I don't mind, so long as I see him first," pouted the girl, mutinously. Sir John smiled drily. "So as to arm him for the fray. Very well. I consent, my dear. You can arrange your campaign, and then I can discuss the matter with this very undesirable suitor. But you must give me your promise that you will not run away with him meanwhile?" Lillian held herself very erect and replied stiffly. "Of course I promise, Uncle John. I am not ashamed of loving Dan, and I shall marry him in a proper manner. But I shan't marry Lord Curberry," she ended, and fairly ran away, so as to prevent further objections. "Oh, my dear, I think you will," grinned Sir John at the closed door, and he sat down to pen a diplomatic letter to Mr. Halliday, as he wished to have the matter settled and done with. "These romantic young nuisances," said the schemer crossly. The new baronet was a slim, well-preserved dandy of sixty, who looked no older than forty-five owing to the means he took to keep himself fit. He was the younger and only brother of Moon, and inherited the title since there was no nephew to take it. He also inherited ten thousand a year for life on condition that he acted as Lillian's guardian. It was no mean task, for the girl had an income of £50,000 coming in every twelve months. There would be plenty of hard-up flies gathering round this honey-pot, and Sir John foresaw that it would not be an easy business to settle the young lady's matrimonial future, especially as the said young lady was obstinate beyond belief. Sir John, being a loafer by nature, had never possessed sufficient money to indulge to the full in his luxurious tastes, since his brother had not financed him as largely as he could have wished. But now that he was safe for the rest of his life on an income which would enable him to enjoy the world's goods, Sir John did not wish to be bothered. It was his aim to get his niece married and settled as soon as possible, so that she would be looked after by a husband. Under these circumstances, and since Lillian was anxious to marry Dan, it was strange that the baronet did not allow her to indulge her fancy. He did not for two reasons: one was that he really did not think Halliday a good match; and, moreover, knew of his late brother's opinion on the matter of the wooing. The second reason had to do with the fact that he had borrowed a large sum of money from Lord Curberry, and did not wish to pay it back again, even though he could do so easily enough in his present flourishing circumstances. Curberry offered to forego the payment if Sir John could persuade Lillian to marry him. And as Moon wanted to be able to talk about the girl as a peeress, and did not want to reduce his new income by frittering it away in paying back debts, he was determined to bring about the very desirable marriage, as he truly considered it to be. "Curberry is sure to go in for politics," thought the plotter, "and he has enough brains to become Prime Minister if he likes. He's got a decent income, too, and a very old title. With Lillian's money and beauty she should have a titled husband. Besides," this was an after-thought, "Curberry can make himself deuced disagreeable if he likes." And perhaps it was this last idea which made Sir John so anxious for the marriage to take place. The late Sir Charles had been a big, burly, broad-shouldered man, with a powerful clean-shaven face--the kind of overbearing, pushing personality which was bound to come up on top wherever men were congregated. And Sir Charles had massively pushed his way from poverty to affluence, from obscurity into notoriety, if not fame. Now his honors and wealth were in the hands of two people infinitely weaker than he had been. Lillian was but a delicate girl, solely bent upon marriage with an undesirable suitor, while Sir John had no desire to do anything with his new income and new title save to enjoy the goods which the gods had sent him so unexpectedly. He was by no means a strong man, being finical, self-indulgent, and quite feminine in his love for dress and luxury. Much smaller and slighter than his masterful brother, he was perfectly arrayed on all occasions in purple and fine linen; very self-possessed, very polite, and invariably quiet in his manner. He had several small talents, and indulged in painting, poetry, and music, producing specimens of each as weak and neatly finished as himself. He also collected china and stamps, old lace and jewels, which he loved for their color and glitter. Such a man was too fantastical to earn the respect of Lillian, who adored the strength, which showed itself in Dan. Consequently, she felt certain that she would be able to force him to consent to her desires. But in this, the girl, inexperienced in worldly matters and in human nature, reckoned without knowledge of Sir John's obstinacy, which was a singularly striking trait of the man's character. Like most weak people the new baronet loved to domineer, and, moreover, when his ease was at stake, he could be strong even to cruelty, since fear begets that quality as much as it fosters cowardice. Moon had removed Lillian and Mrs. Bolstreath to his new house in Mayfair, because it was not wise that the girl should remain at Hampstead, where everything served to remind her of the good father she had lost. Therefore, Sir John wished for no trouble to take place under his roof, as such--as he put it--would shatter his nerves. The mere fact that Lillian wished to marry young Halliday, and that Curberry wished to marry her, was a fruitful source of ills. It stands to Sir John's credit that he did not take the easiest method of getting rid of his niece by allowing her to become Mrs. Halliday. He had a conscience of some sort, and wished to carry out his late brother's desire that Lillian should become a peeress. So far as the girl's inclinations were concerned he cared little, since he looked upon her as a child who required guidance. And to guide her in the proper direction--that is, towards the altar in Curberry's company--Sir John put himself to considerable inconvenience, and acted honestly with the very best intentions. His egotism--the powerful egotism of a weak man--prevented him from seeing that Lillian was also a human being, and had her right to freedom of choice. It must be said that, for a dilettante, Sir John acted with surprising promptitude. He took the two women to his own house, and let the mansion at Hampstead to an Australian millionaire, who paid an excellent rent. Then he saw the lawyers, and went into details concerning the property. Luckily, Sir Charles had gradually withdrawn from business a few years before his death, since he had more or less concentrated his mind on politics. Therefore, the income was mostly well invested, and, with the exception of the line of steamers with which Mrs. Brown's son had been concerned, there were few interests which required personal supervision. Sir John, having power under the will, sold the dead man's interest in the ships, withdrew from several other speculations, and having seen that the securities, which meant fifty thousand a year to Lillian, and ten thousand a year to himself, were all in good order, he settled down to enjoy himself. The lawyers--on whom he kept an eye--received the money and banked it, and consulted with Sir John regarding reinvestments. They also, by the new baronet's direction, offered a reward of £1,000 for the discovery of the murderess. So, shortly after the New Year everything was more or less settled, and Sir John found himself able to attend once more to his lace and jewels, his music and poetry. Only Lillian's marriage remained to be arranged, and after his conversation with the girl, Sir John appointed a day for Dan to call. That young gentleman, who had been hovering round, lost no time in obeying the summons, which was worded amiably enough, and presented himself in due time. Sir John received Halliday with great affability, offered him a chair and a cigarette, and came to the point at once. "It's about Lillian I wish to see you, Mr. Halliday," he remarked, placing the tips of his fingers delicately together. "You can go up to the drawing-room afterwards and have tea with her and with Mrs. Bolstreath. But we must have a chat first to adjust the situation."

"What situation?" asked Dan, wilfully dense. "Oh, I think you understand," rejoined Sir John, drily. "Well?"

"I love her," was all that Dan could find to say. "Naturally. Lillian is a charming girl, and you are a young man of discernment. At least, I hope so, as I wish you to give Lillian up." Dan rose and pitched his cigarette into the fire. "Never," he cried, looking pale and determined and singularly virile and handsome. "How can you ask such a thing, Mr. Moon--I mean Sir John."

"My new title doesn't come easily I see," said the baronet smoothly. "Oh, I quite understand. My poor brother died so unexpectedly that none of us have got used to the new order of things. You least of all, Mr. Halliday."

"Why not 'Dan'?" asked that young gentleman, leaning against the mantelpiece since he felt that he could talk better standing than sitting. "Because, as I say, there is a new order of things. I have known you all your life, my dear boy, as your parents placed you in my late brother's charge when you were only five years of age. But I say Mr. Halliday instead of Dan as I wish you to understand that we are talking as business men and not as old friends."

"You take away your friendship----"

"Not at all, Mr. Halliday. We shall be better friends than ever when we have had our talk and you have done the right thing. Probably I shall then call you Dan, as of yore."

"You can call me what you please," said Dan obstinately, and rather angrily, for the fiddling methods of Sir John annoyed him. "But I won't give up the dearest girl in the world."

"Her father wished her to marry Lord Curberry."

"If her father had lived, bless him," retorted Halliday vehemently, "he would have seen that Lillian loves me, and not Curberry, in which case he would not have withheld his consent."

"Oh, I think he would," said Sir John amiably. "Lillian is rich, and my poor brother wished to obtain a title for her. Very natural, Mr. Halliday, as you must see for yourself. Charles always aimed at high things."

"He loved Lillian and would not have seen her unhappy," said Dan bluffly. "I don't see that Curberry would make her unhappy. He is devoted to her."

"But she does not love him," argued Halliday crossly, "and how can there be happiness when love is lacking. Come, Sir John, you have, as you said just now, known me all my life. I am honorable and clean-living and wellborn, while Lillian loves me. What objection have you to the match?"

"The same objection as my brother had, Mr. Halliday. Lillian is wealthy and you are poor."

"I have only a few hundreds a year, it is true, but----"

"No 'buts' if you please," Sir John flung up a delicate hand in protest. "You can't argue away facts. If you marry Lillian, you will live on her." Dan bit his lip and clenched his hands to prevent his temper from showing itself too strongly. "If another man had said that to me, Sir John, I should have knocked him down."

"Brute force is no argument," rejoined Moon unruffled. "Consider, Mr. Halliday, you have a few hundreds a year and Lillian has fifty thousand coming in every twelve months. Being wealthy, she can scarcely live on your income, so to keep up the position to which she has been born, she must live on her own. Husband and wife are one, as we are assured by the Church, therefore if she lives on the fifty thousand per annum, you must live on it also."

"I wouldn't take a single penny!" cried Dan hotly and boyishly. "Oh, I am not suggesting that you would," said Sir John easily, "but Lillian cannot live in the cottage your few hundreds would run to, and if she lives, as she must, being rich, in a large house, you must live there also, and in a style which your income does not warrant. You know what people will say under the circumstances. Either you must take Lillian to live on your small income, which is not fair to her, or you must live on her large one, which is not fair to you. I speak to a man of honor, remember."

"These arguments are sophistical."

"Not at all. You can't escape from facts."

"Then is this miserable money to stand between us?" asked Dan in despair, for he could not deny that there was great truth in what Sir John said. The baronet shrugged his shoulders. "It seems likely unless you can make a fortune equal to Lillian's."

"Why not? Aviation is yet in its infancy."

"Quite so, and thus accidents are continually happening. If you marry my niece, it is probable that you will shortly leave her a widow. No! No! In whatever way you look at the matter, Mr. Halliday, the match is most undesirable. Be a man--a man of honor--and give Lillian up."

"To be miserable with Lord Curberry," said Dan fiercely, "never!" And he meant what he said, as Sir John saw very plainly. This being the case the baronet used another argument to obtain what he wanted. "I have been young myself, and I know how you feel," he said quietly. "Very good. I suggest a compromise."

"What is it?" muttered Dan dropping into his chair again and looking very miserable, as was natural, seeing what he stood to lose. "My poor brother," went on Sir John smoothly, and crossing his legs, "has been struck down when most enjoying life. The person who murdered him--presumably the woman who called herself Mrs. Brown--has not yet been discovered in spite of the efforts of the police backed by a substantial reward. I propose, Mr. Halliday, that you search for this person, the period of searching be limited to one year. If you find her and she is punished, then you shall marry Lillian; if you fail, then you must stand aside and allow her to marry Lord Curberry."

"You forget," said Dan, not jumping at the chance as Sir John expected, "if I do bring the woman to justice, your arguments regarding my living on Lillian remain in full force."

"Oh, as to that, Mr. Halliday, when the time comes, I can find arguments equally strong on the other side. To use one now, if you revenge my brother's death, no one will deny but what you have every right to marry his daughter and enjoy her income. That would be only fair. Well?"

"Well," echoed Dan dully, and reflected with his sad eyes on the carpet. Then he looked up anxiously. "Meanwhile, Lillian may marry Lord Curberry."

"Oh," said Sir John, coolly, "if you can't trust her----"

"He can trust her," cried the voice of the girl, herself, and the curtain of the folding doors was drawn quickly aside. "Lillian!" cried Dan, springing to his feet and opening his arms. Sir John saw his niece rush into those same arms and laughed. "H'm!" said he whimsically, "I quite forgot that the folding-doors into the next room were open. You have been listening." Lillian twisted herself in Dan's arms, but did not leave them, as she felt safe within that warm embrace. "Of course I have been listening," she cried scornfully; "as soon as I knew Dan was in the house, and in the library, I listened. I told Bolly that I was coming down to listen, and though she tried to prevent me, I came. Who has a better right to listen when all the conversation was about me, and remember I should have seen him first."

"Well," said her uncle unmoved, "it's no use arguing with you. A man's idea of honor and a woman's are quite opposed to one another. You heard. What have you to say?"

"I think you're horrid," snapped Lillian, in a schoolgirl manner, "as if my money mattered. I am quite willing to give it to you and marry Dan on what he has. It's better to love in a garret than to hate in a drawing-room."

"Quite epigrammatic," murmured Sir John cynically. "Well, my dear, I am much obliged to you for your fifty thousand a year offer, but I fancy what I have is enough for me. I never did care for millions, and always wondered why my late brother should wear himself out in obtaining them. I decline." "Whether you decline or not, I marry Dan," said Lillian hotly. "What does Dan say?" The young man disengaged himself. He had kept silent during the passage of arms between uncle and niece. "I say that I can trust Lillian to remain true to me for twelve months."

"For ever, for ever, for ever!" cried the girl, her face flaming and her eyes flashing; "but don't make any promise of letting our marriage depend upon finding the woman who murdered my poor father."

"Ah," said Sir John contemptuously, "you never loved your father, I see."

"How dare you say that?" flashed out the girl, panting with anger. "My dear, ask yourself," replied Moon patiently; "your father has been basely murdered. Yet you do not wish to avenge his death and prefer your own happiness to the fulfilment of a solemn duty. Of course," added Sir John, with a shrug, for he now knew what line of argument to take, "you can't trust yourself to be faithful for twelve months and----"

"I *can* trust myself to be faithful, and for twelve centuries, if necessary."

"No, no, no!" smiled Moon, shaking his head, "you prefer pleasure to duty. I see you love yourself more than you loved your father. Well," he rose and waved his hands with a gesture of dismissal, "go your ways, my dear, and marry Dan--you observe I call you 'Dan,' Mr. Halliday, since you are to become my nephew straight away. When is the wedding to be?"

"You consent?" cried Lillian opening her eyes widely. "I can't stop you," said Moon, still continuing his crafty diplomacy. "You will soon be of age and you can buy your husband at once, since you dare not risk a probation of twelve months."

"I can risk twelve years," retorted Lillian uneasily, for in a flash she understood how selfishly she was behaving, seeing that her father's assassin was still at large, "and to prove it----" she looked at Dan. He understood and spoke, although he had already made up his mind as to the best course to pursue. "To prove it," he said steadily, "we accept your proposal, Sir John. Lillian will wait twelve months, and during that time I shall search for the woman who murdered Sir Charles. If I don't find her----"

"Lillian marries Lord Curberry," said Moon quickly. "No," cried the girl defiantly; "that part of the agreement I decline to assent to. Twelve months or twelve years it may take before the truth comes to light, but I marry no one but Dan." Sir John reflected on the dangers of aviation and swiftly came to a conclusion. "We'll see at the end of the year," he said cautiously, "much may happen in that time."

"So long as Lillian's wedding to Curberry doesn't happen," said Dan obstinately, "I don't care. But it is understood that Lillian is not to be worried about the matter?"

"That depends upon what you and Lillian call worry," said Moon drily, "so far as I am concerned I shall not coerce her in any way. All I wish is the promise of you both that you will wait twelve months before taking any steps to marry. Meantime, you must not see too much of Lillian."

"Oh," cried the girl, indignantly, "you would push Dan out of my life."

"It's a test," explained Sir John, blinking nervously. "You will be in mourning for the next twelve months, and should see few people."

"Of whom Dan will be one," she flashed out. "Occasionally--very occasionally, you can see him, but, of course, if you can't trust yourself to be true without being continually reminded that Mr. Halliday exists, there is no more to be said."

"I can trust myself," muttered the girl uneasily. "And I can trust Lillian," said Dan, promptly and decisively. "It does not look like it since you always wish to see one another. And remember, Lillian, you owe it to your father's memory to put all thoughts of love, which is self, out of your heart until the mystery of his death is entirely solved."

"There is something in that," said Halliday thoughtfully and Lillian nodded; "but of course I can write to Lillian." "Occasionally," said the baronet again, "you must both be tested by a year's separation, with a meeting or a letter every now and then. Duty must be the keynote of the twelve months and not pleasure. Well?" The lovers looked at one another and sighed. The terms were hard, but not so hard as Sir John might have made them. Still both the boy and the girl--they were little else--recognized that their duty was to the dead. Afterwards pleasure would be theirs. Silently they accepted and silently adjusted the situation. "We agree!" said the two almost simultaneously. "Very good," said Moon, rubbing his hands, "how do you intend to begin your search for the missing woman, Mr. Halliday?"

"I don't know," murmured Dan, miserably. "Neither do I," rejoined Sir John with great amiability. "Come to tea?" And to tea the lovers went as to a funeral feast. But Sir John rejoiced.

CHAPTER IV

AN AMATEUR DETECTIVE

Dan left the Mayfair house very mournfully, feeling that Sir John was indeed master of the situation. By a skilful appeal to the generous emotions of youth, to the boy's honor and to the girl's affections, he had procured a respite of twelve months, during which time the lovers could do nothing, bound as they were by silken threads. This would give Curberry time to push his suit, and there was always a chance that Dan would come to grief in one of his aerial trips in which case Lillian would certainly be driven to marry her titled swain. Halliday knew nothing of Moon's reckoning on these points, or he would have only accepted the situation on condition that Curberry was not to meet the girl or write to the girl oftener than himself. Logically speaking, the peer and the commoner should have been placed on the same footing. But Dan's grief at the parting confused his understanding, and he had not been clever enough to seize his opportunity. Therefore Sir John, winning all along the line, had cleared the path for Curberry, and had more or less blocked it for Dan. But, as yet, the young man did not grasp the full extent of Sir John's worldly wisdom. What Halliday had to do--and this dominated his mind immediately he left the house--was to solve the mystery of Sir Charles's death. The sooner he captured the false Mrs. Brown, who, presumably, had murdered the old man, the sooner would he lead Lillian to the altar. Therefore he was feverishly anxious to begin, but for the life of him he did not see how to make a start. He had absolutely no experience of what constituted the business of a detective, and was daunted at the outset by the difficulties of the path. All the same he never thought of halting, but pressed forward without a pause. And the first step he took was to consult a friend, on the obvious assumption that two heads are better than one. It was Freddy Laurance whom he decided to interview, since that very up-to-date young journalist knew every one of any note, and almost everything of interest, being, indeed, aware of much of which the ordinary man in the street was ignorant. He and Dan had been to Oxford together, and for many years had been the best of friends. Laurance had been brought up in the expectation of being a rich man. But over-speculation ruined his father, and on leaving the University he was thrown unprepared on the world to make his money as best he could, without any sort of training in particular. Hearty praise from an expert for three or four newspaper articles suggested journalism, and having an observant eye and a ready pen, the young man was successful from the beginning. For a time he was a free-lance, writing indiscriminately for this journal and for that, until the proprietor of *The Moment*, a halfpenny daily, secured his exclusive services at a salary which procured Freddy the luxuries of life. This was something to have achieved at the age of five and twenty. *The Moment* was a bright shoot-folly-as-it-flies sort of journal, which detailed the news of the day in epigrammatic scraps. Its longest articles did not exceed a quarter of a column, and important events were usually restricted to paragraphs. It, indeed, skimmed the cream of events, and ten minutes' study of its sheets gave a busy man all the information he required concerning the doings of humanity. Also it daily published an extra sheet concerned entirely with letters from the public to the public, and many of these were prolix, as the paragraph rule did not apply to this portion of the journal. People wrote herein on this, that, and the other thing, ventilating their ideas and suggesting schemes. And as many wrote many bought, so that friends and relatives might read their letters, therefore vanity gave *The Moment* quite a large circulation independent of its orthodox issue. The proprietor made money in two ways; by supplying gossip for curious people, and by giving vain persons the chance of seeing themselves in print. Seeing what human nature is, it is scarcely to be wondered at that *The Moment* was a great success, and sold largely in town and country. Freddy's post was that of a roving correspondent. Whenever any event of interest took place in any of the four quarters of the globe, Laurance went to take notes on the spot, and his information was boiled down into concise, illuminative paragraphs. Indeed, the older journalists said that it was hardly worth while for him to make such long journeys for the sake of condensed-milk news; but, as Freddy's details were always amusing as well as abrupt, the editor and the public and the proprietor were all satisfied. A man who can flash a vivid picture into the dullest mind in few words is well worth money. Therefore was Laurance greatly appreciated. Dan walked to a grimy lane leading from Fleet Street with some doubt in his puzzled mind as to whether Freddy would be in his office. At a moment's notice, the man would dart off to the ends of the earth, and was more or less on the move throughout the three hundred and sixty-five days of the year. But, of late, sensational events had concentrated themselves in England, so Dan hoped that his friend would be on the spot. An inquiry from the gorgeous individual who guarded the entrance to the red brick building wherein *The Moment* was printed and published and composed revealed that Mr. Laurance was not only in London, but in his office at the very second, so Dan sent up his name, and rejoiced at the catching of this carrier-pigeon. And it was a good omen also that Freddy saw him straight away, since he generally refused himself to every one on the plea of business. "But I couldn't resist seeing you, Dan," remarked Mr. Laurance, when he had shaken hands, before supplying his visitor with a cigarette and a chair. "I was coming to see you, if the mountain hadn't come to Mahommed!" Dan lighted up, and through the smoke of tobacco stared inquisitively at his friend, wondering what this introductory remark meant. Laurance was rather like Dan in personal appearance, being tall and slim and clean-shaven, with Greek features and an aristocratic look. But he was decidedly fair, as Halliday was decidedly dark, and his eyes were less like those of an eagle than the eyes of the aviator. But then Laurance was not accustomed to the boundless spaces of the air, although he had twice ascended in an airship; therefore the new expression of the new race was wanting. Nevertheless, he looked a capable, alert young man, able to get the full value out of every minute. He was an admirable type of the restless, present-day seeker. "Well, Mahommed," said Dan, leisurely, "here's the mountain. What have you to say to it?"

"That murder of Sir Charles Moon." Halliday quivered with surprise. It was so amazing that Laurance should hit upon the very subject, which employed his own thoughts. "Yes?" he inquired. "You are engaged to Miss Moon; you were in the house when the crime was committed; you saw the body; you----"

"Stop! Stop! I was not in the house when the crime was committed. I returned there from the theatre some time later--in fact about midnight. I certainly did see the body. As to being engaged to Miss Moon--h'm! I came to see about that, Freddy."

"The deuce you did. Great minds jump. What?" Laurance puffed a blue cloud, sat down astride a chair and leaned his arms on the back. "Strange!"

"That you and I should be on the hunt. Well it is."

"On the hunt!" echoed Laurance, staring. "What do you mean?"

"I should rather ask that question of you," said Dan drily. "Sir Charles is dead and buried these many weeks, and the woman who assassinated him can't be found, in spite of the reward and the effort of the police. Why, at this late hour, do you wish to rake up stale news? I thought that *The Moment* was more up-to-date."

"It will be very much up-to-date when the next murder is committed," observed Laurance, grimly and significantly. The legs of Dan's chair grated, as he pushed back in sheer surprise. "What do you mean by the next murder?" he demanded sharply. "Well, this gang----"

"Gang! gang! Who says there is a gang?" and Dan's thoughts flew back to Durwin's reason for visiting Sir Charles. "Humph!" growled Laurance, thrusting his hands into his pockets. "I'm disappointed. I thought you knew more."

"I know a good deal," retorted the other quickly, "but I don't intend to talk to you about what I know until I learn your game."

"What about your own?" "That comes later also," said Halliday promptly. "Go on! I want to know why you rake up Moon's murder."

"Naturally you do, seeing you are engaged to the daughter."

"Am I? I am not quite sure. She loves me and I love her, but the new baronet wants her to marry Lord Curberry. She refused, and I kicked up a row some hours back. Result, we are on probation for one year, during which time I am to discover the assassin of Sir Charles."

"And if you don't?"

"Time enough to talk about that when I fail," said Halliday coolly; "at least I have twelve months to hunt round. I came for your help, but it seems that you want mine. Why?" Freddy, through sheer absence of mind, flung away a half-smoked cigarette and lighted another. Then he rose and strolled across the room to lean his shoulders against the mantelpiece. "We can help one another, I think," was his final observation. "I hope so. In any case I intend to marry Lillian. All the same, to pacify Sir John, I am willing to become a detective. You know my game. Yours?"

"Listen," said Laurance vivaciously. "I forgot all about the murder, since there seemed to be no chance of the truth coming to the light, and so did every one else for the same reason. But a few nights ago I was dining out, and met a chap called Durwin----"

"Scotland Yard man," interrupted Dan, nodding several times. "He came to see Sir Charles on business and found the corpse." "Just so. Well, after dinner we had a chat, and he told me that he was anxious to learn who killed Moon, because he didn't want any more murders of the kind to happen--as a police official, you understand."

"Strange he should be confidential on that point," murmured Halliday thoughtfully, "seeing that he wished his theory regarding a possible gang kept quiet, in the hope of making discoveries."

"He has changed his mind about secrecy, and so has Tenson," said Freddy. "Oh!" Dan raised his eyebrows. "The Inspector. You have seen him also?" Laurance nodded. "After I saw Durwin, and learned what he had to say I saw Tenson, and interviewed him. They told me about the fly on the neck, and remembering the case of the purple fern, and having regard to the fact that the fly in question was artificial, both men are inclined to believe in the existence of a gang, whose trade-mark the said fly is." Dan nodded again. "Quite so; and then Durwin came to see Moon and hear about the gang. He found him dead."

"So you said; so Durwin said," rejoined Laurance quietly. "It seems very certain, putting this and that together, that Sir Charles became dangerous to this gang, whatever it is, and wherever it exists, so was put to death by the false Mrs. Brown, who came expressly to kill him."

"So far I am with you on all fours," said Halliday. "Well?"

"Well, both Durwin and Tenson, dreading lest the gang may commit another crime, wish me to make the matter as public as I can, so as to frighten the beasts."

"H'm!" said Dan, looking at his neat brown boots. "They have changed their minds, it seems. Their first idea was to keep the matter quiet, so as to catch these devils red-handed. However, publicity may be a good thing. How do you intend to begin?"

"I have got facts from Tenson and from Durwin," said Freddy promptly; "and now, since you saw the body and found the fly, I want to get the facts from you. On what I acquire I shall write a letter in that extra sheet of ours, and you can be pretty certain from what you know of human nature that any amount of people will reply to my letter."

"They may reply to no purpose."

"I'm not so sure of that, Dan. If I mention the fly as a trade-mark and recall the strange case of the purple fern, some one may write about matters known to themselves from positive knowledge. If this gang exists, it has committed more murders than one, but the fly being a small insect may not have been noticed as a trade-mark in the other crimes. I wonder you spotted it anyhow."

"It was easily seen, being on the back of the neck near the wound. Besides, flies in November--the month of the murder--are rare. Finally Tenson discovered the fly to be artificial, which shows that it was purposely placed on the dead man's neck, near the wound. H'm!" he reflected, "perhaps someone may know of some crime with the fly trade-mark, and in that case we can be certain that such a gang does exist."

"So I think," cried Laurance quickly, "and for that reason I intend to start a discussion by writing an open letter. Publicity may frighten the beasts into dropping their trade; on the other hand, it may goad the gang into asserting itself. In either case the subject will be ventilated, and we may learn more or less of the truth."

"Yes. I think it's a good idea, Freddy. And the perfume? Did Durwin or the Inspector tell you anything about the perfume. No, I can see by your blank stare that they didn't. Listen, Freddy, and store this knowledge in your blessed brain, my son. It is a clue, I am sure," and Halliday forthwith related to his attentive listener details concerning the strange perfume which had impregnated the clothes of the dead man. "And Sir Charles hated perfumes," he ended, emphatically; "he didn't even like Lillian or Mrs. Bolstreath to use them, and they obeyed him." "Curious," mused the journalist, and idly scribbling on his blotting-paper; he was back at his desk by this time. "What sort of scent is it?"

"My dear chap, you ask me to describe the impossible," retorted Dan, with uplifted eyebrows. "How the deuce can I get the kind of smell into your head? It must be smelt to be understood. All I can say is that the perfume was rich and heavy, suggestive of drowsiness. Indeed, I used that word, and Tenson thought of some kind of chloroform used, perhaps, to stupefy the victim before killing him. But there was an odor about the mouth or nose."

"On the handkerchief, perhaps?" suggested the reporter. "No. Tenson smelt the handkerchief."

"Well, if this Mrs. Brown used this perfume, you and Miss Moon and Mrs. Bolstreath must have smelt it on her in the hall. I understand from Durwin that you all three saw the woman." "Yes. And Lillian, poor girl, persuaded her father to see the wretch. But we did not smell the perfume on the woman. Tenson or Durwin--I forget which--asked us the question."

"Humph!" said Laurance, after a pause; "it may be a kind of trade-mark, like the fly business." He took a note. "I shall use this evidence in my letter to the public. I suppose, Dan, you would recognize the scent again?"

"Oh, yes! I have a keen sense of smell, you know. But I don't expect I shall ever drop across this particular fragrance, Freddy."

"There's always Monsieur Chance, you know," remarked Laurance, tapping his white teeth with a pencil. "Perhaps the gang use this scent so as to identify one another--in the dark it may be--like cats. How does that strike you?"

"As purely theoretical," said Dan, with a shrug, and reached for another cigarette; "it's a case of perhaps, and perhaps not." Laurance assented. "But everything so far is theoretical in this case," he argued; "you have told me all you know?"

"Every bit, even to my year of probation. Do you know Curberry?"

"Yes. He was a slap-up barrister. A pity he got title and money, as he has left the Bar, and is a good man spoiled. Lucky chap all the same, as his uncle and cousin both died unexpectedly, to give him his chance of the House of Lords."

"How did they die?" "Motor accident. Car went over a cliff. Only the chauffeur was saved, and he broke both legs. Do you know the present Lord Curberry?"

"I have seen him, and think he's a dried-up, cruel-looking beast," said Dan, with considerable frankness. "I'd rather see Lillian dead than his wife."

"Hear, hear!" applauded Laurance, smiling. "The girl's too delightful to be wasted on Curberry. You have my blessing on the match, Dan."

"Thanks," said Halliday ruefully, "but I have to bring it off first. Sir John's infernally clever, and managed to get both Lillian and me to consent to let matters stand over for a year, during which time I guess he'll push Curberry's suit. But I can trust Lillian to be true to me, bless her, and Mrs. Bolstreath is quite on our side. After all," murmured the young man disconsolately, "it's only fair that Sir Charles should be avenged. Perhaps it would be selfish for Lillian and me to marry and live happy ever afterwards, without making some attempt to square things. The question is how to start. I'm hanged if I know, and so I came to you."

"Well," said Laurance thoughtfully, "there's a hope of Monsieur Chance you know. In many ways you may stumble on clues even without looking for them, since this gang--if it exists--must carry on an extensive business. All you can do, Dan, is to keep your eyes and ears and nose open--the last for that scent, you know. On my part I shall write the letter, and publish it in the annex of The Moment. Then we shall see what will happen."

"Yes, I think that's about the best way to begin. Stir up the muddy water, and we may find what is at the bottom of the pond. But there's one thing to be considered, and that is money. If I'm going to hunt for these scoundrels I need cash, and to own up, Freddy, I haven't very much." "You're so beastly extravagant," said Laurance grinning, "and your private income goes nowhere."

"Huh! what's five hundred a year?"

"Ten pounds a week, more or less. However, there's your aviation. I hear that you take people flights for money?" Dan nodded. "It's the latest fashionable folly, which is a good thing for me, old son. I get pretty well paid, and it means fun."

"With some risk of death," said Laurance drily. "Well, yes. But that is a peculiarity of present-day fun. People love to play with death--it thrills them. However, if I am to hunt for the assassin of Sir Charles, I can't give much attention to aviation, and I repeat that I want money. Oceans of it."

"Would two thousand pounds suit you?"

"Rather. Only I'm not going to borrow from you, old man, thank you."

"I haven't that amount to lend," said Freddy, drily; "but you must have seen, if you read our very interesting paper, that our proprietor has offered a prize of two thousand pounds for a successful flight from London to York."

"A kind of up-to-date Dick Turpin, I suppose," laughed Dan, rising and stretching his long limbs. "Good, I'll have a shot, I may win."

"You will, if you use a Vincent machine."

"Vincent, Vincent? Where have I heard that name?"

"Everywhere if you know anything of the aviation world," snapped Laurance rather crossly, for at times Dan's indolence in acquiring necessary information annoyed him. "Solomon Vincent, who has been inventing airships and new-fangled aeroplanes for ever so long."

"Yes, yes! I remember now. He's a genius. Every one knows him." "Every one knows of him, except yourself; but no one knows him personally. He lives a secluded life up in Hillshire, on the borders of the moors, where he can find wide space for his experiments in aerial craft. I interviewed him a year ago, and--and----" Laurance blushed red. "Hullo, what's this?" asked Dan shrewdly. "Can it be that the inventor has a daughter fair?"

"A niece," retorted Laurance, recovering; "why shouldn't I be in love as well as you, Halliday? However, that doesn't matter."

"It matters a great deal to you."

"Never mind. What you have to do is to secure one of Vincent's machines and try for this race. If you win the prize you will have heaps of money to search for the gang. But why doesn't Miss Moon----"

"I don't take Lillian's money," said Dan curtly, and blushed in his turn. "It is a good idea, Freddy. How can I get hold of the machine?"

"I shall take you up to Hillshire next week, and you can see Vincent for yourself. He can talk to you, and----"

"And you can talk to the niece. What's her name?"

"Oh, shut up and get out," said Laurance, turning away, "you're interrupting my work."

"Going to write a letter to the beloved," said Dan, leisurely making for the door. "All right, old son, I'll go. You know my address, so write me when you want me. I'd like to see Vincent's machines, as I hear he has made several good improvements, and everything tells in a race. Salaam!"

"Keep your eyes open," Laurance called after him; "remember Monsieur Chance may prove to be our best friend." Dan departed, shrugging his shoulders. "I don't believe in heaven-sent miracles," were his last words. But they were wasted on Freddy, for that alert young man was already buried in his work. It was painful to witness such industry, in Halliday's opinion. In an inquiring frame of mind, the amateur detective strolled along Fleet Street, thinking of Lillian instead of keeping his wits about him, as Freddy had requested. It seemed impossible that he should strike on a clue without deliberately searching for it, which he did not feel inclined to do at the moment. Monsieur Chance, indeed! He was a mythical personage in whom this sceptical young man did not believe. Besides love dominated his thoughts to the exclusion of minor matters, and he dreamed about his darling all along the Strand. Thus he did not look where he was going, and stumbled into the midst of a Charing Cross crowd, where a motor had broken down after colliding with a 'bus. A policeman was conversing with the chauffeur and the 'bus driver, who were conversing abusively with one another. The crowd blocked the street and stopped the traffic in order to enjoy the conversation, which left nothing to be desired in the way of free language. Dan halted idly, as a spectator, not because he wished to be one, but for the very simple reason that he could not get through the crowd into Trafalgar Square. Thrust up against one man, and wedged in by two others, and surrounded by hundreds, he grumbled at the delay, and peered over shoulders to see when the incident would end. As he did so, he suddenly in his mind's eye saw a vision of Sir Charles lying dead in the well-lighted library. While wondering why he thought of the crime at this particular moment, he became aware that a familiar scent assailed his nostrils, the scent about which he had talked to Durwin and Tenson and Laurance. Nosing like a hound, he tried to find the person from whom it emanated, and almost immediately later the man turned, and Dan found himself face to face with Marcus Penn.

CHAPTER V

MUDDY WATER

The secretary of the late Sir Charles Moon smiled irresolutely when he recognized Dan. That young gentleman, who thought Penn a weak-kneed idiot, had never taken much notice of him, but for the fact that he was perfumed with the unusual scent would not have spoken to him now. But as he looked at the lank creature with his yellow face, and scanty moustache, he guessed that he was exactly the effeminate sort of person who would use perfume. What he wished to know was why he affected this particular kind of fragrance, and whence he obtained it. To gain the information he pretended a friendliness for the man he was far from feeling. Dan, strong, virile, and self-confident, was not altogether just to Penn, who was not responsible for his pallid looks and weak character. But Halliday was not a perfect individual by any means, and had yet to learn that the weak are meant to be protected and helped instead of being despised. "You here, Mr. Penn?" said Dan, thus formal to mark the difference between them. "Yes," replied the man in his faint hesitating voice, and, as they moved out of the crowd, Halliday smelt the weird perfume more strongly than ever shaken from Penn's clothes by his movements. "I stopped to look at the accident."

"A very ordinary one," rejoined Mr. Halliday, with a shrug. "By the way, I have not seen you since the funeral of Sir Charles. What are you doing now, if I may ask?"

"I am secretary to Lord Curberry."

"Oh!" The reply gave Dan something of a shock, for he did not expect at the moment to hear his rival's name. But then the whole incident of meeting Penn and smelling the incriminating perfume was strange. Monsieur Chance had proved himself to be an actuality instead of the mythical personage Dan had believed him to be. It was certainly odd that the meeting had taken place, and odder still that Penn should prove to be the servant of Curberry. As Halliday said nothing more than "Oh!" the other man stroked his moustache and explained. "Sir John got me the post, Mr. Halliday," he said, with his shifty eyes anywhere but on Dan's inquiring face. "I was quite stranded after Sir Charles's unexpected death, and did not know where to turn for employment. As I support a widowed mother, the situation was rather serious, so I took my courage in my hands and went to Sir John. He was good enough to recommend me to Lord Curberry, and I have been with his lordship for a month, more or less."

"I congratulate you, Mr. Penn, and Lord Curberry, also. Sir Charles always said you were an excellent secretary," Dan stopped as Penn bowed his acknowledgments to the compliment, and cast a keen side glance at the man. They were walking through Trafalgar Square by this time, passing under the shadow of Nelson's Column. "Do you know what I was thinking of when behind you in the crowd yonder, Mr. Penn?" he asked abruptly, and it must be confessed rather undiplomatically, if he wished to get at the truth. "No," said the secretary, with simplicity and manifest surprise. "No, Mr. Halliday, how can I guess your thoughts?"

"I was thinking of the murder of your late employer," said Dan straightly. Penn blinked and shivered. "It's a horrible subject to think about," he remarked in a low voice. "I can scarcely get it out of my own thoughts. I suppose the sight of me reminded you of the crime, Mr. Halliday?"

"Scarcely, since I was behind you, and did not recognize you until you turned," replied Dan, calmly, and the other appeared to be surprised. "Then how----" he began, only to be cut short. "It's that scent."

"Scent!" echoed Penn nervously, but manifestly still surprised. "I don't understand exactly what you mean, Mr. Halliday. I like scent, and use much of it." Dan's lip curled. "So I perceive. But where did you get the particular scent you are using now, may I ask?" Something in his tone annoyed the secretary, for he drew himself up and halted. "I don't know why you should criticize my tastes, Mr. Halliday."

"I'm not criticizing them, and don't jump down my throat. But you reek of some strange perfume, which I last smelt----" He paused. "You cannot have smelt it anywhere," said Penn indifferently. "What do you mean by that exactly?" asked Dan with considerable sharpness. Penn resumed his walk and drew his light eyebrows together. "I am willing to explain as soon as you tell me why you speak of the scent."

"Hang it, man," rejoined Halliday, dropping into step, "any one would notice the scent and speak of it since it is so strong."

"Oh"--Penn's brow cleared--"I understand now. You have taken a fancy to the scent and wish me to get you some." Halliday was about to make an indignant denial, when he suddenly changed his mind, seeing a chance of learning something. "Well, can you get me some?"

"No," said Penn coolly; "I cannot. This is a particular perfume which comes from the Island of Sumatra. I have a cousin there who knows that I like perfumes, and he sent me a single bottle."

"Can't I buy it anywhere?"

"No, it is not to be obtained in England," said Penn curtly. "In that case," said Halliday slowly, "it is strange that I should have smelt the same perfume on the clothes of Sir Charles after his death."

"Did you?" Penn looked surprised. "That is impossible. Why, Sir Charles detested scents, and I never dared to use this one until I left him for the night."

"You used it on the night of the murder?"

"Of course. I used it every night when I left Sir Charles. On that evening he sent me away with my usual batch of letters, and was going down to the House later. I would not have seen him until the next morning, so I took the opportunity to indulge in this taste."

"Then how did Sir Charles's clothes become impregnated with it?"

"I am unable to say. Why do you ask? Surely"--Penn turned an alarmed face towards the speaker, and looked yellower than ever--"surely you do not suspect me of keeping back anything from the police likely to lead to the detection of the assassin."

"Ask yourself, Mr. Penn," said Dan coldly. "I and Inspector Tenson and Mr. Durwin smelt this particular perfume on the clothes of the dead man, and I do not mind telling you that the police consider it something of a clue."

"A clue to what? To me? It must be, since I alone possess this scent. I certainly came into the library when summoned by Mr. Durwin, and I helped to look after Sir Charles. As I was strongly perfumed with the scent it is not impossible that my employer's clothes took what, doubtless, you will call the taint. I think," ended Penn in a dignified manner, "that such is the proper explanation. You have found a mare's nest, Mr. Halliday."

"Upon my word, I believe I have," said Dan, quite good-humoredly, "but you must forgive me, Mr. Penn. Inspector Tenson agreed with me that the fly and the scent were clues."

"About the fly I know nothing," said the secretary positively, "but this scent is not to be had in England, and Sir Charles's clothes could only have gathered the fragrance from mine. If Inspector Tenson suspects me----"

"No, no, no!" interrupted Halliday quickly. "I assure you that he does not."

"He would if you told him of our meeting," retorted Penn as they passed into Piccadilly Circus, "and as I don't like even a suspicion to rest on me, Mr. Halliday--for my good name is my fortune--I shall go and see him and explain the whole circumstance. Indeed, if he wishes it, I shall give him the bottle which my cousin sent me from Sumatra, and never shall I use the scent again. I do not like these injurious suspicions."

"Don't make a mountain out of a mole-hill," said Dan, drily; "if I have hurt your feelings, I apologize."

"I accept your apology only on condition that you accept my explanation." Dan inwardly chuckled at Penn's dignity, but replied, readily enough. "Oh, yes, for if I did not accept your explanation I should not make any apology. You are probably right since the scent must have got on to Sir Charles's clothes from your own. The clue--as we took it to be--has ended in smoke."

"But don't you think that I should see Inspector Tenson and explain?"

"There is no need," Dan assured him, soothingly. "If the Inspector says anything about the scent, I shall explain; and, after all, it was I who suggested the perfume as a clue." "Would you like what is left of the bottle?" asked Penn, pacified by the very frank apology of the other. "No, thanks, I never use perfumes. I hate them."

"So did Sir Charles," mused Penn, and eyeing Dan with a lack-lustre gaze. "I wonder he did not suspect me of liking them. If he had come upon me scented in this manner, he would have kicked me out."

"It is to be hoped Lord Curberry has not the same dislike," said Dan, who having learned all he wished, desired to escape from such boring society. "No, he has not," said Penn with great simplicity; "he is very kind to me. I suppose he will marry Miss Moon."

"Then you suppose wrong. He will not," snapped Halliday roughly. "He loves her devotedly," insisted the secretary, and with a glint of malice in his pale-colored eyes. "Good-day," rejoined Dan shortly, as he did not wish to argue the matter. He turned into Regent Street--for by this time they had crossed the Circus--when Penn ran after him and seized his arm. "Is there any chance of the woman who killed Sir Charles being found?"

"No," replied Dan, halting for a moment. "Why?"

"Because Sir Charles was good to me, and I should like his death to be avenged. That is only natural. Surely the police will search."

"They are searching, Mr. Penn, and can discover nothing."

"Perhaps Lord Curberry may hunt for this woman. I shall ask him to, and as he loves Miss Moon so devotedly, he will try to learn the truth." Irritated by this speech--for Penn knew very well of the rivalry--Dan became scarlet. "I shall discover the truth. Lord Curberry need not trouble himself." "If you discover the truth----" began Penn, and hesitated. "Well?" asked Halliday sharply. "I think Lord Curberry will certainly marry Miss Moon."

"What do you mean by that?" demanded Dan, but Penn gave no answer. Shaking his head significantly, he stepped back, and in one moment was lost in the midst of the crowd which thronged the corner. Halliday would have followed, for the man's last observation seemed to hint that he knew more about the truth than he was disposed to admit; but many people came between him and the secretary, so it was impossible to get hold of him again. Dan was forced to walk on alone and he walked on pondering deeply. Did Penn know the truth? It seemed impossible that he should know it. The evidence of the typewriting girl went to show that he had not left his private room all the evening until summoned by Durwin when the death was discovered. What Penn said about the perfume appeared to be reasonable enough, as he certainly had handled the body, and if reeking of the scent--as he was reeking on this very day--it was not surprising that the odor should communicate itself to the dress clothes of the dead man. Some odors cling very powerfully, and endure for a considerable time. This Sumatra scent assuredly had done so, for it was quite three hours after the death that Dan himself had seen the corpse, and even then he had smelt the perfume. However, on the face of it, Halliday saw no reason to doubt Penn's statement, and quite understood how he became, through Sir John's mediation, the secretary of Lord Curberry. Only the last speech of the secretary was strange. Why should he say that, if the truth were discovered by Dan, Curberry would marry the girl, when, on the discovery of the truth--so far as Dan could see--the marriage of himself to Lillian depended? Dan could find no answer to this question, and had half a mind to follow Penn to his new employer's house, so as to force an explanation. But as he knew Curberry did not like him, he decided to let matters stand as they were, and only reveal what he had heard to Laurance. For the next four or five days, young Halliday went about his business in a quiet, determined manner, and thought as little as possible of Lillian. He did not even write or call to see her, since he wished to give up his whole attention to discovering the truth about Moon's death. If he thought of love and Lillian, he certainly could not concentrate his mind on the necessary search. And it was very necessary, if he intended to marry the girl. He became certain that in some way Sir John intended to trick him, but if he found out the false Mrs. Brown, and solved the mystery, Sir John would be forced out of sheer justice to sanction the marriage. It was heroical of Halliday to turn his thoughts from his beloved and it was no easy task to one so deeply in love as he. But he saw the need of it, and manfully set himself to endure present pain for future joy. Whether Lillian saw things in the same light, or resented his neglect, he did not know, as he had no word from her, neither came there any letter from Mrs. Bolstreath. Dan had, certainly been pushed out of the girl's life by her astute uncle; but it was his own common sense that kept him out of it--for the time being--be it understood. Love demands its martyrs, and Halliday had become one for Love's sake. By doing so, although he knew it not, he was displaying more real love towards her than he had ever done in his life before.

Meanwhile, Laurance lost no time in publishing his letter, which dealt with the mystery of Moon's death. As *The Moment*, including its extra letter-writing sheet, had a large circulation, and as it was a season devoid of news, the letter caused great discussions. It was sufficiently alarming to those who loved law and order, since it boldly announced that a gang of criminals existed which coldly and cautiously and deliberately employed its members to put people to death. The letter called attention to the fly--and that an artificial one--on Sir Charles's neck near the poisoned wound, and declared that such was the sign-manual of the accursed society. No mention was made of the scent, since Dan had explained what Penn had said to Laurance, and Laurance had accepted the explanation as valid. But there was quite enough in the letter to startle the most dull, especially when the writer called attention to the happening of various mysterious murders, and suggested that such were the work of this misguided set of people who constituted the unknown gang; finally, Freddy ended his letter by saying that Moon had knowledge of the gang, and had sent for a Scotland Yard official--name not given--to explain the whole matter, when he met with his death. It was a fact, therefore, that the false Mrs. Brown was an emissary of the gang who had been sent to murder Sir Charles, and had performed her vile errand only too well. A postscript to the epistle invited discussion, and particularly called upon any person who knew of an artificial fly being found on a corpse to give evidence. In two days the sheet was filled with letters from various people, and the matter was much discussed. Some of the writers laughed at the idea of such a society existing in a civilized country such as England, while others expressed alarm and asked what the police were doing not to arrest the criminals. These last scribes evidently entirely forgot that no one knew where the central quarters of the gang were, and that the letter of Mr. Laurance was an attempt to root out the heart of the mystery. Those who appeared in print and aided the circulation of *The Moment* by buying their own lucubrations certainly did not help much. The generality of the letters were discursive and ornate, wandering very much from the point, and giving no positive information such as would assist Freddy's purpose. But three or four epistles drew attention to certain mysterious crimes, the perpetrators of which had never been brought to justice, and who were not even known. There was the case of a young girl found dead on the Brighton railway line, near Redhill, and who must have been thrown out of the train. Then some one wrote about a miser in the East End who had been strangled, and another person recalled the drowning of a well-known philanthropist in the Serpentine. A verdict of suicide had been brought in as regards this last victim, but the writer of the letter positively asserted that the philanthropist had not the slightest intention of making away with himself. Finally came a batch of letters concerning children who had been murdered. But only in one case did it appear that any fly was seen on the victim, and that was when a schoolmistress was stabbed to the heart while in bed and asleep. The assassin had entered and escaped by the window, and the victim's mother--who wrote the letter drawing attention to this case--had found the fly on her daughter's cheek. She had thought nothing of it at the time, and had brushed away the insect. But after the mention of the fly on Sir Charles Moon's neck, she remembered the incident. Also it turned out that the schoolmistress, had she lived, would have inherited a large sum of money. It was this last circumstance that suggested the intervention of the gang to murder the girl, so that someone else might inherit. But all the letters dealing with the various cases were vague, and no enlightening details could be given. All that could be said was that there were many unusual deaths, the mystery of which could not be solved. Laurance, reading the letters during the week of their appearance, felt sure that the gang existed, but he was more or less alone in his opinion. Even Dan was doubtful. "It seems such a large order for a number of people to band themselves together, to murder on this comprehensive scale," he objected; "and I don't quite see the object. Many of the victims mentioned in these letters are poor."

"You seem to have changed your mind about the matter," said Laurance drily, "for when my letter appeared you were assured that there was such a gang."

"Only because of Sir Charles's remarks to Durwin."

"It was a pity Sir Charles was not more explicit," retorted Freddy crossly. "He had no time to be explicit," said Dan patiently, "since he died before he explained. But let us admit, for the sake of argument, that such a gang exists. Why should the members murder poor people?"

"Folks have been murdered by way of revenge, as well as for money. And let me remind you, Dan, that four or five of these victims mentioned in the letters had money, or were about to inherit money. I am quite convinced," said Laurance, striking the table, "that there is such an association."

"An association for what?"

"You are very dull. To get undesirable people out of the way. Remember, in the reign of Louis XIV there were dozens of poisoners in Paris who undertook to kill people when engaged to do so. The reason was for revenge, or desire for money, or--or--or for other reasons," ended Laurance vaguely. "Hum!" Dan stroked his chin, "it may be as you say. Certainly Sir Charles was got rid of, because he knew too much."

"About this gang," insisted Laurance, "since he was to see Durwin about the same. I am certain that such an association exists."

"You said that before," Halliday reminded him. "And I say it again. At all events there is one thing certain--that we have learned from these letters of many mysterious crimes."

"But only in one case was the fly discovered," objected Dan again. "That is not to be wondered at," replied the journalist; "the wonder is that such a small insect should be noticed at all. No one would ever think of connecting a fly, whether dead or alive, with the death. The mother of this schoolmistress did not, until your experience with regard to Moon was quoted in my letter. The fly business is quite ridiculous."

"And perhaps means nothing."

"Oh, I think it does, seeing that in Moon's case, the fly was artificial. Probably in the case of the schoolmistress it was artificial also, only the mother who noticed it did not make an examination. Why should she? I wonder the gang don't have a better trade-mark."

"Perhaps the gang may think it would be spotted if it did."

"Then why have any trade-mark at all," answered Laurance, sensibly. "If there is to be a sign, there should be some sensible one. If the fly was stamped on the skin, as the purple fern was stamped, there would be some sense in the matter. But a fly, artificial or real, is----" Freddy spread out his hands, for words entirely failed him. "Well," said Dan after a pause, "I don't know what to say, since everything is so vague. However, I shall assume that such a gang exists, and shall do my best to aid you to bring about its destruction, as that means my marriage to Lillian. To help, I must have money, so the sooner we get North and engage one of Vincent's machines with all the latest improvements, the better shall I be pleased." He moved towards the door, as they were in Laurance's rooms when this conversation took place, and there he halted. "I think, Freddy, you will have a chance of proving in your own person, as to the truth of your supposition regarding this gang!" "What do you mean?" asked Laurance somewhat startled. "Well," murmured Dan, "the gang knows you started the hunt for its destruction, as I expect the members read the papers. If that is the case you will be a source of danger, such as Sir Charles was and----"

"I'll look after myself," interrupted Laurance grimly. "Well, if you don't, and the worst comes," said Dan agreeably, "I shall carefully examine your corpse for the celebrated fly."

"I'll look after myself," said Laurance again, "and if you think I am going to give up doing business through fear of death, you are much mistaken. If I can find the gang and exterminate the gang, I'll get a much larger salary, and so will be able to marry Mildred."

"Oh, that's her name, is it? Mildred Vincent! Is she pretty?" "You might not think so, since Miss Moon is your ideal," said Freddy, with a blush. "Mildred is dark and tall, and well-proportioned--none of your skimpy women, old man."

"Lillian isn't skimpy," cried Halliday indignantly. "I never said she was. Let us call her fairy-like."

"That's better. And your Mildred?" "You'll see her when we go North the day after tomorrow."

"Good!" Dan nodded thankfully, "we go to Vincent the day after to-morrow?"

"Yes. Meet me at a quarter to twelve at St. Pancras Station; the train leaves at mid-day and we change at Thawley for Beswick about four o'clock. I expect we'll arrive--all going well--at Sheepeak about six."

"Good. But why shouldn't all go well?" inquired Dan, after a pause. Laurance chuckled. "According to you, the gang will hunt me down, and as you are in my company--well!" he chuckled again. "Oh, I don't care a cent for the gang, no more than yourself," retorted Dan with a shrug. "I'm not even going to think of the beasts. We go North to get the machine which will enable me to win this two thousand. And then----"

"And then?" echoed Laurance with a grin. "Then I shall discover the truth, crush the gang, and marry Lillian." In this way, therefore, the muddy water was stirred up.

CHAPTER VI

THE INVENTOR

Freddy Laurance usually opened his mouth to ask questions, rarely to talk about himself. In the newspaper world, confidences may mean copy, given that such are worthy to appear in print. Therefore, as the young man found, it is just as well to be sparing of personal details, and having made this discovery, he was careful to keep his tongue between his teeth in all matters dealing with his private life. This reticence, useful in business, but wholly unnecessary in friendship--particularly when the friendship had to do with Dan Halliday--had grown upon Laurance to such an extent that he said very little about his love affair. Dan, being a genial soul, and a fellow-sufferer in the cause of Cupid, and having a heart-whole liking for the journalist, resented being shut out in this way. He therefore made it his business to extract Freddy's love story from him when the two were in the train making for Sheepeak, *viâ* Thawley and Beswick. "Where did you meet her?" asked Dan abruptly, as they had the compartment to themselves, and he had exhausted not only the newspapers but the magazines. "Her?" repeated Laurance, who was calmly smoking, with his feet on the opposite seat, "what her?"

"The her. The one girl in the world for you?"

"Oh, bosh!" Freddy colored, and looked pleasantly embarrassed. "Is it? Perhaps you are right!" and Dan began to hum a simple little American song, entitled, "I wonder who's kissing her now." Laurance took this personally. "No one is! I can trust her."

"Trust who?" asked Dan innocently. "The person you mentioned now. Miss Vincent, Mildred."

"Did I mention her? Well, now you recall her name, I did. Old man, we are the best of friends, but this fourth estate habit of holding your confounded tongue is getting on my nerves. Give yourself a treat by letting yourself go. I am ready to listen," and he leaned back with a seraphic smile. Freddy did not fence any longer, but came out with details. After all, since he could trust Dan, he was beginning to think that it would be delightful to talk his heart empty. "She's the dearest girl in the world," was the preamble. Dan twiddled his thumbs. "We all say that. Now Lillian----"

"Mildred! We are speaking of her." Freddy spoke very fast lest his friend should interrupt. Since Dan wanted confidences, Dan should have them given to him in a most thorough manner. "Mildred is an angel, and her uncle is an old respectable, clever beast."

"Yes!" said Halliday persuasively. "I thought in that way of Sir Charles when he interrupted private conversations between Lillian and myself. I am of the same opinion as regards Sir John Moon because----"

"Yes, I know what you mean by because. But with regard to Mildred----"

"Who is an angel. Yes?"

"I met her a year ago in London--Regent Street, to be precise as to locality. A snob spoke to her without an introduction, so she appealed to me, and I punched his head. Then I escorted her home----"

"To Hillshire? What a knight-errant," chuckled Dan. "Don't be an ass. I escorted her to the Guelph Hotel in Jermyn Street, where she and her uncle were staying. The uncle appreciated the service I did for his niece, and made me welcome, especially when he found that, as a newspaper man, I was able to talk in print about his machines. For an inventor the old man had an excellent idea of business."

"Inventors being generally fools. So you called the next day to see if Miss Vincent's nerves were better." Freddy cast a look of surprise at Dan's dark face. "How did you guess that, Halliday? Well, I did, and I got on better with Solomon Vincent than ever."

"Undoubtedly you got on better with the niece," murmured Dan, mischievously. "Well," Laurance colored, "you might put it that way."

"I do put it that way," said Dan firmly, "and from personal experience."

"Not with Mildred. Well, to make a long story short, I saw a great deal of them in town, and took them to dinner and got them theatre seats, and fell deeper in love every day. Then Vincent asked me to Sheepeak to inspect his machines and I wrote several articles in *The Moment*."

"Ah! I thought I remembered Vincent's name. I read those articles. But you didn't mention the niece."

"Ass!" said the journalist scornfully, "is it likely! Well, that's the whole yarn. I've been several times to Sheepeak and Vincent likes me."

"To the extent of taking you as a nephew?" inquired Dan, thoughtfully. "No, hang him! That's why I call him a beast. He says that Mildred is necessary to his comfort as a housekeeper, and won't allow her to marry me. She is such a good girl that she obeys her uncle because he brought her up when her parents died, and has been a father to her."

"A dull romance and a league-long wooing, with the lady in Hillshire and the swain in London. How long is this unsatisfactory state of things going to last, my son?"

"I don't know," rejoined Fred mournfully, "until her uncle dies, perhaps."

"Then let us hope he'll fly once too often," said Dan cheerfully; "but do not be downhearted. I am sure it will be all right. I shall dance at your wedding and you will dance at mine. By the way, there's no necessity to talk to Vincent or his niece about our endeavors to spot this gang."

"Of course not. The matter won't be mentioned. All I am talking about is private, and you come to Sheepeak with me to get a machine so as to win the London to York race. It will be an advertisement for Vincent." "That's all right. And Mildred--talk about her, old man. I know you are dying to explain the kind of angel she really is. Lull me to sleep with lover's rhapsodies"--a request, with which Freddy, now having broken the ice, was perfectly willing to comply. He described Mildred's appearance with a lover's wealth of details, drew attention to her many admirable qualities, quoted her speeches, praised her talents, and thus entertained his friend--and incidentally himself--all the way to Thawley. Dan closed his eyes and listened, puffing comfortably at his pipe. Occasionally he threw in a word, but for the greater part of the time held his peace, and let Laurance babble on about his darling's perfections. Secretly, Dan did not think these could match Lillian's in any way. At the great manufacturing town of Thawley, which was overshadowed by a cloud of dun smoke, the travellers left the main line, and crossed to another platform where they boarded the local train to Beswick. This station was only six miles down the line, and they turned on their tracks to reach it, since it branched off from the main artery into the wilds. It nestled at the foot of a lofty hill covered from top to bottom with trees, now more or less leafless. Laurance informed his companion that there was a ruined abbey hidden in the wood, and also pointed out several interesting places, for he was well acquainted with the locality. At Beswick they piled their bags on a ramshackle old trap, and proceeded in this to climb up a long, winding, steep road, which mounted gradually to the moors. As the year was yet wintry and the hour was late, the air became wonderfully keen, and--as Freddy said--inspiriting. Dan, however, did not find it so, as he felt quite sleepy, and yawned the whole way until the trap stopped at the solitary hotel of Sheepeak, a rough stone house, with thick walls and a slate roof. The landlady, raw-boned, sharp-eyed, and not at all beautiful, met them at the door, smiling in what was meant for an amiable manner when she saw Laurance. "Oh, you're here again?" she said defiantly, and Dan noticed that beyond the Northern burr she did not reproduce the country dialect. "Yes, Mrs. Pelgrin, and I have brought a friend to stay three or four days. We want two bedrooms and a sitting-room, and supper straight away."

"You shall have them," said Mrs. Pelgrin, still defiantly. "And the price will be a pound each for the four days," ventured Freddy. "With ten shillings extra for the sitting-room," said Mrs. Pelgrin, fiercely. "Oh, come now."

"I'll not take you in for less." "Well," put in Dan, shrugging, "sooner than stand here in the cold and argue, I shall pay the extra ten shillings."

"Cold, do you call it? Cold!" Mrs. Pelgrin's tone was one of scorn. "Ha, cold!" and she led the way through a flagged stone passage to a large and comfortable room at the back of the house. "Will this suit you?"

"That's all right, Mrs. Pelgrin," said Freddy, throwing himself down on a slippery horse-hair sofa--"and supper?"

"You'll have it when it's ready, no sooner and no later," barked the ogress, leaving the room. "Cold is it?" and she laughed hoarsely. "I say, Freddy," observed Halliday in a lazy tone, "why is the good lady so very savage?"

"She isn't, Mrs. Pelgrin is quite fond of me. I've stayed here often."

"Fond of you?" echoed Dan, with a chuckle. "Good Lord, how does she speak to those she isn't fond of?"

"It's Northern brusqueness. She's honest----"

"But rude. The two seem to go together with many people. They think they will be taken for rascals if they are decently polite." Laurance remonstrated. "Mrs. Pelgrin is a rough diamond."

"I like my jewels polished. However, here we are and here we stay, and here we eat, if that amiable lady will bring in supper. Then I shall go to bed, as I shall certainly yawn my head off if I don't."

"But it's just after six," cried Laurance. "I want to take you to see Vincent to-night--this evening, that is."

"Go yourself, and see the beautiful Mildred," muttered Dan drowsily. "Two's company and three's a crowd. I'm going to bed"; and, in spite of Laurance's arguments against such sloth, to bed he went, after a brisk fight with Mrs. Pelgrin over a fire in his sleeping apartment. He said that he wanted one, while the landlady declared that it was unnecessary. Finally Dan got his own way, and when the fire was blazing, Mrs. Pelgrin said good-night. "But you're no more nor a butterfly," she informed her guest, and went out banging the door, with muttering remarks concerning people who felt cold. "No doubt this weather is here regarded as tropical," murmured Dan, getting into bed and referring to the weather, and he smiled over Mrs. Pelgrin's manners until he fell asleep. Next morning Laurance woke him at eight, and Dan grumbled about getting up, although he was assured that he had slept the clock round. However, a cold bath soon brisked him up, and he came down to the sitting-room with an excellent appetite for breakfast. Mrs. Pelgrin brought it in, and again joked in her fierce way about the cold, which the butterfly--as she again termed Dan--was supposed to feel so keenly. Laurance talked about Mildred, who had been delighted to see him, but mentioned regretfully that he did not think that Dan would get the machine he was in search of. "Why not?" asked Mr. Halliday, lighting his pipe and finishing his third cup of coffee. "Vincent wants his aeroplanes exploited, doesn't he? And where will he find a better chance than for an experienced man, such as I am, flying his latest invention in *The Moment's* London to York race?"

"Vincent's a queer fish. That's all I can say," retorted Laurance. "Well, you can't say more and you can't say less, I suppose. We'll go and have a look at the queer fish in his pond whenever you like."

"At eleven o'clock then."

"Right oh! I can talk to the uncle and you can talk to the niece. It's a fair division of labor." This arrangement was willingly agreed to by Laurance, as Dan was certain it would be since he saw that his friend was fathoms deep in love. Afterwards, the two went out of doors and surveyed the landscape. Sheepeak was situated on the top of a lofty tableland, the village being a tolerably large collection of substantial stone houses, whence the moors spread north and south, east and west. From where they were, the friends could see the green squares of cultivated fields, the purple bloom of the heather, and the azure hues which distance gave to the distant mountains. Here and there the vast country, which looked enormously large from the elevation whence they surveyed it, dipped into verdant dales, snugly clothed with forests, and sprinkled with manor-houses and villages, big and little. The lands were so far-stretching and the prospect so extensive, that Dan became mightily impressed with the magnitude of the sky. It covered them like a huge inverted cup, and as there was nothing to break its league-long sweep, Dan felt quite small in the immensity which surrounded him above and below. "I feel like a pill in the Desert of Sahara," said Mr. Halliday, sighing. "What is the sensation of feeling like a pill," rejoined Laurance drily, for he was not an imaginative individual. "Only a poet can explain, Freddy, and you are very earthy."

"I never knew you were a genius," snapped Laurance, with a shrug. "You have much to learn," replied Dan reprovingly; "and as it's near eleven o'clock, suppose we light out for Vincent." Freddy agreed, and skirting the village for three-quarters of a mile, they suddenly came upon a small cottage, with walls and roof of yellowish stone covered with lichen, and standing in a small garden of wind-tormented vegetation. A low stone wall divided this from the high road, and the visitors entered through a small wooden gate to pass up a cobble-stone walk to the modest door. But the cottage itself was dwarfed wholly by huge sheds of wood covered with roofs of galvanized tin, which loomed up suddenly behind it, on a vast scale more in keeping with the character of the landscape. These were the workshops of Vincent, where he built his machines and housed them from prying eyes. The fields at the back cultivated into smooth lawns were where the aeroplanes started to fly over hill and dale, to the wonderment of the inhabitants. "Though they are pretty well used to Vincent's vagaries by this time," said Freddy, ending his explanation. Mildred received them in the small parlor of the cottage which was about the size of a doll's drawing-room, and expressed herself as pleased to make the acquaintance of Mr. Halliday. Her uncle, she mentioned, was busy as usual in his workshop, but would see the visitors in half an hour. While she explained, Dan took stock of her, and admitted that she was really a very amiable and pretty girl, though not a patch on Lillian. But then Dan did not care for tall ladies with olive complexions, blue eyes, dark hair, and the regal melancholy look of discrowned queens. Mildred--the name suited her--was too tall and stately for his taste, which approved more of little golden-haired women, fairy-like and frolicsome. Miss Vincent looked serious and thoughtful, and although her smile was delicious, she smiled very seldom. It seemed to Dan that her solitary life in these moorlands and in the company--when she enjoyed it--of her morose uncle, made the girl sober beyond her years, which were not more than two-and-twenty. However, many minds many tastes, and Dan could not deny but what Freddy's fair Saxon looks went very well with the Celtic mystic appearance of the inventor's niece. They were a handsome couple, indeed, but much too solemn in looks and character for Dan, whose liking leaned to the frivolous side of things. "Don't you find it dull here, Miss Vincent?" asked Halliday casually. "Dull!" she echoed, turning her somewhat sad eyes of dark blue in his direction, "oh, not at all. Why I have a great deal to do. We have only one servant and I assist in the housework. My uncle is not easy to cater for, as he has many likes and dislikes with regard to food. Then he employs a certain number of workmen, and I have to pay them every Saturday. Indeed, I look after all the financial part of my uncle's business."

"Is it a business, or a whim--a hobby?" inquired Dan respectfully, for, being frivolous, he was struck with awe at the multitude of Miss Vincent's employments. "Well, more of the last than the first perhaps," said Mildred smiling at his respectful expression. "Uncle Solomon really doesn't care for publicity. All his aim is to construct a perfect machine, and he is always inventing, and improving, and thinking of new ways in which to obtain the mastery of the air."

"His machines have been tried by other people, though," remarked Freddy. "Oh, yes, and with great success. But uncle doesn't even read the papers to see what is said about his aeroplanes, although he is always anxious to read what other inventors are doing, and takes a great interest in races across Channel and over the Alps, and from city to city. But he is wrapt up in his own schemes, and works for twelve and more hours out of the twenty-four in perfecting his machines. Public applause or public rewards don't appeal to him, you see, Mr. Halliday; it's the work itself."

"Ah, that is the true spirit of genius," said Dan approvingly, "a man like that is sure to arrive."

"He will never arrive," said Miss Vincent quietly, "for as soon as he arrives at one point, he only regards it as a resting-place to start for a further goal. He doesn't care for food or drink, or clothes, or politics, or amusements, or anything for which the ordinary man strives. His machine takes up all his attention."

"Happy man. To have one strong aim and to be allowed to work at that aim, is the true happiness of any man. I shall be glad to have a talk with him."

"He doesn't talk much, Mr. Halliday."

"A man obsessed with one idea seldom does," retorted the young fellow. "I hope, however, he will let me have a machine for this race. I can handle any aeroplane, once it is explained to me, and Freddy here, says that your uncle's machines have many improvements likely to tell against competitors."

"I am not sure if he will let you have a machine," said Mildred, her face clouding; "he is very jealous and whimsical you know." "Like all inventors," murmured Laurance rising; "let us go and see him."

"Yes," added Dan, also getting on his feet, "and then you take Freddy away, Miss Vincent, and let me talk to your uncle. I shall get what I want, somehow." Mildred laughed and led the way out of the cottage by the back door. "It is not an easy task you have set yourself to do," she said, doubtfully; "here are the workshops and the buildings where the machines are housed, and yonder is Uncle Solomon." The buildings looked plebeian and gimcrack with their flimsy wooden walls and tin roofs, impressive only in their magnitude. They must have cost a deal to erect in this neighborhood where all the houses, great and small, were of stone; and wood was comparatively scarce. Vincent, as Dan considered, must be well-off to indulge in so expensive a hobby. To be sure by racing he could gain prizes, and if successful could also sell machines at a good figure; but from what Mildred said, it seemed to Dan that her uncle had the true jealous spirit of an inventor, and did not let his darlings go out of his hands if he could help it. To live on this vast moorland, working at his inventions and experimenting with his ideas, was enough for Solomon Vincent, without the applause and rewards of the world. Undoubtedly to carry out his plans he must have a private income, and not an inconsiderable one at that. "Uncle, this is Mr. Laurance and Mr. Halliday," said Mildred, introducing the two young men, though the first did not require mention. But Vincent, like most inventors, was absent-minded, and it took him quite a minute to recognize Laurance, whom he had not seen on the previous night. "Mr. Laurance and Mr. Halliday," he said casually, and turning from the workman to whom he had been speaking--"yes, of course. You understand about the propeller, Quinton," he added, again taking up his conversation with the workman, "it must be seen to at once," and quite oblivious of the company he went on giving instructions, until the man went away to do his task, and Mildred touched her uncle's arm. "This is Mr. Laurance and Mr.----"

"Of course I know it is Mr. Laurance," said Vincent testily, "do you think I am blind? How do you do, Laurance? Good-by, I am busy."

"And this is Mr. Halliday who wants a machine," went on Mildred persuasively. "Indeed. Then Mr. Halliday shan't get one," retorted Vincent, and sauntered into the nearest shed with a scowl on his lean face. He was an acrid-looking man of fifty, with untidy gray hair and an untrimmed beard. "Follow him, and he will talk," said Mildred hastily, "I shall remain here with Freddy, as uncle doesn't like many people to be about him."

"He is not easy to get on with," sighed Dan, "I can see that." However, he took the girl's advice and went into the shed after the ungracious inventor, leaving the lovers to return to the cottage parlor, which they did forthwith. Laurance was quite astute enough to lose no time, since the moments spent with Mildred were all golden and not easily obtainable. Dan marched into the shed with a fine air of possession, and again surveyed Vincent, who was examining some specifications near a window. The man was carelessly dressed in a shabby suit of blue serge, and seemed to care little about his personal appearance. Marking once more his shaggy hair and beard, and yellow skin considerably wrinkled, the young man went up to him. As if waking from a dream, Vincent looked up, and Dan met the gaze of two very keen dark eyes, whose expression was anything but amiable. "Who are you, and what do you want?" demanded the owner of the eyes crossly. "My name is Halliday. I want a machine to race between London and York. I have just been introduced to you by your niece."

"My niece should have more sense than to have brought you here," cried the inventor fiercely; "you come to spy out my ideas and to steal them."

"I assure you I don't," said Dan drily. "I am not a genius as you are."

"All the more reason you should pick my brains," snapped Vincent in no way mollified by the compliment as Dan intended he should be. Halliday laughed. "If I did, I could make no use of my pickings, Mr. Vincent, as you may guess. I can handle a machine, but I can't put one together."

"Who told you about me?" demanded the man suspiciously. "Laurance."

"He's a meddlesome fool."

"Well," said Dan cheerfully, "there may be two opinions about that you know."

"I don't want him, and I don't want you, and I don't want any one. Why do you come and bother me when I don't want you?"

"Because my wants are to be considered. See here, Mr. Vincent," added Halliday in a coaxing voice, for he saw that it was necessary to humor this clever man like a child, "there is to be a race between London and York for a big prize given by *The Moment*, the paper Mr. Laurance works for. I wish to compete, but my machine isn't so good as I should like it to be. I hear that you have made several improvements which make for speed and easier handling of aeroplanes. Let me have one of your latest, and I'll share the prize with you. It's two thousand, you know."

"I don't want money," snapped Vincent abruptly. "I congratulate you," said Dan coolly; "and yet large sums must be needed to help you to build machines. You must be rich. Are you rich?" Vincent grew a dusky red, and glanced in an odd way over his shoulder, as if he expected to find some one at his elbow. "Mind your own business," he said in a harsh voice, and with suppressed fury; "whether I'm rich or not is my business. You shan't have an aeroplane of mine. Clear out." Dan did clear out, but as he went, wondered why the man was so angry and confused. He seemed quite afraid of the simple question that had been put to him.

CHAPTER VII

THE HERMIT LADIES

Dan was not naturally of a suspicious nature, but since taking up the profession of a detective, he had become so. Slight matters that formerly he would not have noticed, now attracted his attention, and, as the saying goes, he saw a bird in every bush. For this reason while returning slowly to the cottage, he considered Vincent's backward glance, which hinted at nervousness, and his unnecessarily angry reply to the question as to whether he was rich. Usually dreamy and absent-minded, the turn taken by the conversation had awakened the tiger in the man, and apparently he regarded Halliday as over-inquisitive. Yet why the inventor should take this view, Dan could not conjecture. But after musing for a few minutes, the young man began to think he was making a mountain out of a mole-hill. And whatever secret Vincent had in his life, as his suddenly aggressive attitude showed, it could have nothing to do with the particular quest upon which Dan was bent. Halliday, therefore, dismissed the matter from his mind with a shrug, and went into the cottage to disturb the lovers. "Well, Mr. Halliday," remarked Mildred, whose cheeks were flushed and whose eyes were bright, "what did my uncle say?"

"Very little, but what he did say was to the point. He refuses to let me have a machine."

"How like him," ejaculated Laurance quickly; "but upon what grounds?" Dan scratched his chin. "Really, I don't know. He seems to think that I am a spy desirous of learning his trade secrets. He called you a meddlesome fool, Freddy."

"Ah, that is because I wish to marry Mildred," replied Freddy drily; "it is very natural that Mr. Vincent should object to a man who comes to rob him of his treasure, so I don't mind his abuse."

"I am not a treasure," cried Mildred, becoming pink. "You are. Who knows that better than I, my darling."

"You think too well of me."

"Impossible. You are the best and dearest----"

"Stop! Stop!" Mildred covered her face. "Remember we are not alone."

"Oh, don't mind me," said Dan phlegmatically, "I'm in love myself, Miss Vincent." She nodded comprehendingly. "With Miss Moon. Freddy has told me."

"Has he told you that my marriage depends upon my finding out who murdered her father?" questioned the young man dismally. "Yes, and that you need money for the search."

"Which money," continued Laurance determinedly, "must be obtained by Dan winning this London to York race. That can be done, I am certain, with one of your uncle's aeroplanes, Mildred, as he has made wonderful improvements in their structure, and----"

"But he declines to furnish me with a machine," interrupted Halliday in a vexed tone, "not even my offer to share the £2,000 prize tempts him. He is too rich, I suppose?" He cast an inquiring glance at the girl. Mildred shook her head. "Uncle Solomon is not rich," she replied quietly. "He must be," insisted Dan sharply; "he could not indulge in such an expensive hobby otherwise."

"Mrs. Jarsell helps him with money, though, to be sure, he has a little of his own. Still, unless she supplied money, Uncle Solomon could not go on building aeroplanes, especially as he rarely sells one, and wishes to keep all his inventions to himself. His idea is to invent a perfect machine and then sell it to the Government, and he fancies that if he allows any one else to handle his aeroplanes, his secrets may be prematurely discovered."

"Well, I can see his objection in that way," assented Dan, "since more ideas are stolen than pocket handkerchiefs, as Balzac says. But Mrs. Jarsell?"

"She is a rich and rather eccentric lady, who lives at The Grange," said Mr. Laurance, before Mildred could reply. "I am as wise as I was before, Freddy. It's an odd thing for a lady to finance an inventor of flying-machines. She must be large-minded and have a very great deal of money."

"She is large-minded and she has plenty of money," admitted Mildred vivaciously; "her influence with my uncle is extraordinary."

"Not at all if she supplies the cash," said Dan cynically, "but I have an idea, Miss Vincent. Suppose we enlist Mrs. Jarsell's sympathies."

"About the murder?"

"No," said Halliday, after thinking for a moment or so. "I don't see the use of talking too much about that. The more secret Freddy and I keep our hunt, the better prospect have we of success, since the gang will not be on guard, as it were. No, Miss Vincent, introduce me to Mrs. Jarsell as a young and ardent lover who wishes to make money in order to marry the girl of his heart. If she is romantic--and nine old ladies out of ten are romantic--she will induce your uncle to, give me his newest aeroplane."

"If she decides to help you, Uncle Solomon certainly will give you what you want," Mildred assured him, "since Mrs. Jarsell has supplied him with so much money for his experiments." She thought for a second, then raised her head cheerfully. "We shall see Mrs. Jarsell and Miss Armour this afternoon."

"Who is Miss Armour?"

"Mrs. Jarsell's companion and relative and confidential friend. She's a dear old thing, and is sure to sympathize with your romance."

"All the better, so long as she can influence Mrs. Jarsell."

"She can influence her, as Mrs. Jarsell swears by her," put in Freddy. "Oh, I think you'll pull it off, Dan. It's a good idea to work old Vincent through the hermit ladies."

"The hermit ladies," echoed Dan wonderingly, "an odd reputation. Hermits are usually masculine."

"Mrs. Jarsell and Miss Armour are an exception," said Laurance laughing, "in fact they are modern representatives of that eccentric couple of ladies who lived at Llangollen. You remember them."

"I have heard the names," murmured Dan reflectively. "The old ladies of Llangollen, who eloped together and lived in Wales. I should rather like to see this pair that follow so strange an example. When are we to go?"

"This afternoon," repeated Mildred, nodding brightly, "I really think something may come of the visit, Mr. Halliday. You and Freddy go back to 'The Peacock' for dinner and then call for me later--say at three o'clock. I am a favorite with the hermit ladies and have leave to bring any one to afternoon tea. Especially nice young men. Mrs. Jarsell and Miss Armour are fond of young men."

"Giddy old things," said Dan gaily. "I hope they will take a fancy to me, as I shall do my best to charm them. Well?" "You must go now, Mr. Halliday, as I have much to do before taking an hour off." "Vincent works you too hard, Mildred," said Laurance impatiently, as he took up his cap, "you can't call a moment your own."

"I shall call two hours or so my own this afternoon," replied Mildred amiably, and sent the young men away quite happy, since there was a promising chance that Dan would gain his ends. "That's a delightful girl," said Dan, when the two were seated at dinner. "I should like to marry her if Lillian were not in existence."

"I'm glad that Lillian is, Dan, since I want to marry Mildred myself. Don't poach, you animal."

"I won't," promised Halliday generously, "I don't like dark hair. But it's no use arguing. Let us eat and drink, for I have to fascinate Mrs. Jarsell and her bosom friend. I'll get hold of that aeroplane, somehow."

"We are here for that purpose," said Laurance, determined to have the last word, and as Dan was hungry he let him have it. The Grange--at which they arrived late in the afternoon, the two men escorting the one girl--was a large, rambling mansion built of yellowish stone, its original color more or less washed out by rain and burnt out by sunshine. The surface of the massive walls was grimy with black and rough with lichens, while the broad, flat stones of the roof were covered with damp green moss. The house, although in two stories, was of no great height, and stood on the uttermost verge of the hill, which sloped abruptly down into the valley. The view should have been very fine, but sundry tall houses had been built round The Grange, which prevented the owner from enjoying the magnificent prospect. This shutting-in--according to the legend--was due to the malice of a disinherited brother in Jacobean times, who had created quite a village round about the estate so as to block out the view. But the present inhabitants did not mind much, for, as Mildred explained, both Miss Armour and Mrs. Jarsell stayed within doors a great deal. "In fact, Miss Armour is more or less paralyzed, and sits in a big chair all day, reading and knitting, and talking and playing Patience," said Mildred, as the trio turned into a small courtyard, and found themselves facing a squat door, set in a porch sufficiently massive to serve for the entrance to a mausoleum. An elderly maid, in an incongruous dress of brilliant scarlet, admitted them into a darkish hall, whose atmosphere, suggestive of a Turkish bath in a mild way, hinted that the house was heated by steam pipes, as indeed was the case. There were some carved boxes of black oak in the hall and three or four uncomfortable high-backed chairs, but the walls and floor were bare, and the general aspect was somewhat bleak. However, when the visitors were conducted along a narrow passage, ill-lighted and dismal, they were introduced to a large low-ceilinged room, richly and luxuriously and picturesquely furnished. The brilliant garb of the maidservant suited this room much better than it did hall or passage, and there was a suggestion of tropical splendor about the woman and the sitting-room, which revealed in Mrs. Jarsell a strong love of color, warmth, and light. Indeed, although there were three large windows looking out on to a garden, and immediately facing the door by which they had entered, yet the light which was admitted being insufficient--perhaps because of the wintry gloom--the apartment was brilliantly illuminated by six lamps. Three of these stood at one end of the room, and three at the other, on tall brass stands, and the light, radiating through opaque globes, filled the place with mellow splendor. The vivid scene it revealed was a strange and unexpected one to find in these barren wilds. What impressed Dan straight away, was the prevalence of scarlet. The walls were covered with brightly toned paper, the floor with a carpet of violently brilliant hue, and even the ceiling was splashed with arabesque designs, blood-red against the white background. The furniture was of black oak upholstered in satin of the same fiery tint, while the draperies were of a dense black, funereal in aspect. A large fire glowed on a wide hearth in a vermilion-tiled alcove, and the poker, tongs, shovels, and pincers were of brass. Also there were brass candlesticks, a tripod of the same alloy in which incense slowly smoldered and even brazen warming-pans of antique pattern were ranged on either side of the fireplace. Thus, the general color-scheme was of black, scarlet, and yellow. What with the barbaric hues, the warm atmosphere, and the faint scent of incense, Dan felt as though he had stumbled on the den of a magician, malicious and dangerous. But this may have only been an impression caused by coming suddenly into this tropical room out of the chill air and neutral-tinted landscape. Neither Mrs. Jarsell nor Miss Armour, however, carried their love of violent color into their personal attire, as both were arrayed--somewhat incongruously, considering the season--in unrelieved white. The former lady was tall and bulky and somewhat assertive in manner, with a masculine cast of countenance and watchful dark eyes. From the smooth olive texture of her skin, she had probably possessed jet-black hair, before age turned her still plentiful locks completely white. She was not, as Dan concluded, more than fifty, as she possessed great vitality, and gripped his hand in a vigorous, manly way, quite in keeping with her commanding looks. Her white gown was made perfectly plain; she did not display even a ribbon, and wore no jewellery whatsoever, yet her whole appearance was distinguished and dignified. Indeed, when she welcomed the young people she assumed something of a motherly air, but if the hint conveyed by the barbarically decorated room was to be taken, she was anything but maternal. Mrs. Jarsell, as Dan mentally confessed, was something of a puzzle; he could not place her, as the saying goes. Miss Armour had also an unusual personality, being the antithesis of her friend in looks and manner. To Mrs. Jarsell's massive assertiveness, she opposed a fragile timidity, and was as small of body as the other was large. Her oval, many-wrinkled face was the hue of old ivory, her features were delicate, and her small head drooped in a rather pensive manner. Her white hair, not so plentiful as that of Mrs. Jarsell, was smoothly arranged under a dainty cap of white lace, decorated, oddly enough, with diamond ornaments. And, indeed, she wore enough jewellery for both ladies; rings on her slender fingers, and chains round her neck, and bracelets on her wrists, with a belt of turquoise stones, a ruby brooch, and earrings of pearls. On a less refined person, this overloading of ornaments would have looked vulgar, but Miss Armour, although she glittered at all points like a heathen idol, preserved a calm dignity, which caused her sumptuous display to appear perfectly natural. It was very strange that such a mild-looking woman should deck herself out in this manner, so she, also, was a puzzle to Halliday's intelligence. Indeed, the two ladies, in their splendid room, suggested to Dan dreams of the Arabian Nights, and gave him the impression of being concerned in some gorgeous romance. Miss Armour, seated in the big chair which Mildred had mentioned, looked over Dan with mild, brown eyes, and evidently approved of his good looks. "I am glad to see you, Mr. Halliday," she said in a soft and musical voice, quite silvery in its sound. "To an old person, such as I am, the young are always welcome." Dan felt called upon to pay a compliment. "You don't look old," he said bluntly. "Well, now-a-days, sixty cannot be called old," said Miss Armour with a pretty laugh, "as I am assured that women of that age actually dance in London."

"The age-limit has been extended since Victorian times," laughed Laurance, who had seated himself near one of the windows beside Mildred. "Yes," assented Mrs. Jarsell, in deep tones suggestive of a mellow-sounding bell. "In those times, women went on the shelf at thirty-five, and lived again in their children. Now-a-days, there are no old people."

"Certainly not in this room," said Dan courteously. "You are Irish, I should say, Mr. Halliday," remarked Miss Armour, smiling, as she resumed her knitting of a red and white striped shawl; "only an Irishman could pay such a pretty compliment."

"My mother was Irish," admitted Dan amiably, "and I made a special journey to kiss the Blarney stone in the hope that it might oil my tongue." Mrs. Jarsell in her heavy way seemed amused. "You have certainly accomplished your purpose, Mr. Halliday. But what does a gay young man, as I see you are, do in this solitary neighborhood?" and her keen black eyes swept over him from head to foot inquiringly. "Ah," put in Freddy quickly, "that question brings out the reason of our visit to you, Mrs. Jarsell. Behold in my friend a lover."

"Delightful," cried Miss Armour with great animation, "and the lady?" "Miss Moon, the daughter of Sir Charles Moon."

"Moon? Moon?" murmured Miss Armour, as though she were invoking the planet. "I seem to have heard that name somewhere. Eliza?" she glanced at her friend. "Don't you remember the murder we read about some months ago?" replied Mrs. Jarsell heavily. "It was much talked about."

"It would need to be to reach my ears, Eliza; you know that I don't like hearing about crime. In this neighborhood," she addressed herself to Dan, "we live a quiet and uneventful life, and although we take one London newspaper daily, we know little of what is going on in the world. My friend reads to me about the theatres and dresses, and sometimes politics, but rarely does she inflict murder cases on me. I don't like to hear of crime."

"I read that particular case because it caused so great a sensation," said Mrs. Jarsell, in a deprecating tone. "You remember Sir Charles was poisoned by

- 61 -

some unknown woman. And now I recall the case, Mr. Halliday, your name was mentioned in connection with it."

"Probably," said Dan lightly, "I am engaged to Miss Moon."

"Have the police discovered who murdered Sir Charles?"

"No. Nor is there any chance that the police will make the discovery. The woman came and the woman went after doing her work, but she has vanished into thin air, like Macbeth's witches."

"I wonder why she murdered Sir Charles?" asked Mrs. Jarsell, after a pause. Halliday glanced at Laurance, and it was the latter who replied in a most cautious manner, wishing to say as little as possible about the quest. "The reason is not known, Mrs. Jarsell."

"But, why--" began Mildred, only to be cut short somewhat impatiently by Miss Armour, who had been moving uneasily. "Don't talk any more about the horrid thing," she broke out impetuously, "I don't want to hear. Tell me of your love affair, Mr. Halliday."

"There is little to tell," said Dan, relieved that the conversation was changed in this manner, since he did not desire to say too much of his business in connection with the crime, "and I would not tell you that little, but that I wish to enlist your sympathies and those of Mrs. Jarsell."

"You have mine already," declared the old lady vivaciously, "but why Eliza's?"

"Mrs. Jarsell can help me."

"Indeed," said that lady, looking at him hard, "in what way?"

"Let me explain," chimed in Freddy, impatient of Dan's slower methods, "Mr. Halliday wishes to marry Miss Moon and wants money."

"But she has plenty, Mr. Laurance. The papers said that the late Sir Charles was a millionaire."

"So he was, and Miss Moon is his heiress," cried Dan quickly; "all the same, I don't wish to live on my wife, and so desire to be in a position to offer her a home however humble. Now I am an aviator, Miss Armour, and there is to be a race for £2,000 between London and York. I wish to compete and desire one of Mr. Vincent's machines, as they are the most improved kind on the market."

"They are not on the market," said Mrs. Jarsell frowning. "Mr. Vincent will not part with his machines until he perfects a masterpiece, and then hopes to sell it to the Government. I don't wonder you failed to get an aeroplane from him."

"I did not say that," said Dan swiftly. "Not in so many words," rejoined Mrs. Jarsell deliberately, "but I can guess why you want my assistance, Mr. Vincent will give you a machine if I ask him."

"And you will?" said Halliday eagerly. "Oh, Eliza, you must," put in Miss Armour quickly. "Vincent will do anything for you, since you have helped him so much with money."

"I shall be delighted to help," said Mrs. Jarsell, in her quiet, slow manner; "you shall have the machine, Mr. Halliday, and I hope you will win the race and marry Miss Moon. But you are a bold man to offer to wed an heiress on £2,000. Don't you want more money?"

"I want heaps and heaps," said Dan laughing, "but I have no chance of getting it. However, two thousand will do to start with. Lillian--Miss Moon, that is--loves me well enough to marry me at once, even on the prize given by *The Moment*."

"Well, Eliza, will get you the machine, that is certain, Mr. Halliday. As to the rest, I have no doubt you will be successful and win the money; but you must have much more in order to marry Miss Moon, since I can see that you are much too honorable a man to live on her millions. The cards"--Miss Armour hastily put away her knitting and took a small box from a drawer in the tiny table which stood at her elbow--"my patience cards, Mr. Halliday, for you know, having few amusements, I am devoted to the game. Also I can tell fortunes. I shall tell yours," and she opened the box to take out two packs of cards. "Dan isn't superstitious," laughed Freddy, and approached with Mildred. "I don't know," said Halliday gravely. "I have known cases----"

"Well, have your fortune told now," broke in Mrs. Jarsell, going to the door, "it will amuse Miss Armour to reveal your future while I see about the tea. I am sure you young people must be hungry."

"But I haven't thanked you for your promise to get me the machine." Mrs. Jarsell nodded in a friendly manner. "When you win the race and marry the young lady, you can thank me," she said, with ponderous playfulness. "Miss Armour will tell you if the Fates will be kind to you in both respects," and she disappeared to get the tea, or rather to instruct the red-robed servant to bring it in. Meanwhile, Miss Armour, her mild face quite flushed with excitement, was spreading out the cards after Dan had shuffled them. She used only one pack, and Freddy looked on at the disposition of the colored oblongs with the deepest interest. Dan idly took up the unused pack, and the moment he brought them near his eyes to examine them, he became aware that there clung to them the same mysterious scent which Penn had stated came from Sumatra. New as he was to the detective business, he yet had enough sense to suppress his excitement at this discovery. Seeing that the ex-secretary had stated very positively that no one but himself in England possessed the perfume, it was strange indeed, that Dan should come across it in these wilds, and connected with the personal possessions of a harmless old lady, confined to her chair by partial paralysis. In spite of his coolness, he was so thunderstruck that he could scarcely stammer a reply to Miss Armour, when she asked him if his colored-card was clubs or spades. She saw his confusion immediately. "What is the matter?" she demanded sharply, and her face grew pale. "The heat of the room, the scents, make me feel rather faint," said Dan haltingly. "Remove the incense burner to the end of the room, Mr. Laurance," said Miss Armour, and when the young man did so, she turned to Halliday. "Are you, then, so susceptible to scents?"

"Yes. I don't like strong perfumes. You do apparently, Miss Armour. Why, even your cards are scented," and he held out the odd pack. The lady took the cards and smelt them, but showed no sign of emotion. "I expect it's some scent Eliza gave me a few weeks ago. I had it on my handkerchief, and it must have got on to the cards. Have you ever smelt a perfume like it before?" she asked suddenly. "No," said Dan, lying promptly, as he thought it best to be on the safe side, "and I hope I shan't again. It's too rich for my taste."

"And was for mine," said Miss Armour indifferently. "I only used it once or twice. Strange that you should be so susceptible to scents. However, you feel better now. That's right. And the cards? See! There is great good fortune coming to you."

"That's jolly," said Dan, now quite recovered. "In a few weeks," said Miss Armour impressively, "a wonderful chance will be offered to you. If you take it, a large amount of money will be yours within the year. You will marry Miss Moon if you seize this chance. If you do not, she will marry another person," and the fortune-teller gathered her pack. "In that case, I shall take the chance at once," said Dan promptly. Miss Armour looked at him hard. "I advise you to do so," she said briefly.

"WHY EVEN YOUR CARDS ARE SCENTED!"   *Page* 107.

CHAPTER VIII

AVIATION

The tea that followed the fortune-telling was quite a success, as Miss Armour was a most amusing talker, and the rest of the party proved themselves to be good listeners. The old lady, being an invalid, had ample time for reading, and concerned herself chiefly with French Mémoires, the cynical light-hearted tone of which appealed to her. But she was also well-posted in English literature of the best kind, and could converse very ably--as she did--on leading authors and their works. Dan complimented her on the knowledge she had attained. "Oh, but it is no credit to me, Mr. Halliday," Miss Armour protested. "I have so much time unoccupied, and grow weary of playing patience and of knitting. It would be strange if I did not know something, after years and years of reading. Books are my best friends."

"Then Mrs. Jarsell is also a book, or say a human document," said Dan politely. "She is the best woman in the world," cried Miss Armour, while Mrs. Jarsell bent her heavy white eyebrows in acknowledgment of the compliment. "You can have no idea how kind she is to me."

"And to whom should I be kind, but to my old governess," said Mrs. Jarsell in a gruff way. "Why, you have taught me all I know."

"And I should think Miss Armour could teach a lot," said Laurance in his pleasant manner; "you know so much and have such tact, that you should be out in the world governing people, Miss Armour." She sent a sharp glance in his direction, as if to inquire exactly what he meant. Then she accepted the compliment with a charming laugh. "But for this dreadful paralysis, I should, indeed, love to be out in the world. I love to deal with human nature, and make people do what I want."

"Can you?" asked Mildred anxiously. "Yes, child," replied the ex-governess quietly, "because I base my diplomacy on the knowledge that every one, with few exceptions, is ruled by self. Harp on that string, and you can manage any one."

"Miss Armour," put in Mrs. Jarsell, in her deep voice, "rather talks of what she would do than what she does. Here, we see few people. I go up to town on occasions, but very rarely."

"You must find it dull," said Dan candidly. For some reason Miss Armour appeared to think this speech amusing. "Oh, no; I don't find life dull at all, I assure you. There is always a great deal to be done, when one knows how to set about the doing."

"As how?" questioned the young man, somewhat puzzled. "Books and music, and card-games and knitting-work," said Mrs. Jarsell quickly, as if she did not approve of Miss Armour's observations; "nothing more."

"Quite so nothing more," assented the governess, but with a sudden flash of her brown eyes directed towards her friend. "Here we are out of the world. Do you stay long, Mr. Halliday?"

"Only for another couple of days, until I can get the machine."

"You shall get it, I promise you," said Mrs. Jarsell graciously, when the trio arose to depart. "Mr. Vincent owes me too much to disregard my request."

"Of course," chimed in Mildred. "Uncle Solomon would never be able to build his aeroplanes if you didn't help him with money. Good-by, Miss Armour."

"Good-by, dear child. I shall say *au revoir* to you, Mr. Halliday, as I shall expect you to come and see me again, if only to let me know that your fortune has come true."

"Will it, do you think?"

"Yes," said Miss Armour positively. "I am quite certain that the chance foretold by the cards will be given you." Dan hoped it would, and thanked the lady for her happy prediction, after which he and Freddy, with Mildred between them, left the weird house, and walked up the darkened road toward the village. Halliday went at once to the "Peacock," wishing to give Freddy and his beloved chance of a *tête-à-tête*. They took it readily enough, as Laurance escorted the girl home. It was an hour before he returned to an overdue supper, which Mrs. Pelgrin served with fierce grumbling. After supper, Dan spoke his mind to Laurance. "When I took up that extra pack of cards," he said abruptly, "I smelt that same perfume that hung about Sir Charles's clothes when he was dead."

"What!" Freddy sat up aghast in his corner of the room, "the perfume about which Penn explained?"

"The same. But did he explain? It seems to me that he told a lie. If he only had one bottle, and the perfume is not procurable in England, seeing it is manufactured in Sumatra, how did Miss Armour become possessed of it?"

"It may not be the same scent," said Laurance, still aghast; "you see a bird in every bush, Dan."

"This is not a question for the eyes, but for the nose. I tell you, Freddy, that the perfume is exactly the same."

"Why did you not ask Miss Armour about it?"

"I did; you heard me. She got it from Mrs. Jarsell, so she said. Now where did Mrs. Jarsell get it? From Sumatra?" "Perhaps. Why not ask her straight out?"

"No," said Dan decisively. "I shall not mention the subject to Mrs. Jarsell until I have questioned Marcus Penn once more. He told me a lie once, by saying that no one in this country possessed this especial perfume. He shan't tell me another."

"How do you mean to get him to tell you the truth?" asked Freddy dubiously. "Never mind. I have some sort of a plan. I shan't explain until it comes off. There is some connection between that perfume and the crime, I am certain," concluded Dan, with a positive air. Laurance wriggled uneasily. "Oh, that is absurd. On such assumption, you suggest that Miss Armour knows about the matter."

"About what matter?"

"You know--the gang."

"Well," said Halliday, smoking thoughtfully, "we are not entirely certain yet if such a gang exists. It's all theory anyhow, in spite of the letters you drew from this person and the other. Penn certainly explained the scent, but told an obvious lie, since Miss Armour has it. I don't say that she knows anything, but it is strange that she should possess the Sumatra perfume."

"Other people can send the same perfume to England," retorted Freddy. "Penn isn't the sole person who has friends in Sumatra. Mrs. Jarsell, since she gave the scent to Miss Armour, may have friends in that island. Ask her."

"No," said Dan, very positively. "I shall ask no one until I make Penn speak out. In any case, I want to know why he told a lie."

"Perhaps he didn't."

"I'm jolly well sure that he did."

"Then, to put it plainly--you suspect Mrs. Jarsell?"

"To answer plainly, I don't. There can be no connection between two harmless old ladies living in these wilds and the murder of Sir Charles. Yet this confounded scent forms a link between the dead man, Mrs. Jarsell, and Penn." Laurance rubbed his chin reflectively. "It's odd, to say the least of it. I suppose you are certain the perfume is the same?"

"I'll swear to it." Dan rose and knocked the ashes out of his pipe. "And I intend to learn how Mrs. Jarsell became possessed of it. I may be on a wild goose chase. All the same, with the stake I have, I can't afford to lose an opportunity."

"So Miss Armour said, when she told your fortune," commented Freddy thoughtfully. "Yes. I wonder what she meant?" Dan stretched himself. "I'm for bed. Ring the bell, and ask Mrs. Pelgrin for the spirits." Laurance, not feeling called upon to resume the conversation, as he was tired himself, did as he was told, and Mrs. Pelgrin, raw-boned and grim, bounced aggressively into the room, to demand fiercely what they required. She sniffed when whiskey was ordered, but as its consumption would increase her bill, she brought in a bottle of "Johnny Walker" and a siphon of soda, without argument. When she turned to depart, and wished them good-night in tones suggestive of a jailer, a sudden thought struck Dan. It would not be amiss, he thought, to question Mrs. Pelgrin concerning the hermit ladies. Not that he expected a great deal to result from his examination, as the worthy woman was a she-cat, and what she knew would probably have to be clawed out of her. "We had tea at The Grange to-day, Mrs. Pelgrin," said Dan casually. The landlady wrapped her hands in her apron and wheeled grimly at the door to speak aggressively. "Ho!" she grunted. "What's that?"

"I said 'Ho,' and 'Ho's' all I'm going to say."

"Well," drawled Freddy with a shrug, "you can't say much less, you know."

"Less or much, I don't say anything," retorted Mrs. Pelgrin, screwing up her hard mouth and nodding. "Nobody wants you to say anything," remarked Dan lazily, but on the alert. Of course this speech opened the landlady's mouth. "People say as it's queer two ladies should live like dormice in a haystack," she observed significantly. "That's like people. They will meddle with what doesn't concern them."

"Not me," snorted Mrs. Pelgrin violently and epigrammatically. "I don't say what I could say, for what I could say wouldn't be what's right to say."

"Wouldn't it?" inquired Freddy innocently. "No, it wouldn't, sir; I'm not to be pumped," cried Mrs. Pelgrin, "try you ever so hard. So there!" and she screwed up her mouth tighter than ever. "Who is pumping?" asked Dan coolly; "I simply remarked that we had tea with Mrs. Jarsell and Miss Armour to-day."

"Friends of yours, no doubt?" snapped the landlady. "I never saw them before to-day, Mrs. Pelgrin." "Then don't see them again," advised the woman sharply. "Thank you for that advice. Anything wrong?"

"Wrong! Wrong! What should be wrong?" Mrs. Pelgrin became more violent than ever. "There's nothing wrong."

"Then that's all right," said Halliday coolly. "Goodnight." Mrs. Pelgrin stared hard at him, evidently wondering why he did not press his questions, seeing how significant a remark she had made. The idea that her conversation was trivial in his eyes hurt her self-esteem. She gave another hint that she knew something. "I wonder how those ladies make their money," she observed casually to the ceiling. "Ah, I wonder," agreed Dan, making a covert sign that Freddy should restrain the question now on the tip of his tongue. "Three motor-cars," said Mrs. Pelgrin musingly, "four servants, women all and sluts at that, I do say, with a house like a palace inside, whatever it may be to look at from the road. All that needs money, Mr. Halliday."

"Quite so. Nothing for nothing in this greedy world."

"Ten years have those ladies been here," continued the landlady, exasperated by this indifference as Dan intended she should be, "and dull they must find that old house. To be sure, Miss Armour is ill and never moves from her chair--so they say," she ended emphatically and stared at Halliday. "So who say?" he inquired phlegmatically. "Every one, sir. She's paralyzed--so they say."

"And Mrs. Jarsell attends to her like an angel," remarked Dan suavely; "they say that also, you know."

"Why do you advise us not to see the ladies again?" asked Freddy, who could no longer rein in his curiosity. Halliday was annoyed by the question, as he thought it would dry up the stream of Mrs. Pelgrin's hinted information. But instead of this happening, she became excessively frank. "Well, it's this way, Mr. Laurance," she said, rubbing her nose in a vexed manner. "You are two nice young gentlemen, and I don't want either of you to step in and spoil George's chance."

"George?"

"My nephew, he being the son of my late husband's brother, and a porter at the Thawley Railway Station. Mrs. Jarsell had taken quite a fancy to him, he being a handsome lad in his way, and the chances are she will leave him a lot of her money, if you two gentlemen don't take her fancy. Now you know my reason for not wanting you to see her again."

"Oh, I don't think Mrs. Jarsell will leave either my friend or me money," said Dan affably. "George Pelgrin is quite safe. I suppose one good turn deserves another."

"What do you mean?" said the landlady, sharper than ever. "Well, George Pelgrin must have done something for Mrs. Jarsell to make her leave him money."

"He's done nothing, and she don't say she'll leave him her money, but George thinks she might, seeing she has taken a fancy to him. I don't want you, or Mr. Laurance here, to spoil my nephew's chances."

"Oh, we shan't do that," rejoined Halliday calmly. "I suppose George finds it dull at the Thawley Station, when there are no Sheepeak friends there with him. Working at the station, that is."

"Oh, he doesn't find it dull," replied Mrs. Pelgrin innocently; "he has made friends with plenty of Thawley folk. Are you going away to-morrow?"

"Perhaps, and perhaps the next day," said Dan, wondering at the direct question. "You see I wish to get an aeroplane from Mr. Vincent, and as soon as I do, I shall go back to London."

"You'll be seeing Mrs. Jarsell again?" Halliday shook his head. "I shall be too busy to spare the time." Mrs. Pelgrin drew a breath of relief, and again became fierce. "I ain't ashamed of what I've said," she declared, pulling open the door violently; "you can tell the whole village if you like," and she bounced out as she had bounced in, leaving Laurance overcome with surprise. "Now what's the meaning of all that chatter?" he asked, staring at Dan. "Oh, it's very plain. Mrs. Jarsell has taken a fancy to her nephew, and Mrs. Pelgrin thinks our fascinations may spoil his chance of getting money. What I want to know is what George has done for Mrs. Jarsell to warrant the deep interest she apparently takes in him. Evidently," mused Dan to himself, "there are not other Sheepeak people employed at the Thawley Station." "What of that?" Laurance stared harder than ever. "Nothing. Only George Pelgrin would be the only person likely to know Mrs. Jarsell at the Thawley Station. There are motor-cars also, remember."

"I really don't see what you are driving at, Dan."

"I scarcely see myself, save that I want to learn the secret of that perfume, and why it forms a link between Moon and Penn and Mrs. Jarsell."

"But how can this chatter of Mrs. Pelgrin's help?" asked Freddy, more and more puzzled. Dan lighted his bedroom candle and walked slowly to the door before he replied. "I shall have to sleep upon what I know before I can answer that," he said, nodding. "Good-night, old chap."

"But Dan, Dan, Dan!" called out Laurance, who had heard just enough to make him wish to hear more, "tell me----"; he stopped speaking, as he saw that Halliday was out of hearing. It was in a very dissatisfied frame of mind that Laurance retired to his bed. Next morning Dan had evidently quite forgotten the conversation of the landlady, for he made no remark, and although Freddy tried to start the subject again he declined to revert to it. Halliday declared that he did not know what to say, that he was putting two and two together, but as yet could not make four, and that it would be just as well to seek Mr. Solomon Vincent, to hear if he was disposed to supply an aeroplane. "Only I wonder," he remarked irrelevantly, as he walked up the road with his friend, "how it comes that Mrs. Pelgrin speaks more like a Londoner than a Derbyshire woman."

"I thought we discussed that question before," replied Laurance. "School-boards are doing away largely with the local dialect. Also Mrs. Pelgrin, as Mildred told me, was in service for some years at Reading. Why do you ask?"

"Oh, I ask nothing," said Dan easily; "it was only an idea I had."

"Connected with the case?"

"Yes, and with Mrs. Jarsell."

"Pooh. You see a bird in every bush, Dan."

"So you said before," rejoined Halliday drily; "why repeat yourself? Hullo, there is our inventor!" he added, as they drew near to the cottage, "and, by Jove! he's smiling. Mrs. Jarsell had evidently spoken to him." It was as Dan said, for Vincent received the young men with a sour smile, which sat uneasily on his face, since he was more accustomed to frowning. However, as he was disposed to be amiable, Dan was thankful for small mercies, and expressed his feeling loudly when the inventor graciously placed at his disposal an aeroplane of the latest construction. "I owe Mrs. Jarsell much," said Vincent, leading the way toward the shed, "so her requests must be granted. Here is the machine, Mr. Halliday."

"It's very good of you----"

"It isn't. Don't thank me, but Mrs. Jarsell. Speaking for myself, I shouldn't allow you to have the aeroplane," said Vincent sourly. "I want to keep all my improvements to myself until I make a perfect machine."

"Oh, I'll keep all your secrets," Dan assured him cheerfully as they entered the vast shed, "and I'll share the prize money with you."

"I don't want it. Win the race and prove that my machine is the best. That is all I ask. By the way, where is Laurance?"

"Don't you remember? We left him in the cottage with your niece."

"I don't want him to marry her, and he shan't," said Vincent with a frown, speaking on the subject unexpectedly, "and, what is more, since he's a newspaper man, I don't want you to talk too freely to him about my improvements."

"Laurance can hold his tongue," rejoined Dan somewhat stiffly; "your trade-secrets are safe with him. So this is the machine," he ended, to avert further discussion on the inventor's part. "Yes," said Vincent, forgetting all else in the passion of his hobby, and he began to explain matters. "A biplane, as you see, and it can carry enough oil and essence for a twelve hours' flight. Wheel it out," he added, turning to a quartette of workmen. "Mr. Halliday will try a flight." Dan was only too ready, as the beauty of the machine appealed to him immensely, especially when he beheld it in the pale light of the sun, when it was brought into the open. The men wheeled it out of the back part of the shed on to a level lawn, which could serve as a starting-place. Vincent talked all the time in a great state of excitement, and pointed out the various improvements and beauties of the masterpiece. The planes were not exactly horizontal, since Vincent considered that he gained more power by making them branch at a slight angle. The wings were doubly covered with fine canvas, and a broad streak of crimson ran through their white, which the inventor informed Dan was a characteristic of all his machines. "A sort of distinguishing mark, as it were," said Vincent. Another improvement was that the aviator could steer with his knees on occasions, which gave freedom to the hands when necessary. The engine was light and powerful, with tremendous driving-power considering its size. Finally, the steering-seat--the bridge of the airship, as it might be--was fenced in comfortably with aluminium, and a broad expanse of mica protected the controller of the aeroplane from the force of the winds. It was really an admirable machine and Halliday was loud in his praises, to which, however, its maker paid little attention. Genius does not require laudation, talent does. Dan inspected the machine in every direction, tried the steering gear which ran easily, saw that the engine was well supplied with fuel, and tested, as well as he could, the various spars and ropes and bolts. Then he took his seat in the pilot-box, and prepared for a trial flight. "Not that she hasn't been out before," said Vincent, while Dan gathered his energies to start. "Ready, Mr. Halliday. Let her go." The workman ran the machine along the lawn, Dan set the propeller going, and after lightly spinning along the ground for some distance the aeroplane rose into the gray sky like an immense bird. A side glance showed Dan that Mildred and her lover were running out of the shed, and had arrived just a moment too late to witness his start. However, he had no time to pay attention to terrestrial matters, for all his capabilities were given to handling the new craft. Up and up he went to a considerable height, with the engine running true and sweet, then dived nearly to earth in switch-back fashion, only to tower again like a hawk. Shortly he was at a lofty elevation, travelling along at top speed in the direction of the ten-mile-distant Thawley. Vincent and his workmen, Laurance and the girl, became mere black dots, and beneath him the earth slipped past at more than railroad speed. Once in the vast spaces of the firmament Dan let his engines travel at their fastest, and the vanes of the propeller spun, as an American would say, like greased lightning. Halliday's pulses raced almost as fast, as the joy of playing with death seized him. In the delicate structure of the aeroplane--being its soul and controlling power--he felt like a bird and swooped in mighty arcs in proof of his mastership of the sky. In a few minutes he was over Thawley, and a downward glance showed him innumerable black insects running with excitement here, there, and everywhere, as the machine was sighted. Dan dipped nearly to the weathercock of the parish church, then slid out toward the northern portion of the town. Making his aerial way with the speed of the wind Thawley was soon left behind and the aviator hovered over a wide country dotted with villages, intersected with streams, and rough with more or less high hills that divided the many vales of the country. Ten minutes took him out of Hillshire, and he flew over the mild Yorkshire moors. The air sang past him on either side of the mica screen, which prevented his breath being taken away. Everything was taut and fit and neat, and in its right place, and the engine sang a song of triumph, which mingled with the droning hum of the screw. Below was the painted earth, above the gray sky, faintly illuminated by the wintry sunshine, and between the two Halliday flew with the swiftness of a kestrel sighting its prey. Dan was used to this sublime excitement, and could control his feelings--otherwise he would have shouted for joy, which would have been from his point of view, a mere waste of energy. He finally reached York, circled round the Minster, and then turned his craft homeward in glee. The machine was certainly the best he had yet handled, and he made sure that given moderately decent conditions he would win the race and gain the £2,000 necessary to continue his search for Moon's murderess. And the capture of her, as he reminded himself, meant his marriage with Lillian. No wonder the young man's heart beat high, for it was not easy to come by so magnificent an aeroplane, and he felt as grateful to Vincent for building it as he felt to Mrs. Jarsell for procuring him the mastership of the same. Those left behind on the lawn behind the Sheepeak shed stared steadily into the gray distance, and shortly saw a dim spot moving toward them with the swiftness of an eagle. Larger and larger it grew, until they could distinguish the aeroplane's construction, like a delicate tracery against the clouds. In a wide circle it moved gracefully and then like a bird folding its wings, settled gently at the very feet of its inventor. The trial was a complete success in every way.

CHAPTER IX

MAHOMET'S COFFIN

The aeroplane acquired by Halliday could be dismounted in three parts, so that it could easily have been taken to pieces and packed for transfer to London. But the race for *The Moment* prize was to take place within seven days, and Dan wished to familiarize himself with the machine as much as was possible in the interval. For this reason he decided to go by air to the metropolis, taking the journey in easy flights, with intervals of rest between. He therefore arranged to send his baggage back to town with Freddy, and carried only a small black bag containing absolutely necessary personal effects. Freddy did not object to this plan, as he did not wish to leave Mildred sooner than was necessary. Therefore Dan started and Laurance remained behind to pass golden hours in the girl's society. However, he promised his friend to be in London within two days. And as Halliday, besides covering the hundred and sixty-odd miles in short flights, desired to practise aviation in the open spaces of the country before getting to the capital, it was not needful for Freddy to return to his business until forty-eight hours had passed. This arrangement suited both the young men very well. Vincent, who was now as hot in Dan's favor as he had been cold, presided at the start, and again and again went over various details in connection with the machine, which was much dearer to him than any child could have been. Now that his objections had been set aside by the intervention of Mrs. Jarsell, the inventor was desperately anxious that Dan should win the race, as such a triumph would undoubtedly show the value of the new-fangled biplane. Not that Vincent wished for the money, or even for the glory, but he very greatly desired to show other inventors that he was their master. His vanity, being purely concerned with the result of nights and days of meditation, could only be gratified by actual proof that he had conquered the air. Not entirely that is, for Vincent was far too thorough in his genius to believe that Rome could be built in a day; but, at all events, he trusted that his machine would reveal itself as the best that any man had yet constructed. So far as that was concerned, Halliday, accustomed to aviation, believed that the sour old man had succeeded. "If I don't win the race, it won't be your fault, Mr. Vincent," Dan assured him, as he stepped into the pilot's box, and, with this farewell speech, the inventor expressed himself very well content. He did not expect impossibilities, and he saw that the man to whom he had entrusted his darling airship was both cool and enthusiastic, qualities which go far toward complete success. It was a calm day, with scarcely any wind, when Dan began his flight, and as the biplane could easily attain sixty miles an hour he would have had no difficulty in reaching London early in the afternoon. But he did not make straight for the south, but circled gradually down to Rugby, where he proposed to remain for the night. Dawdling in the air, it was five hours before he alighted outside the town, and feeling weary with the strain on his nerves--for the machine required dexterous handling--he determined to rest. Without much difficulty he found a friendly farmer, who was willing that the airship should be housed in an empty barn for the night. When all was safe and Halliday had arranged that no one should enter the barn, he sought out a cheap inn on the borders of the place to rest for the night, within watching-distance of his craft. Next morning, after breakfast, he concluded to start again, but after a visit to the barn to see that all was well, he returned to the inn for an hour. It was necessary, he thought, to consider the situation and his future plans, and he wished for solitude to do so. Owing to his fatigue, he had not been able to think much on the previous night before sleep overtook him. The plan, which Dan intended to carry into effect when he reached Town, was to force Penn into confessing what he actually knew concerning the perfume. He had obviously spoken falsely as to his being its sole possessor in England, since Mrs. Jarsell had given the like scent to her old governess. Yet, why should Penn lie in this fashion, unless there was some secret connected with the perfume, which he desired to keep concealed. And assuredly the scent had clung round the clothes of the dead man. Dan determined to force Penn into confession, and that could only be done by frightening him greatly. To carry out this plan, Halliday wrote to the man asking him for an interview, and when he came--as Dan was certain he would--intended, in some way, to inveigle him into taking a flight. Once Penn was in the air his fears could be played upon to some purpose. At least Dan thought so, and was eager to make the experiment. Of course, the young man did not suspect Mrs. Jarsell of being connected in any way with crime of any sort. Still it was strange that the perfume from Sumatra should form a link between her and Sir Charles Moon, with Penn intervening. It was also strange that Mrs. Pelgrin should hint that Mrs. Jarsell had secrets. She had not said as much in so many words, but the general trend of her cautious conversation went to show that Mrs. Jarsell was not entirely open and aboveboard. The landlady had wondered where the owner of the Grange got her money. Now why should she so wonder, unless she had proofs that the said money was not come by honestly? And why, also, should she, in a quite unnecessary way, mention her nephew, who was the Thawley station porter--friendly with Mrs. Jarsell to such an extent that there was a chance of his getting a legacy? Ladies of wealth do not make friends of railway porters without reason, and Dan wished to learn the reason in this particular case. By a diplomatic question he had ascertained from Mrs. Pelgrin that her nephew was the sole Sheepeak person employed at the station. Consequently he would naturally be the sole person who knew Mrs. Jarsell and all about her; therefore it was not impossible that the lady befriended the man so that he might not speak of her visits to town. Yet why should he not do so, should Mrs. Jarsell's doings be entirely honest? Then there were three motor cars, a quite unnecessary number for a lady to keep, especially as, according to her own story, she went out little and spent most of her time in attending to Miss Armour. On the whole, although his suspicions were vague, Dan had an idea that Mrs. Jarsell's doings would not bear the light of day. Still--and especially since she had procured him the biplane--he would not have troubled about her rustic affairs save for the fact of the perfume. It might be--and this he hoped to discover--that Penn's confession would show more plainly the link which connected Mrs. Jarsell with the Hampstead crime. Yet, on the face of it, the very idea seemed monstrous, and Dan scorned himself for his folly as he wrote the letter to Penn. Nevertheless, something stronger than himself drove him to post the letter. Afterwards, to get the unpleasant taste of conspiring out of his mouth, the young man wrote a lover-like epistle to Lillian, telling her about his capture of the aeroplane. "You and Mrs. Bolstreath must come and see the start of the race at Blackheath," wrote Dan, "and your mere presence will inspire me to do my very best to win. So much hangs on my gaining this race, as I want the money to prosecute the search for your father's assassin!" Then Halliday left business for pleasure, and, telling Lillian that he adored her to distraction, urged her not to see too much of Lord Curberry. Finally, he declared that he was hungering for a glimpse of her angel face, and now that he was returning to London intended to call and see her, despite the prohibition of Sir John. There was much more passionate writing to the same effect, and the letter ended with sentiments of lively and lofty devotion. If another man had written the letter Dan would have smiled at its vehemence, since the scribe cast himself under Miss Moon's dainty feet to be trampled upon. But as Dan was the author of the epistle, he only regretted that he could not say more ardent things than he had set down. To such lengths does the passion of love carry the most matter-of-fact of men; and Halliday certainly prided himself upon being a very up-to-date child of this materialistic age, believing in nothing he could not see, or touch, or feel. The letters having been posted, and the bill paid, and the black bag packed, Dan took his way to the barn of the friendly farmer. He found quite a number of people before the great doors, as the news that an aviator was in the neighborhood had spread rapidly. The farmer did not wish to take any rent for the night's lodging of the aeroplane, but as it had been guarded so carefully and was housed so comfortably, Halliday insisted on the man having some recompense for his kindness. Then, with the assistance of three or four willing onlookers, the machine was wheeled out into the meadow wherein the barn stood. It was close upon mid-day when Dan started, and the spectators gasped with awe and delighted surprise when the biplane, like a big dragon-fly, soared into the cloudy sky. Willing to give them pleasure, since an airship was not a common sight in the neighborhood, Halliday did some fancy flying, and circled and dipped and towered directly over the town before finally waving his hand in farewell. A thin cry of many throats came to his ears as he sped southward, and he was delighted to find how readily the machine answered to every motion of his hand. He almost felt that he was riding on a live thing, all nerves and energy, so obedient was the craft to his will. The machine was like a flying beetle, the planes motionless to sustain the body like the front wings of the insect, while the propeller, spinning vigorously, acted like the back wings to drive ahead. Dan had a faint idea of seeing some comparison of this sort in a magazine, and wondered if Vincent, having seen it also, had constructed his aeroplane on insect lines. But he soon dropped all conjecture to attend strictly to his business, which was to reach London as speedily as possible; no very difficult task, considering the swiftness of his vehicle. It was convenient that Dan should know a shed at Blackheath where he could house his machine, as Lord Curberry's house was in that neighborhood. Once on the spot it would be easy to have an interview with Marcus Penn, and perhaps not difficult to induce him to take the air in the loft spaces of the sky. The neighborhood was well known to Halliday, for his occupation of aviation brought him often there, and he had experimented with various inventions at various times, where the land afforded room for the departure and arrival of the machines; therefore, when he reached London's outskirts he made for Blackheath, and without difficulty brought the aeroplane to earth, a stone-throw from the shed in question. It said a great deal for the capabilities of the biplane that her pilot was enabled to strike his destination so exactly. Of course, the usual concourse of people gathered when the great bird-like structure fluttered down from the sky, but Dan sent a messenger to the man who looked after the shed, and soon had Vincent's masterpiece safely put away under lock and key. As he had been practising flying and strenuously testing the qualities of the machine, it was quite five o'clock before he was free to do what he would. As the distance from Rugby was just over eighty miles he could have arrived much earlier had he wished. But there was no need to do so, and every need to accustom himself to handling the biplane easily in view of the great race. When Dan had given certain instructions to the man who looked after the shed and was responsible for the safety of the machine, he walked across the Heath to a comfortable inn, where he was well known, as he had put up at it many times previously. It was here that he had appointed the meeting with Marcus Penn, for the next morning, but so eager was he to come face to face with the man and wring the truth out of him, that he almost decided to walk to Lord Curberry's house, which was two miles distant. But a swift reflection that he could do nothing until the next morning--since Penn had to be coaxed on to the aeroplane and certainly would decline a night-run--decided him to wait. The "Black Bull" was a particularly comfortable hotel and the landlady supplied tasty dinners; therefore Halliday took the good the gods sent him and settled down for a quiet evening. After a stroll to the shed to see that Vincent's creation was all right he returned to the inn and went to bed. His nerves speedily relaxed, and he slept deeply until nine o'clock in the morning. As he had invited Penn to see him at eleven, he had just time to take his breakfast comfortably, read the newspaper, and saunter; out to take the fresh air before his visitor arrived. Marcus Penn had not improved in looks since Dan had last seen him. His thin face was still yellow, his hair and moustache still scanty, and he appeared to be as nervous as ever. When he sat down he looked apprehensively at Halliday with his pale eyes, and passed his tongue over his dry lips. It seemed to the aviator that Penn's conscience was not quite at rest, else he would scarcely look so scared, when--on the face of it--there was no need to do so. Dan, however, soon set him at his ease, which was the first necessary step towards gaining his confidence. For, unless that was gained he assuredly would not set foot on the aeroplane. "How are you getting along, Mr. Penn?" said Halliday, genially. "Have a cigarette and something wet? Oh, I forget you don't drink so early in the day. I am glad you are up to time, as I am just starting out on a fly."

"Really," remarked the secretary eagerly. "I should like to see you make a start. Is your flying-machine near at hand?"

"In the shed over yonder, on the verge of the Heath," said Dan, jerking his head over his left shoulder; "but I daresay you wonder why I asked you to see me, Mr. Penn?"

"Well, er--that is--er--I did wonder a trifle," hesitated the pale man, and again looked anxious. "It has to do with your literary ambitions," said Halliday slowly. Penn flushed, looking both relieved on learning why he had been summoned to the meeting and pleased that the subject should be of such personal interest. "What do you know of my literary ambitions?" he asked doubtfully. "All that Miss Moon could tell me," said Dan, promptly, and this was absolutely correct, as Lillian had long ago asked him to aid the secretary, although he had never troubled about the matter until now. "Yes, I certainly did tell Miss Moon that I wished to become a novelist. I found her sympathetic."

"Yes, she would be; she always is. I suppose," said Dan darting off at a tangent, "that you are comfortable with Lord Curberry?"

"Oh, yes," assented the man, cheerfully. "I have good pay and little to do, and Lord Curberry is very kind. I have plenty of time to write my stories."

"Have you had any published?"

"No," sighed Penn, sadly, "I have tried again and again to get some short tales printed, but so far, without success. "Well, then, you know that I have a friend--Mr. Frederick Laurance--who is on that newspaper *The Moment*. I suggest that you should send me some of your manuscripts for him to read. If he approves of them he will see what he can do, as he knows nearly every one of any note in the literary world." "Oh, you are too good. I shall be delighted. All the same," Penn hesitated, and writhed, "why should you do this for me?"

"It is Miss Moon who is doing this for you," rejoined Halliday, saying what was perfectly true; "she asked me to help you. I suppose she comes sometimes to Lord Curberry's house?"

"Oh, yes," said Penn, with a swift glance at him, "her uncle, Sir John, and Miss Moon and Mrs. Bolstreath dined with Lord Curberry last week. I am afraid, Mr. Halliday," added the secretary timidly, "that you will lose Miss Moon." Dan laughed cheerfully. "I don't think so. Why should I?"

"Her uncle is very anxious for her to marry Lord Curberry, who is also very desirous to make Miss Moon his wife."

"That shows Curberry's good taste," said Halliday rising, and putting on his cap. "However, she is to be my wife, and Curberry and Sir John can go hang."

"I should not be so sure, Mr. Halliday," said Penn, in a mysterious manner, "when Lord Curberry wants anything, he generally gets it."

"He is crying for the moon just now," said the other man making a pun, "and the moon is no man's property. However, I must go off to start for my flying practise. I am going to compete in the London to York race next week. Come with me and see me start. As to your stories, you can send them to me at my old address, which you knew when you were with Sir Charles. I shall see Mr. Laurance about them."

"You are good," murmured Penn, drawing a long breath and following Dan out of the inn. "I am obliged to you."

"To Miss Moon, you mean. She is the one who takes an interest in your literary efforts. But come along and see my machine. I got it from an inventor called Vincent," and Dan turned suddenly to shoot an inquiring glance at his companion. It occurred to him that Penn might have heard the name since Penn had the perfume as well as Mrs. Jarsell, who knew the inventor. But evidently Penn had not heard the name, for he gave no sign of knowledge. "I hope it is a good machine," he said innocently and weakly. "Very good," said Halliday, as they halted near the great doors of the shed, "a clipper. Why not try a fly with me?" "Oh!" Penn shrank back. "I should be afraid."

"Nonsense, man!" joked the aviator while the aeroplane was wheeled out, and the usual crowd of onlookers began to gather. "As a literary man you ought to experience all sensation so as to write about it. Coming stories will be full of flying-machines and airships."

"Isn't it dangerous?" asked Penn, looking at the delicate structure which appeared almost too fragile to sustain one person, let alone two. "Not at all, especially if one doesn't do any fancy flying, which I shall avoid if you come with me."

"I should like to have the experience," hesitated the secretary, "that is if you will not fly too high or too far."

"I'll take you across the Heath and back again and will keep within a tolerably safe distance from the ground."

"It's tempting," quavered Penn, wistfully, while Dan busied himself in getting things square. "Please yourself," rejoined Halliday carelessly, and satisfied that the timid man was nibbling at the bait. "I can't stay here all day." He slipped into the pilot's seat. "Well, well?"

"I really think I should like--where am I to sit?"

"In this place." Dan touched a spring and the pilot box of aluminium lengthened out so that there was room for two people. This was one of Vincent's improvements upon which he prided himself, as the vehicle could, by adjusting the closed-in car, seat two people or one, as the need arose. "But don't come, if you feel the least fear." Those of the idle spectators close at hand grinned at Penn's pale face, and he was stung into accepting hastily what he would have rejected in a cooler moment. "I am not afraid," he said, trying to steady his voice, and with an air of bravado he stepped in beside the aviator. "Oh, I say," he gasped. And no wonder. Dan did not give him a moment to change his mind. Having captured his prey, he intended to keep him, so set the engine going almost before Penn was comfortably seated. In less time than it takes to tell the aeroplane whirled along the ground swiftly and lifted herself gracefully upward. Penn gasped again, and glanced down at the sinking ground, where the spectators were already beginning to grow smaller. But the motion of the biplane was so easy, and the face of her pilot was so composed, that after the first thrill of terror Penn began to feel that flying was not such a very dangerous pastime as he had imagined. "Wonderful, wonderful," he murmured, as the great artificial bird glided smoothly through the air, "but don't--don't go too high, Mr. Halliday."

"I shall go high enough to smash you," said Dan, coolly. He was circling in swallow flights round the Heath, now high now low, now swift now slow, and had the machine so entirely under command that he was enabled to give a certain amount of his attention, though not all, to his companion. Penn gasped again, and his terror revived. "Smash me! Oh!!" he almost shrieked. "Yes," said Dan, not looking, since he had to watch where he was going, but speaking rapidly and clearly all the same. "I want to know the truth about that perfume. About the Sumatra perfume you told me was possessed alone by you. That was a lie, and you know it was a lie."

"I--I--I don't know anything more about it," whimpered the secretary. "Yes you do. Out with the truth," said Dan relentlessly, "if you don't I shall drop you overboard to smash like an egg." Penn clung to his seat desperately. "That would be murder."

"I daresay, but I shouldn't suffer. Accidents will happen in aeroplanes you know. You are like Mahomet's coffin, slung between heaven and earth, and overboard Mahomet's coffin will go in a few minutes unless----" Dan swerved the machine which tilted slightly and Penn went green with terror. "What--what--what do you want to know?" he wailed, as the biplane dipped nearly to earth, to sweep upward in a graceful curve. "Who is Mrs. Jarsell?"

"I--oh, Lord--I don't know."

"You do. She has this perfume also. Has it anything to do with a gang?"

"Yes, yes." Penn's teeth were chattering, and the sinking motion made him sick. "What has it to do with a gang?" "It's--it's a--a sign."

"Was Sir Charles murdered by this gang?"

"I don't know--I don't know. Oh!" Penn screamed and clutched again at the side of the car. "You do. This false Mrs. Brown belonged to the gang."

"I can't say. I daren't tell you. If I say anything I shall die."

"You shall die if you don't say what I want you to say," said Dan between his teeth, and again the machine dipped and towered. "I'll tilt you out, I swear, if you don't tell me who murdered Sir Charles."

"I don't know, I tell you," cried Penn desperately, "the perfume has to do with a society of people, who--who--but I daren't speak. I should be killed. I have said too much as it is. And if you reveal what I have said, you will be killed also."

"I don't care. Is Mrs. Jarsell connected with this gang?"

"I don't know Mrs. Jarsell," said Penn sullenly, although his terrified face showed that he was nearly frightened out of his wits. "Do you belong to this-----" started Dan, when a sudden action of Penn took him by surprise. In endeavoring to frighten the man he had flown too low, and the aeroplane was only six feet off the ground, preparing to swing skyward again. The secretary, in desperation, flung himself sideways out of the machine, as it curved at the lowest and fell heavily on the herbage of the Heath. Dan could not stop to see if he was safe or hurt, but soared aloft again to a considerable height. Circling widely he came sailing directly over the spot where the secretary had tumbled out in his desperate endeavor to escape. Already the man had picked himself up and was limping off toward the town as quickly as he was able. "Now," said Dan grimly to himself, "he will have me arrested for attempted murder. That's all right," and he chuckled, although not entirely successful in his endeavor to make Penn confess.

CHAPTER X

ANOTHER MYSTERY

In his anxiety to learn the truth Dan was perfectly willing to be arrested on whatever charge Penn might wish to bring against him. After all, publicity was what he chiefly aimed at, and if he gave his reasons for threatening the secretary, he felt confident that the man would find it difficult to clear his character. Certainly Halliday had not intended to take Penn's life, and had not the man been such a coward he would have simply laughed at the idea of being tilted out of the machine. But his nerves, shaken by the possible danger, had given way, and he had said much which he would have preferred to keep locked up in his heart. But that the aeroplane, by dipping so low, had afforded Penn the chance of escape at the risk of a rough fall, he would have spoken at greater length. And yet, after turning the matter over in his own mind, Dan could not be sure of this. But this much Halliday had learned. A gang assuredly existed, and the perfume was a sign of recognition amongst the members, who apparently followed each other's trails by scent. Penn declined to say if his late employer had been done to death by the fraternity, but the perfume on the dead man's clothes answered this question very positively. Also the secretary had denied that the false Mrs. Brown belonged to the gang, a statement which was absurd, as undoubtedly she was the emissary employed to bring about the death. Finally, the fact that Mrs. Jarsell used the Sumatra scent brought her into connection with the Hampstead crime; whatever Penn might say Dan felt that he had struck a trail, which would end in the capture of Moon's assassin and the breaking up of a dangerous organization. On reflection he concluded that Penn would have said very little more, even though face to face with what he believed to be imminent death. He had hinted sufficiently to show that revelation was dangerous not only to himself but to Halliday, for if the gang learned that their secret was betrayed, it was certain that death would be portioned out to the man who heard, as well as to the man who spoke. On this assumption Dan felt confident that Penn would take no action in the matter, and would probably hold his tongue about the adventure. If he told any of the gang to which he presumably belonged, he would have to admit that he had betrayed the secret of the perfume, in which case he would assuredly be killed by his unscrupulous associates. The death of Dan, as the young man believed, would follow, but he also believed that by taking care of his own skin Penn would remove any risk of vengeance following himself; therefore he was not surprised when he heard nothing from Penn, or of Penn during the days that passed before the morning of the great race. Meanwhile he detailed the conversation to Laurance. That young gentleman had returned to town with some regret since Mildred Vincent was not by his side. But to assure himself of an early marriage by securing a steady income, he flung himself into journalistic work with redoubled energy, working night and day to gain an increased salary. He was in his office employed on a political article when Dan presented himself, and was not overpleased to give up even a moment of his precious time. In fact, he grumbled. "I wish you would come after business hours, Halliday," he said testily. "Oh, fudge," retorted Dan lightly. "A journalist hasn't any business hours. Like a king, he is always in harness. Why do you require me to tell you such elementary truths, Freddy?"

"I have an important article to write."

"Well, then, you can write it in ten minutes or so. I shan't keep you long." Laurance pushed away his writing paper, leaned back in his chair, and reached for a cigarette. "What is it, then?" he asked resignedly. Dan paced the office and related his adventure. "So you see, old son, that the perfume is of great importance, as I always suspected." Laurance nodded gravely. "It appears so. But if what you think is true, would the man have disclosed a secret dangerous to his own safety?"

"People will disclose anything when on the rack," replied Dan with a shrug, "and the aeroplane was my rack. The fool really believed that I would tilt him overboard, and therefore said what he did say to save his confounded skin. If he had not escaped so cleverly he would have admitted more." "I doubt it. From the hint he gave, if it was death for him not to confess to you, because you could kill him, it was equally death for him to speak, if his associates are prepared to murder him for babbling. However, we are now certain that the gang alluded to by Sir Charles does exist. Undoubtedly he was got out of the way since he knew too much."

"It is a pity he did not reveal his knowledge to Durwin."

"He intended to do so, but was murdered before Durwin arrived, as we know. By the way, Durwin is as keen as we are over this search. I met him the other day and he said that he was hunting everywhere for evidence. Why not tell him what you have learned, Dan? He can make Penn speak out."

"Penn won't speak further," denied Dan abruptly. "I think, as it is, he dreads the vengeance of his comrades."

"Durwin belongs to Scotland Yard, and has powers to drive Penn into a corner, so he may be able to force confession. I think you should consult with Durwin about the matter."

"After the race then."

"Why not before the race, which does not take place for a couple of days?"

"I don't like doing things in a hurry," said Halliday uneasily. "I want to question Mrs. Jarsell, and see if she knows anything."

"If she does, which is doubtful, she will assuredly refuse to speak. So far, I see no connection between her and the gang."

"You forget the perfume."

"H'm, yes," said Laurance meditatively, "perhaps you are right. I want to have more evidence before I can give an opinion. But since Penn told you so much, aren't you in danger from the gang yourself, Dan?"

"I think not. Penn, for his own sake, will hold his tongue. At all events he has not moved so far."

"That doesn't say he won't move. I should examine that aeroplane very carefully before the race, if I were you."

"Oh, I'll do that. I know the machine thoroughly by this time, and if it has been tampered with I shall soon spot the trickery. Well, now that I have brought you up to date with my information I shall leave you to work."

"One moment. Is Miss Moon going to see you start for York?"

"Yes. I got a letter from her this morning. She and Mrs. Bolstreath come to the aviation ground with Lord Curberry, confound him," and with a frown, Dan took his leave. He was anything but amiably disposed towards his rival. Everything was quiet as regards the criminal business for the next two days, as Penn made no attempt to punish Dan for the fright he had given him. Halliday himself was much too eager over the race to trouble about the matter, but he kept a sharp eye on the Vincent machine, still stored at Blackheath, so as to guard against any tampering. The start was to take place at Blackheath, and on the appointed day five competitors were on the spot surrounded by a large crowd of curious people anxious to witness the conquest of the air. Amongst those present was Durwin, who pushed his way to where Dan was looking over his aeroplane. The aviator did not see the lean, keen-eyed man until he was touched on the elbow. "Is it all right, Halliday?" asked Durwin, nodding toward the machine. "Perfect. She's a beauty, and it won't be her fault if I don't lift York Minster before sunset. What are you doing here, Mr. Durwin? I didn't know that you took an interest in aviation."

"I take an interest in this search for Moon's assassin," said Durwin drily, but in low tones. "Laurance saw me and related your discovery. I am looking about for Marcus Penn and intend to ask him questions."

"He may be on the ground," said Dan, glancing around, "since Lord Curberry's place is a stone-throw away. But he won't speak."

"I'll make him speak," said Durwin with a grim look. "Well, I hope you'll win, Halliday. When you return to town look me up. I may have something to tell you," and he moved away with a significant look. Dan could not leave his machine, or he would have followed, as there were several questions which he greatly desired to ask. The day was cold and dry, with few clouds, and a good deal of sunshine, so the conditions for the race were fairly good. The wind was rather high, and that vexed the aviators, as the art of flying is not yet so perfect as to control the winds when they are over-strong. However, to go against these strong air-currents would be an excellent test of the qualities of the various machines. The start was to take place at one o'clock, and the competitors hoped to reach their destination before five o'clock. Some of the aeroplanes could travel at forty miles an hour; others at fifty, but so far as Dan knew, his was the sole machine which could gather sixty-miles-an-hour speed. If Vincent could be believed, the aeroplane ought to travel the hundred and eighty-odd miles, if the conditions were tolerably good, in a trifle over three hours. Dan, now having perfect mastery of the biplane, hoped to accomplish the wonderful journey in a shorter space of time. But this hope had yet to be verified. Meanwhile, having seen that all was in order, he turned to speak to Lillian who had just come up accompanied by Mrs. Bolstreath. Lord Curberry was in attendance, and in the distance Dan caught a glimpse of the yellow-faced secretary, looking unhappy and nervous. "Oh, Dan, I do hope you will win," cried Lillian, who looked extremely pretty, but more than a trifle anxious; "it does seem so dangerous to fly in such a light machine."

"She's the best I have yet struck," Dan assured her. "Don't you think she's as perfect as Lillian, Mrs. Bolstreath?" The elderly lady laughed and cast a sideglance at Curberry, to see how he took Halliday's complimentary speech. "Well, I suppose you cannot think of anything prettier to say. I have heard of a woman being compared to a gazelle and to a ship, but never to a flying-machine."

"Mr. Halliday is very up to date in his compliments," said Curberry with a slight sneer. He was a tall, bilious-looking man, with pale blue eyes and a thin-lipped sinister mouth, not at all prepossessing in appearance, although immaculate in dress. Dan laughed. Being confident that Lillian would never marry this spectre, he could afford to laugh. "We young people," he said with emphasis, "go with the times, Lord Curberry." "Meaning that I belong to the past generation," retorted the other with a flash in his pale eyes; "you will find that I don't in some ways," and he glanced significantly at Lillian. Mrs. Bolstreath looked nervous, but Miss Moon was supremely indifferent. She did not care for Lord Curberry, and in spite of her uncle's advocacy had not the slightest idea of marrying the man; therefore she ignored him as consistently as she could considering the way he thrust himself into her company. Without taking notice of this passage-at-arms, she began to question her lover about the airship, and gathered quite a stock of information before the start. Curberry being ignorant of aviation was out of the picture, as the saying goes, so fumed and fretted and looked daggers at Dan. It took all Mrs. Bolstreath's diplomacy to keep him in a moderately good temper. Luckily Laurance strolled up, note-book in hand, as he was reporting for *The Moment*, and greeted the party gaily. He knew Curberry slightly and nodded to him without any word or salutation. In common with many other people, Freddy did not like the man, who was by no means a popular character. "Isn't it a splendid day for the race, Miss Moon?" said Laurance, casting an upward glance at the grey sky. "I look forward to chronicling Dan's triumph in *The Moment* to-morrow morning. Well, old fellow," he slapped Halliday jovially on the back, "are you prepared for what Jules Verne would call the very greatest journey of the century?"

"The century is yet young," replied Dan drily, "and it's only one hundred and eighty odd miles I have to travel. Considering that aviators have reached a successful distance of five hundred miles this race is a trifle."

"Well," said Lord Curberry, trying to be amiable--a hard task for him, seeing how much Lillian was taken up with the hero of the moment--"aviation has certainly accomplished wonders since Santos Dumont took his flight of ten yards some four years ago." "Oh, you do know something about aviation, Lord Curberry," said Dan coolly. "I know that it is dangerous, Mr. Halliday."

"Oh, Dan," Lillian grew pale, knowing what the spiteful speech meant. "I think flying looks more dangerous than it is," said Dan with a reassuring glance, "and Miss Moon has come here to be my mascot."

"You will wire your safe arrival as soon as you get to York," said Mrs. Bolstreath anxiously. "Oh, every one will wire," cried Freddy, taking out his field-glass, "the telegraph offices will be kept hard at work all the night. As sure as I stand here, Mrs. Bolstreath, Dan will be the richer to-morrow by £2,000."

"If he is safe, I shall be content," breathed Lillian, and she looked as though she would have kissed Dan then and there, in spite of the presence of the crowd and Lord Curberry. That unsuccessful suitor scowled, and was about to make one of his acid speeches, when those authorities arranging the race came to declare that all was ready for the start. Already the cinematographs were at work taking pictures of the crowd and the machines and their various pilots. Policemen drove back the throng to some distance, so that the aeroplanes might have a clear space to run in, and just as the hour of one sounded the start was made amidst a breathless silence. The aeroplanes ran along the ground like startled hens, and sprang into the air at various points. The eyes of the people from looking level now began to stare upward at the diminishing dots which towered and raced for the north. A zigzag monoplane was leading, but Lillian had only eyes for Dan's craft. Freddy gave her his field-glasses so that she might get a better view. Three of the aeroplanes bunched, but two circled away some distance in wide arcs, and of the two, one machine belonged to Dan. The onlookers saw him increase the speed of his propeller and then, like an arrow from the bow, he sped swiftly out of sight in a straight line. A cheer rose from the throng, as the Vincent airship was leading by some lengths, and Lillian gave Freddy back his glasses. "I hope he'll come back safe," she said with quivering lip. "Of course he will," Laurance assured her. "Dan is one of the most cautious aviators we have."

"But there is always a risk," sneered Lord Curberry. "Probably. Only a brave man would take the risk."

"You don't fly yourself, Mr. Laurance."

"As you see," was the calm reply, as Curberry's enmity was too paltry to trouble about. "Well, Miss Moon, we can't see anything more, so I suppose you will go home."

"Miss Moon is coming to luncheon with me," said Lord Curberry, "and Mrs. Bolstreath also."

"I am very hungry," said that lady pensively, "so I don't say----"

"Hallo!" interrupted Laurance, as a clamor arose on the outskirts of the now fast diminishing crowd, "what's the matter? In the interests of my paper I must see what is taking place," and with a hasty raising of his hat to the ladies he left them to the care of Lord Curberry. As he pushed his way toward the commotion he heard a voice asking if the man was quite dead, and fancied that someone must have fallen down in a fit. But when he broke through the ring of policemen, and beheld Durwin lying on the ground, with staring eyes and a ghastly, expressionless face, the sight so startled him that he caught a constable's arm. "What's all this?" he demanded hoarsely. "Is Mr. Durwin dead?" "Durwin," echoed the policeman sharply, "do you know the gentleman?"

"Of course. He is Mr. Durwin, one of the Scotland Yard officials. I wonder you don't know that."

"I never heard of him, sir. He must belong to the detective department." "What's the matter with him; has he had a fit?"

"He's been murdered," said the constable shortly. "Murdered?" Laurance stared at the man in a horrified manner, and his thoughts flew to the gang which he and Dan and Durwin were trying to root out. Was this another crime similar to that committed at Hampstead, when Sir Charles was killed for knowing too much? "Is there a fly on him?" asked the reporter hastily; "see if there's a fly."

"A fly!" The policeman evidently thought the speaker was crazy. "What has a fly to do with the matter? Here's the Inspector, who was sent for some time ago. You had better speak to him, sir." Laurance did so, and advanced toward the soldierly-looking official who made his appearance. In a low and rapid voice, Laurance hastily explained that the prone man was Mr. Durwin, of Scotland Yard, and also handed the Inspector his own card. Meanwhile a doctor was examining the body, and found that the deceased had been murdered by having a dagger thrust under his left shoulder-blade. He was quite dead, and must have passed away almost immediately the blow was delivered. The Inspector received this uncompromising statement with natural surprise, and knelt down beside the corpse to verify the declaration. There was no doubt that the medical man spoke the truth, for a stream of blood stained the back of Durwin's coat, and had soaked into the ground. The thrust must have been made with a very sharp instrument, and was undoubtedly delivered with great force. "Who knows anything of this?" demanded the Inspector, rising and looking at the awestruck faces of the crowd sharply. A slim lady-like girl stepped forward. "I was standing close to the gentleman," she explained nervously, "and we were all looking at the airships as they went away. I heard him give a gasp, and when I turned at the sound, he was slipping to the ground. That's all I know."

"Did you see any one strike him?"

"No, I didn't. How could I, when with the rest I was staring at the airships going away. The gentleman was staring also, I think. But of course I didn't take much notice of him, as he was a stranger to me."

"I saw him fall," put in a rough man, something like a navvy; "he was crushed up against me in the crowd, and I felt him tumbling. I heard him gurgle, too, and heard this young lady cry out. Then I saw him on the ground, and pushed back the folk, saying there was a cove dying. But I didn't think it was murder," ended the man, shuddering. "Nor did I," chimed in the slim girl. "I fancied it was a fit. I'm sure we were all so crushed up with the lot of people, that I shouldn't have been surprised if he had taken a fit." This was all that could be learned, and the Inspector took the names and addresses of the two who had spoken. There were other people who had noted the man on the ground, but these were the sole ones to see the fall. They had, as it were, almost caught the assassin red-handed. But it was impossible to say who was guilty, for the throng was so dense and every one's attention had been so earnestly fixed skyward on the airships that no one could say who had struck down the unfortunate gentleman. The Inspector was much impressed when he learned the identity of the dead man. Once or twice he had received official letters from Durwin, but he had never set eyes on him until he beheld him dead. But for Laurance he would not have known who he was, and therefore questioned that young gentleman closely when the body was carried by four policemen off the ground to the nearest place where it could be placed under shelter. "And what about this fly?" asked the Inspector, who had heard of the question from the policeman who Laurance had first addressed. "Don't you remember the case of Sir Charles Moon?"

"Yes. The woman who killed him was never discovered. I remember about the fly, and also I remember the letters written to that newspaper of yours."

"I wrote the first letter that brought forth the correspondence," said Freddy quickly. "Sir Charles had some idea that a gang of criminals was in existence, and invited Mr. Durwin to his house to explain. Before Mr. Durwin arrived Sir Charles was murdered. Since then he had been looking into the matter, and I believe that he also learned too much."

"You think that this gang you mention had him put out of the way?"

"Yes, I do, and that is why I asked if there was a fly on him. It's the trademark of these devils, I fancy."

"Well, there didn't appear to be any fly on him," said the Inspector in an uneasy tone. "All the same, I think your idea is right. Moon was murdered because he knew too much, and Mr. Durwin has been got out of the way for the same reason; at least I think so. However, we shall learn more between this and the inquest. You will attend, Mr. Laurance?"

"Of course. I am only too anxious to find out all I can about this dangerous gang. It must be broken up."

"The breaking up will be attended with considerable danger," said the Inspector in a very dry tone. Then he noted Freddy's address and let him go. Laurance returned to the office of *The Moment* and hastily wrote his description of the start for the London to York race, after which he saw the editor and related what he knew about the death of Durwin. Permitted to write the article dealing with the subject, Laurance gave a concise account, and although he did not say too much, yet hinted very plainly that the death of the Scotland Yard official was connected indirectly with the murder of Sir Charles Moon. Remembering that Penn was now Lord Curberry's secretary, and that Lord Curberry's house was near the aviation ground, Freddy wondered if Penn had been amidst the crowd. Dan could have told him that he had been, but, at present, Laurance did not know this. However, he had a shrewd idea that as Penn was connected with one murder, he was probably connected with the other. Then Freddy cursed himself for not having observed if there was any special perfume hanging about the dead man's clothes. As he did not know the particular smell of the Sumatra scent he could not say if it was the one Dan had traced to Mrs. Jarsell, but if there was any scent at all, it was worth while looking into the matter. To repair his negligence he finished writing the article--which was very short--and then started for Blackheath to view the corpse again. As he was leaving the office of the paper a telegram was put into his hand. It proved to be from Dan, and had been sent from Bedford. "Had an accident," ran the wire, "rudder broke. No bones broken, but shaken by fall. I return this evening to town and will call. Halliday."

"Now I wonder," murmured Laurance, when he read the telegram, "if that machine was tampered with, after all. If so, the gang must be getting scared. First Moon, then Durwin, now an attempt on Dan's life. By Jove, I'll be the next." The idea was by no means a pleasant one.

CHAPTER XI

ON THE TRAIL

When Dan, looking rather pale and sick, presented himself at *The Moment* office late that same evening, the first question Laurance put to him was relative to the accident. "Was your machine tampered with?" asked Freddy in a breathless manner, and the second almost the door was closed. "No, it wasn't," replied Halliday, sinking with a tired sigh into the nearest chair. "I was making a quick turn and the rudder gave way; I put too great a strain on it, and came fluttering to the ground like a shot partridge. That was a few miles beyond Bedford. However, I had the aeroplane dismounted and packed away in a village close at hand, then after a rest caught the express to St. Pancras. You got my wire?"

"Yes, and I fancied this tumble must be the work of the gang."

"Not a bit of it. My bad flying, that's all. Well, I have lost the race, and the man who flew the Zigzag monoplane has won, though he took his own time in arriving at York. A dashed bad machine I think he had, even though it's come out top for the time being. I'm a bit shaken, and feel sick, but a night's rest will put me square."

"Why didn't you go straight home and get it?" inquired Freddy anxiously, for there was no denying that Dan looked considerably fagged. "I read about this death of Durwin in a late edition of an evening paper, and couldn't rest until I knew the truth. The paper only gave a hint. Tell me what you know." Laurance did so, and then handed Halliday a proof of his article on the subject which was to appear in the morning issue of *The Moment*. He supplemented the same with further information. "I went down to see if there was any scent on the clothes of the corpse," he explained, "it's still at Blackheath, you know, in charge of the Inspector. There's no perfume, anyhow."

"And no fly?"

"No. I asked that the moment I saw Durwin stretched out on the ground. If this crime is the work of the gang, the sign-manual is absent."

"All the same it is the work of the gang, I truly believe," remarked Dan in grim tones. "Durwin has been on the hunt, and very probably, since he discovered the death of Moon first of all, he has been watched. One of the gang got behind him in the crowd, and knifed him in the crush. It would be perfectly easy for the assassin to slip away, without being noticed, since every one was watching the flight of the aeroplanes." Laurance nodded. "I agree with you. But who is the assassin?"

"Well," said Dan reflectively, "I saw Penn on the ground."

"The deuce you did," cried Freddy jumping up, "did he----"

"Don't be in too great a hurry. He seems to me much too nervous a man to handle this job."

"But he belongs to the gang," insisted Laurance sharply. "He has as good as admitted that much by what he said of the perfume."

"Oh, yes, I believe he has something to do with the association, which, by the way, appears to be a kind of joint-stock company, like that one mentioned by Balzac in his story 'Histoire des Treize,' and----"

"Oh, hang your literary references," interrupted Freddy, anxiously pacing the office, "do you believe that Penn struck the blow?"

"No, I don't. The gang must have better men than he to strike."

"Or women," muttered Laurance, thinking of the false Mrs. Brown. "However, since Penn was in the crowd, and is plainly in the secret of the gang, don't you think we ought to tell the Blackheath Inspector about the matter, and also Inspector Tenson, who had charge of the Hampstead crime?"

"No," said Dan, after a pause. "If Penn is arrested and questioned, he will say nothing. As he hinted, he would be killed if he gave away the gang; so as he wouldn't split, when I threatened him on the aeroplane, he certainly won't speak out if questioned by the police. And we haven't got enough evidence to prove his complicity, remember. Better keep silence, Freddy, and let the police fog out this crime alone. Meanwhile, we can look round and keep an eye on Penn." After some argument, Laurance agreed to act as his friend suggested. It was no doubt the wiser course to take no action until absolute proof could be procured that the secretary was a member of the gang. Also, if Penn were arrested, the organization might break up and scatter out of sheer alarm, in which case all the villains would not be caught. Dan deemed it best to work quietly until the whole of the scoundrels could be netted, and to do so it was necessary to preserve silence. Thus it came about that, at the inquest on Durwin, nothing came to light likely to connect this crime with the preceding one. The hint given by Freddy in *The Moment* was not taken, and, indeed, was laughed at. There was neither perfume nor fly on the corpse of the unfortunate man, and consequently no link between Blackheath and Hampstead. An open verdict was brought in, and Durwin was buried without the truth becoming known in any detail. Then a new sensation took up the attention of the public. Nevertheless, both Dan and his friend were convinced that Darwin, having learned too much, had been done to death by the gang for its own safety in the same way as Sir Charles Moon had been put out of the way. They employed a private detective to watch Penn, but gave him no hint that they suspected him in any way. Through Penn, who was the sole person they knew for certain--and on the evidence of the perfume was connected with the gang--they hoped to arrive at the truth, but the time was not yet ripe for questioning him as regarded his nefarious doings. But they kept him well in sight so as to watch the path he took in life. There was no doubt that by following the same they would arrive at a gathering of the dangerous persons, whose association threatened to disintegrate society. As Dan, quoting Balzac's fiction, had observed, it was Ferragus and his fellow-conspirators in a modern setting. Dan, having lost the race, and consequently the £2,000, was short of funds, and Laurance not being rich could not lend him any money. However, the two managed to borrow a certain sum from a grasping money-lender, which supplied the sinews of war for the time being. Halliday had the Vincent aeroplane brought to Blackheath again, and made some money in his usual way by taking various people trips for short distances. Aviation was now quite a Society craze, especially for ladies desirous of a new sensation, so Dan did extremely well. A few months later he intended to attempt a cross-Channel flight, for which a French millionaire was offering a large prize, but in the meantime he got along as best he could. Nothing happened for a week or two likely to stir up the muddy water which concealed the doings of the gang, and there were no new murders. Then Dan took Lillian to a cinematograph exhibition, and made a discovery. Of course Lillian was profoundly grieved that her lover should have lost the race, but comforted herself with the reflection that he was safe. Had she been able, she would have interdicted Dan from trying further flights, especially in the face of the many accidents which were occurring in connection with aviation all over the world. Dan, however, laughed at her fears, and insisted upon continuing his dangerous vocation. Nevertheless, he promised in a moment of tenderness, to give up aviation when he and Lillian were married, though at present affairs in this direction did not look bright. As yet Dan had discovered very little likely to lead to the detection of Moon's assassin, and until that individual was brought to justice, Sir John would never consent to the match. The course of true love in these dark days was by no means running as smoothly as the pair desired. Lord Curberry haunted Sir John Moon's house, and pestered Lillian with undesired attentions until she was openly rude to him. But this did not at all damp his ardor; he merely smiled acidly and continued to send flowers and theatre seats, and lastly articles of jewelry, which she declined to accept. And always Sir John was at her elbow, croaking out what a lucky girl she was to attract the attention of the peer. With her money and his title, to say nothing of his talents, the marriage would be an ideal one. Lillian did not think so, and with the obstinacy of a woman in love with the wrong person, preferred to think of and long for Dan Halliday. More than that, with the connivance of Mrs. Bolstreath, who was heart and soul with the poor suitor, Lillian contrived to meet him at various times, and enjoy herself not a little. On these occasions they were like children let loose from an over-severe nursery. Sometimes Mrs. Bolstreath came as chaperon, and sometimes, knowing that Dan was a gentleman, she allowed them to be together alone, which, naturally, they liked much better. But on the whole, and so that no one might talk, the good-natured smiling woman followed their restless footsteps to restaurants and theatres--matinees that is--even to cinematographs. It was at one of these last entertainments that Dan received a shock. On this particular occasion, Mrs. Bolstreath was not with them, as she had gone shopping in Regent Street. An appointment had been made by her to meet Lillian and Dan at five, when the trio intended to have afternoon-tea in New Bond Street. Meantime, as it was only three o'clock, the lovers had the whole of London to themselves. The day was rather fine, so Lillian proposed to go to the unfashionable spaces of the park, where she was not likely to meet with any acquaintance. Dan was willing, and they walked along Piccadilly in a leisurely manner. Then Lillian stumbled on a biograph theatre, and read the programme. When she saw that a set of pictures represented the aviation ground at Blackheath, and the start for the London to York race, nothing would serve her whim, but that she must go in and see the film. Dan was willing to oblige her, as he also was curious to see himself in a moving-picture. Therefore, they soon found themselves being guided by an attendant with an electric-torch, through the warm darkness of the hall to a couple of well-cushioned seats. The performance was a continuous one, the pictures repeating themselves again and again, so the lovers arrived in the middle of an interesting story of which they did not know the beginning. Anxious to see what had gone before, Lillian exacted a promise from her complaisant swain that they should wait until the repetition. Dan agreed, but reminded her that this delay would mean no walk in the park. "Never mind," said Lillian, slipping her hand into his, under cover of the friendly twilight, "we can stay here until we meet Bolly in New Bond Street; you know I adore cinematographs." "And me also I hope," insinuated Dan, to which the answer was a friendly and very emphatic squeeze. As is usual with such entertainments the pictures were a mixture of comedy and tragedy, so as not to dwell too long on one note. But Lillian, in an impatient mood, waited anxiously for the aviation scenes. These were in due time thrown on the screen, and the girl gave a little cry of pleasure when she saw Dan tinkering at his aeroplane, every gesture being faithfully reproduced. Halliday himself was greatly amused by this resurrection of his doings and felt an odd feeling at coming face to face with himself in this way. But he started, greatly surprised, for in front of the crowd and disproportionately large, in comparison with the rest of the figures, he beheld the massive form of Mrs. Jarsell moving across the illuminated picture. She even paused to look round at someone in the mob, so he had a distinct front view of her powerful face. There could be no mistake, as she was a singularly noticeable woman, and when she finally passed away from the screen, he sat wondering at the odd chance which had shown him that she had been on the Blackheath aviation ground on the very day and about the very time Durwin had met with his mysterious death. Her presence suggested the possession of the Sumatra scent perfume, which in its turn recalled Penn's ownership of the same, and the scent of the dead Sir Charles Moon's clothes. More than ever Dan was convinced that Mrs. Jarsell was connected with the gang, and therefore with the two tragedies which were perplexing justice. He was glad that he had promised to wait for the repetition, and when Lillian wished to go, after she had seen the start of the picture, which had met them half-finished on their entrance, Dan urged her to stop and witness the aviation scenes once more. "It is so amusing to see one's self in this way," said Dan artfully. Lillian pouted. "I wish I could have been taken also," she said with a sigh of pleasure, and willingly consented to wait. The second view convinced Halliday absolutely that he was right. It was Mrs. Jarsell who moved so royally across the screen, and what puzzled him was that she appeared to be well dressed, without any attempt at disguise. Yet, if she had come to Blackheath bent upon crime, she would surely have worn a veil, so as not to be noticed. Still, Mrs. Jarsell, living a secluded life at Sheepeak, would not be known to any one in London, and might not think it necessary to disguise herself in any way. Moreover, if by chance she was recognized through any possible disguise, such a thing would mean the asking of leading questions. However, there was no doubt that she had been on the aviation ground when Durwin was murdered, and Dan determined to go that same night to Sheepeak and make inquiries. He was very silent when at the afternoon tea with the ladies, but Lillian chattered enough for two, and gave Mrs. Bolstreath a vivid account of the animated pictures. The companion certainly did hint that Halliday was not quite himself, but he averted further inquiries by saying that he had a headache. Then he took leave of the pair, and went to see what train he could catch to Thawley, being in so great a hurry that he did not even call on Freddy Laurance to acquaint him with his wonderful discovery. Thus Halliday most unexpectedly found himself standing on the Thawley Station platform, a few minutes after nine o'clock, as he had left St. Pancras by the six o'clock express. It was now too late to travel by the local to Beswick, for when he reached that place there was the long hill to climb to Sheepeak, and The Peacock Hotel would probably be closed by the time he got to his destination. Dan therefore decided to remain in Thawley for the night, and secured a bed at an hotel near the station. Early next morning he came to look for George Pelgrin with whom he wished to talk, and had no difficulty in finding him. A brother-porter brought the man to him and handing over his bag, Halliday requested to be led to the platform whence the Beswick local departed. Then he began to ask artful questions. Pelgrin was a big bovine creature, with sleepy blue eyes, and a slow, ponderous manner, which argued small intelligence. Dan wondered why a clever woman like Mrs. Jarsell should interest herself in such a creature, and to find out cautiously introduced the lady's name. "I was staying at your aunt's hotel in Sheepeak some time ago," said Dan, as George carried his bag over the bridge, "and she told me that you are quite a favorite with my friend, Mrs. Jarsell of The Hall."

"Aye," grinned George amiably, "that I be, sir. I come from Sheepeak, and Mrs. Jarsell she takes interest in Sheepeak folk. 'Send for George,' she says, when coming to London, and I puts her straight as she likes."

"She comes to town pretty often I expect," said Halliday lightly, "which is all the better for your pocket."

"Why, no," said Pelgrin thoughtfully, "she don't go away much from Sheepeak, not even to come to Thawley. Once in a few months she goes to London to see things. 'George,' she says, 'I'm going to look up friends,' or 'George, I'm after lawyer's business this day,' she says. Oh, she's good to me and Aunt Marian, is Mrs. Jarsell. I wish she'd come to London oftener," ended George in dismal tones, "for she gives me half-a-crown always, and don't come as often as I'd like, seeing as I wants money."

"Ah, she's a stay-at-home," commented Halliday. "Looking after that friend of hers, Miss Armour, she is," agreed George. "Well, she has been a good friend to me," said the other man, shuffling into a first-class compartment, "for she got me an aeroplane from Mr. Vincent."

"Aye," said Pelgrin, "I know him. Crosspatch he is, sir."

"I think so, too. But Mrs. Jarsell promised to come to London and see me in the London to York race. You heard of it, I suppose."

"Aye, that I did," said Pelgrin, and mentioned the exact date, "we'd a heap of traffic that day, folk going to York to see them airships arrive. But Mrs. Jarsell wasn't one of them, sir."

"She wouldn't go to York, but to London."

"She didn't go nowhere," said George doggedly, "on that day anyhow. 'Send for George,' she always says, and on the day of that flying-race send for me she did not. So she stayed at home, I reckon."

"Oh," Dan looked disappointed. "I did so want her to see me flying in this race, Pelgrin, since she got Mr. Vincent to give me the aeroplane." "Well, she didn't see you, sir, for she never went to London on that day early or late, I swear. She don't go much away from Sheepeak, and hasn't been there--to London that is, sir--for months. And she always tips me half a crown," ended George once more. Dan took the hint and handed over the money. "There you are. And I hope Mrs. Jarsell will travel oftener so that you may become rich."

"Aye, I need money, me being engaged as it were," said Pelgrin with a grin, touching his forelock, and he went on explaining his private affairs, which had to do with a girl, until the train steamed out of the station. Dan was puzzled. According to the cinematograph Mrs. Jarsell had certainly been in town on the day of the race, yet this yokel swore that she had not travelled from the Thawley Station. Yet there was no other route by which she could come. Of course, according to Mrs. Pelgrin, the woman owned three motors and could go to London in that way. There was just a chance that she might have done so, but Dan did not know how he was to find out. It would be no use asking Mrs. Jarsell, as she would deny having been out of Sheepeak. Yet since she was wholly undisguised on the Blackheath ground, why should she deny her identity. It might be that she would admit having gone to the big city--say by motor--and would defy him to credit her with the death of Durwin. Not that Dan would be foolish enough to accuse her of the same, as he had no evidence to go upon, save the fact of the perfume, and that was a weak reed upon which to lean. Mrs. Pelgrin might know something, however, and to Mrs. Pelgrin he determined to apply for information. At the end of his journey, and when he arrived in a ramshackle fly, he was welcomed by her as usual--that is, she bounced out of the inn, and placing her arms akimbo, smiled grimly. "Oh, so you are here again," she said in exactly the same way in which she had greeted Laurance. "Yes," said Halliday, readily having his excuse cut and dried, "I lost the flying race, and have come to apologize to Mr. Vincent for misusing his machine. I only want a mid-day meal as I leave again this afternoon."

"You shall have your dinner," snapped Mrs. Pelgrin, leading the way into the inn after Dan had arranged for the driver of the trap to wait for three or four hours. "So you didn't win that race. Aye, Mr. Vincent will be rare mad with you, thinking what he does of those kites he makes." Halliday sat down in the well-remembered room and laughed. "The fortune of war, Mrs. Pelgrin. But I am sorry I lost the race. Mrs. Jarsell, who got me the aeroplane, will also be disappointed. Did she tell you about the start?"

"Eh! man, would a lady like her come chattering to a humble body like me," was the landlady's reply, as she laid the table rapidly, "not that she saw the race, mind you, Mr. Halliday."

"Oh, but she must have," replied Dan, with pretended surprise, "she promised to come and see me start from Blackheath."

"She did not go to London," persisted Mrs. Pelgrin, her eyes becoming angry at the contradiction, "I mind that well, because she came to see me about some eggs on the very day you were flying, and says she, 'It will be a good day for Mr. Vincent's machine to win the race.'" "Are you sure?" asked Dan, more puzzled than ever to find that the stories of Mrs. Pelgrin and her nephew were in accordance with one another. "Do you take me for a fool," cried Mrs. Pelgrin, her sallow face becoming a fiery red; "am I not telling you again and again that Mrs. Jarsell never went to see your rubbishy race. She came here to get some eggs from me, and sat in this very room at nine o'clock, or a little after. You take me for a liar, you--you--oh, I'll best see to the dinner, or I'll lose my temper," and the sharp-tongued woman, having already lost it, bounced out of the room. "Mrs. Jarsell was here at nine o'clock, or a little after," repeated Dan, in a wondering tone, "then she could not have been in London. All the same, I swear I saw her on that cinematograph." Here he opened his bag and took out an "A.B.C.," to see the trains from Thawley to London. An examination showed him that, even if Mrs. Jarsell had left Thawley Station at nine o'clock exactly, she would not have reached St. Pancras until twelve-five. This would scarcely give her time to arrive at Blackheath. The aeroplanes had started in the race at one o'clock, and, according to the evidence at the inquest, the people had been looking at them flying northward at the moment Durwin was stabbed. Mrs. Jarsell could not have arrived on the ground by one o'clock if she only got to St. Pancras at mid-day. And then, to do that, she would have been obliged to leave Thawley at nine o'clock. According to George she had not been near the station on that day, and if Mrs. Pelgrin was to be believed, she was in the very room he now occupied at the hour when the express departed. It was clearly impossible that she could have got to Thawley for the nine o'clock train, let alone it being impossible that had she caught the express she could have arrived in London to execute the crime by one o'clock, or a trifle later. Yet, on the other hand, was the evidence of Mrs. Pelgrin and her nephew, while on the other hand was the evidence of the cinematograph. One or the other must assuredly be wrong. Of course the landlady and George might be telling lies, but on the face of it there was no need for them to do so. Moreover, as Dan had sprung his questions on them unexpectedly, they could not have been ready with false answers. "She must have used a motor-car," thought Halliday, restoring the "A.B.C." to his bag, "yet even so, she was here at nine o'clock, and could not have reached town in the three hours and odd minutes. D---- it!" Mrs. Pelgrin brought in the dinner with compressed lips and showed small disposition to chatter. Anxious not to arouse her suspicions by asking any further questions, Dan began to talk of other matters, and gradually she became more friendly. He told her that he had employed George and had given him half-a-crown, since the mention of money appeared to melt her into civility more than did anything else. Mrs.

Pelgrin smiled grimly and observed that "George was a grasping hound," an amiable speech which did not argue that she was on the best of terms with the sleepy-eyed man at Thawley Station. After Dan had learned indirectly all he could from her he sought out Vincent's cottage, only to learn that the inventor and his niece were absent for the day. As he could frame no excuse to visit Mrs. Jarsell there was nothing left for him to do but to travel back to town; therefore he found himself once more in St. Pancras Station, comparatively early in the evening, wondering what was the solution of this new problem.

CHAPTER XII

AN AMAZING ADVENTURE

Next day Dan went to look up Laurance and have a consultation, as he was considerably puzzled over the new problem and did not know exactly how to act. But Fate was against him, so far as having a second opinion was concerned, for Laurance proved to be absent. An anarchistic plot, of which *The Moment* desired to know the details, had taken him to Vienna, and it was probable that he would not return for at least a week. Halliday might have expected something of the sort, as in the prosecution of his business Freddy was here, there, and everywhere, never knowing his next destination, which depended entirely on the latest sensation. But hitherto few startling events had summoned Laurance out of England, and Dan had been accustomed to always finding him on the spot for a consultation. He left the office of *The Moment* in a rather disconsolate frame of mind. There was no doubt that Halliday badly needed someone to talk to about the matters which occupied his thoughts. But, failing Freddy, who was working with him, he did not know any one worth consulting--anyone, that is, whose advice would be worth taking. Certainly there were the two inspectors of police--one at Hampstead, and one at Blackheath--who were deeply interested in the respective deaths of Moon and Durwin. They would have been delighted to discuss the entire business threadbare in the hope of solving the mystery of the two crimes. But Dan did not wish to bring the police into the matter until he had more evidence to go upon. After all, what he knew concerning Mrs. Jarsell and Penn was both vague and uncertain, while the clue of the perfume being so slight might be scouted as ridiculous by these cut-and-dried officials. What Halliday wished to do was to establish a connection between the doings at Sheepeak, Blackheath, and Hampstead on evidence that could not be questioned, so that he might submit a complete case to the police. He could not do this until he acquired positive proof, and he desired to acquire the same by his own endeavors supplemented by those of Laurance. Therefore, as Freddy was away on business, and Dan did not care about placing his unfinished case before the inspectors, he went about his ordinary affairs, waiting for his friend's return. This was all that he could do, and he did it reluctantly. A hint from Lord Curberry had evidently made Sir John more vigilant as regarded his niece. Dan called at the house and was denied an interview; he wrote a letter and received no answer; and although he haunted Bond Street and Regent Street, the parks and the theatres, he could catch no glimpse of Lillian. After three days of unavailing endeavor he went to Bedford and attended to the transfer of his aeroplane to Blackheath, bringing it up in the train personally. Then he put it together again, and took short flights in the vicinity of London, after repairing the damage done to the propeller. All the same, his heart was not in the business of aviation at the moment as the detective fever had seized him and he felt that he could not rest until he had solved the mystery of the two crimes. But at the moment, he saw no way by which he could advance toward a consummation of his wishes, and simply fiddled away his time until the return of Laurance. Then, after a threshing out of details, he hoped to make some sort of move in the darkness. But Fate decreed that he should act alone and without advice, and the intimation of Fate's intention came in the form of a short letter from Marcus Penn, asking for an interview. "I am confident," wrote the secretary, "that from what you threatened in the aeroplane you suspect me of knowing something relative to Sir Charles Moon's murder. As I am entirely innocent I resent these suspicions, and I wish you to meet me in order that they should be cleared away. If you will meet me at the booking-office of the Bakerloo Tube, I can take you to the person who gave me the perfume. He will be able to tell you that I have no connection with any criminal." Then the letter went on to state day and hour of the appointment, and ended with the feeble signature of the writer. Dan always thought that Penn's signature revealed only too plainly the weakness of his character. Of course he intended to go, even though he remembered that Penn had declared the identity of the person who had given him the perfume. His cousin in Sumatra had sent the same to him, the secretary had said, yet he now proposed to introduce Dan to another person, who was the donor of the scent. Unless, indeed--and this was possible--the Sumatra cousin had come to England with the intention of exonerating Penn. Certainly, Penn might mean mischief, and might be dexterously luring him to a trap. But Halliday felt that he was quite equal to dealing with a timid personality such as the secretary possessed. Also, when going to keep the appointment, he slipped a revolver into his hip-pocket, to be used if necessary. It might be--and Dan's adventurous blood reached fever heat at the mere idea--that Penn intended to introduce him to his brother scoundrels, who constituted this mysterious gang. If so, there was a very good chance that at last he might learn something tangible concerning the organization. Undoubtedly there was a great risk of his losing liberty if not life, and it was impossible to say what precautions this society of cut-throats might take to preserve its secrets. But Halliday was not of a nervous nature, and, moreover, was willing to risk everything on one cast of the die, instead of lingering in suspense. He therefore got himself ready without saying a word to any one, and kept the appointment. And, indeed, now that Laurance was absent, there was no one to whom he could speak. It chanced to be a somewhat foggy night when Dan descended to the underground in Trafalgar Square, but out of the darkness and in the light he had no difficulty in recognizing Penn. The secretary was well wrapped up in a heavy great-coat, and welcomed the young man with a nervous smile, blinking his pale eyes furiously, as was his custom when much moved. However, he spoke amiably enough, and appeared to bear no malice against his companion, notwithstanding the threat in the aeroplane. "I am glad you have come, Mr. Halliday," said Penn in a would-be dignified tone, "as I wish to clear my character from the grave doubts you cast upon it when we last met."

"Your admissions favored the grave doubts," retorted Dan lightly. "I spoke foolishly, Mr. Halliday, as I was quite upset by your threats."

"H'm! I wonder to see you trust yourself again to such a bloodthirsty being as I am, Mr. Penn."

"Oh, I knew you were only bluffing in the aeroplane," said the secretary in a meek voice and with a shrug. "The means you took to escape further questioning showed me that!" The dry tone of Dan stirred the man's chilly blood to greater heat. "You have no right to interfere with my private affairs," he said furiously. "But when those affairs have to do with a crime----"

"They have not. I know nothing about the matter," Penn's breath was short, and he tried to keep his voice from quavering. "When you see my cousin he will prove that he gave me the scent."

"Oh! then your Sumatra cousin is now in England?"

"Yes! Otherwise, I should not have asked you to come."

"Are we to meet him here?" questioned Dan, glancing round curiously. "No. We can go to him in a taxi. I thought of the tube first, but we can get to our destination quicker in a motor. Come!" and Penn, leading the way, ascended the stairs, down which Halliday had lately come. "Where are we going to?" asked Dan, but the secretary, being some distance ahead, either did not hear the question, or did not desire to reply to the same. "I suppose," added Halliday, as the two stood once more in the foggy upper-world, "that your cousin wishes to see Mrs. Jarsell?"

"My cousin doesn't know Mrs. Jarsell, neither do I," retorted Penn sharply. "Curious that she should possess the perfume," murmured Dan sceptically, "and one which you say is unique."

"In England that is," said the secretary, as they stepped into a taxi-cab which evidently was waiting for them, near the Trafalgar Square lions, "but, this lady whose name you mention may know someone in Sumatra also, and in that way the perfume may have come into her possession."

"Ah!" Dan made himself comfortable, while Penn pulled up the windows of the taxi, so as to keep out the damp air, "the long arm of coincidence?"

"The improbable usually occurs in real life and not in novels, Mr. Halliday." Dan laughed and watched the street lights flash past the blurred windows as the taxi turned up the Haymarket. He wondered where they were going, and as he believed that Penn would not give him any information he carefully watched to see the route. His companion adjusted his silk muffler well over his mouth, with a murmured explanation about his weak lungs, and then held out a silver cigarette case to Dan, clicking it open as he did so. "Will you smoke, Mr. Halliday?"

"No, thank you," replied the other cautiously, "for the present I don't care about it," and Penn shrugged his shoulders, evidently understanding that Dan did not trust him or his gifts. After a time he took out a cigarette and lighted a match. "These cigarettes are of a particular kind," he remarked, and blew a cloud of smoke directly under Halliday's nose, after which he readjusted the muffler, not only over his mouth, but over his nose. Dan started, for the whiff of smoke filled the close confinement of the taxi with the well-known flavor of the Sumatra scent. He was about to make a remark when the scent grew stronger as the cigarette burned steadily with a red, smoldering tip, and he felt suddenly faint. "Pull down the window," he gasped, and leaned forward to do so himself. For answer, Penn suddenly pulled the young man back into his seat, and enveloped him in a cloud of drowsy smoke, keeping his own mouth and nose well covered meanwhile with the silk muffler. Halliday made a faint struggle to retain his senses and the control of his muscles, but the known world receded rapidly from him and he seemed to be withdrawn into gulfs of utter gloom. The last coherent thought which came into his mind was that the pretended cigarette produced by Penn was a drugged pastil. Then an effort to grasp the undoubted fact that he had been lured into a skilful trap which had shut down on him, used up his remaining will-power, and he remembered no more. Whither he went into darkness, or what he did, Dan never knew, as there seemed to be no break in the time that elapsed from his becoming unconscious in the taxi and waking with the acrid smell of some reviving salts in his nostrils. He might have been on earth or in sky or sea; he did not know, for he opened his eyes languidly in a dense gloom. "Where am I?" he asked, but there was no reply. His senses came back to him with a rush, owing perhaps to the power of the stimulant applied to bring him round. He sat up alertly in his chair, and felt immediately that his arms were bound tightly to his sides, so that he could not use his revolver, or even strike a match. He certainly would have done this latter, had he been able to, for he greatly desired to be informed as to the quality of his surroundings. He presumed that he was in a large room of some kind, and he became convinced by his sixth sense that the room was crowded with people. When fully himself Dan could hear the soft breathing of many unseen beings, but whether they were men or women, or a mixture of the sexes, he could not say. Even when his eyes became accustomed to the gloom he could discern nothing, for the darkness was that of Egypt. And the silence, save for the steady breathing, was most uncanny. Dan felt it incumbent on him to make some attempt towards acquiring knowledge. "What is the meaning of this outrage?" he demanded loudly and in a resolute tone. "I insist upon knowing!" From the near distance came a whispering voice, which made him shiver. "No one insists here," said the unknown speaker, "all obey."

"Who is it that all obey?" demanded the prisoner undauntedly. "Queen Beelzebub!" murmured the voice, soft and sibilant. There flashed into Dan's mind some teaching, secular or sacred--he could not tell which at the moment--relative to a deity who had to do with flies. A Phœnician deity he fancied, but surely if his memory served him, a male godling. Beelzebub, the god of Flies! He remembered now, and remembered also the trade-mark of the mysterious society formed for the purpose of murdering various people for various reasons, known and unknown. "So you have got me at last," he said aloud. "I might have guessed that Penn would trap me."

"No names," said the unseen speaker coldly; "it will be the worse for you if you mention names."

"Am I addressing Beelzebub?" asked Dan, and for the life of him he could not keep the irony out of his tones, for the whole thing was so theatrical. "Queen Beelzebub!"

"I see; you have given the god of Flies a consort. May I ask why I have been brought here?"

"We intend to make you an offer."

"Who we? What we?"

"The members of the Society of Flies, of which I am the head."

"H'm, I understand. Don't you think you had better loose my hands and turn up the lights?"

"Be silent," ordered the voice imperiously, and, as Dan fancied, with some hint of temper at the flippant way in which he talked; "be silent and listen!"

"I can't help myself," said Halliday coolly, "go on, please." There was a soft rustle, as if the unseen company admired his courage for behaving calmly in what was, undoubtedly, a weird and trying situation. Then some distance away a disk of red light, like a winter sun, appeared with nerve-shaking swiftness. It revealed none of the company, for all were still in the gloom, but concentrated its angry rays on a large and solemn visage, unhuman in its stillness and awful calm. It was an Egyptian face, such as belongs to the statues of the gods of Kem, and the head-dress, stiff and formal, was also suggestive of the Nile. Of more than usual size, Dan could only see its vast features, but fancied that a red robe fell in folds from the neck downward.

There was something grand about this severe face, and in the darkness, with the scarlet light gleaming fiercely on its immobility, it was assuredly effective, if somewhat theatrical. The lips did not move when Queen Beelzebub began to speak, but the eyes were alive; the eyes of the person concealed behind the mask. Dan noticed that, when the face became visible in the angry red light, the speaker ceased to whisper, and the voice became deep, voluminous, and resonant as that of a gong. The tone was that of a man, but it might have been a woman speaking through an artificial mouthpiece. The final thing which Dan noticed was that the whole atmosphere of the room reeked with the rich fragrance of the Sumatra scent. "You are very daring and meddlesome," said the voice, issuing in chilly tones from behind the stately mask, "for you have intruded yourself into affairs which have nothing to do with you."

"They have everything to do with me," retorted Halliday decisively and feeling reckless, "if you and your society are omniscient, you should know."

"Omniscient is a good word. We know that you love Lillian Moon and wish to marry her; we know that her uncle is willing this should be, if you discover the truth about his brother's death. You have been searching for the assassin, and you are still searching. That search must stop."

"I think not."

"If you refuse to obey," said Queen Beelzebub coldly, "we can put you out of the way as we have put others out of the way."

"The Law----" A faint murmur of laughter was heard, suggestive of scorn. "We care nothing for the law," said the speaker contemptuously. "Oh, I think you do, or you would not have taken all this trouble to have me brought here."

"You are here to receive an offer."

"Indeed. I shall be glad to hear the offer."

"We wish you to join the Society of Flies and swear to obey me, the queen."

"Thank you, but an association of cut-throats does not appeal to me."

"Think twice before you refuse," the voice became threatening. "I think once, and that is sufficient," returned Dan drily. "You are at our mercy. We can kill you as we have killed others."

"There are worse things than death. Dishonor."

"You talk like a fool," scoffed Queen Beelzebub. "What is dishonor? Merely a word. It means nothing."

"I can well believe that it means nothing to you and your friends," said Dan, who was weary of this fencing: "may I ask what advantage I gain by becoming a member of your bloodthirsty gang?"

"We are an association," boomed the great voice, "banded against the injustice of the world. We resent few people having wealth and the majority going without the necessaries of life. Being limited in number, the Law is too strong for us, and we cannot gain our objects openly; therefore we have to strike in the dark."

"And your objects?" "To equalize wealth, to give our members wealth, position, comfort, and power." "Oh. It's a kind of Socialistic community. You work for the poor."

"We work for ourselves. "Rather selfish, isn't it?"

"People will only work for self, and to those who labor for us we give all that they wish for. Become a member and you will realize your heart's desire."

"Perhaps," said Halliday in a caustic tone, "I may realize that without your aid."

"We think not. To marry Lillian Moon you must find who murdered her father, and that person will never be found."

"Then why stop me from searching?"

"It is a pity you should waste your time," said Queen Beelzebub sarcastically, "besides you are one who would do honor to our society."

"Perhaps. But would the society do honor to me?"

"We can give you what you desire, on certain conditions."

"What are they?"

"You must take the oath and sign the book; swear to obey me, who am the head of this association, without question; promise to be secret, and give all your talents to forwarding the aims of the Society of Flies."

"H'm," said Dan coolly, "a very comprehensive oath indeed. And the aims?"

"Wealth and power. We are banded together to get what we want, independent of the law, and we think that the end justifies the means. We accept money from those people who desire to get rid of their enemies, or of those who stand between them and their desires. We supply plans of English forts to foreign powers on condition that large sums are paid to us. We trade on the secrets of people, which we learn in various ways. If we are asked by any member to get him something, all the resources of the society are at his disposal. Rivals can be removed if he wants to marry; relatives can be put out of the way, if he wishes for their money. There is no height to which an ambitious man cannot climb with our aid. Join us and you shall marry Lillian Moon within the year and also shall enjoy her large fortune." Desirous to learn more of the villainies with which this precious band of scoundrels were concerned, Dan temporized. "And if I refuse?"

"You will be put to death!"

"Now? At this very moment?" Dan's blood ran cold, for, after all, he was yet young, and life was sweet to him. "No. You will be allowed to go, and death shall fall upon you when you least expect it. Thus your agony will be great, for death may find you to-morrow, or in a week, a month, or a year. We are not afraid you will tell the police, for if you do it will only hasten your end. Besides, you do not know where you are, and shall be taken away as secretly as you have been brought here. The Law cannot touch us, because we work under ground like moles, and even if you told the police, your story of what has happened would only be laughed at. The police," here the voice sneered, "think everything is known and refuse to believe that we exist."

"Well," said Dan, as if making up his mind, "can I ever leave the society if I once join it?"

"Yes," said Queen Beelzebub unexpectedly, "when you take the oath you must swear to be sober, chaste, and secret, since these qualities are needed to keep a member in good working trim. A certain amount of work you must do in connection with our aims, so that you dare not speak without being implicated in our doings. But, after a time, you can leave with money, position, or power--whatever you desire, and then can lead your own life, however profligate it may be. But while a member you must be a saint."

"A black saint," murmured Dan, wondering at the solid ground upon which this association was founded, and thinking how dangerous it could be with its misdirected aims, "well, I don't say 'No' and I don't say 'Yes.' I must have time to think what my answer will be."

"You shall have one month to consider, and then you shall be brought here secretly again," said Queen Beelzebub authoritatively, "but you will be wise if you join us. We wish you to do so because you have brains, and we want brains. Our society will rule the world if we get clever men to join, as the training of our members in sobriety, chastity, self-control, and secrecy is that of the so-called saints."

"I see," said Dan cheerfully, "the Lord's Prayer said backward, so to speak, your Majesty. Well, the whole business is clever, and extremely well managed as I can see. I shall take my month's respite, and then----"

"And then if you say 'Yes,' you will have all that the world can give you; if you say 'No,' prepare for death." A murmur, vague and indistinct, went round the dark room. "Prepare for death."

"And if I speak to the police in the meantime?" asked Dan yawning. "You have been warned that if you do, death will follow immediately," declared Queen Beelzebub, "no human law can protect you from us. Enough has been said, and you have thirty days to decide what to do." As she spoke, the red light vanished as abruptly as it had come. Dan could only hear the steady breathing of many people in the gloom, and wondered how many members of this devilish society were present. At that moment, and while the thought was yet in his mind, he felt that a pastil was being held under his nose. The drowsy scent stole into his brain, although he tried to avert his head, and almost immediately he became again unconscious. Again he fell into gulfs of gloom, and remembered nothing. When he recovered his senses, he was seated in a four wheeler, driving in an unknown direction, and he was alone. His head ached, but he struck a match and looked at his watch. It was eleven o'clock. "Where did you find me?" he asked the cabman, putting his head out of the window, and noticing that he was in a well-lighted street. "A friend of yours brought you to my cab," said the man, "saying you was drunk--dead drunk. He gave me your address, and I'm taking you home."

"Clever," said Dan to himself, accepting the explanation without comment.

CHAPTER XIII

A BOLD DETERMINATION

Dan went to bed with an aching head, doubtless induced by the power of the drug which had been used to stupefy him. The Sumatra perfume was evidently both powerful and useful, as it was used by the Society of Flies not only as a means of recognition in the form of a harmless scent, but as a soporific to bring about insensibility. Probably many a person had been rendered unconscious by the drowsy smoke, and taken to the headquarters of the infernal association, there to become members. But where the headquarters were to be found, Dan had not the slightest notion. And, as his head pained him greatly, he decided to wait until the next morning before thinking out the matter. Off and on he managed to sleep a trifle, but it was not until the small hours that true slumber came to him. It was nine o'clock when he woke, and then he found his head clear, and the pain absent. Only an evil taste remained in his mouth, and after a cold bath he felt more himself, although a touch of languor remained to recall to his recollection what he had been through. After breakfast he lighted a pipe, and began to think over late events as carefully as was necessary. On alighting at his own door he had paid the driver of the four-wheeled cab, and had asked questions, which the man was willing enough to answer. Halliday hoped by learning where the cabman had picked him up, to discover at least the neighborhood wherein the headquarters were situated. It was difficult to think that an unconscious person, as he had been, could have been taken any great distance along streets, or roads, or lanes, without attention being attracted. But the cabman explained that the friend who had placed his fare in the four-wheeler, had removed him from a taxi, which the friend declared had broken down. "And he wanted to get you home, you being drunk," explained the driver, "so he shoved you into my trap, and I drove off, having the address I was to take you to, leaving your friend to look after the broken-down taxi, along with the chauffer." From this explanation it was apparent that on being removed from the dark room Dan had been transported for some distance, long or short, in the taxi. He did not believe that the same had broken down, but that his friend--probably Marcus Penn--had hailed the first cab he saw, and on pretence of an accident had got rid of him in this clever way. It was West Kensington where this exchange had taken place, according to the cabman's story, but since he had been driven an indefinite distance by Penn in the taxi, the headquarters might be in Hampstead, or Blackheath, or Ilford, or, indeed, anywhere round about London, if not in the heart of the metropolis itself. All bearings were lost by the clever way in which the return had been carried out. And now Halliday scarcely knew what to do, or how to act. He did not dare to tell the police, as the first sign of activity on the part of the authorities would mean his own death in some mysterious way. He also would be found with an artificial fly near the wound and the odor of the Sumatra scent on his clothes. As Dan did not wish to die, he therefore hesitated to make any statement to Inspector Tenson of Hampstead, who was so anxious to learn the secret and gain the reward. In fact, he hoped that the man would not come to his rooms--he had been there several times in quest of information--lest he should smell the Sumatra scent. Dan found that he had brought the perfume away on his clothes when he examined them, which was scarcely to be wondered at considering how powerfully the dark room had reeked of the odor. Certainly Tenson did not know the scent so well as Halliday did, although he had experienced a whiff of it when examining the body of Sir Charles Moon. But he might have forgotten the smell. While Dan turned over his clothes--the blue serge suit he had worn on the previous night--he found a piece of paper in one of the trousers pockets, which contained a message typewritten in crimson ink. It was set forth in the third person, by no less an individual than Queen Beelzebub herself, and ran as follows--

"QUEEN BEELZEBUB warns Daniel Halliday that not only his own life depends upon his secrecy but the life of Lillian Moon also. Should he apply to the authorities, or in any way recount his adventures, the girl he loves will be put out of the way, and afterwards Daniel Halliday will be dealt with. At the end of thirty days Queen Beelzebub expects to receive homage from her new subject, who will receive notice of time and place fixed for the ceremony. Remember!"

"Quite a Charles-the-First ring about that last word," thought Dan, frowning at the threatening message; "the scoundrels: they have tied my hands with a vengeance. What the deuce am I to do?" It was useless for him to ask himself this question as the only answer could be, "Nothing!" If he moved in any way likely to harm the society he ran the chance of sacrificing, not only himself, but Lillian. It was bad enough that he should be done to death; but he might have risked that so as to break up the organization; but it was impossible to place the girl he loved in so dangerous a position. Queen Beelzebub knew what she was about when she used the phrase. And Halliday was well aware that the Society had a long arm, and that nothing could protect Lillian from these moles who were working in darkness--clever, deadly, and unscrupulous. For the next two days the young man went about in a dream, or rather in a nightmare. He did not dare to see Lillian, or to write to Lillian, lest the members of the Society should believe he was betraying them. They appeared to have spies everywhere, and there was no move on the chessboard which he could make which might not be detected. Yet he could not wait passively for the rest of the thirty days, since he had no idea of joining the band and had only asked for a respite so as to think out some means of escape. More than ever he longed for the return of Laurance. He could trust him, and a consultation between the two might evolve some scheme by which to baffle the subjects of the accursed woman who called herself Queen Beelzebub. Dan wondered if she was Mrs. Jarsell, but the evidence of the perfume seemed too slight a link to join her with this deadly organization. Of course there was Marcus Penn who was a member and knew everything; but he would not speak, since he ran also a risk of death should he betray too much. Still, Dan, being in the same boat and under the same ban, fancied that the secretary might be frank, as his confidence could not be abused. Now, if he could get Penn to state positively that Mrs. Jarsell was Queen Beelzebub, he might have something tangible upon which to work. But, taking into consideration the Egyptian mask, and the alteration of the voice by means of the artificial mouthpiece, Dan believed that she wished to keep her identity secret; always presuming that Queen Beelzebub was the "she" in question. On this assumption Halliday concluded that Penn would not speak out, and bothered himself for hours as to whether it would be worth while to ask the secretary questions. While still in this undecided frame of mind he received a morning visit from Laurance, who turned up unexpectedly. Freddy, in pursuit of his business, played puss-in-the-corner all over the world, coming and going from London in the most unexpected manner. He reminded Dan of this when the young man jumped up with an exclamation at his sudden entrance. "You might have known that I would turn up, anyhow," he said, sitting down, and accepting an offer to have breakfast. "I never know where I shall be on any given date, and you must be always prepared for the unexpected so far as I am concerned. I heard you were looking for me, when I returned last night from Vienna, so I came along to feed with you." Halliday ordered his man to bring in a clean cup, and poured out coffee, after which he heaped Freddy's plate with bacon and kidneys. "There you are, old fellow, eat away and get yourself ready for a long talk. I have heaps to tell you likely to be interesting."

"About the murder of Durwin?" questioned Laurance, reaching for toast. "Yes, and about the murder of Sir Charles Moon also. You don't mind my smoking while you eat?"

"No. Smoke away! Have you seen *The Moment* this morning?"

"No. Anything interesting in it about your Austrian excursion?"

"Oh, yes," said Laurance indifferently, "I managed to learn a good deal about these anarchistic beasts and it's set all out in print. But that's not what I meant," he fumbled in his pockets. "Hang it, I haven't brought a paper, and

I meant to. There's a death chronicled this morning." Dan sat up and shivered. "Another of the murders?"

"Yes. Marcus Penn this time."

"Penn!" Halliday dropped his pipe, "the devil," he picked it up again, "I wonder why they killed him?"

"He told you too much, maybe," said Laurance drily; "anyhow, the gang has got rid of him by drowning him in an ornamental pond in Curberry's grounds."

"He might have fallen in," suggested Dan uneasily, "or he might have committed suicide out of sheer terror."

"Well, he might have," admitted Freddy, thoughtfully, "but from what I saw of the man I should think he was too great a coward to commit suicide." Dan smoked in a meditative manner. "I suppose she killed him, or had him killed," he said aloud, after a pause. "She? Who?"

"The she-devil who presides over the Society of Flies. Queen Beelzebub." Laurance dropped his knife and fork to stare hard at his friend. "So you have learned something since I have been away?" "Several things. Wait a moment." Dan rose and retired to his bedroom, while Freddy pushed away the breakfast things as he did not wish to eat further in the face of Halliday's hint which had taken away his appetite. In a few minutes Dan came back to the sitting-room carrying the clothes he had worn on the night of his kidnapping, which still retained a faint odor of the fatal scent belonging to the gang. "Smell that," said Dan, placing the clothes on his friend's knee. Laurance sniffed. "Is this the Sumatra scent?" he asked; "h'm, quite a tropical fragrance. But I thought you proved to your satisfaction that there was nothing in this perfume business?"

"I always had my doubts," said Halliday drily, "they were lulled by Penn's lies and reawakened when I found the scent at Mrs. Jarsell's. Now I know all about the matter. I place my life in your hands by telling you."

"Is it as serious as that?" asked Laurance uneasily. "Yes. Serious to me and to Lillian also. Read that." The journalist scanned the crimson typewriting, and his eyes opened larger and larger as he grasped the meaning of the message. "Where the deuce did you get this?" he demanded hurriedly. "I found it in my pocket when I got back the other night."

"Where from?"

"From the headquarters of the Society of Flies."

"There is a gang then?" asked Laurance, starting. "Yes. A very well-organized gang, presided over by Queen Beelzebub, the consort of the gentleman of that name, who is the god of Flies."

"Where are the headquarters?"

"I don't know."

"We may be able to trace the gang by this," said Freddy, examining the typewritten paper. "If Inspector Tenson----"

"If Tenson gets hold of that and learns anything, which by the way I don't think he can, from that paper, my life won't be worth a cent; neither will that of Lillian's. I might not care for my own life, but I care a great deal for hers. I want to have a consultation as to what is best to be done to save her from these devils."

"Well, you can depend upon my saying nothing, Dan. It seems serious. Tell me all about your discoveries." Halliday did so, starting with his visit to the cinematograph with Lillian, and his recognition of Mrs. Jarsell in the animated picture. Then he recounted his journey to Hillshire, and what he had learned from Mrs. Pelgrin and her nephew. "So on the face of it," concluded Dan earnestly, "I don't see how Mrs. Jarsell could have got to London. She didn't go by train and could not have gone by motor. Yet, I'm sure she was on the Blackheath grounds."

"It is a puzzle," admitted Freddy, drawing his brows together, "but go on; you have something else to tell me."

"Rather," and Dan detailed all that had taken place from the time he received Penn's invitation to meet him in the Bakerloo Tube to the moment he arrived at his rooms again in the four-wheeler. "What do you make of it all, Freddy?" asked Halliday, when he ended and relighted his pipe. "Give me time to think," said Laurance, and rose to pace the room. For a time there was a dead silence, each man thinking his own thoughts. It was Dan who spoke first, and said what was uppermost in his mind. "Of course my hands are tied," he said dismally, "I dare not risk Lillian's life. The beasts have killed her father, and Durwin and Penn, all because they got to know too much. They may kill Lillian also and in the same mysterious way."

"But she knows nothing," said Freddy anxiously. "No. But I do, and if I speak--well, then you know what will happen. Queen Beelzebub saw that I cared little for my own life, so she is striking at me through Lillian. 'The girl he loves!' says that message. Clever woman Mrs. Jarsell; she has me on toast." "But, my dear fellow, you can't be sure that your masked demon is Mrs. Jarsell, since you did not see her face, or recognize her voice."

"I admit that the mask concealed her features, and I believe that she spoke through an artificial mouthpiece to disguise the voice. Still, there is the evidence of her possessing the perfume, which plays such a large part in the gang's doings. Also her appearance in the animated picture, which proves her to have been on the Blackheath ground."

"But Mrs. Pelgrin and her nephew declare positively that she could not have been there."

"Quite so, but Mrs. Pelgrin and her nephew may be paid to keep silence," retorted Dan in a worried tone; "then Miss Armour, if you remember, prophesied that I should have a wonderful offer made to me. If I accepted I should marry Lillian and enjoy a large fortune. Well, an offer in precisely the same words was made to me, on condition that I joined the gang." "But surely you don't believe that a paralyzed woman like Miss Armour has anything to do with this business?" questioned Laurance skeptically. Dan shrugged his shoulders. "Miss Armour is the friend of Mrs. Jarsell, whom I suspect, and certainly told my fortune as you heard. Mrs. Jarsell may have told her what to say, knowing that the prophecy would be fulfilled. I don't say that Miss Armour knows about this infernal organization, as the very idea would horrify her. But Mrs. Jarsell may use the poor woman as a tool."

"I can't believe that Miss Armour knows anything," said Freddy decidedly; "to begin with, the Society of Flies needs useful people, and an invalid like Miss Armour would be of no use."

"I admit that Miss Armour is in the dark," replied Halliday impatiently; "all the same, her prophecy, together with the perfume and the cinematograph evidence, hints at Mrs. Jarsell's complicity. Again, the false Mrs. Brown who murdered Sir Charles was stout and massive. Mrs. Jarsell is stout and massive."

"Plenty of women are stout and massive," asserted the reporter, "but you saw the false Mrs. Brown yourself. Did you recognize Mrs. Jarsell as that person?"

"No. But Mrs. Brown was so wrinkled for a fat woman that I remember thinking at the time she might be a fraud. I daresay--I am positive, in fact-- that her face was made up, and while I looked at her she let down her veil-- another hint that she did not wish to be examined too closely."

"If you think that Mrs. Jarsell murdered Moon and Durwin, and you have the evidence you speak of, you should reveal all to the police."

"And risk Lillian's life and my own? Freddy, you must take me for a fool." Laurance shook his head. "No. I don't underrate your cleverness, and I see that you are in a tight place. You can't move with safety to yourself and Miss Moon. Yet if you don't move, what is to be done?"

"Well," said Dan, after a pause, "I have a month to think matters out. My idea is to hide Lillian somewhere under the care of Mrs. Bolstreath, and then take action. So long as Lillian is safe I am ready to risk my own life to bring these mysteries to light."

"I am with you," cried Freddy enthusiastically, "it's a good scheme, Dan. I wonder how Miss Moon is to be hidden though; since the Society of Flies may employ spies to find her whereabouts?"

"Oh, every member of the society is a spy," was Halliday's answer, "although I don't know how many members of the gang there are. Penn could have told us, and perhaps could have proved the identity of Mrs. Jarsell with Queen Beelzebub. But he's dead, and----"

"And was murdered," broke in Laurance decisively. "I am quite sure that--because he could prove too much for Mrs. Jarsell's safety--he was got rid of."

"Oh!" Dan looked up with a smile, "then you believe that Mrs. Jarsell----" "I don't know what to believe until more evidence is forthcoming," said the reporter impatiently, "but Miss Moon's hiding-place? Where is it best to place her, with Mrs. Bolstreath as her guardian?" Halliday reflected, and then made the last answer Freddy expected to hear, considering the circumstances. "At Sheepeak with Miss Vincent," he declared. "Dan, are you serious. You place her under the guns of the enemy."

"Quite so, and there has been proof that under the guns is the safest place in some cases. It is in this, I am sure. Should Mrs. Jarsell be the person we suspect her to be, she will not foul her own nest at Sheepeak. Therefore she will not dare to have Lillian killed within a stone-throw of her own house. By daring all, we gain all."

"It's a risk," said Laurance pondering. "I can see that."

"So can I. Everything is risky in this business."

"Then there's Mildred," rejoined the journalist uneasily. "I really do not want her to be brought into the matter."

"It will be all right, Freddy, and much the safer for Lillian. Mrs. Jarsell won't have the courage to hurt my promised wife, when your promised wife is in her company. Still, if you have qualms----"

"No, no, no!" interrupted Laurance eagerly, "after all, I cannot be half a friend, and if Mildred is willing--when she learns the whole circumstance that is, I shall agree. After all, if anything does happen, we can accuse Mrs. Jarsell, and if she is Queen Beelzebub she will end her career in jail. I don't think she will risk that by hurting the girls."

"Oh, she would never hurt Miss Vincent, I am sure, and would only harm Lillian because I have to be frightened into joining her gang. No, Freddy, a daring policy is the best in this case. We'll place Lillian with Mrs. Bolstreath under Mildred Vincent's charge--under the guns of the enemy as you say. I am sure the result will be good."

"But Sir John Moon will make a row if you take his niece away."

"Let him," retorted Dan contemptuously. "I can deal with that fribble of a man. After all, Lillian need only be absent from London for a month, and during that time we must break up the gang, with or without the aid of the police. If we don't, I shall certainly be murdered, like Moon and Durwin and Penn have been, and on the same grounds--that I know too much. But I daresay Lillian will then be left alone, and Sir John can carry out his pet scheme and marry her to Curberry."

"I wonder," said Laurance musingly, "if Curberry has anything to do with the gang in question."

"I think not, he has nothing to gain."

"Now he hasn't," said Freddy drily, "but he had a good deal to gain when he was a barrister and two lives stood between him and a title and a fortune." The two men looked at one another. "I see what you mean," said Dan slowly, "h'm. Of course he may be a member and the society may have cleared his uncle and cousin out of the way. But we can't be sure. One thing at a time, Freddy. I am going to see Lillian and Mrs. Bolstreath and get them to fly to Sheepeak."

"But you will have to reveal what we know, and that will frighten them." Dan looked vexed and gnawed his nether lip. "I don't want to say more than is necessary," he replied, "as for their own safety, the less they know of the business, the better. Perhaps I may induce Lillian to elope with me to Sheepeak, and need not explain to her. But Mrs. Bolstreath must know more."

"Well," said Freddy, putting on his hat, "I leave these matters in your very capable hands. So far as I am concerned, I am going to Blackheath to see about this death of Penn. I may get into the house--" he paused. "Well?" asked Halliday, raising his eyebrows. "Well, if Curberry does favor this Society of Flies, who knows what I may discover? Also some truths may come out at the inquest. Penn belonged to the gang as we know, and when he wanted a situation, he was taken on by Lord Curberry. That hints at much. However, we shall see; we shall see!" and with a careless nod Freddy took his leave, while Dan changed his clothes with the intention of calling at Sir John Moon's house. Owing to a late breakfast, and the long conversation with Laurance, it was quite one o'clock before Dan reached his destination. He half expected to be refused admittance as usual, especially when he learned from the footman that Miss Moon was not in the house. But failing Lillian, who had no doubt gone out on a shopping expedition and would shortly return to luncheon, Dan sent in his name to Mrs. Bolstreath, with a request for an interview. It was best to explain the situation to her, he thought, since no time could be lost in assuring Lillian's safety. The chaperon saw the young man at once, and when introduced into the room where she was seated, he was struck by her worried air. His thoughts immediately flew to the girl. "Lillian?" he asked anxiously, "is anything the matter with Lillian?"

"Oh, that girl will break my heart with her freaks," said Mrs. Bolstreath in an irritable tone, "she knows that Sir John does not approve of her going out by herself, and that my retaining my situation depends upon my looking after her closely. Yet she has gone out without telling me."

"Where has she gone to?"

"Well," said Mrs. Bolstreath, looking at him, "I think she has gone to Lord Curberry's house." Dan's lip curled. "That ought to please Sir John. Is he with her?"

"No. Sir John is in the country for a few days. He would not be pleased at Lillian going to see Lord Curberry without my being present."

"But why has she gone to see a man she hates?" asked Halliday perplexed. "It is not Lord Curberry she wishes to see," Mrs. Bolstreath hesitated. "I suppose you saw that Mr. Penn is dead?" she asked irrelevantly. "It was in the morning paper, I know--that is, the announcement of his death," said Dan. "Laurance came and told me. Well?"

"This morning Lillian received a letter from Mr. Penn, written a few days ago, saying that if anything happened to him, she was to go to Lord Curberry and find some important paper he has left behind him for her perusal."

"Oh," Dan started to his feet, "then Penn has left a confession?"

"A confession?" Mrs. Bolstreath looked puzzled. "He must have guessed that his death was determined upon," said Halliday to himself, but loud enough for his companion to hear, "perhaps the truth will come out in that confession."

"What truth? For heaven's sake, Mr. Halliday, speak plainly. I am worried enough as it is over Lillian's escapade. Is anything wrong?"

"A great deal. Mrs. Bolstreath, I have to confide in you in order to save Lillian from death--from a death like her father suffered." Mrs. Bolstreath screamed. "Oh, what is it, what is it?"

"You must be silent about what I tell you."

"Of course I shall. I can keep a secret. But tell me, tell me," she panted. "If you don't keep the secret all our lives are in jeopardy. There is no time to be lost. I must follow Lillian to Curberry's house at once. Listen, Mrs. Bolstreath, and remember every word I say is important." Then Dan hastily related much that he knew, though not more than was absolutely necessary. However, he told enough to make Mrs. Bolstreath almost crazy with terror. "Keep your head and my confidence," said Halliday sharply, "we must beat these demons at their own game. Get ready and come with me to Blackheath; on the way I can explain."

"You think Lillian is safe?" implored Mrs. Bolstreath, preparing to leave the room and assume her out-of-door things. "Yes. Yet, if Curberry is connected with the gang and thinks she is hunting for Penn's confession, he may--but it won't bear thinking of. We must go to Lillian at once. You will work with me to save Lillian?"

"With all my heart and soul and body," cried the chaperon wildly. "Then get ready and come with me at once," said Dan imperiously.

CHAPTER XIV

A BUSY AFTERNOON

Lord Curberry was something of a student and a great deal of a man-about-town, so his residence at Blackheath was an ideal one for an individual who blended such opposite qualities. His pleasant Georgian mansion of mellow red brick stood sufficiently far from London to secure privacy for study, and yet was sufficiently near to enable its owner to reach Piccadilly, Bond Street, the clubs and the theatres, easily when he felt so disposed. The chief seat of the family, indeed, was situated in Somersetshire, but Curberry, not possessing a sporting nature, rarely went to live in the country. The Blackheath estate was not large, consisting only of a few acres of woodland, surrounded by a lofty stone wall; but this wall and the trees of the park so sequestered the house that its seclusion suggested a situation in the very wildest parts of England. In every way, therefore, this compact place suited Lord Curberry and he lived there for the greater part of the year. When Dan and Mrs. Bolstreath arrived they found that the house had been thrown open to the public, so to speak. That is, there was a crowd at the entrance-gates, many people in the grounds, and not a few in the very mansion itself. There was not much difficulty in guessing that Marcus Penn's death had drawn a morbid multitude into the neighborhood wherein he had come to his untimely end. Moreover, the inquest was to be held in the house, and the public desired ardently to hear if the verdict would be "Suicide!"

"Murder!" or merely "Accident!" In any case, sensational developments were expected, since the death of the secretary was both violent and unexpected. As a barrister, Curberry assisted the law in every possible way and had permitted the inquest to take place in the house instead of ordering the body of the unfortunate man to be removed to the nearest mortuary. Every one commented on his kindness in this respect, and approved of his consideration. For the time being Curberry was more popular than he had ever been before. As Dan walked up the short avenue and noted the disorganization of the establishment, he made a significant remark to the agitated chaperon. "I don't think that Curberry will have much time to give to Lillian. All the better, isn't it?"

"I'm sure I don't know what you mean," said Mrs. Bolstreath, much flustered. "Well, Penn must have concealed his confession somewhere about the house, so if Lillian wishes to find it, she must get rid of Curberry somehow." "But wouldn't it be wise of her to tell him and ask him to assist in the search?" suggested the lady. "No. If Penn wished Curberry to see his confession, he would have given it to him for delivery to Lillian. He doesn't want Curberry to see what he has written. H'm," Dan reflected that he had used the present tense, "I forgot that the poor chap is dead."

"But surely," Mrs. Bolstreath's voice sank to a horrified whisper, "surely you don't think that Lord Curberry has anything to do with these horrible people you have been telling me about?" "I say nothing--because I know nothing--for certain, that is. I only suspect--er--well--that Curberry may be in the swim. Now don't go and give away the show by changing your manner toward the man," continued Halliday hastily; "act as you have always acted and, indeed, I want you to make yourself as agreeable as possible. Take him away if you can, and leave me alone with Lillian."

"But for what reason?"

"Well, if Curberry is mixed up in this shady business he will not leave Lillian alone. He may wonder, and probably does, at her unexpected presence here, on this day of all days; therefore he may suspect a confession by his secretary and will keep his eyes open."

"Oh, you go too far," cried Mrs. Bolstreath, fanning herself with her handkerchief. "Perhaps I do," assented Dan in a very dry tone, "but in a case like this it is just as well to take all necessary precautions. And in any case Curberry will haunt Lillian's footsteps until she is out of the house, if only to find out why she paid this unnecessary visit."

"He can ask her," said the chaperon curtly. "He won't, if he is what I suspect him to be. But there, I may be accusing the man wrongfully."

"I'm sure you are. Lord Curberry is a perfect gentleman."

"Perfect gentlemen have been discovered doing shady things before now. However, you know what comedy we have arranged. You have come to fetch Lillian back, and I came to escort you. Then get Curberry away on some pretext and let me have ten minutes talk with Lillian. Understand?"

"Yes," gasped Mrs. Bolstreath, "but I don't like these things."

"One can't touch pitch without being defiled," quoted Dan cynically, as they arrived at the open hall door, "we wish to see Lord Curberry." This last question was addressed to a footman, who came to meet them. He recognized Mrs. Bolstreath as having been in the house before with Miss Moon, so readily explained that the young lady was with his master in the drawing-room. Everything was so upset with the inquest, that he never thought of asking for a card, so conducted the visitors to where Lord Curberry was entertaining the girl. Having announced the names and fairly pushed them into the room, the footman departed in a hurry, as there was much excitement amongst the servants and he wished to hear all that was being said. Had not Curberry been attending to Lillian, he would have kept better order, as he was a severe master, and expected decency under all circumstances. But no doubt he also was disturbed by the unusual invasion of his house. "My--dear--Lillian," cried Mrs. Bolstreath in large capitals, and advancing toward the end of the room, where Lillian was seated, looking uncomfortable, "my dear Lillian!" She glared at Lord Curberry. The gentleman had evidently been pressing his suit, a proceeding which sufficiently explained Miss Moon's discomfort. He was as cadaverous as ever in his looks, and his pale-blue eyes, thin lips and general sneering expression struck Dan afresh as uncommonly unpleasant. The man flushed to a brick red under Mrs. Bolstreath's glare and hastened to excuse himself. "I am not to blame, I assure you," he said hurriedly. "Blame!" echoed Lillian with a thankful glance at the sight of her lover, "why do you say 'blame,' Lord Curberry?"

"You ask that?" said Mrs. Bolstreath, plumping down indignantly, "when you go away without my knowledge to pay an unauthorized visit to a-a-a bachelor. If I thought that Lord Curberry----"

"I am not to blame," said that gentleman again with a scowl, for he did not like to stand on the defensive. "Of course you aren't," remarked Miss Moon easily, and with another glance at Dan to point her words. "I saw in the paper that poor Mr. Penn was dead, and as he had been my dear father's secretary I came on the impulse of the moment to learn exactly what had happened." Curberry nodded acquiescence. "I have explained the circumstance to Miss Moon and I shall explain matters to you, Mrs. Bolstreath! As for Mr. Halliday," he frowned at Dan, "I don't know why he has come."

"To escort me, at my request," said Mrs. Bolstreath coldly. "It was necessary for me to call here and take Lillian home. Why did you come?" she asked again. "To hear about Mr. Penn," repeated Lillian rather crossly. "I have been telling you so for the last few minutes."

"I am curious about Penn's death myself," said Dan agreeably, "did he commit suicide?" Curberry wheeled at the word. "Why should he commit suicide?" he demanded with suspicion written on every line of his clean-shaven face. Dan shrugged his shoulders. "I'm sure I can't say," he answered good-humoredly, "only a man in good health isn't found drowned unless he has some reason to get into the pond."

"Penn was not in good health," said Curberry sharply. "He was always complaining and did his work so badly that I intended to give him notice."

"Perhaps he committed suicide because you did." "No. I did not tell him to go, and after all, I can't say that he did kill himself. He was all right at luncheon yesterday, which was when I last set eyes on him. I went to town and returned at five o'clock to hear that he was dead. One of the servants walking in the park found his body in the ornamental water at the bottom of the garden."

"Did any one push him in?" asked Mrs. Bolstreath. "I think not. He was on good terms with the servants, although not popular in any way. No one in my employment would have murdered him, and, as the gates were closed and no one called between luncheon and five o'clock yesterday, it is quite certain that he was not murdered by a stranger. In fact, I don't believe he was murdered at all."

"Suicide, then?" suggested Dan once more, and again Curberry looked at him unpleasantly, as if not relishing the idea. "So far as I saw he had no intention of committing suicide," he said in a cold manner, "however, the evidence at the inquest will settle the matter."

"I expect he didn't look where he was going and fell in," said Lillian suddenly. "Mr. Penn was always absent-minded you know."

"I frequently found him so," remarked Curberry grimly. "He made a great mess of his work occasionally. I am inclined to agree with you, Miss Moon."

"Well," said Dan, after a pause, "let us settle that Penn fell in by accident until we hear the verdict of the jury. When does the inquest take place?"

"In another hour," responded the host, glancing at his watch. "I was just impressing upon Miss Moon the necessity of returning home when you arrived. I have to be present, of course, so as to state what I know of Penn."

"You will give him a good character?" asked Halliday pointedly. Curberry stared in a supercilious way. "The best of characters," he said. "I had no fault to find with him save that he was absent-minded, a quality which no doubt accounts for his death, poor chap."

"Well, well, it's all very sad," said Mrs. Bolstreath in a matter of fact way, "but all our talking will not bring the poor man back. Lillian, child, we must go home, now that your curiosity is satisfied. But first I shall ask Lord Curberry to give me some of those hot-house flowers I see yonder," and she nodded toward a conservatory, which could be entered from the drawing-room by means of a French window. "Oh, I shall be charmed," said Curberry with alacrity, "and perhaps Miss Moon will come also to choose the flowers."

"I can wait here," replied Lillian carelessly. "I have every confidence in Mrs. Bolstreath's choice." Curberry scowled at Dan, for he understood well enough that Lillian wished to remain with his rival. However, he could make no further objection without appearing rude, so he moved reluctantly toward the conservatory beside the chaperon. Yet Dan saw plainly that he was determined not to lose sight of the two, for he plucked the flowers which were directly in front of the French window, and thus could gain a view of the young couple every now and then, when facing round to speak with Mrs. Bolstreath. Lillian noticed this espionage, also, and whispered to Dan, who had sauntered across the room close to her elbow. "He won't let us out of his sight," said Lillian rapidly, "and I can't get to the library, although I have been trying all the time."

"Why do you wish to get to the library?" asked Dan in a low voice. Lillian rose suddenly and dropped a piece of paper. "Put your foot on it and pick it up when he is not looking," she said swiftly; "hush, he's coming back," and then she raised her voice as Curberry returned to the room. "Of course Mr. Penn was always nervous. I really think his health was bad."

"Still on the disagreeable subject of the death," remarked Curberry, who had a handful of flowers to offer. "I wish you wouldn't think of these things, Lillian--I beg pardon, Miss Moon. Please take these flowers and let me escort you and Mrs. Bolstreath out of the house. It's atmosphere is uncomfortable just now." He took no notice of Dan, but offered his arm to Lillian. With a swift glance at her lover, at Mrs. Bolstreath, at the room, the flowers, at anything save Dan's right foot, which was placed firmly on the scrap of paper, she accepted his offer. The chaperon followed, and when Curberry's back was turned she noticed that Halliday stooped swiftly to pick up the paper. But that he gave her a warning glance she would have asked an indiscreet question. As it was she went after her host and pupil, walking beside Dan, who had now slipped the paper into his trousers pocket. But Mrs. Bolstreath could not restrain her curiosity altogether. "What is it?" she whispered, as they walked into the entrance hall. "Nothing! Nothing!" he replied softly, "take Lillian home at once. I shall follow later," and with this Mrs. Bolstreath was obliged to be content, although she was desperately anxious to know more. "I wish I could escort you home," said Curberry, as the two ladies and he stood on the steps, "but my duty keeps me here for the inquest. Perhaps Mr. Halliday will oblige."

"I am afraid not," said Dan stolidly. "I promised to meet my friend Mr. Laurance here. He is coming about the matter of Penn's death. Why, there he is," and sure enough, at a moment that could not have been better chosen, Freddy appeared up the avenue. "Well," said Mrs. Bolstreath, catching a significant glance from Dan. "We are not able to wait and chat. Lord Curberry, we detain you."

"No! no! Let me walk for some distance with you," cried Curberry, and bareheaded as he was he strolled down the avenue between the two ladies. Laurance took off his hat and Lillian bowed graciously, as did Mrs. Bolstreath. But Lord Curberry took no notice of the reporter beyond a rude stare. "That's just as it should be," remarked Halliday, watching the man's retreating form, while Freddy came up to him, "you're just the man we want."

"We?" echoed Laurance, glancing round. "Lillian and myself. See here, this is the note sent by Penn to her, and it asks her to do something which she has not been able to accomplish owing to our noble friend's vigilance."

"What's that?"

"I'm just going to find out. I haven't read the note as yet," and with a second glance to make sure that Curberry was at a safe distance Dan opened the piece of paper, and read it hurriedly. A moment later he slipped it again into his pocket and took Freddy's arm. "It's only a few lines saying that Penn has left a document which he wishes Lillian to read. It is to be found between the pages of the second volume of Gibbon's 'Decline and Fall.' Hum! So that is why Lillian wished to get into the library."

"Let me go," said Freddy eagerly. "No! no! You catch Curberry as he returns and keep him in conversation on some plea or other. Then I can slip into the house and seek the library without being noticed."

"Won't the servants----"

"Oh, the house is all upset this day with the inquest, and every one is wandering about more or less at large. I'll chance it."

"But if Lord Curberry asks for you?"

"Say that I am in the library and that I am waiting to have an interview."

"On what subject?" asked Laurance, rather puzzled by this scheming. "I'll find the subject," said Dan, retreating toward the door of the house; "all I want is five minutes in the library to find the confession. Detain Curberry for that time. Here he is coming back and here I am going forward." As he spoke Dan vanished into the house and came face to face with the butler. "I am waiting for Lord Curberry," said Dan, "will you show me into the library, please." Suspecting nothing wrong and impressed by Dan's cool manner, the butler conducted him to the room in question, and after intimating that he would tell his lordship, departed, closing the door. Halliday ran his eye round the shelves, which extended on three sides of the large compartment from floor to ceiling. It seemed impossible to find the book he was in search of, in so short space of time as would probably be at his disposal. He wished that Penn had indicated the position of Gibbon's masterpiece. However, Halliday, by a stroke of luck, suddenly realized that Curberry numbered his shelves alphabetically, and catalogued his books, so to speak, by the initial letter of the author's name. Those beginning with "A" were placed on the shelf, ticketed with that letter, as Allison, Allen, Anderson, and so on, while the shelf "B" contained Browning, Bronte, Burns, and others. Going by this way of finding the whereabouts of books, Dan discovered Gibbon's "Decline and Fall" on shelf "G" and laid his hand on the second volume. But as luck would have it, Lord Curberry suddenly entered the room just as he was about to open it. Halliday looked up, retaining the volume in his hand. "I am rather surprised to see you here, Mr. Halliday," said Curberry in a cold and haughty tone, "you know that I am busy with this inquest and have no time for conversation. Besides," he looked hard at his visitor, "you could have explained your business out of doors."

"Not in the presence of the ladies," said Dan promptly; "however, I won't keep you more than five minutes," and he wondered how he was to secure the confession without the knowledge of his host. "I am waiting to hear what you have to say," said Curberry, throwing his lean figure into a chair, "you have been making yourself at home," he added with a sneer, glancing at the book. Dan laid it on the table. "I took up Gibbon's second volume just to pass the time," said he carelessly, "I apologize if you think me presuming."

"I don't think anything," rejoined Curberry with a shrug, "except that I am anxious to know why you desire a private conversation."

"It is about Lillian----"

"Miss Moon, if you please."

"Lillian to me, Lord Curberry." "Nothing of the sort, sir," cried the other suitor furiously, and his pale eyes grew angry. "Sir John Moon wishes me to marry his niece."

"Probably, but his niece wishes to marry me."

"That she shall never do."

"Oh, I think so. And what I wish to say, Lord Curberry, is this--that you annoy Miss Moon with your attentions. They must cease."

"How dare you; how dare you; how dare you!"

"Oh, I dare anything where Lillian is concerned," retorted Halliday, and again in a careless manner took up the book, leaning against the table and crossing his legs as he did so. "Leave my house," cried Curberry, starting to his feet, for this nonchalant behavior irritated him greatly. "Oh, willingly. I simply stayed to warn you that Lillian must not be annoyed by you in any way."

"And if I do not obey you?" sneered the other, quivering with rage. "I shall make myself unpleasant, Lord Curberry."

"Do you know to whom you are speaking?"

"Well," said Dan slowly, and with a keen glance at the angry face, "I am not quite sure. I am not Asmodeus to unroof houses, you know." Curberry's yellow face suddenly became white, and his lips trembled nervously. "I don't understand you."

"I scarcely understand myself, and----"

"Wait," interrupted Curberry, as a knock came to the door, "there is no need to let every one overhear our conversation. Come in!" he cried aloud. The butler entered. "You are wanted at the inquest, my lord," he said, and as Curberry's face was bent inquiringly on that of the servant, Dan seized the opportunity to slip a stiff sheaf of papers out of the Gibbon volume. As a matter of fact, it was three or four sheets joined at the corner by a brass clasp. Scarcely had he got it in his hand when Curberry wheeled, after hurriedly telling the butler that he would come shortly. "What have you there?" demanded the host, advancing menacingly. "Some papers of mine," said Dan, preparing to put the sheets into his pocket. "It's a lie. You must have taken them from the table, or out of that book, Mr. Halliday. Yes, I am sure you did. Give me what you have taken."

"No," said Dan, retreating before Curberry's advance, "you are not to----" Before he could get another word, the man flung himself forward and made a snatch at the papers. Held loosely by the corner clasp they flew into a kind of fan, and Curberry managed to grip one or two of the sheets. In the momentary struggle these were torn away, and then the owner of the house released himself suddenly. The next moment he had flung the sheets into the fire, apparently thinking he had got them all. Dan cleverly thrust the one or two remaining sheets into his pocket, and played the part of a man who has been robbed. "How dare you destroy my papers," he cried indignantly. "They were mine," said Curberry, gasping with relief, "and now they are burnt."

"They were Penn's," retorted Halliday sharply, "perhaps that is why they have been destroyed by you."

"What do you mean; what do you mean?"

"Never mind. I think you understand."

"I don't. I swear I don't."

"In that case," said Dan slowly, "you can make public the fact that I came into your library to find a document in the second volume of Gibbon, which was placed there by Marcus Penn. But you won't, Lord Curberry."

"If the papers were not destroyed, I would place them before the Coroner at once," said Curberry, wiping his face and with a glance at the fire on which fluttered a few black shreds--all that remained of what he had thrown in. "I think you must be mad to talk as you do."

"If I am, why not make the matter public?" asked Dan drily. "I don't care about a scandal," said Curberry loftily. "Well," Halliday retreated to the library door, "perhaps the death of Penn will be scandal enough. Those papers doubtless contained an account of the reasons which led to his death."

"I'm sorry that I burnt them then," said Curberry in a studied tone of regret. "I am an impulsive man, Mr. Halliday, and you should not have annoyed me in the way you did. How did you know that the papers were in the second volume of Gibbon?"

"Never mind."

"Were they addressed to you?"

"Never mind."

"What were they about?"

"Never mind!" "D---- you, sir, how dare you?"

"Good-day, Lord Curberry," interrupted Dan, and walked out of the room, leaving his host looking the picture of consternation and dread.

CHAPTER XV.

ABSOLUTE PROOF

It did not require a particularly clever man to guess that Lord Curberry was connected with the Society of Flies. Had he been entirely ignorant of that association, he would not have displayed such agitation when he saw the papers in Dan's hand, nor would he have struggled to gain possession of them, much less have destroyed them. Penn certainly was one of the gang, and on that account, probably Curberry had engaged him as a secretary after the death of Moon. Also he may have had some suspicion that Penn was a traitor, and had guessed that the papers betrayed the society. Otherwise, he would have placed the same before the Coroner, so as to elucidate the reason why the secretary had been done to death. That he had been, Halliday was quite convinced, as Penn was too nervous a man to commit suicide and must have been assisted out of the world by some other person. "But the verdict of suicide has been brought in," argued Laurance, when Dan related his adventure. "I daresay. Curberry's evidence was to the effect that Penn had been considerably worried of late. Of course, that is true, but he wouldn't have killed himself, I'll swear. However," Dan chuckled, "I have a sheet or two remaining of the confession, and we may learn much from that."

"Will it state that Curberry belonged to Queen Beelzebub's gang?"

"I think so. If Curberry does not, he would have made a row and kicked me out of the house. I had no business in the library and no right to take the papers, you know. But I defied Curberry to create a scandal, and left him in a pleasing state of uncertainty as to what I knew and what I intended to do. He was green with fright."

"You had better take care, Dan, or the society will murder you," warned Laurance in an uneasy tone. "Oh, I'm safe enough for the given month," returned Halliday positively; "so far I have said nothing, and until I do notify the authorities all will be well with me."

"But Miss Moon?"

"I join her and Mrs. Bolstreath, at St. Pancras this evening, to catch the six o'clock express to Thawley. Have you written to Miss Vincent?"

"Yes. There is no time to receive a reply, but she is aware that the ladies will stay at The Peacock Hotel, Sheepeak, under the wing of Mrs. Pelgrin. I only hope," added Freddy emphatically, "that you are doing right in placing Miss Moon in the lion's mouth."

"Under the guns of the enemy, you said before. Oh, yes, I am right, especially that I now hold a part of Penn's confession. I shall contrive to let Mrs. Jarsell know that I do, and that if anything happens to Lillian, I can make it hot for her."

"Does the confession implicate Mrs. Jarsell?"

"Yes, it does. I have not had time to decipher the crooked writing of our late friend, but intend to do so when in the train this evening. But the little I saw hinted that Mrs. Jarsell was in the swim."

"I wish you would leave the confession with me," said Laurance, who was desperately anxious to know the exact truth. "Can't, my dear fellow, nor have I time to let you read it, even if I had it on me, which I haven't. My taxi is at the door of this office, and I'm off to St. Pancras in five minutes. Remember, Freddy, that this confession is my sole weapon to protect Lillian. When Mrs. Jarsell learns that I have it, she will not dare to move, and will keep her subjects off the grass also."

"But Curberry will tell her that he has destroyed the confession."

"So he thinks," chuckled Halliday, "but I shall tell her that I rescued enough of it to damn her and her precious gang."

"But how can you tell her without danger?"

"I shall find a way, although I haven't formulated any scheme as yet. Perhaps she will ask me what all this--the story of Queen Beelzebub you know--has to do with her. I shall reply that it has nothing to do with her, but that I know she desires to assist in my love affair. Oh, I'll manage somehow, old son, you may be certain. Good-by."

"Wait a moment," said Laurance, following Dan to the door, "what about Sir John Moon? He will make a row over Lillian's flight, and you will get into trouble."

"He may make a row if he likes, but as Lillian is under the wing of Mrs. Bolstreath, her duly-appointed chaperon, I don't see what he can say. She is quite ready to take all blame."

"Of course," said Laurance thoughtfully, "Sir John may belong to the society himself, in which case, like Curberry, he dare not make a row."

"No," rejoined Dan positively, "I don't believe Sir John belongs to the gang. I wish he did, as it would smooth things. Curberry dare not make open trouble, because he is one of Queen Beelzebub's subjects, but Sir John may because he isn't. However, I shall risk taking Lillian away with Mrs. Bolstreath to play the part of dragon, and Sir John can do what he jolly well likes. Luckily, he is in the country on a visit just now, so we can get clear away without a fuss. By the way, you were at the inquest. Was there any fly found on Penn's body, or was there mention of any scent?"

"No. The man was drowned, and it was not possible for either scent or fly to be on his corpse or clothes. The evidence clearly pointed to suicide."

"H'm. Curberry brought that about," said Dan grimly; "however, I am jolly well sure that Penn was murdered by one of the gang."

"Not by Curberry. He was away at the time of the death." "Perhaps. I'd like to be certain of that. But in any case, he may have others of the gang in his employment, who could polish off the traitor. Queen Beelzebub's subjects are of all classes. Well, I'm off." Halliday took his way to St. Pancras forthwith, and found Mrs. Bolstreath and her charge waiting for him. Lillian was greatly excited and curious, as she did not yet know the reason for this sudden trip northward. Instructed by Dan, the chaperon had refused to impart knowledge, as the young man intended to tell the girl everything when they were in the train. However, Miss Moon was enjoying the unexpected journey and had every faith in her companion. Also, so long as she was in Dan's company, she did not care where she went, or why she went, or when she went. She loved Halliday too completely for there to be any room for distrust in her mind. "Dan," said Mrs. Bolstreath, when they were stepping into the first-class compartment which Halliday had wired to reserve to themselves. "I have written to Sir John saying that Lillian required a change, and that I was taking her to Hillshire, to see some friends of mine. When he has this explanation he will not make any trouble, or even any inquiries. He has every trust in me."

"Good," said Dan, heartily, "you make an excellent conspirator."

"Conspirator," echoed Lillian, gaily, "now what does that mysterious word mean, Dan? I am quite in the dark."

"You shall know all before we get to Thawley. Make yourself comfortable!" "Do we stay at Thawley?" asked the girl, arranging her rug. "For the night. I have telegraphed, engaging rooms for you and Mrs. Bolstreath at the best hotel. To-morrow we go to Sheepeak."

"Where is that?"

"Some miles from Thawley. You must live quietly for a short time, Lillian."

"It's all immensely exciting, of course," cried Miss Moon, petulantly, "but I should like to know what it all means."

"Patience! Patience!" said Dan in a teasing tone, "little girls should be content to wait. By Jove, we're off." The long train glided out of the station, gathering impetus as it left the lights of London behind. Mrs. Bolstreath made herself comfortable in one corner of the compartment, and Lillian did the same in another corner, while Dan sat on the opposite seat and addressed his conversation to both impartially. The girl could scarcely restrain her impatience, so anxious was she to learn the reason for this unexpected journey. "Now, Dan, now!" she cried, clapping her hands, "there is no stop until Bedford, so we have plenty of time to hear the story."

"One minute," said Halliday, who was now in possession of the three sheets of foolscap, which he had rescued from Curberry's grip, "I must bring the story up to date, and cannot do so until I read this statement. By the way, Lillian, why should he send to you about the matter?"

"I'm sure I don't know. But, of course, he knew how grieved I was over my father's murder, and perhaps wished to set my mind at rest." Dan looked at her curiously. "Why should you think that Penn knew of anything likely to set your mind at rest on that point?" Lillian cast down her eyes thoughtfully. "I always thought that Mr. Penn knew much more than he would confess about poor father's death. I quite forgot that I thought so until I got the letter asking me to look into the second volume of Gibbon's 'Decline and Fall' in Lord Curberry's library. Dear me!" murmured the girl, folding her hands, "how I did try to get into the library."

"Curberry would not let you?" "No, I think he was puzzled why I wished to go. But he did not ask me any questions."

"I quite believe that," said Dan, grimly; "asking questions was a dangerous game for him to play. However, when he found me in the library, he evidently recalled your desire to go there, and it flashed across him that we were working in consort. No wonder he destroyed the papers on the chance that Penn might have left incriminating evidence behind him."

"I don't know what you are talking about," said Lillian, fretfully. "Well," observed Dan, smoothing out the foolscap, "Penn, no doubt, left the clue as to the whereabouts of the confession to you, so that you might learn who murdered your father."

"Ah, I always believed Mr. Penn knew. Is the name in that paper?" she asked eagerly, and leaning forward. "It may or it may not be, dear. You see the greater part of the confession was destroyed by Lord Curberry. He was afraid."

"Dan!" Lillian caught her lover's hand, "you don't think that Lord Curberry killed my father?" "No, no, no!" said Halliday, quickly. "I am sure he did not. However, you shall hear all that I know, and Laurance knows, and all that Mrs. Bolstreath is acquainted with. Only let me read these few sheets first." The girl, on fire with curiosity, would have objected, but that Mrs. Bolstreath touched her shoulder significantly. With an effort to restrain her curiosity, which was creditable considering the circumstances, she nestled into her corner of the carriage, while Dan glanced through the manuscript. In spite of Penn's crooked handwriting--and it was very bad indeed--it did not take much time for the young man to master the contents of the confession. He uttered an exclamation of vexation when he reached the end. "Like a serial story, it breaks off at the most interesting part," he said crossly. "However, I have learned something." "What have you learned?" demanded Mrs. Bolstreath immediately. "All in good time," said Halliday, quietly. "I must first tell Lillian what we both know, and then I can bring our discoveries up to date by saying what is in this confession," and he tapped his breast-pocket, wherein he had placed the sheets. "Now then, Lillian."

"Now then, Dan," she mocked, "just tell me all, for I cannot keep silence any longer."

"You will have to, if you desire to hear the story. Only don't be worried by what I am about to tell you. You are safe with me." Lillian shrugged her shoulders, as if to imply that there was no need for him to state such a plain truth, and looked at him with inquiring eyes. As she appeared to be brave and collected, Dan had no hesitation in relating to her all that he had already told Mrs. Bolstreath, and thus the girl became thoroughly informed of the underhand doings which had taken place since the death of her father. As Halliday explained, her eyes became larger and rounder and more shining. Still the color did not leave her cheeks and although she was intensely interested she did not display any fright. This was creditable to her courage, considering that the revelation hinted at many possible dangers to herself and to her lover. Dan brought the story up to the time they started from London, and then waited to hear her opinion. "It's dreadful and wonderful, and very horrid," said Lillian, drawing a deep breath; "do you think that Mr. Penn murdered my father?"

"No. The evidence of the girl to whom he was dictating letters to be typewritten proves that he did not enter the library at the time when the death was supposed to have taken place."

"Then Lord Curberry? He----"

"I don't believe Lord Curberry, either directly or indirectly, had anything to do with the matter," said Dan, decisively. "Sir Charles approved of his suit rather than of mine, so it was to Curberry's interest to keep your father alive and well. My dear, it was the false Mrs. Brown who killed Sir Charles, and she came as an agent of this ghastly Society of Flies, because he got to know too much about the association."

"Then Mrs. Brown is Mrs. Jarsell?" asked Mrs. Bolstreath, anxiously. "I can't be sure of that," said the young man, thoughtfully; "of course, the sole evidence that proves Mrs. Jarsell to be connected with the gang is the presence of the Sumatra scent in her Hillshire house, and her presence on the Blackheath grounds when Durwin was murdered."

"But, by your own showing, she could not have reached London in time."

"That is quite true and yet I recognized her plainly enough on the day Lillian and I saw the animated pictures. However, we can leave that fact alone for the moment. I am certain that Mrs. Jarsell is Queen Beelzebub, for Penn says as much." He tapped his breast-pocket again. "Oh," cried Lillian, eagerly, "what does the confession say?"

"I'll give you the gist of it," replied Halliday, quietly. "Penn begins with a statement of his early life. He was the son of a clergyman, and his mother is still alive. From a public school he went to Cambridge, and thence to London, where he tried to make a living by literature. Not being clever he did not succeed, and fell into low water. I am bound to say that he did not trouble much about his own poverty, but seemed to be greatly concerned on account of his mother, who is badly off--so he says. Then he was tempted and fell, poor devil."

"Who tempted him?" demanded Mrs. Bolstreath. "A young man whom he met when he was staying in a Bloomsbury boarding-house, very hard up. The man said that he belonged to a society which could make its members rich, and proposed to introduce Penn. This was done, in the same way, I presume, in which I was taken to these mysterious headquarters. The first fruits of Penn's connection with Queen Beelzebub was that Sir Charles Moon engaged him as secretary, so, getting a good salary, he was enabled to give his mother many comforts." Lillian looked alarmed. "But my father did not belong to the association."

"No. Of course he didn't. But Penn was placed as his secretary--the business was managed through Curberry, who *does* belong to the gang--so that he might inveigle Sir Charles into becoming a member. Penn appears to have lost his nerve, and did not dare to persuade Sir Charles, so another person was put on to the business. The name is not given."

"But why did Queen Beelzebub wish my father to belong to the gang?" asked Lillian, with natural perplexity. "The reason is plain, my dear. Sir Charles was an influential man, and could be of great service to the association. He learned enough to show him what a dangerous organization existed, and then sent for Mr. Durwin, who belonged to New Scotland Yard, so that he might reveal what he knew. Penn learned this, since he saw the letter written by your father, Lillian, and at once told the society. Then the false Mrs. Brown was sent to stop Sir Charles, and----" Dan made an eloquent gesture with his hands. There did not seem to be much need of further explanation. "Mrs.

Brown undoubtedly murdered Sir Charles," commented Mrs. Bolstreath, in a thoughtful way, "but is she Mrs. Jarsell?"

"Penn says as much," repeated Dan, who had made the same remark earlier, "but it is just at that point he ends. Listen and I shall read you the last sentence," and Halliday took the papers from his pocket. The three sheets were intact, as Curberry did only rend away the remainder from the brass clasp. At the end of the third page Halliday read, "Mrs. Jarsell of the Grange, Hillshire, can explain how Mrs.----" Dan broke off with a frown. "Here we come to the end of the page, and can learn no more. Curberry burnt the most important part of the confession, which doubtless gave full details of Mrs. Jarsell's connection with the gang."

"She could explain about Mrs. Brown, I suppose," said Lillian, quietly. "Yes. The first word over the page is, I am certain, Brown. What is more, I believe Mrs. Jarsell and Mrs. Brown are one and the same."

"If I see Mrs. Jarsell, I may recognize her, Dan. I saw the false Mrs. Brown, remember, and it was because of me that she was admitted to an interview with my father." "If you do recognize her, which I doubt, you must not let on you know who she really is," Dan warned the girl; "our business just now, and until we get more evidence, is to pretend entire ignorance of these things. You are up in Hillshire for a change of air, Lillian, and know nothing. Mrs. Jarsell, relying on the clever way in which she was disguised, will never dream that you connect her with the poor woman who came on that fatal night to see your father. You understand?"

"Quite," put in Mrs. Bolstreath, before the girl could speak, "and I shall see that Lillian acts her part of knowing nothing."

"Remember you deal with an extraordinarily clever woman, Mrs. Bolstreath."

"I am a woman also, so diamond can cut diamond."

"But, Dan," asked Lillian, timidly, "do you think that Mrs. Jarsell really did murder my father?"

"On what evidence we have, I believe she did. She murdered your father and Durwin because they knew too much, and I should not be surprised to learn, in spite of the verdict at the inquest, that she got rid of Penn."

"Why should she?"

"Penn let out too much to me," explained Dan, putting away the confession, "and, in any case, was a weak sort of chap, who was a source of danger to the society. Queen Beelzebub, who is, I believe, Mrs. Jarsell, evidently thought it was best to silence him. I am sure that Penn did not commit suicide, and was drowned by Mrs. Jarsell. Still, in the absence of further evidence, we can do nothing."

"What action will you take now?" asked Mrs. Bolstreath, quickly. "Before leaving Thawley to-morrow morning," said Halliday, after a pause, "I shall post this confession to Laurance, and tell him to make use of it only should he hear that anything happens to me."

"Or to me," chimed in Lillian, and looked a trifle nervous. "My dear, nothing can happen to you," said Dan, decidedly, "cheek by jowl, as it were, with Mrs. Jarsell, you are perfectly safe. Queen Beelzebub confines her doings to London and keeps the name of Mrs. Jarsell clean in Hillshire, for obvious reasons. The Grange is her place of refuge, and no one would connect an innocent country lady with criminal doings in London. If she is what we think her to be, she will not hurt a hair of your head in Hillshire."

"All the same, I don't intend to see her," said Lillian, determinedly. "There is no reason that you should. She may call and try to learn why you are staying at the Peacock Hotel, and, if so, will probably ask you to The Grange. Don't go," ended Dan, emphatically. "Of course not," put in Mrs. Bolstreath, equally decisive, "leave that to me, since I am responsible for Lillian."

"You can say that I am ill with nerves or consumption, or something," said the girl, vaguely. "I don't want to meet the woman if she murdered my father."

"If you do," said Dan, impressively, "don't reveal your suspicions," and then he went on to instruct the two ladies how they were to behave in the enemy's country. That they were safe there, so long as they pretended ignorance, Dan did not doubt, but, should Mrs. Jarsell learn that they knew so much about her, she might adopt a counsel of despair and strike. It did not do to drive so dangerous a woman into a corner. For the rest of the journey very little was said. The subject had been thoroughly threshed out. Lillian had been informed of what was going on, and all plans had been made for the future. The girl was to live at the Peacock and see Miss Vincent, and chat with Mrs. Pelgrin, and take walks and admire the country, and to conduct herself generally as one who came simply for a change of air. If she did not go to The Grange--and on the plea of illness, she could excuse herself from going--Mrs. Jarsell could not harm her in any way. And, indeed, even if Mrs. Jarsell did succeed in getting her to come to afternoon tea, Dan had a plan in his head whereby to ensure Lillian against any use being made of the Sumatra scent. It was a daring thing to take Miss Moon into the jaws of the lion, yet that very daring would probably prove to be her safeguard. But Halliday had done what he could to guard against the events of a threatening future, and now could only wait to see what would take place. At the moment there was nothing more to be done. In due course the train arrived at Thawley Station, and Dan singled out George Pelgrin to convey luggage to a cab. Mindful of his last tip, George displayed great alacrity in performing his duties as porter, and, what is more, when he received another half-crown gave inadvertently a piece of valuable information, which Halliday was far from expecting. "That's the second two-and-six since yesterday," said George, spitting on the coin for luck. "Mrs. Jarsell gave me the same when she came back yesterday evening."

"Oh," Dan was startled, but did not show it, "your Sheepeak friend has been to London then?"

"Went a couple of days ago, and came back last night," said Pelgrin, "and she says to me, 'George, look after my traps, for you're the only smart porter in this station,' she says. Ah, she's a kind lady is Mrs. Jarsell, and that civil as never was. There's the luggage in the cab all right, sir. The Vulcan Hotel? Yes, sir. Drive on, cabby." Mrs. Bolstreath and Lillian had not heard this conversation, but Dan pondered over it on the way to the hotel. Mrs. Jarsell had, then, been in London at the time of Penn's death, and probably--although he could not prove this--she was responsible for the same. When the young man arrived at the hotel, and the ladies went to rest, he wrote a letter to Laurance, detailing the new fact he had learned, and instructed him what use to make of the confession if anything happened to himself in Hillshire. Then he enclosed the confession and went out personally to register the packet. Once it was posted he felt that he had done all that was possible. "And now," said Dan, to himself, "we'll see what move Queen Beelzebub will make."

CHAPTER XVI

DAN'S DIPLOMACY

Mrs. Pelgrin welcomed her unexpected guests with great delight and showed her appreciation of their coming by emphatic aggressiveness. Why she should mask a kind heart and an excellent disposition by assuming a brusque demeanor is not very clear, but certainly the more amiable she felt the more disagreeable did she become. In fact, the landlady appeared to believe that honesty of purpose was best shown by blunt speeches and abrupt movements. Consequently, she did not get on particularly well with Mrs. Bolstreath, who demanded respect and deference from underlings, which Mrs. Pelgrin positively declined to render. She termed the chaperon "a fine madam," in the same spirit as she had called Dan "a butterfly," and was always ready for a war of words. But, admiring Lillian's gay and lively character, she waited on the girl hand and foot, yet with an air of protest to hide the real satisfaction she felt at having her in the house. To Mrs. Pelgrin, Lillian was a goddess who had descended from high Olympus to mingle for a time with mere mortals. Out of consideration for Halliday's desire to seek safety for Lillian by placing her under the guns of the enemy, Mrs. Bolstreath decided to remain a week at the Peacock Hotel. Later she arranged to go to Hartlepool in Durhamshire, where she and her charge could find shelter with two spinsters who kept a school. The chaperon admitted that she felt uneasy in the near vicinity of Queen Beelzebub, and all Dan's assurance could not quieten her fears. She thought that he was playing too bold a game, and that ill would come of the stay at Sheepeak. Lillian was more confident, always confident that Dan could do no wrong, and she was quite indifferent to Mrs. Jarsell's doings. However, she agreed to go to Hartlepool, and as Mrs. Bolstreath was bent upon the change, Halliday accepted the situation. Meanwhile, he decided to call at The Grange on some innocent pretext and diplomatically give Queen Beelzebub to understand that he held the winning card in the game he was playing with the Society of Flies. This could be done, he ventured to think, by assuming that Mrs. Jarsell knew nothing about the nefarious association, and he did not believe that she would remove her mask, since it was to her interest to observe secrecy in Hillshire. However, he left this matter of a call and an explanation in abeyance for the time being, and for a couple of days attended to the three ladies. The third, it is needless to say, was Mildred Vincent, who called at The Peacock Hotel on receipt of her lover's letter. She gave Dan to understand that he was out of favor with the inventor. "Uncle has never forgiven you for not winning the race," said Mildred, at afternoon tea, "he says you should have gained the prize."

"I wish I had," said Halliday, dryly, "the money would have been very acceptable. It was my fancy-flying did the mischief, as I broke the rudder. However, I shall call and apologize."

"He won't see you, Mr. Halliday."

"Ah, that's so like an inventor, who is as touchy as a minor poet."

"Mrs. Jarsell is annoyed also," continued Mildred, sadly, "she says you should have made a better use of the favor she procured for you."

"It seems to me that I am in hot water all round, Miss Vincent. All the same, I shall survive these dislikes."

"It is absurd," cried Lillian, with indignation. "Dan risked his life to win the race, and if he hadn't had such bad luck he would have won."

"Thanks, my dear girl, but it was less bad luck than carelessness, and a certain amount of vanity, to show how I could handle the machine."

"You are very modest, Dan," said Mrs. Bolstreath, laughingly. "It is my best quality," replied Halliday, with a twinkle in his eyes. "Where is Mr. Vincent's machine now?" questioned Mildred. "At Blackheath stored away. I suppose, as it was only lent, I shall have to return it to your uncle. But I shall have a final fly on it when I go back to London in a few days."

"Does Miss Moon go back also?"

"Not to London," interposed Mrs. Bolstreath, "we propose to visit some friends in Scotland." Lillian looked up in surprise, as Hartlepool certainly was not in Scotland, and she thought that Mrs. Bolstreath's geography was at fault. But a significant look from Dan showed her that he understood why the wrong address had been given. Mrs. Bolstreath, with too much zeal, mistrusted Mildred, although she had no cause to do so. Certainly Mildred, in perfect innocence, did she know the actual destination, might tell her uncle, who would assuredly tell Mrs. Jarsell, and, for obvious reasons, it was not necessary that Mrs. Jarsell should know where the city of refuge was situated. All the same, Dan did not think for a moment that Mildred knew anything about the Society of Flies. But he was beginning to fancy that Vincent had some such knowledge, as Mrs. Jarsell financed him, and that she would not do so, he was positive, unless she made something out of the matter. It was very convenient for Queen Beelzebub to have an inventor at her elbow who could construct swift aeroplanes. And it was at this point of his meditations that Dan jumped up so suddenly as to spill his tea. "What's the matter?" asked Lillian, making a dash at the cup and saucer to save breakage. "I've got an idea," said Halliday, with a gasp. "I must go out and think it over," and, without excusing himself further, he rushed from the room. "That's not like Dan," remarked Mrs. Bolstreath, uneasily, "he is calm and cool-headed as a rule. I wonder what is the matter?"

"Oh, he'll tell us when he comes back," replied Lillian, philosophically. "I can always trust Dan." Then she turned the conversation in a somewhat heedless manner. "Do you like living here, Miss Vincent?"

"Well," admitted Mildred, "it is rather too quiet for my taste. But I have plenty to do in looking after my uncle and his business. He depends so much on me, that I wonder what he will do when I get married."

"When do you intend to get married?" asked Mrs. Bolstreath, curiously. She could not disabuse herself of the idea that, living so close to Mrs. Jarsell, and having an uncle who was helped by Mrs. Jarsell, the girl knew something about the Society of Flies. "Next year, the year after--I don't exactly know. It all depends upon my dear Freddy's success. We must have a home and an income. But I suppose we shall marry, sooner or later, and then Mrs. Jarsell can look after Uncle Solomon."

"Who is Mrs. Jarsell?" asked Lillian, artfully and cautiously. "She is an old lady who lives at The Grange with another old lady, her former governess, Miss Armour. Both are charming. If you are dull here, perhaps, Miss Moon, you would like to meet them?"

"Later, later," put in Mrs. Bolstreath, hurriedly, "thank you for the suggestion, Miss Vincent. Meanwhile, we wish to explore the country. It is a charming neighborhood, although very quiet in many respects." Mildred agreed and then began to plan excursions to this place and that, with the idea of making the stay of the visitors at Sheepeak pleasant. So agreeably did she behave and took such trouble in designing trips that Mrs. Bolstreath revised her opinion and began to believe that so nice a girl could not possibly know anything of Mrs. Jarsell's doings, whatever knowledge her uncle might be possessed of. And Dan, walking at top speed along the high road in a vain attempt to quieten his mind, was convinced that the inventor had some such knowledge. The idea which had brought him to his feet, and had sent him out to work off his excitement, was that the inventor was responsible for Mrs. Jarsell's presence in London at unexpected moments. She financed him and retained him at her elbow, so to speak, that she might utilize his capabilities and his clever inventions. If, on the day of the London to York race, Mrs. Jarsell was at the Peacock Hotel about the hour of nine o'clock--as she certainly was, on the evidence of Mrs. Pelgrin, who had no obvious reason to tell a lie--she could not have got to London by train or motor in time to murder Durwin. Yet she was assuredly at Blackheath, if the cinematograph was to be believed. Dan had hitherto been puzzled to reconcile apparent impossibilities, but at tea-time the solution of the problem had suddenly flashed into his mind. Mrs. Jarsell had travelled to town on an aeroplane. "It is about one hundred and sixty miles from this place to town," muttered Dan, walking very fast, and talking aloud to himself in his excitement, "so she could accomplish that distance with ease in three hours, considering that Vincent's machine can fly at sixty miles in sixty minutes. He said so and I proved that he spoke truly when I experimented with the machine he lent me. Mrs. Jarsell was at the Peacock Hotel at nine o'clock, and the cinematograph showed she was at Blackheath at one o'clock. The race started then, and Durwin was killed shortly afterwards. Sixty miles an hour means one hundred and eighty miles in three hours. Say she started at half-past nine--which she could easily do, leaving Mrs. Pelgrin immediately for Vincent's place--she could reach London by half-past twelve, if not earlier, seeing she had just one hundred and sixty miles to go. There would be no difficulty in her reaching Blackheath and stabbing Durwin at the time the death took place." Halliday was convinced that in this way the miracle of Mrs. Jarsell had taken place. No other means of transit could have landed her at the place where Durwin had met with his death. Of course, this assumption intimated that Mrs. Jarsell was an accomplished aviator, and that there had been no hitch in the journey from Sheepeak to Blackheath. But these were not impossibilities, for Vincent probably had taught the woman how to fly, and perhaps had handled the machine himself. There was room for two in the aeroplane, as Dan very well knew, since he had taken Penn for a flight himself, and the vehicle used was probably built on the same lines as the one lent. Since aviation was yet in its infancy, there was certainly a possibility that such a journey could not take place without accidents or hindrance. But, as inferior machines had accomplished greater distances, Dan quite believed that Mrs. Jarsell, with or without Vincent as pilot, had reached London in one smooth stretch of flying. On other occasions she might not have been so successful, but on this one she probably had, for to get to Blackheath in time to commit the crime, it would have been necessary for her to use rightfully every second of the given time. No wonder with such a means of transit at her disposal she could prove an advantageous alibi, when occasion demanded. Also, since the late conquest of the air afforded her the opportunity of swift travelling, greatly in excess of other human inventions, it was quite reasonable that she should live so far from the scene of her criminal exploits. Thinking thus, Halliday stumbled across the very person who was in his thought. He rushed with bent head along the roads and unconsciously mounted towards the vast spaces of the moorlands, stretching under gray skies. Thus--and he swiftly decided that the collision was meant--he ran into Mrs. Jarsell, who approached in the opposite direction. She laughed and expostulated, as if Dan was in the wrong, although she must have seen him coming, and the road was wide enough for her to move to one side. "Really, Mr. Halliday, you require the whole country to move in," said Mrs. Jarsell in her heavy way, and with an affectation of joviality. "I--I--I beg your pardon," stammered

Dan, not quite himself, and stared at her as though she had suddenly risen out of the earth. Indeed, so far as he was concerned, she had done so, ignorant as he was of her approach. The woman was arrayed in her favorite white, but, as the day was chilly, she wore a voluminous cloak of scarlet silk quilted and padded and warm both in looks and wear. Her black eyes, set in her olive-hued face, peered from under her white hair as watchfully as ever. At the present moment, her heavy countenance wore an expression of amusement at the startled looks of the young man, and she commented on them with ponderous jocularity. "One would think I was a ghost, Mr. Halliday. You will admit that I am a very substantial ghost," and she shook her silver-mounted cane playfully at him. "I didn't expect to meet you here," said Dan, drawing a deep breath, and thinking how best he could introduce the subject of Lillian. "Nor did I expect to meet you," responded Mrs. Jarsell, still phlegmatically playful. "Have you risen from the earth, or dropped from the skies? I did not even know that you were in the neighborhood." Dan grimly decided that this last statement was false, since he had been a whole two days at the Peacock Hotel, and he was certain Mrs. Jarsell must have heard of his visit. Also of the ladies sheltering under Mrs. Pelgrin's wing, for in the country gossip is more prevalent than in town. "I came up for a day or two, or three or four," said Dan, still staring. "You don't appear to be very decided in your own mind," rejoined Mrs. Jarsell, dryly, and sat down on a large block of granite, which was embedded amongst the heather; "our neighborhood evidently has a fascination for you," her eye searched his face carefully. "I am pleased, as we are proud of our scenery hereabouts. Those who come once, come twice; quite a proverb, isn't it? Is your friend, Mr. Laurance, with you?"

"Not on this occasion," answered Dan, coolly, and coming to the point. "I came with two ladies, Miss Moon and her companion. They are stopping at the Peacock Hotel for a short time."

"Miss Moon! Miss Moon!" mused Mrs. Jarsell, "oh, yes, the young lady you are engaged to marry. The daughter of that poor man who was murdered." "You have an excellent memory, Mrs. Jarsell."

"We have little to exercise our memories in this dull place," said the woman graciously, and with a motherly air, "you don't ask after Miss Armour, I observe. That is very unkind of you, as you are a great favorite with her."

"Miss Armour is my very good friend," responded Halliday, cautiously, "and so are you, since you induced Mr. Vincent to lend me the aeroplane."

"I am as glad that I did that as I am sorry you lost the race, Mr. Halliday."

"Fortune of war," said Dan, lightly, "we can't always be successful you know, Mrs. Jarsell. I wish you had seen the start; it was grand."

"I wish I had," said the woman, lying glibly, "but it was impossible for me to leave Miss Armour on that day, as she had bad health. In fact, Mr. Vincent wished to go also and see how his machine worked; but he could not get away either. Still," added Mrs. Jarsell, with a cheerful air, "perhaps it is as well, so far as I am concerned, that I could not go. Aviation seems to be very dangerous, and I should have been afraid for your safety."

"Oh, I shall never come to harm in the air, I hope," responded Dan, with emphasis, "you must let me take you up some day." Mrs. Jarsell shuddered. "I should be terrified out of my wits," she protested, "fancy a heavy woman, such as I am, trying to emulate a bird. Why, I am quite sure I would fall and smash like an egg, even supposing there is any machine capable of bearing my none too trifling weight."

"Oh, I think there is, Mrs. Jarsell. Some machines can carry two, you know, and lately in France an aviator took five or six people from one given point to another. It is quite safe." Mrs. Jarsell shook her head seriously. "I think not, since aviation is yet in its infancy. In five years, if I live as long, I may venture, but now--no, thank you, Mr. Halliday."

"Most ladies are afraid, certainly. Even Miss Moon, who is plucky, will not let me take her for a fly."

"Miss Moon, of course. I was quite forgetting her. I hope you will bring her to see me and Miss Armour."

"If she stays here, certainly. But I think of returning to town to-morrow, so I may not be able to bring her. I daresay Mrs. Bolstreath will, however," ended Dan, quite certain in his own mind that the chaperon would find some good excuse to avoid the visit. "I shall be delighted," Mrs. Jarsell murmured vaguely, "how have you been, Mr. Halliday, since I saw you last?" It seemed to Dan that she asked this question with intention, and he was entirely willing to give her a frank answer. In frankness, as in taking Lillian under the guns of the enemy, lay the safety of both. Halliday was convinced of this. "I have been rather worried," he said, slowly, and with a side-glance at Mrs. Jarsell's watchful face. "I had an adventure."

"I love adventures," replied the woman, heavily, "and this one?"

"Well. I was hustled into a taxi-cab and carried in a drugged condition to some place where I met with a collection of scoundrels. A kind of murder-gang, you might call it, who slay, blackmail, and thieve for the sake of power."

"Rather a strange reason," said Mrs. Jarsell, equably, and not at all moved, "I should say the reason was for money."

"That, with power," explained Dan, "but, indeed, this society appears to be governed on wonderful principles, such as one would ascribe to honest men."

"In what way?" Mrs. Jarsell was quite curious in a detached manner. "Well, the members are chaste and sober and industrious."

"They must be virtuous. You are describing a society of saints."

"Quite so; only these saints apply their virtues to crime. They have a head who is called Queen Beelzebub." Mrs. Jarsell shuddered and drew lines on the dust of the road with her cane slowly and carefully. "Did you see her?" she asked, "it's a horrid name, full of horrid possibilities."

"No, I did not see her or anyone," said Dan, frankly, "the room was in darkness save for a red light around Queen Beelzebub's mask."

"Oh, this person wore a mask! How did you know she was a woman?"

"Well, you see, the name is Queen Beelzebub."

"That might be taken by a man to hide the truth."

"It might," admitted the other carelessly, "and, indeed, I don't think that any woman would have the nerve to belong to such a gang."

"I agree with you," said Mrs. Jarsell, gravely, "well, and what happened?"

"I was asked by Queen Beelzebub to join the gang and share the profits, which you may guess are large. I have a month to think over the matter." Mrs. Jarsell looked at him keenly. "Surely, you would never belong to such an organization," she said with a reproachful tone in her heavy voice. "Oh, I don't know. I have my own axe to grind like other people, and, if this gang helps me to grind it, I may consider the offer. Do I shock you, Mrs. Jarsell? Your voice sounded as though I did."

"You shock me more than I can say," she replied, decisively, "that an honest man should even think of such a thing is dreadful. This gang should be denounced to the police. I wonder you have not done so already." Dan shook his head and admired the cool, clever way in which she was playing a very dangerous game, though, to be sure, she was far from suspecting he guessed her connection with Queen Beelzebub. "I can't do that yet."

"What do you mean by--yet?" questioned Mrs. Jarsell, and this time there was a distinct note of alarm in her voice. "I risk death if I denounce the gang, not only to myself, but to Miss Moon. I am sure she and I would be killed as her father was killed, if I moved in the matter. Also, I am not sure of many things." Mrs. Jarsell, still drawing patterns, spoke thoughtfully. "I don't think you are wise to speak of this gang if it is so dangerous, even to a country mouse such as I am. Of course, I shall say nothing, as I have no one to say anything to, and if I had I should not speak. But if you talk to a stranger like me about things you were told to keep secret, you or Miss Moon may be murdered."

"I thought so a week ago," admitted Halliday, candidly. "Then you don't think so now."

"No. Not since Marcus Penn died." Mrs. Jarsell drew a long breath and wriggled uneasily. "Who is Marcus Penn?"

"Well, he was the secretary of Sir Charles Moon, and afterwards he was the secretary of Lord Curberry. Now he's a corpse."

"Oh," cried Mrs. Jarsell, suddenly, "I wish you wouldn't talk of these horrible things. Has this gang----"

"Murdered him?" finished the young man, "yes, I believe so, although a verdict of suicide was brought in. But poor Penn's death may be the means of saving me and Miss Moon."

"Indeed!" the woman's tone became harsh and imperative, but she did not ask any questions. "Yes. He left a confession." Even the side-glance Dan sent in Mrs. Jarsell's direction showed him that her olive cheeks had turned to a dead white. However, she said nothing, although she moistened her lips slowly; so he went on easily, as if he were telling an idle story. "This confession was concealed in Lord Curberry's house, but Penn sent a note of its whereabouts to Miss Moon, who told me. I got the confession and placed it in safe keeping."

"That was wise," said Mrs. Jarsell, with an effort. "And the safe keeping?"

"Oh, I shall only tell the whereabouts of the confession and the name of the person who holds it when there is no necessity for the confession to be used."

"I don't see quite what you mean, Mr. Halliday."

"Well, you see, Mrs. Jarsell, I have to protect myself and Miss Moon from the machinations of the society. The person who holds the confession will not open the sealed envelope in which it is placed unless something happens to Miss Moon or to myself. Therefore, so long as no member of the gang hurts us, the secrets of the gang are quite safe." To his attentive ear it seemed that Mrs. Jarsell drew a long breath of relief. With a command of herself which did her credit, she displayed no emotion, but observed playfully, "It is very clever of you and very wise to guard yourself in this way. Certainly the gang cannot hurt you in any way so long as there is danger of the confession being opened in the event of things happening to you or to Miss Moon. Suppose the confession is a very dreadful one, Mr. Halliday?"

"It is not so dreadful or so full as I should like it to be," said Dan, in his calmest manner, "but there is sufficient set down to warrant the interference of the authorities. If that confession comes into the hands of the Scotland Yard officials, they can lay hands on the gang;" he was bluffing when he said this, as he was not quite sure if Curberry had not let Mrs. Jarsell know that the confession--as Curberry thought--had been destroyed. "I think the police should know," said Mrs. Jarsell, rising. "Thank you for nothing," said Dan, following her example, "but, if I move in the matter, I run the risk of death. Besides, I may accept the offer of the society. Who knows?"

"Don't do that," implored Mrs. Jarsell, so earnestly that Dan was convinced Curberry had not told her of any confession, "it's so wicked."

"Perhaps it is. However, if the society leave me and Miss Moon alone, the confession won't be opened and the gang is safe. Otherwise----" "Otherwise the whole association will be exposed to the danger of arrest," said Mrs. Jarsell, lightly, "well, it sounds all very dreadful to a country lady as I am. I wish you had not told me. Why did you tell me?"

"Because," said Dan, ironically, "I look upon you as a friend." Mrs. Jarsell's face cleared and she smiled. "I am your friend," she said in an emphatic way, "and, believe me when I say that I am sure Miss Moon is safe."

"Thank you," replied Dan, agreeably, "I am sure also." Then they parted with mutual compliments, smiles and handshakes.

CHAPTER XVII

AT BAY

When Dan left Mrs. Jarsell he was very well pleased with the promise she had given concerning the safety of Lillian. He fully believed that she, in her role of Queen Beelzebub, would keep that promise faithfully, if only because her own interests demanded such honesty. The fact that the confession of Penn was in the hands of a third party, to be made use of should anything happen to Miss Moon, prevented the Society of Flies from carrying out the threat made to him at the secret meeting. To save their own lives, the members would be forced--much against their will no doubt--to spare those of Lillian and himself. Dan chuckled at the way in which he had circumvented the deadly organization. But he had only scotched the snake; he had not killed it, and, until he did so, there was always that chance that it would strike when able to do so with safety. But, while Penn's confession remained in Laurance's hands, all was well. One thing struck Halliday as strange, and that was the persistence with which Mrs. Jarsell kept up the comedy of having-nothing-to-do-with-the-matter during so confidential a conversation. She knew that Penn had been a doubtful member of her gang; she knew that he had been despatched--as Dan truly believed--because he was not to be trusted, and now she knew that he had left a confession behind him, which was in the hands of her enemies. Also, she was aware that the man who spoke to her had read the confession and must have guessed that her name, as Queen Beelzebub, was mentioned therein. This being the case, it is to be presumed that she would speak freely, but, in place of doing so, she had pretended ignorance, and for his own ends he had humored her feigning. Either she doubted that such a confession existed, or she guessed in whose possession it was, and intended to regain it. "Queen Beelzebub knows well enough that Freddy is my best friend," thought Dan, as he returned to the Peacock Hotel, "and it would be reasonable for her to believe that he had Penn's confession, which is certainly the case. I should not be at all surprised if Freddy was inveigled into a trap as I was, so that he might be forced to surrender the document or rather what remains of it. If that were managed, Queen Beelzebub would revenge herself on Lillian and on me, since there would be nothing left to shield us from her spite. And, in any case, Freddy is in danger, as I am certain she guesses that he holds the confession," he mused for a few moments, and then added, aloud, "I shall return to town at once and see him." The more he thought the more he saw the necessity of doing this. Mrs. Jarsell's first move to counterplot him would be to seek out Lord Curberry and learn what she could, relative to what Penn had left behind him. Certainly Curberry would assure her that he had burnt the confession, in which case Queen Beelzebub would think that she would be free to act. But Halliday believed she was of too suspicious a nature to be quite convinced that he had only bluffed. Before taking any steps, she would decidedly ascertain for certain--although in what way it was difficult to say--if there really was any compromising document in Laurance's hands. To do so, she would, as Dan had thought a few minutes before, set a trap for him, and browbeat him into stating what he knew and what he held. Therefore, for Freddy's sake, it was necessary to go to London, and report in detail the conversation on the moor. Then the two could arrange what was best to be done. They were dealing with a coterie of daring scoundrels, who would stop at nothing to secure their own safety, and it behoved them to move warily. "We are walking on a volcano," was Halliday's concluding reflection. Of course, as it was useless to alarm the ladies, Dan said nothing of his meeting with Queen Beelzebub on the moor. However, on being questioned, he confessed the sudden thought which had sent him out of doors, and both Lillian and Mrs. Bolstreath agreed that it was entirely probable that Mrs. Jarsell did travel in up-to-date aeroplanes, like a mischief-making fairy. Then, in turn, they told him that Mildred had stayed for quite a long time and was altogether more charming each time she appeared. She suggested many trips and Mrs. Bolstreath was inclined to stay at Sheepeak longer than she intended, in spite of the near menace of Queen Beelzebub. Lillian was delighted with the lovely scenery, so gracious after the drab hues of London. "I don't see why we shouldn't get a house here after we are married," she said to her lover, "one of those delicious old manor houses of faded yellow stone. I could live quietly with Mrs. Bolstreath, while you ran up to business on your aeroplane."

"And all the time you would be fretting lest any harm came to him," said the chaperon, shaking her head, "besides, my dear, when you are married, you won't want me to be with you."

"Dear Bolly, I shall always want you, and so will Dan."

"Nonsense," said Mrs. Bolstreath, briskly, "two's company and three's none."

"Well," remarked Halliday, leisurely, "we can settle the matter when we are married, Lillian. Remember, before your uncle will consent, I shall have to discover who murdered your father."

"You have discovered who murdered him. It was the false Mrs. Brown, who is Mrs. Jarsell, who is Queen Beelzebub."

"So I believe, but I have to prove my case," said Dan, dryly, "and, moreover, I won't find it easy to place the woman in the dock when she has this accursed society at the back of her."

"You don't think there is danger?" asked Lillian, hastily. "No, no, no! Things are safer than ever, my dear. I go to town this evening, and can leave you here with the certainty that all is well."

"You go to town this evening?" said Mrs. Bolstreath, anxiously, "isn't that a very sudden resolution?"

"Oh, I think not," answered Dan, in an easy way. "I came down here only to settle you and Lillian. By the way, Sir John----"

"I wired our address, and he wrote me," interrupted Mrs. Bolstreath, "he is quite pleased that we are away. I rather think," the lady added, thoughtfully, "that Sir John is not ill-pleased we are away. At his age the constant presence of two women in his house is rather disconcerting. Finding we had left town he returned there to enjoy his own house to himself."

"In that case," said Dan, cheerfully, "he will be glad to see Lillian married."

"But to Lord Curberry, not to you."

"I would die rather than marry Lord Curberry," said Lillian, decisively, and with her chin in the air. "You won't be asked to do either one or the other, my dear," replied Dan, in his calmest tone. "We shall marry, right enough, whatever opposition Sir John may make. As to Lord Curberry," he hesitated. "Well?" asked Mrs. Bolstreath, impatiently. "I intend to see him when I return to town."

"I think it will be as well. Better have a complete understanding with him so that he will not worry Lillian any more."

"He won't," answered Dan, grimly, "and now I shall have to get away. I see Mrs. Pelgrin has had the trap brought round. Take care of Lillian." Lillian kissed her lover and followed him to the door of the sitting-room with a gay laugh. "Lillian can look after herself," she said lightly, "I am not afraid of Mrs. Jarsell or of anyone else. But you take care, Dan. I fear much more for you than for myself."

"I'm all right!" Dan, with an Englishman's dislike for an emotional scene, kissed the girl again and slipped out of the door. They saw him drive away in the gloom of the evening, and then settled to make themselves comfortable. Neither Lillian nor Mrs. Bolstreath would admit as much, but both felt rather downcast at Dan's sudden departure. Luckily, as he had been so cool and composed, they did not connect it with any fresh development likely to give trouble. In some vague way Mrs. Bolstreath guessed that Dan had spiked the guns of the enemy under which they were encamped, and, her certainty of safety, being infectious, Lillian also felt quite at her ease. Meanwhile, Dan reached the Beswick station in the ramshackle trap and was lucky enough to catch the in-going train to Thawley, just as it started to glide past the platform. The fortunate connection enabled him to board the seven-twenty express to London, where he hoped to arrive shortly before eleven that same evening. Knowing that Laurance's work kept him up late at night, he wired from Thawley, asking him to come to St. Pancras Station. Important as was Freddy's time, Dan knew that he would respond to the call at once, knowing that large issues would be the outcome of the present situation. Therefore, as the train dropped south, Halliday felt quite comfortable, as he had done all he could to arrange matters for the moment. Indeed, so assured did he feel that he had taken all possible precautions, that he did not even trouble to think over the matter, but fell asleep and refreshed his weary brain and body. Only when the train arrived at St. Pancras did he tumble out, sleepy still, to catch a sight of his faithful friend on the platform. "Nothing wrong?" asked Laurance, hurrying up. "Nothing wrong," responded Dan, with a yawn, "but I have much to talk to you about. Get a four-wheeler."

"A taxi you mean."

"I don't mean. I wish to travel as slowly as possible, so as to explain matters. Tell the man to drive to *The Moment* office. There I can drop you and go on to my rooms." Thus understanding the situation, Freddy selected a shaky old cab, drawn by a shaky old horse, and the rate at which it progressed through the brilliantly lighted streets was so slow that they were a very long time arriving at *The Moment* office in Fleet Street. In the damp-smelling interior of this antique conveyance, Halliday, now quite alert and clearheaded, gave his friend a full account of all that had happened, particularly emphasizing the interview with Mrs. Jarsell. "H'm," commenced Freddy, when he ended, "so she didn't give herself away?"

"No; and very wisely, too, I think. She didn't know how much I knew, and wasn't keen on giving me rope to hang her."

"But she knows you have read Penn's confession--what there is of it."

"I didn't tell her that I had anything else than the full confession, old son. She may think I have the whole document intact, or--and this I fancy is probable--she may believe that there isn't any confession in existence."

"Curberry may have written to her, telling her that he burnt the confession."

"No," said Dan, after a pause, "I really don't think he has done that. Mrs. Jarsell went dead white when I mentioned a confession."

"Then she believes that you spoke the truth," persisted Laurance, hopefully. "She may, or she may not, as I said before," retorted Halliday, "anyhow, as she can't be sure if I'm in jest or earnest, she will delay proceedings until she sees Curberry. If he swears that he burnt the confession, Mrs. Jarsell may act;

therefore I want you to send him an unsigned telegram, containing these three words, 'All is discovered!'"

"What will that do?"

"Put the fear of God into Curberry, into Queen Beelzebub, and into the Society of Flies as a whole. The warning will be so vague that they won't know who will strike the blow."

"They will suspect you, Dan."

"In that case," replied Halliday, promptly, "Queen Beelzebub will leave Lillian alone, and my object will be obtained. I want to gain time, and can only do so with safety to Lillian by keeping these beasts in a state of uncertainty as to how much or how little is known."

"I see," Laurance thought the plan a good one, "since you say that you have the confession and Curberry will say that he destroyed it, Queen Beelzebub will be undecided. This telegram, like a bolt from the blue, will clinch matters and make her and her gang pause before they take steps to hurt you or Miss Moon. I'll send the wire. What then?"

"Then--to-morrow that is--I go down to see Curberry, and have it out with him. His name is mentioned in the portion of the confession which you hold and we know enough to ensure his arrest."

"That is doubtful," protested Freddy, thoughtfully, "I have read the confession. Penn hints a lot about Curberry, but doesn't say enough to----"
"Never mind, he says enough for my purpose, which is to scare Curberry; belonging to the Society of Flies, as he does. I believe he got his uncle and cousin put out of the way to inherit the title and property. I'll harp on that string. If Queen Beelzebub calls----"

"There's the danger, Dan," interposed Freddy, quickly and anxiously. "I know. I am far from suggesting that there is not danger, as we are driving these people into a corner. If I don't turn up at your office by five o'clock to-morrow, Freddy, or if I don't send a wire saying that I am safe, you get Inspector Tenson, tell him all, show him the confession, and come down with him to Blackheath to see the Inspector who had charge of the Durwin murder. Then, armed with the authority of the law, you can go to Curberry's house. If I am missing, you will know how to act." Laurance drew a deep breath as the cab turned into Fleet Street. "It's a big risk for you, Dan."
"Pooh. As an aviator I am always taking risks. I must settle this business somehow, if I wish to marry Lillian and save her life as well as my own from these infernal beasts. Here you get down, Freddy. Don't forget to do as I tell you," and Laurance promised to faithfully adhere to his instructions, while the four-wheeler lumbered away in the direction of the Strand. Halliday

possessed one of those rare natures which invariably reveal their best in time of danger. He knew what to say and how to act when in a tight corner, and his training as an aviator had learned him to take risks from which less level-headed men would have shrunk. At the present moment he required all his energies to cope with unforeseen emergencies, since he did not quite know what action would be taken against him. Of course, he was confident that some sort of action would be taken, since he had aroused the wrath of a brilliantly clever and intensely evil set of people. Fearful for their own safety, the Society of Flies would do its best to get rid of him and to get rid of Lillian, as they had gotten rid of others who had stood in their crooked path. Both he and the girl were safeguarded so far by the confession, but it all depended upon what Curberry said to Queen Beelzebub as to how long such a safeguard would be efficacious. He had told the woman one story, but Curberry would tell her another, so it was doubtful which she would believe. The telegram from an unknown source might turn the balance in his favor, and lead both Mrs. Jarsell and her friend to believe that there was a chance of their devilish doings coming to light. Having arrived at this conclusion, Dan fell asleep, quite indifferent to the fact that the sword of Damocles hung over his head, and that the single hair might part at any moment. Herein he showed the steadiness of his nerves, and the value of a nature trained to face the worst smilingly. Next morning Halliday arose brisk and cheerful with the expectation of having a most exciting day, and as soon as he finished his breakfast made his way, by train, to Blackheath. On arriving there, somewhere about twelve o'clock, he did not go immediately to Curberry's house, but walked to the place where the Vincent aeroplane was housed. It had just struck him that Mrs. Jarsell might have wired to one of her friends to damage the machine, so that it could not be used. She had procured it for him and he--to put it plainly--had abused her friendship, so it was not likely she would permit him to retain, unharmed, a wonderful airship, with which he could make money and win fame. But, when he reached the shed and saw the man whom he had engaged to watch the machine, he found that his fears were groundless. No one had been near the place, and, so far as he could ascertain, the aeroplane was in perfect condition. Then it struck Dan, as it was yet too early to call on Lord Curberry, that he might indulge in a little fly. His enemy's house was only a stone's throw distant, on the borders of the open space, and Halliday did not intend to lose sight of the entrance gate, lest Mrs. Jarsell should steal in unobserved. In the air, and hovering directly over the grounds, he could see all who came and went. Also, incidentally, he might gain information as to what was going on in the gardens. Somewhat oddly, it occurred to him that if Queen Beelzebub came, she might push Curberry into the ornamental pond, as Marcus Penn had been pushed. There was no knowing what she might do in her despair. In brutal English, Queen Beelzebub was at bay, and could fight, like the rat she was, in the corner into which she was being slowly driven by circumstances, engineered by Mr. Daniel Halliday. Therefore, Dan saw to the fittings of the biplane, and ascertained by sight and touch that they had not been tampered with. He oiled the engine, saw that it did not lack petroleum, and, in fact, was as careful of all and everything connected with the structure as though he was preparing for a long race. Of course there was the usual crowd of loafers who came to see him start, and he swept upward from the ground in a graceful curve. The aeroplane acted easily and truthfully, according to its very excellent design, and the aviator, after making a wide circle, dropped down, to pass slowly over the grounds of Curberry's mansion. He could see no one about, even though the day was fine and sunny, so concluded that the owner, having received the anonymous telegram, was shivering within doors, terrified to venture out. In his impatience to learn the absolute truth, Dan turned his machine back to the shed, and came to rest almost at the very door. Owing to the examination of the aeroplane, and the experimental flight to test its working order, time had passed uncommonly swiftly, and it was now fifteen minutes past one o'clock. Dan made up his mind to beard Curberry in his library, without waiting for the arrival of Queen Beelzebub, who, after all, might not arrive. His man and some willing onlookers wheeled the machine into the great shed, and the doors were about to be closed when one of the crowd uttered an exclamation, which was echoed by many others. Halliday, always on the alert for the unexpected, came quickly to the door of the building, and saw everyone looking upward and northward, to where a small black dot spotted the blue of the sky. It increased in size rapidly, and there was no difficulty in seeing that it was a flying-machine. At once a thought entered Dan's mind that there was Mrs. Jarsell on a Vincent biplane, paying her expected visit, although he had no reason to suppose that she was the pilot. Wondering if he was right or wrong in his surmise, he waited with a fast-beating heart, and became certain of the truth of his guess very shortly. Travelling at a great height, the strange biplane poised itself directly over the open space, and then began to drop slowly into the enclosed grounds of Lord Curberry's mansion. Not having field-glasses, Halliday could not make out if the pilot was a man or a woman, but, when the machine, cleverly managed, disappeared below the trees and walls of the park, he was convinced that Queen Beelzebub had arrived. At once he determined to make a third at her interview with Curberry, whatever objections might be raised. But first he arranged what to do in order to guard against future events of a dangerous nature. "Wheel my machine out again," he ordered the man and those who had assisted, "see that everything is in order, and have everything prepared to start. Do not let anyone touch this," and he tapped the aeroplane, "you understand?"

"Yes, sir," said the man stolidly, "you're going for another fly?" "Exactly. The person who arrived is a friend of mine. I am going into yonder house to ask if a race can be arranged." Knowing that he could trust his man to guard the machine, and certain it would not be tampered with when hundreds of eyes were watching it, Halliday walked across the open space with serene confidence. It struck him that if Mrs. Jarsell wished to escape, she would certainly use her biplane, and it was just as well to follow in his own and run her to earth. As both machines were made by Vincent, the speed of each would be about equal, and, in any case, Dan hoped to keep Queen Beelzebub in sight, if it was necessary to give chase. Having thus prepared for possible emergencies, the young man entered the big gates of the park and hastened up the short avenue. Soon he found himself at the front door, and, as he rang the bell, glanced around for Mrs. Jarsell's flying-machine. It was not visible, so he presumed she had left it on the broad and spacious lawn on the further side of the house. It was in his mind to go and tamper with the engine to prevent her further flight, but, before he could make up his mind to this course, the door opened and the footman appeared. "I wish to see Lord Curberry," said Halliday, giving the man his card, "on most important business. Can he see me?"

"I'll inquire, sir. He is with a lady just now, and has been for the last ten minutes. Please wait here, sir," and he introduced Dan into the hall. Again, when left alone, Halliday had the impulse to go out and look to the gear of the machine, with the idea of putting things wrong, and again the footman appeared before he could decide if it would be wise to do so. "His lordship will see you, sir," said the man, who looked rather uncomfortable, "but he seems to be ill."

"Ill," echoed Dan, wondering what new deviltry was taking place, "and the lady?"

"She is not with his lordship now, sir," said the footman, in a bewildered manner, "yet I showed her into the library a few minutes ago."

"Do you know the lady?" asked Halliday, sharply. "No, sir. At least, I can't tell, sir. She came in one of them flying-machines, and wears a thick veil. She's a stout lady, sir, with a sharp manner."

"Take me to your master," commanded Dan, not caring to ask further questions, since it was best to ask them of Lord Curberry himself, and the man obeyed, still bewildered and nervous in his manner. The entrance of Queen Beelzebub into the house had evidently upset things. Ushered into the library, Dan waited for the closing of the door, and then advanced to where Curberry was seated at his desk, near the window. The man looked gaunt and haggard, and very sick. When the young man advanced, he rose as if moved by springs, and held out a telegram in a trembling hand. "You--you--sent this," quavered Curberry, and Halliday could see that the perspiration beaded his bald high forehead. In a flash Halliday guessed that this was the wire which Laurance had dispatched according to arrangement. "No, I did not send you any telegram," he denied, calmly, and with perfect truth. "You sent this, saying that all is discovered," stuttered Curberry again, and dropped back into his seat, "you have learned too much. She says that you know everything."

"Queen Beelzebub?"

"Ah, you know the name. I guessed as much. She is here; she is furious!"

"Who is Queen Beelzebub?" demanded Dan, anxiously. "You know. Why do you ask questions you know the answer to? I know why you have come; to have me arrested. I thought I destroyed the confession of that infernal Penn. But she says----"

"I retained sufficient to show me----"

"Yes, yes! You know all. You have won. I fought you for Lillian, and there is no chance of my gaining her for my wife. You won't either. You have to reckon with Queen Beelzebub. As for me--as for me----" he faltered, and trembled. Dan stepped right up to the desk. "What's the matter?"

"I--I--I have taken poison," gasped Curberry, and dropped his head on his hands with a sob.

CHAPTER XVIII

THE FLIGHT

"Poison!" echoed Dan, startled out of his composure, for he was far from expecting such a word, "the doctor----"

"No doctor can do me any good," sobbed Curberry, lifting his haggard face, and looking up with wild, despairing eyes, "there is no antidote to this drug I have taken. It is painless, more or less, and in an hour I shall be dead, as it works but slowly. Time enough for me to speak."

"Let me get a doctor," insisted Halliday, for so distraught did the man look that he was not surprised that the servant had been uncomfortable, "you must not die without----" Curberry struggled to his feet, and laid hands on his visitor. "No, no! I am ready to die," he said in a harsh, strained voice, "why should I be kept alive to be hanged--to be disgraced--to be----"

"Then you admit----"

"I admit everything in this--this," he touched a few loose sheets of paper lying on the desk, "this confession. Like Penn, I have made one."

"You must have a doctor," said Halliday, and ran to the bell. Curberry, with a wonderful strength, seeing how ill he looked, rose swiftly, and sprang after him. "If you call a doctor I shall shoot myself," he said, hoarsely, and pulled out a small revolver. "I would rather die by means of the poison I have taken, since it is more painless. But, sooner than be taken by the police, I shall shoot myself--and you, too--and you, too." Halliday waived aside this threat. "You won't see the police----"

"The doctor would try to save me," insisted Curberry, fiercely, "and I will not be saved only to be hanged. Stay here and listen to me. I have something to say. Touch the button of the bell and I shoot!" As he spoke he levelled the revolver. "Quick, quick, what will you do?"

"Have your own way," agreed Halliday, and moved to the desk, where he sat down on a convenient chair. Curberry, with a groan, returned to his seat, and laid the revolver on the blotting paper, ready for instant use should necessity arise. Even as yet he did not wholly trust Halliday. And there was cause for his suspicion. Since Dan was unarmed, he could do nothing against a man with a quick-firing weapon, but he made up his mind to snatch at the revolver the moment Curberry was off his guard. Yet, even as he decided upon this course, he said to himself that it was foolish. The man's recovery, supposing a doctor did arrive, meant the man's arrest, and, in Dan's opinion, as in Curberry's, death was better than disgrace. It was a most uncomfortable situation, but Halliday did not see anything to do but to listen to what his host had to say. The poor wretch had poisoned himself, and was keeping all help at bay with his revolver. He would be dead in an hour, or half an hour, as he hinted, so the best thing was to hear his story in the hope that by its means those who had brought him to this pass could be punished. But it was a weird experience to sit beside a tormented man, who declined to be saved from a tragic death. "Did Queen Beelzebub give you the poison?" asked Halliday, shivering at the gray pinched look on Curberry's face. "Long ago; long ago; not now," muttered the man, groaning. "Every member of the Society of Flies has this poison to escape arrest, should there be danger. It is a painless poison, more or less, and acts slowly, and--but I have told you all this before. There is not much time," he pressed his hands on his heart, "while I retain my strength and my senses, listen!"

"But where is this woman you call Queen Beelzebub," demanded Dan, looking round anxiously. "I saw her arrive in an aeroplane."

"She did; she came to tell me that you knew all about our society."

"You belong to it?"

"Yes, curse it, and those who dragged me into the matter. I was getting on all right in the law, when I was tempted and fell."

"Your uncle and your cousin----"

"Yes, yes!" broke in Curberry, with another groan, "she said that if I joined the society, they could be got rid of. They were got rid of because I wished for the title and the money."

"But for what reason?"

"So that I could marry Lillian. Moon refused to listen to me so long as I was merely a struggling barrister. But, when I became wealthy and--and--oh, this pain. The poison is a lie like all the rest of the business."

"She declared it was painless, and now--and now----" he broke off, to wipe the perspiration from his face. Dan half rose. "Let me call assistance. It may not be too late----" Curberry pointed his revolver at him as he moved. "It *is* too late," he said, setting his teeth, "if I do not die, I must face the worst. You--you have brought me to this."

"I!" echoed Halliday, sitting down again, "in what way?"

"You meddled and meddled, and--and you sent that telegram."

"I did not."

"Then your meddling has brought the police into the matter. That telegram may have been sent by a friend or an enemy; in either case it is true, for all is discovered. I was----" Curberry gasped with pain again, and moistened his dry lips. "I was sitting with it, wondering if it was best to end things or to wait and see if the warning was a true one. Then she came in through yonder door," he nodded towards the entrance from the terrace into the library. "She told me that you--that you--oh--oh!" he groaned, and rocked himself from side to side, yet kept a grip on the revolver, lest Dan should call or ring for assistance, or endeavor to secure the weapon. "So you took the poison?" said Halliday, wondering how he could manage to evade being shot and summon a doctor. "When she said that all was known, I did. Then she--she----" "Queen Beelzebub you mean?"

"Curse her, yes. Like Eve, she tempted me, and, like Adam, I fell."

"Where is she?"

"Up in Penn's old rooms, searching for any further confession he may have left. Oh," Curberry rocked and moaned, "I thought when I snatched it from you, and burnt it, that all evidence was destroyed."

"I saved a few sheets."

"Do they contain mention of my name?"

"Yes; they do, and----"

"I thought so. I thought so. It's just as well that I took poison. The title and money I paid such a price to obtain will go to my cousin, who is at Oxford--a young fool with no brains. Oh, to lose all when everything was so bright. I could have married Lillian and served my country, and----"

"You could not have married Lillian," interrupted Dan, positively, "for she loves me and me only. As to serving your country, how could you, with an easy conscience, when you have broken its law by taking the lives of your uncle and cousin?"

"I did not. The society saw to that," gasped Curberry with a twisted grin. "You engaged the society to end their lives, you--you--murderer."

"Don't call names," moaned the man, "at least I have not murdered you, although I have every reason to. You meddled with matters which do not concern you."

"I meddled in matters which concern every honest man who loves law and order, Lord Curberry," said Dan, sternly, "apart from the death of Sir Charles Moon, which I was bound to avenge for Lillian's sake, it was my duty to stop this wholesale murder. Perhaps you had Moon killed yourself."

"I didn't; I didn't. It was to my interest that he should live, for if he had I should have been married to his daughter by this time. Queen Beelzebub murdered him because he was offered a chance of belonging to the society and refused."

"In that," said Dan, sternly, "acting as an honest man."

"He acted as a foolish man. For, learning too much, he sent for Durwin to reveal what he knew. Penn found out his intended treachery, and told the Queen. She came--you saw her when she came--and she killed him."

"She killed Durwin?" "Yes," gasped Curberry, who was growing whiter and more haggard every moment. "And Marcus Penn?"

"I killed him. I had to, or be killed myself. He betrayed too much to you."

"Only out of fear," said Dan, looking at the murderer more with pity than with anger, for he was suffering greatly. "Not even fear should have made him reveal anything about the scent. He confessed his folly and was doomed to death. I went away on that day, and then came back secretly, having ordered Penn to meet me by the ornamental water, to speak about the society. He suspected something, because he wrote that confession and let Lillian know where it was concealed. But he came, and I managed to stupefy him with the Sumatra scent, after which I thrust him under water, and, when I was sure he was dead, I got away secretly, returning openly to hear that his body had been found."

"You wicked wretch," said Dan, scarcely able to restrain his disgust, although he felt he should not be too hard on one already being severely punished for his crimes. "Don't call names," said Curberry, with an attempt at a laugh, "after all, I am better than you think, since I am trying to save you. I want you to live and marry Lillian, and keep this confession," he laid his hands on the loose sheets of paper "from Queen Beelzebub, so that you can put an end to her wicked doings. Hide the papers when she comes back, or she will destroy them." As this was very probable, Dan stretched out his hand for the papers. Curberry feverishly gathered them together, speaking in a halting manner, as he did so. "Wait till I put them together," he said, painfully, "this is a full account of my connection with the society and its evil doings. It accounts for the death of Moon, of Durwin, of Penn, and of myself. But, take care, Halliday, for Queen Beelzebub will not give in without a fight."

"She can do nothing," said Dan, watching Curberry pinning the loose papers together. "Laurance has what remains of Penn's confession, and will inform the police shortly. If you would let me get a doctor."

"No, no, no! I refuse to live and face the reward of my wickedness. I prefer to pay the cost of my folly in joining the society. My name is disgraced, but I won't be on earth to suffer for the disgrace. That brainless young fool who succeeds me will not trouble you so long as he gets the money and the title, which he is certain to. But marry Lillian, and take care of her. Queen Beelzebub will strike at you through her."

"She dare not while I hold the confession of Penn," said Dan, grimly, "sooner or later she shall stand in the dock."

"That she never will, believe me. She has a means of escape if the worst comes to the worst. Oh," Curberry half rose, and then fell back in his chair, "the end is coming; my eyes are growing dim, and--and--ah," he uttered a shriek, "save yourself!" and, with a shaking hand, he grasped the revolver. As Curberry's eyes were looking past him, Dan, with the subconscious instinct of self-preservation, had just time to rise and swerve to one side, when a hand grazed his shoulder. The young man gripped his chair, and swung it up as a barrier between himself and a stout woman, who was immediately behind him. She was dressed in a long, black cloak, with a close-fitting cloth cap, and wore a heavy veil of the motor style, with pieces of mica let in as eyeholes. Not a word did she say, but, seeing Dan's action, drew back with a deep, indrawn breath like the hiss of a baffled snake. "Take care; take care; she has--the serpent poison," gasped Curberry, who was sitting loosely in his chair, gripping his revolver. Halliday remembered the wicked wound on Sir Charles Moon's neck, and his flesh grew cold, for the slightest touch of that morsel of shining steel in Queen Beelzebub's hand meant swift death. "You fiend!" he shouted, and, with a cry of anger, flung the heavy chair fairly at her. With the leap of a pantheress, she sprang to one side, and the chair crashed against the opposite wall, while the woman glided rapidly round to the open door of the terrace. A shot rang out as she reached it, and Dan knew that the dying man had fired on his enemy. Apparently the bullet did not reach its mark, for Queen Beelzebub still moved on, silent, sinister, and dangerous. Halliday flung himself forward to get between her and the door, so as to prevent her escape, but with a faint snarl like a beast at bay she stabbed at him with the death-tip's piece of steel. He leaped back to save himself from being scratched, while Curberry dragged himself painfully to the bell-button near the fire-place, and pressed it with his remaining strength. "I'm done for--call the police. You--you, oh!" He fell prone on the hearth-rug, and the revolver dropped beside him. Halliday ran forward on the impulse of the moment to offer aid, hastily picking up the weapon meanwhile, and as he did so, Queen Beelzebub sprang through the door into the open. "She's making for the aeroplane," cried Dan, and would have followed on the instant, but that Curberry gripped him fast. "Stay, stay! A priest; a clergyman. I'm dying," and a deadly fear became apparent in his glazed eyes, "get a--a--a help!" As he cried, retaining Dan's coat in a grip of iron, the door of the room opened, and the butler with the footman beside him rushed in. The shot, as well as the ringing of the bell, had brought them immediately to the spot. Trying to disengage himself, Dan gave hasty orders. "Send for a doctor; send for a clergyman; send for the police. That woman has murdered your master."

"Catch her; stop her--oh--oh!" Curberry's grip loosened, and he rolled over with a moan. Whether he was dead or alive, Dan did not wait to see. Every moment was precious, if he intended to stay the flight of Queen Beelzebub. The terrified men came to assist their dying master, and more servants, attracted by the noise, poured in at the library door. A backward glance showed Dan that Curberry was being attended to, and then he sped along the terrace towards the lawn at the side of the house. Here he arrived, just a moment too late, for already the aeroplane was spinning along the turf, with Queen Beelzebub in the pilot's seat. Like the wicked fairy of nursery tale, she was escaping in her dragon-car, and even in that hour of success she did not utter a sound. Silent and menacing she mounted into the air, and Halliday dashed forward with a cry of rage as she lifted above his reach. There was not a moment to be lost, and without another glance, he raced down the avenue, and made for the entrance gates. Queen Beelzebub might make for her lair in Hillshire, or it might be that she would cross the Channel to seek safety on the Continent; but, wherever she went, Dan intended to follow. She would not escape him this time, and he flew like an arrow from the bow across from the open space outside the park, to where his man still stood guard by his own machine. The little crowd around had their faces turned heavenward, and were shouting at the sight of the biplane, now dwindling to a black dot, as it receded swiftly from Blackheath. Dan felt a throb of satisfaction as he saw that Queen Beelzebub was making for the north. "Out of the way; out of the way," gasped the young man, charging through the throng, and it scattered at his approach, "let her go, let her go!" and he sprang into the pilot's seat to start the engine. Immediately the screw began to spin, slowly at first, but gathering in speed every second. The aeroplane moved, and ran with bird-like swiftness along the ground, then soared with the hum of a giant bee. Halliday swept in a vast circle, like an actor taking the stage, then turned the nose of his machine in the direction of the black dot. This was to be his pole-star towards which he was to continually direct his course, until the goal, wherever it might be, was attained. The many men, women and children standing round the Blackheath shed shouted and cheered, thinking that they were witnessing the start of an exciting race; but they little knew that it was a chase dealing with the serious issues of life and death. Halliday heard the thin sound of their voices reach him faintly, then settled down to handle his biplane in a masterly manner. Since both aeroplanes were made by Vincent, it was probable that both were equal in durability and speed. But Queen Beelzebub had gained a very fair start, and Dan knew that it would require all his knowledge of aviation to catch her up. Her escape or capture depended entirely upon the dexterity with which he manœuvered the delicate structure which bore him. On her part, the woman would use all her knowledge to get away safely, but Dan did not believe that her capability as an aeronaut was equal to his own. In this contest it was science against despair, and given the machines as equal, yet the pilots as unequal, it was hard to say what would be the result. Halliday, racing to save Lillian's life, and to gain her as his wife, believed that the final victory would remain with him. It was an unusually pleasant day, with a pale blue sky, lightly sprinkled with feathery white clouds. A gentle wind was blowing, which was not sufficiently strong to impede the speed of the aeroplanes. Yet it was chilly in these high altitudes, and in his haste Dan had not put on his overcoat. Before the end of the chase he grimly expected to be well-nigh frozen, but did not mind so uncomfortable a prospect so long as he gained his aim. Before him fled the woman he was determined to capture and place in the criminal dock to answer for her manifold sins. Thinking of what she had done, and how her path was strewn with victims, the young man set his teeth and tried his best to force the pace. But this was useless, as the biplane could not do more than it was intended to do. Although he had now been racing northward for over an hour, the distance between pursuer and pursued appeared to be much the same, and the receding black dot did not seem to be growing larger. Dan was irritated, yet felt that even though he was not gaining, he was not losing, and that was much, taking all things into account. There was always the chance that Queen Beelzebub's machine might break down, and then she would be as helpless as a bird with a broken wing. Also--and Dan did not blind himself to this possibility--his own aeroplane might come to grief, as it had done during the London to York race. But, benefiting by his former experience, he did not try any fancy-flying, and held to a straight undeviating course. Both machines were making a bee-line for the goal, which Halliday now guessed very plainly was The Grange in Sheepeak, Hillshire. It had been about two o'clock when the chase started, but already those taking part in it were miles upon miles distant from London, since the aeroplanes were flying at the rate of between fifty and sixty miles an hour. Harrow, St. Albans, Luton, Bedford and Northampton had long since dropped behind, and Queen Beelzebub, swerving to the left, was making for Rugby, so as to get into the straight line for Hillshire, and particularly for Thawley. Passing over the famous school-town the pace slackened somewhat, and Dan managed to secure the advantage of a few miles. But when her machine lifted Birmingham, she increased her speed, a fact which made Dan curse. He had been under the impression that she was running short of oil and petroleum, but apparently this was not the case. She had simply reduced her speed so as to nurse her resources, since she could take this bold step because of the start she had gained at the outset. Halliday grudgingly confessed to himself that the woman, knew her business, as she wasted no time. Her machine neither rose nor fell, nor deviated to right or left overmuch, and all she did was to hold to a straight line at a moderate height above the earth, humoring her engine, and straining as little as might be the wings, spars, bolts, and such-like gear of the biplane. Vincent had taught her admirably, and Dan no longer undervalued her as an antagonist. She was dexterous, bold, resourceful, and venturesome. His admiration, now freely given, was mixed with pity that so clever a human being should debase her gifts to harry mankind. Such qualities as she possessed made her more dangerous, as she was an intellectual animal, slaying with taught skill rather than with instinctive cunning. As the afternoon drew on, and the chase still continued, the night began to shut down. Gliding over Derby the town was veiled in the gray mists of swiftly-falling dusk, and when Nottingham came in sight it was distinguished by a thousand glittering pin-points of light, the usual nightly illumination. Matlock, and Mansfield, Holdbrook and Wayleigh, gleamed beneath like jewelled crowns, and when the stars began to appear the aeroplanes were flying between two firmaments, radiant with multi-colored orbs of light. At last Thawley rose into view burning like a furnace under its veil of smoke and the dim shroudings of twilight, while a vague murmur like the swarming of bees came muffled to the ears of those who drove the machines. Yet at these heights the coming dark was not yet very intense, and Queen Beelzebub's aeroplane, beginning to slacken speed, Dan was able to keep it well in view. He saw it rather vaguely closer at hand, a shadow against the shadow of the gray sky. Minute by minute he drew nearer and began to discern the outlines more or less clearly. But it must be admitted that at the best the clearness was not quite that which deserved the use of such a word. However, Dan, cold, hungry, and weary with the strain on his nerves, could think of none better at the moment. Queen Beelzebub was decidedly losing speed. Her machine seemed to falter after it left Thawley, as if it was doubtful how to find its way home in this world of shadows. But at Beswick the woman made a last effort, as it seemed, like a wounded animal dragging itself faster homeward as it neared its den, and her aeroplane towered aloft to the vast tableland of the moors. Halliday was close behind, and when they hovered over Sheepeak the two biplanes were only a stone throw from one another. He exulted, for now he had driven the woman to her citadel, and for her there was no escape even by her machine, as that was--so to speak--worn out. She was at her last gasp, and would have to fight or yield. She elected to fight when the airships swung in the foggy air over the fields near The Grange. If she alighted, Queen Beelzebub knew that her pursuer would alight also and capture her, so she described a rapid circle with what motive power was left her, and plunged downward on her enemy to ram his machine. Dan saw the movement, and with his hand on the steering gear, swerved to one side, dropping lower as he did so. The other machine swooped harmlessly overhead, but, recovering quickly, once more came down with the dip of a hawk on a heron. Halliday dodged again, then thinking that two could play at the dangerous game, he watched his chance and rushed straightly at his prey. Queen Beelzebub saw him coming, and adopted his tactics--that is, she dropped below his onset, and Dan's aeroplane swept on without result. Once more he came down to her level, and by this time the machines were only twenty feet from the ground. This time, as he dashed forward, the woman was not dexterous enough to get out of the way, and the two clashed violently with a ripping, breaking, smashing sound. With the engines still spinning, but with broken wings, the biplanes dropped to the earth, tangled together, Dan's uppermost, clutching at its prey, so to speak, like a hawk clutching a partridge. Down they came, and the rising earth met them with a smashing blow. Halliday was shaken, but did not become unconscious. Clearing his feet and arms from the tangle of ropes and canvas, he emerged from the confused heap, and dragged out the woman by her dress, which fluttered out from the wreckage. To tear off her veil and light a match took a single minute. "Miss Armour!" cried Dan, greatly amazed. And Miss Armour it was, quite senseless.

CHAPTER XIX

TREACHERY

In the chill gray gloom of the fields, damp, depressing and misty, with the wreckage of the airship piled up around him, and the insensible woman lying at his feet, Dan stood bewildered, his nerves jangling like ill-tuned bells. The twenty feet fall had not harmed him in limb or body; but the violent contact with the earth, broken in some measure by the fact that his enemy's aeroplane had been underneath, resulted in a displacement of his normal powers. He felt battered and bruised, deadly sick and wished to lie on the wet grass, indifferent to everything and everyone. But with a dangerous creature at his elbow, this was not to be thought of, even though that same creature was unable to exercise her wicked will. Moreover, The Grange was only a stone's throw distant, and doubtless Mrs. Jarsell had been watching for the coming of her friend. If this were the case, she would come out with help--for Queen Beelzebub, that is. How Halliday would be treated he was much too muddled in his brain to consider. Finally, he dropped on his knees, longing for brandy to pull him together, and began to think with difficulty. This woman was not Mrs. Jarsell, but Miss Armour. Seeing that he knew her to be old, feeble, and paralyzed, this was most remarkable. Curberry had called her Queen Beelzebub, so Miss Armour, and not Mrs. Jarsell, was the head of the Society of Flies, and the cause of all the trouble. In a weak way, Dan considered that she evidently was not so old as she had made herself out to be, and certainly she was not paralyzed. No woman without the use of her limbs could have escaped so swiftly, or have worked the aeroplane so dexterously. Miss Armour, the delicate, kind-hearted old lady, was the infernal Queen Beelzebub who had spoken behind the mask when in the darkness the scarlet light had made an accursed halo round her head. And now she was dead--stone dead. A moment's reflection assured him that he could not be certain on this point without examination, so he tore open her dress, and laid his hand on her heart. It beat feebly, so he knew that she was still alive, although she was crumpled up in a heap amidst the wreckage. This knowledge restored Halliday more positively to his senses. She was so dangerous that, even helpless as she appeared to be, he could not tell what devilry she might not make use of to get the upper hand. She still had the piece of steel tipped with the deadly snake poison, and even a feeble woman could inflict death with that. The idea made Dan search in her pockets to secure the subtle weapon of defence, but even while he fumbled and hunted, he was pulled violently backward. "Mr. Halliday!" gasped Mrs. Jarsell, holding a lantern to his white face, "hold him," she added to a couple of men who were beside her. "I've--I've caught Queen Beelzebub red-handed," muttered Dan, striving to get on his feet, and thinking in a muddled way that Mrs. Jarsell had seen the arrival of the aeroplanes, the battle in the air, and the catastrophe. She must have come stealthily across the intervening fields with her myrmidons, and thus he had been caught unawares. He knew well that, once in her grip, since she was an accomplice of Queen Beelzebub's, he could expect no mercy, and, what was worse, Lillian would be in danger. He, therefore, in a weak way, fought his best to escape. If he could only reach Mrs. Pelgrin's hotel he would be safe. But the men were too strong for him, and he was beaten to his knees. Then, what with, the hunger that gnawed him, the bitter cold, the fall, and the general surprise of the situation, his senses left him. He uttered a weary sigh, and slipped to the ground, limp and unconscious. Then, again, as had happened when Penn had drugged him in the taxi-cab, he felt himself swallowed up in gloom; felt himself falling interminably, and lost sight of the physical world and its surroundings. To all intents and purposes he was dead, and from the moment he closed his eyes in that misty meadow he remembered nothing more. When his eyes opened again, they shut at once, for the blaze of light was painful. Dimly he fancied that he heard a telephonic voice give an order, and he felt that some ardent spirit was being poured down his throat. The fiery liquor put new life into him; his heart began to beat more strongly and he felt that his weak limbs were regaining a fictitious strength. With a thankful sigh he opened his eyes again, and a bewildered look round made him understand that he was in the barbaric sitting-room of The Grange. He saw the violent contrasts of red and yellow and black, he realized the glare and glitter and oppressive splendor of the many lamps and his nostrils were filled with the well-known Sumatra scent. Reason came back to him with a rush, and he knew in what a dangerous position he was placed. Here he was in the power of Queen Beelzebub and her factotum, Mrs. Jarsell- -at their mercy completely, as it were, although he was assured that he would receive none at all. He had hunted down the gang; he was breaking up the gang; and now in his hour of triumph he was at the mercy of the gang. Queen Beelzebub was top, tail, and bottom of the society, and he was in her grip. She would not relax it, he knew very well, until the life was squeezed out of him. The realization of his danger and the memory of what his helplessness meant to Lillian, nerved him to recover full control of his consciousness. While there was life there was hope, and as his captors had not murdered him while he was insensible, Dan concluded that they would not do so when he had recovered his wits. Queen Beelzebub would play with him, he fancied, as a cat plays with a mouse, and in that case he might find some means of escape. So far he had beaten her all along the line, and he might beat her still, although she certainly held the winning cards at the moment. As these things flashed across his brain, he yawned and stretched himself, looking round in a leisurely way as he did so. Still feeling a trifle stiff and sore, his thinking powers were nevertheless in good working order, as they at once responded to the command of his indomitable will. Therefore, with wonderful self-control, he smiled amiably, and stared into every corner, in order to spy out the weakness of the land. But he was being watched, as he soon knew, and his thought was read. "No," snarled a silvery voice, higher in tone than that of Mrs. Jarsell, "I have you and I mean to keep you." Queen Beelzebub, alive and well, and as completely in possession of her senses as he was, sat in her big carved chair near the open fireplace just as she had sat when he paid that long distant visit with Freddy Laurance and Mildred. Her face was as wrinkled as ever, but instead of being of the ivory hue which had impressed him on a former occasion, it was deadly white, and looked particularly venomous. Her white hair had been smoothly brushed and she wore a loose cloak of scarlet velvet, which fell to her feet. But in the fall she had suffered, since Dan noticed that her right arm was bound up in bandages and splints, resting in a black silk scarf against her breast. His eyes fastened on this and Miss Armour laughed in a thin, spiteful manner, which hinted at the wrath that consumed her. "Yes," she said, in answer to his mute query, "I have broken my arm, thanks to you, Mr. Halliday. You smashed my aeroplane and sent me to the ground."

"That is what you tried to do with me," said Dan, drily, and settling himself comfortably in his chair, since he felt convinced that he was in no immediate danger. "Tit for tat, Queen Beelzebub, or shall I call you Miss Armour?"

"The real name or the feigned name, doesn't matter," rejoined the lady very coolly, "you can call me what you like for the time you have to live." "Oh!" said Halliday, equally coolly, and aware that the cat-and-mouse torment was beginning, "so that's it, is it?" Mrs. Jarsell stood beside her friend's chair, and was handing her food in an anxious manner. The large and ponderous woman looked like a child overcome with terror. Her eyes were sunken, her cheeks were hollow, and the immense vitality she possessed appeared to be at a very low ebb. She was arrayed in white, as usual, but her garb was not so colorless as her face. She even looked smaller than formerly, and was shrunken in her clothes. There was something pitiful in the spectacle of this large phlegmatic female broken down, worn out, and overcome with dread of the future. As she attended to Miss Armour the tears rolled down her face, which had so suddenly grown old. The sight seemed to irritate the other woman, who was much more frail, but who had a much more powerful will. Dan saw in a flash that he had been mistaken in thinking that Mrs. Jarsell was strong. Her strength lay in her imposing looks, but she was the mere tool of that fragile, delicate old lady, whose glittering eyes revealed the iron will which dominated her weak age-worn body. Here, indeed, was the true Queen Beelzebub, driven into a corner and prepared to fight to the last. Halliday felt, with a creeping of the flesh, that he had come to grips with an evil power, which it would be desperately hard to conquer. Miss Armour saw the shadow in his eyes. "You're afraid," she taunted him. Dan agreed. "Not physically, you understand," he said quietly, "but you seem to be so thoroughly wicked that the spiritual part of myself quails for the moment. But it doesn't matter much, you know, seeing that you have much more cause to fear that I may shoot you at sight," and he fumbled in his pocket for Curberry's revolver which he had picked up when leaving the room. "I removed that when you were insensible," gasped Mrs. Jarsell, wiping her eyes and turning a heavy white face in his direction. "Of course," said Miss Armour, in a hard voice. "I ordered the search to be made in case you had any weapons. Now you are quite defenceless, and at my mercy, you meddling ape."

"How long have I been insensible," asked Dan, ignoring the feminine spite which led her to call him names. "For quite an hour," sighed Mrs. Jarsell, whose great body was shaking as if with the ague. "I had you brought here along with Miss Armour. You were both in a kind of faint. Now you are all right, and----"

"And I am all right," finished Miss Armour, imperiously, "which is much more to the purpose. Better had you died when you fell from the aeroplane, Mr. Halliday, than have recovered so completely as you seem to have done."

"You mean mischief?"

"Oh, yes, I mean mischief," replied Queen Beelzebub amiably, "and I mean torture, such as will make you wince. I'll prove what sort of a man you are."

"You had better make haste, then," said Dan, with a shrug, and bracing up his courage to beat this fiend with her own weapons, "by this time the police know all about Curberry." "What's that to me. The police can't connect me with his death?"

"Not so far as you know, but as my friend, Laurance, promised to take action at five o'clock, if he did not hear from me, I expect with the Blackheath and Hampstead inspectors he is now in Lord Curberry's house. An explanation from him will soon bring the authorities to this den." Mrs. Jarsell burst into hysterical tears. "I knew there was great danger," she wailed. "I knew the end had come!" and she sank at Miss Armour's feet in a fit of despair, the picture of a beaten woman. "Oh, shut up, Eliza," said Queen Beelzebub savagely, and her eyes glittered more venomously than ever, "you always play the fool when wits are needed to keep things straight."

"You can't keep them straight," said Dan calmly, lounging in his chair, "your career is at an end, Miss Armour."

"We'll see about that, Mr. Halliday. Oh, you needn't look at me in that way, my friend. I still have the snake-poisoned lancet, you know, and if you try to spring on me, even though my arm is broken, you will meet with a sudden and unpleasant death."

"I don't want to touch you," retorted Halliday. "I shall leave the hangman to finish you off." "That he never shall do," snapped Miss Armour, her eyes flashing and her nostrils dilating, "not one member of that glorious society I have founded shall ever be done to death by those accursed people in authority. I, and my subjects who obey me so loyally, will vanish."

"Will you? Not while the ports and railway stations are watched," sneered Halliday, with contempt, "and I don't think your friend Vincent can supply aeroplanes in sufficient quantity for you all to get away. Even if you did by some extraordinary chance, the world would be hunted for you."

"It can be hunted from the North Pole to the South, Mr. Halliday, but neither the members of the Society of Flies nor its queen will be discovered. We will be as if we had never been," she concluded triumphantly, and as she spoke the big woman, sobbing at her feet, shivered and shook, and uttered a muffled cry of terror. Queen Beelzebub kicked her. "Get up, Eliza, you fool," she said contemptuously, "you know quite well that I have made ready for everything this long time."

"But I don't want to----"

"If you say another word," interrupted Miss Armour, viciously, "you shall afford sport for this society as this meddling beast shall do." Dan laughed gaily, determined not to show the white feather, although his heart was filled with fear. He did not mind a clean, short, sharp death, but he did not wish to be tortured and mutilated, as he believed this incarnate demon intended he should be. Curiously enough, his laugh, instead of exciting Queen Beelzebub to further wrath, seemed to extort her unwilling admiration. "You are a brave man, Mr. Halliday," she muttered reluctantly; then burst out furiously, "oh, you young fool, why did you not accept the offer I made you?"

"The offer you prophesied in this very room would be made," said Halliday complacently, "well, you see, Miss Armour, or Queen Beelzebub, or whatever you like to call yourself, I happen to have a conscience."

"That is your weakness," said the woman calmly; "throw it on the rubbish heap, my friend. It is useless."

"Now it is, so far as joining your infernal organization is concerned, I am quite sure. To-morrow the police will be here, and the Society of Flies will cease to exist."

"That is possible, and yet may not be probable, Mr. Halliday. If the Society does cease to exist, it will not do so in the way you contemplate. Eliza!" added Miss Armour impatiently, "if you will sniff and howl, go and do so in some other room. I can't stand you just now. My nerves are shaken, and my arm is hurting me. Go away."

"And leave you with----" Mrs. Jarsell cast a terrified look at Dan. "Pooh!" cried Queen Beelzebub contemptuously, "you don't think that I am afraid of him. I have the lancet with the snake-poison, and if he tries to get out of the door or the window you know very well that every exit is watched. Go away and employ your time better than sobbing and moaning. You know what you have to do, you poor silly fool?"

"Yes," sighed Mrs. Jarsell, and stumbled towards the door like a rebuked infant. "I'll send the telegrams before eight. But the village post-office will learn too much if I send them."

"Never mind. The whole world will learn too much before to-morrow night, my dear Eliza. However, neither you nor I, nor anyone else concerned, will be here to get into trouble." Mrs. Jarsell threw her hands above her head. "The end has come; the end has come," she wailed tearfully, "we are lost, lost, lost!"

"I know that as well as you do," said Miss Armour cheerfully, "thanks to this idiot here. However, he shall pay for his meddling."

"But if the police----"

"If you don't get out," interrupted Queen Beelzebub in a cold fury, "I shall prick you with the lancet--you know what that means."

"It would be better than the other thing," moaned Mrs. Jarsell, clinging to the door, which she had opened. "What other thing?" inquired Halliday, on the alert for information. Queen Beelzebub replied. "You shall know before you die! Eliza, will you go and send those telegrams, you silly fool? If you don't obey me----" the woman's face took on such a wicked expression that Mrs. Jarsell, with a piteous cry, fled hastily, closing the door after her. Then Miss Armour drank a little of the wine that was on the table beside her and looked smilingly at her prisoner. "I never could make anything of Eliza," she explained, "always a whimpering cry-baby. I wouldn't have had her in the society but that I wished to use this house, which belongs to her, and of course when we started her money was useful." Halliday, being alone, glanced around to see if he could escape. He could not attack Miss Armour, old and feeble as she was, because of the poisoned piece of steel which she had concealed about her. He had seen the effects on Sir Charles Moon, and did not wish to risk so sudden a death. For the sake of Lillian it was necessary that he should live, since, if he did not, there was no one left to protect her; therefore, he did not think of meddling with Queen Beelzebub, but cast an anxious look at windows and door. Escape that way was equally impossible, as all were guarded. There seemed to be nothing for it but to wait and take what chance offered itself later. He could see none at the moment. The position was unpleasant, especially when he remembered that he was to be tortured, but his manhood prevented his showing the least sign of fear. To intimate that he cared nothing for her threats, he took out his pipe and tobacco pouch. "Do you mind my smoking, Miss Armour?"

"Not at all, unless you would rather eat. There's food on the table behind you. Oh," she laughed, when she saw the expression on his face, as he glanced around, "don't be alarmed, I don't intend to poison you. That death will be too easy. You can eat and drink and smoke with perfect safety. I intend to end your life in a less merciful manner."

"Well," said Dan, going to the table and taking a sandwich, together with a glass of port wine. "I think you are spiteful enough to give me a bad time before dying, so I am quite sure that I can eat and drink with safety!"

"Oh, what a pity; what a pity," said Miss Armour thoughtfully, when the young man returned to his seat and began to make a hurried meal. "What's a pity?" asked Dan carelessly. "That you and I should be enemies. I gave you the chance to be friendly with me, you know, but you wouldn't take it. Yet I admire you, and have always admired you. You have courage, brains, coolness, and persistence. These are valuable qualities such as I needed for a member of my society. If I had not seen that you possessed them and wished to make use of them by binding you to my society, I should have ended your life long ago."

"As Sir Charles Moon's life was ended; as Durwin's life was cut short; as Penn was disposed of, and as Lord Curberry was dispatched."

"Well, no. Curberry poisoned himself because he feared that everything was about to come out."

"As it will."

"Probably," said Queen Beelzebub indifferently, "but there are yet some hours before the end. No, my friend, you will not die like those you have mentioned. Your cleverness demands a more ingenious death."

"You are a very clever woman," said Dan, finishing his glass of port. "I am. You will admire my cleverness when you----" she checked herself and laughed. "I knew a Chinese mandarin once and he told me many things, Mr. Halliday. You can guess what he told me."

"Something about torture?" said Dan, lighting his pipe, "quite so. You go to the Chinese to learn how to hurt a man. I thought you were more original." Miss Armour sneered. "Isn't this indifference rather overdone, Mr. Halliday?"

"Well, it is a trifle. I'm in a blue funk, and can you blame me," he shuddered, "a man doesn't like to die by inches, you know. However, as we understand one another, suppose we wile away the time by your telling me how you came to start this damned gang of yours."

"My dear young friend, I admire your courage so much that I can refuse you nothing," mocked Miss Armour, wincing as she moved her broken arm. "I really should be in bed with my hurt."

"You'll get feverish if you don't lay up," Dan advised her. "Oh, I don't think so. I know about other drugs than the Sumatra scent, Mr. Halliday. Of course, a broken arm," she added with a sigh, "can't be mended by all the drugs in the world. Time alone can put it right, and, thanks to you, I shan't have time to get cured. If you had only fought with me instead of against me, this would not have happened. Well, my society----"

"Yes. What about your society?" questioned Dan, politely and easily. Queen Beelzebub cast an admiring look in his direction and began to speak in a quiet lady-like manner, as though she were presiding at a tea-table, and the subject of conversation was quite an ordinary one. "I was left an orphan at an early age," she said leisurely, "poor and honest and friendless. For years I led what you fools call a decent life, earning my bread by going out as a governess. But poverty and honesty did not please me, especially since the first was the outcome of the last. I never wished to marry, as I did not care for men. I did not wish for society, or fame, or flirtation, or, indeed, anything a woman usually longs for. I desired power!" and as she uttered the last word an infernal expression of pride came over her white and delicate face. "Power for a bad purpose?"

"Well, you see, Mr. Halliday, I could not get power for a good one. The sole way in which I could obtain my ends was to appeal to people's self-love. I read of those Italian societies, and the way in which they terrorized the world. Whatever the members of those societies want they get, because they work by blackmail, by threats, by the knife, and with poison. I always wished to found a society of that sort, but I noticed how frequently things went wrong because the members of various societies got mixed up with women, or drank too much, or gave themselves away in a moment of profligacy."

"Ah," Dan smoked calmly, "now I understand why your rules were so stringent."

"You speak of them in a past tense," said Miss Armour curiously. "Well," Dan pressed down the tobacco in his pipe, "the society is done for; it's gastados, used up, busted, and all the rest of it. Well?"

"Well," echoed the woman, passing over his remark with a sneer. "I wished to collect a body of men and women who were to live like saints and use all the power such self-denial gave them to gain all they wanted for themselves."

"A devilishly clever scheme." "But not original, like my tortures," Queen Beelzebub assured him. "In Australia--Sydney, New South Wales--I fancy there are societies who have the same rules. They call such an organization there a 'Push!' I think." Dan nodded. "I have heard of such things."

"Well, then--to make a long story short, as I want to go to bed, and can't enjoy your delightful society much longer--I intended to work on those lines. Years and years ago Mrs. Jarsell was a favorite pupil of mine. We parted and she married a man with money. He died," Miss Armour laughed, "in fact, since he treated Eliza badly, I got rid of him."

"Oh, so that is the hold you have on her."

"Quite so. I met her again and got rid of the husband. He left her his money and I came to live with Eliza as a companion. For a time we went into London society, and I soon managed to get a few people together by appealing to their egotism. Some kicked at my ideas--others did not, and in the end I collected quite a large number. Then I made Eliza take this house, as it struck me that aeroplanes might be utilized for criminal purposes. I don't say that when this idea struck me aeroplanes were so good as they are now, but I believed that aviation would improve, and that the air would be conquered. Chance brought Vincent into my life. He became a member of the Society of Flies, and manufactured the machines. He also taught me how to handle them----"

"I am bound to say that he had an excellent pupil," put in Dan politely. "Thank you," Miss Armour smiled and nodded. "I fancy I am pretty good. But you see that by using an aeroplane I was able to get up and down to London without people knowing. I was, so to speak, in two places at once, by travelling fast, and so could prove an alibi easily."

"Then Durwin?"

"No. Eliza murdered him. She went up in an aeroplane along with Vincent, since she is too silly to handle one herself. To kill Moon--that was my work because he learned too much and refused to join me--I went to town by train in the character of the false Mrs. Brown. Penn was killed by Curberry, who had to obey me or suffer himself. Oh, I assure you I am quite autocratic, Mr. Halliday," finished the woman merrily. "I quite believe that," said Halliday drily, "but did all this villainy give you pleasure?"

"Oh, yes," Miss Armour's nostrils again dilated, and her eyes again flashed triumphantly, "think of the power I held until you interfered. I pretended for greater safety to be paralyzed, and no one ever connected a poor invalid lady with Queen Beelzebub."

"I did not, I assure you. I believed Queen Beelzebub to be Mrs. Jarsell."

"Eliza," Miss Armour scoffed, "why, she's a poor weak fool, and only did what I ordered her to do because I implicated her along with myself in the murder of her husband. However, she has been useful, as, without her money, I could not have started the business. Power!" she repeated, "yes, I have a great power. High or low, rich or poor, there was no one I could not remove if I chose. My subjects worked for me willingly, or unwillingly."

"You are a kind of 'Old Woman of the Mountain,' like the gentleman of that name who invented the Assassins--that gang about the time of the Crusades."

"Quite so, although it is not polite of you to call me an old woman. By the way, I got Curberry his title by getting rid of his uncle and cousin."

"Yes. So he told me," said Dan, marvelling that the woman could speak so calmly about her wickedness. "Oh, you are shocked," she laughed gaily, "what a fool you are. I could tell you much concerning many murders and disappearances which the police knew nothing about. For some years I have ruled like a despot, and--and--well," she yawned, "it's all over. Oh, what a pity."

"I think not. People will sleep quieter when they know Queen Beelzebub and her demons are harmless."

"Harmless," she echoed the word with a laugh, and touched a silver bell that stood at her elbow, "we shall all be harmless enough to-morrow, if indeed you speak truly, and your friend Laurance is coming up here with the police."

"He is, I assure you," said Dan, wondering why she rang the bell, "but who are the members of your gang?"

"You'll see them to-morrow, when you afford sport for them," said Queen Beelzebub in a weary way, and looking fagged out, "meanwhile, I must have you safely locked up," and as she spoke, two big men entered the room. "Hang you, I shan't," began Dan, and sprang to his feet. But the two men had their hands on him, and shortly he was trussed up like a Christmas turkey. "You are less clever than I thought," said Queen Beelzebub, sneering, "or you would not fight against impossibilities. Good night! Take him away." And as they were commanded, the two big men took him away in silence.

CHAPTER XX

QUEEN BEELZEBUB'S END

Unable to resist superior force, Dan ceased to struggle, thinking it was best to play a waiting game, until chance afforded him the opportunity of escape. Hitherto his good fortune had saved him from grave perils, and he trusted that finally it would prove strong enough to extricate him from this last difficulty. He was taken down a short flight of damp steps and thrust into what he took to be a disused coal-cellar. Here the two big men released him from his bonds and retired, locking the door behind them. Once or twice he asked questions, but, receiving no reply, he asked no more. They left a lantern for his use, and the light, although only that of a candle, was very acceptable in the cimmerian darkness of this underground dungeon. When left alone, the prisoner stretched himself, swung his arms and stamped with his feet to get warm, after which he made an examination of his surroundings. Halliday found that the cellar was small, with stone floor, stone roof, and stone walls, all more or less humid. Light and air came through a shaft on the right of the entrance, which was too narrow to permit of escape. Evidently the place had been used before as a prison, and no doubt for refractory members of the society, since there was some spare furniture. In one corner was a low bed, in another a deal table, in a third a washstand, and finally there was one kitchen chair, on which Dan took his seat to think over matters. He had eaten, so did not feel hungry, and solaced himself with his pipe, a luxury for which he felt very grateful. It could not be said that his thoughts were pleasant; they could scarcely be so, under the circumstances, as there was no denying he was in a most uncomfortable plight. So Miss Armour, the delicate maiden lady, was Queen Beelzebub, and the imposing Mrs. Jarsell was only her tool. Dan was surprised when he reflected on this, and could not help admiring the infernal cunning of the woman who had arranged matters. Miss Armour was without doubt a born criminal, who much preferred doing evil to doing good. As Mrs. Jarsell's companion, she could have led a blameless existence, surrounded by attention and comfort and luxury, but her craving for power had led her into dark paths. For all her care, she might have guessed that in a law-abiding country the truth of her murderous association would come to the notice of the authorities sooner or later. And, when the knowledge had become public, with all her cunning, she was unable to cope with the situation. Like the fox in the fable, her many wiles had proved useless, and here she was driven into a corner. What she intended to do Dan could not think. He did not see in what way she could escape punishment. Of course, the young man was perfectly satisfied that Freddy was moving in the matter down South. According to instructions, he must have gone to

Lord Curberry's house at Blackheath when he failed to receive news of his friend, and what he discovered there would assure him that it was time to take public action and inform the police of what was going on. The servants would be questioned and Curberry's body would be examined, while the visit of the veiled woman and her flight in the aeroplane would be explained. Laurance would guess at once that the unknown lady was Queen Beelzebub attending to her iniquitous business, and an inquiry at the shed would soon inform him of the pursuit. Halliday believed that on the morrow Laurance, together with the police, would arrive at Sheepeak, and then the end would come. Meanwhile he was in great danger unless Freddy appeared in time to rescue him, for Miss Armour was very spiteful and her last act of power would undoubtedly be to murder him for the action he had taken in bringing about her downfall. But this had to be faced, and, if death was certain, he hoped that it would be immediate, since even his brave nature quailed at the idea of suffering ingenious Chinese tortures. As to Lillian, Dan was quite sure she would not be harmed, because Queen Beelzebub had her hands full and would not have time to kill her. Indeed, if she decided to do so, it would not be easy for her to find anyone to execute her commands, for every member of the Society of Flies must by this time have been aware of the danger which threatened their organization. Halliday believed that the telegrams alluded to by Miss Armour and which were to be sent by Mrs. Jarsell were intended to summon the members to a conference. Yet, what use such a meeting would be, the young man could not think. The net of the law would capture the entire gang without doubt. And yet Queen Beelzebub was so infernally cunning that Dan could not be sure she would not find some means of saving herself and her subjects, even at the eleventh hour. In thoughts such as these the night passed slowly and the hours seemed interminable. The candle in the lantern burned itself out, and he found himself in complete darkness, while the silence was only broken by the drip of water from the walls, or by his own breathing and restless movements. Dan felt as though he were in a tomb, and his lively imagination conjured up all kinds of horrors until, worn out physically and mentally, he fell into a profound slumber. When he opened his eyes again, it was dawn, for he saw the cold light streaming down through the air shaft. A glance at his watch assured him that it was seven o'clock, and he wondered if food would be brought to him shortly. As he had only eaten a sandwich and drank a glass of port-wine since a yesterday morning breakfast, he felt most uncommonly hungry, and, in spite of the peril in which he stood, he longed ardently for food. In the meantime, for comfort, he lighted his pipe again, sat on his bed, and watched the thin beam of sunlight move slowly across the stone floor of his cell. This was an unexpected adventure, sure enough, and, unpleasant as it was now, it promised to be still more unpleasant before it was concluded. All that Halliday could hope for was that Laurance, with the police, would arrive in time to save his life, and deliver him from imprisonment. At ten o'clock--Dan looked again at his watch when the door opened--Mrs. Jarsell entered with a tray, on which were two boiled eggs, bread and butter, and coffee. Placing this on the table, she was about to leave, as she had entered, in silence, when Dan caught her dress. At once, with a shiver, she drew back and displayed the lancet tipped with the serpent-poison. "If you try to escape, I shall kill you," she said in her heavy voice. Dan looked at her curiously, and saw that she was less imposing than ever for all her massive looks. All her self-restraint was gone, her eyes were red; her face was disfigured with tears; and her big body looked flabby and inert. A greater collapse or a more pitiful spectacle can scarcely be imagined, and Dan felt quite sorry for her, even though he knew she was banded against him with others to bring him to a cruel death. "I shall not try to escape," he said, slowly; "that is, I shan't try just now." Pausing at the door, Mrs. Jarsell, still on guard with the lancet, looked at him sorrowfully. "You can never escape," she said brokenly, "try as you may, for the house is guarded by four men, who are sworn to obey Miss Armour."

"Queen Beelzebub, you mean," said Halliday with a shrug. "I wish I had never heard the name," cried Mrs. Jarsell with a sob. "I quite believe that. I am very sorry for you."

"You have every need to be. Thanks to you, we are all caught in a trap, and there is no means of escape."

"Really. I thought that Miss Armour----" Mrs. Jarsell shuddered. "She has an idea, but I hope it will not be necessary for her to carry out her idea. After all, things may not be so bad as they seem, Mr. Halliday."

"If you mean the police, I am afraid they are," he retorted with another shrug and with great emphasis; "by this time my friend Laurance has informed the Scotland Yard authorities of what we know."

"What do you know?" demanded Mrs. Jarsell, with a gasp, and she was forced to lean against the door for support. "Everything," said Dan, briefly; "so with your permission I shall have my breakfast, Mrs. Jarsell," and he began to eat with a good appetite. "Oh, how can you; how can you?" cried the big woman, convulsively; "think of the danger you stand in."

"I shall escape!"

"Escape, and from Queen Beelzebub? Nobody has ever escaped her." "I shall, and you will be the means of my escaping."

"Me?" Mrs. Jarsell used bad grammar in her astonishment; "how can I----"

"That is your affair," broke in Halliday, pouring out the coffee. "Why should I help you to escape?"

"Because you are a woman and not a fiend. Miss Armour is one, I admit, but I can see very plainly that you are a most unwilling accomplice."

"I am, I am," cried Mrs. Jarsell, vehemently; "years ago I was a decent woman, a good woman. She came into my life again and poisoned my existence. She worked on my jealousy and on my fear and----"

"I know; I know. She enabled you to get rid of your husband." "Ah!" Mrs. Jarsell reeled back as though she had been struck; "she told you that, did she?"

"She told me everything."

"Then you will never escape; she would never let you go free with the knowledge you have of her secrets. You are doomed. As to my husband," Mrs. Jarsell appeared to be speaking more to herself than to Dan, "he was a wicked and cruel wretch. He starved me, he beat me, he was unfaithful to me, and led me such a life as no woman could endure. Miss Armour showed me how to rid myself of him, when I was distraught with misery and passion. I thought it was sympathy with me that made her help me. It was not. All she desired was to gain some hold over me, and use my money for her own vile ends."

"You don't appear to love her," said Halliday, coolly. The woman closed the door, placed her back against it and clenched her hands in a cold fury. "I hate her; I loathe her; I detest her," she cried, in a guttural voice, evidently consumed with rage. "For years and years and years I have been her slave. After I killed my husband, under her directions--although I don't deny but what he deserved death--there was no retreat for me, as she could have, and would have, informed the police. I should have been hanged. She made use of her power to use my money in order to create this wicked society. It murders and slays and blackmails and----"

"I know; I know," said Dan, soothingly; "she told me all about it."

"Then you know how evil she is! I have had to commit crimes, from which my better self shrank, at her command."

"Such as the murder of Durwin," put in Dan, quickly. "That is only one out of many. Deeper and deeper I have sunk into the mire and now the end has come. I am glad of it."

"Why not turn king's evidence, and denounce this woman and her gang? Then you would be pardoned."

"There is no pardon for my wickedness," said Mrs. Jarsell, in a sombre tone. "I have sown, and I must reap as I have sown. It is too late. I know that your friend will come with the police. They will find the whole wicked lot of criminals here, which constitute the Society of Flies."

"Ah! those telegrams?"

"Yes. I sent off thirty last night, for now Penn and Curberry are dead there are just thirty members. Today all will come up, since the danger to all is so great. I sent the wires last night, and I am confident that the members have started for Sheepeak this morning. This afternoon everyone will be under this roof. All the worse for you." Dan quailed. "Does she really mean to torture me?" he asked nervously, and it was little to be wondered at that such a prospect did make him feel sick. "Yes, she does," rejoined Mrs. Jarsell, gloomily; "when the members find that there is no escape, they will be delighted to see the man who had brought this danger on them mutilated and done to death by inches."

"A pleasant set of people," muttered Dan, bracing himself to meet the worst, "but I think you would not care to see me tortured."

"No, I wouldn't. You are brave, and young, and clever, and handsome----"

"And," added Dan, quickly, thinking of a means to move her to help him. "I am to marry Lillian Moon. Surely you have some sympathy with me and with her?"

"Supposing I have; what can I do?"

"Help me to escape," said Dan, persuasively. "It's impossible," she growled, and went suddenly away, closing the door after her with a bang that sounded in Dan's ears like his death-warrant. All the same, with the courage of a brave nature, and the hopefulness inseparable from youth, he went on with his meal, hoping for the best. Mrs. Jarsell was moved by his plight; he saw that, and, deeply stained as she was with compulsory crimes, she might hope to atone for them by doing one good act. At the eleventh hour she might set him free, and undoubtedly she would think over what he had said. This woman, unlike the others, was not entirely evil, and the seeds of good in her breast might bring forth repentance and a consequent help. Dan knew that he was clinging to a straw, but in his present dilemma there was nothing else to cling to. After breakfast he lay down again, and again began to smoke. For hours he waited to hear his fate, sometimes stretched on his bed, sometimes seated in the chair and occasionally walking up and down the confined space of his cell. He could not disguise from himself that things were desperate. His sole hope of escape lay with Mrs. Jarsell, and that was but a slight one. Even though her remorse might wish to aid him, her terror of Queen Beelzebub might be too strong to let her move in the matter. Halliday was uncommonly brave and extraordinarily hopeful, yet the perspiration beaded his forehead, and he shivered at the prospect of torture. Without doubt he was in hell, and the devils presided over by the infernal queen were waiting to inflict pains and penalties on him. It terrified him to think that---- "But this won't do," said Dan to himself, as he heard the key grate in the lock, late in the afternoon. "I must pull myself together and smile. Whatever these beasts do to me, I must die game. But--but--Lillian." With a quiet smile he turned to greet Mrs. Jarsell, who did not look him in the face, nor did she even speak. With a gesture, he was invited to come out, and for the moment had a wild idea of escape as soon as he reached the upper portion of that wicked house. But the sight of the lancet in her hand prevented him from making a dash for liberty. He knew that the merest scratch would make him a corpse, so it was not worth while to risk the attempt. Only when he was at the door of the barbaric sitting-room he whispered to Mrs. Jarsell, "You will help me to escape. I know you will. Even now you are thinking of ways and means."

"Perhaps," she gasped in a low whisper; then hastily flung open the door and pushed him into the room. With that word of hope ringing in his ears, Halliday faced his judges with a smile on his lips. The room was filled with people, who greeted his entrance with a roar of anger. He was spat upon, struck at, kicked and shaken by those despairing creatures, whom he had brought to book. Queen Beelzebub, seated in her big chair, at the end of the apartment, smiled viciously when she saw his reception, but did not interfere for some moments. Then she waved her hand. "Let him be; let him be," she said, in her malicious, silvery voice; "you shall have all the revenge you desire. But let everything be done in order." Left alone by the furies, Halliday stood with his back to the door, and with Mrs. Jarsell on guard beside him. He glanced round at the pallid faces and thought that he had never seen such an assemblage of terror. There were old men and young men, mixed with women of the higher and lower classes. Some were well-dressed, while others were badly clothed; some were handsome and others were ugly. But one and all bore the mark of despair written on their white faces and in their agonized eyes. It was like a gathering of the damned and only the individual who had damned them, one and all, seemed to be unmoved. Queen Beelzebub appeared calm and unshaken, looking at her prisoner quietly and speaking in a tranquil manner. Dan found himself wondering if this creature was indeed a human being or a fiend. "We are all here," said Miss Armour, in a dignified manner, and, waving her hand again, this time to indicate the assembly, "this is the Society of Flies which you see face to face for the first and the last time. You have brought us together for an unpleasant purpose----"

"To torture and murder me, I suppose," said Halliday, with studied insolence, and bracing his courage with the memory of Mrs. Jarsell's whispered word. "No. That part of our business is pleasant," Queen Beelzebub assured him. "I look forward to enjoyment when I see you writhing in torment. But the unpleasant purpose is the disbanding of our society." A wail of terror arose from those present. Some dropped on their knees and beat the ground with their foreheads; others stood stiff and terror-struck, while a few dropped limply on the floor, grovelling in despair. Since all these people were criminals, who had inflicted death and sorrow on others, it was strange how they hated a dose of their own medicine. Even in the midst of his fears, Dan found himself wondering at the illogicality of the degenerate mob, who expected to do evil and yet enjoy peace. Then he remembered that cruelty always means cowardice, and no longer marvelled at the expression of dread and fear on every ghastly face. "How I propose to disband our society," went on Queen Beelzebub, quite unmoved by that agonized wail, "there is no need for you to know. It may be that we shall break up, and each one will go here, there, and the other place. It is certain that we cannot keep together since I have received news of the police being after us."

"Headed by Laurance."

"Exactly. Headed by your friend Laurance. I should like to punish him, but there is no time, so you will have to bear his punishment as well as your own, Mr. Halliday. What have you to say why we should not torture you and kill you, and force you to die by inches?" Fists were shaken, feet were stamped, and a dozen voices asked the same question. Dan looked round at his foes calmly, and shrugged his shoulders in contempt. There was a burst of jeering laughter. "You won't look like that," said Queen Beelzebub, significantly, "when----" she broke off with a dreadful laugh and glanced at the fire-place. There Dan saw irons of curious shape, pincers and files and tongs, and, what was worst of all, in the centre of the flames reddened a circle of steel. He could not help turning pale as he guessed that this would be placed on his head, and again he comforted himself with the memory that Mrs. Jarsell, even at the eleventh hour, might help him. When he changed color, there was a second burst of laughter, and Halliday glared fiercely around. "Are you human beings or fiends?" he asked, "to think of torturing me. Kill me if you will, but shame as men and women should prevent you mutilating a man who has done you no harm."

"No harm?" It was Queen Beelzebub who spoke, while her subjects snarled like ill-fed beasts. "You dare to say that when you have brought us to this pass?"

"I acted in the cause of law and order," said Dan, boldly. "We despise law and order."

"Yet you are now being brought to book by what you despise," retorted the prisoner, and again there came that unhuman snarl. "The more you speak in that way the worse it will be for you," said Miss Armour, coldly; "yet you can escape some tortures if you will tell us all how you came to learn the truth about us."

"I don't care a damn about your tortures," said Dan, valiantly, "and I will explain what you ask just to show that, clever as your organization is, it cannot escape discovery. Nor has it. You are all snared here like rats in a trap, and, should you venture out of this house, you will be caught by the authorities, to be hanged as you deserve." A howl of rage went up, and Queen Beelzebub waved her hand once more. "All in good time," she said, quietly; "let us hear what he has to explain."

"It was the Sumatra scent on the body of Sir Charles Moon which put me on the track," declared Dan, folding his arms. "I traced it to Penn, who told me a lie about it. I believed him at the moment and disbelieved him when I smelt the same perfume in this very room."

"Here?" questioned Miss Armour, and for the first time her face wore an expression of dismay, as if she had been caught napping. "Yes. If you remember, I spoke about your cards being scented. You told me a lie about it. But that clue connected you with Moon's murder. I watched you and I watched Mrs. Jarsell. I saw her face in a cinematograph which was taken on the day of the London to York race when Durwin was murdered."

"Oh!" Mrs. Jarsell gasped and moaned, and Dan could hear some of the men in impotent fury grind their teeth. Queen Beelzebub was as calm as ever. "Penn told me much when I was taking him for that flight in which I said I would throw him overboard unless he confessed. Then I was taken to the headquarters of your society in London, and again smelt the perfume. I believed that Queen Beelzebub was Mrs. Jarsell, and was astonished when I found Miss Armour played that part. Penn's confession was not all destroyed, and my friend Laurance has by this time shown what remains of it to the police."

"And the telegram which Curberry received?" demanded Queen Beelzebub. "Laurance sent that in vague terms so as to frighten Curberry. It did, and he committed suicide after declaring to me that he murdered Penn by your damned orders, Miss Armour. Then----"

"Thank you, we know the rest," she said in a quiet tone, which was infinitely sinister in its suggestion; "you followed me in the aeroplane, and smashed us both up."

"He broke my machines, the two of them," said a hoarse voice of wrath, and Dan looked sideways to see Vincent glaring at him furiously. "Well, you have fallen into your own trap," said Queen Beelzebub, savagely. "I caught you, and I hold you, and, after we have had a conference as to how you will be tortured, you will expiate your crimes."

"Crimes," echoed Dan; "that's a nice way to put the matter. I have done a service to the State by ridding the world of all you devils. You can't escape hanging, not one of you," and he looked defiantly round the room. "We shall all escape," said Queen Beelzebub, quietly; "those who think that they will not have no trust in me." She rose and stretched out her arms. "I have never failed you; never, never. I shall not fail you now. I swear that not a single one of you will suffer on the gallows." Apparently her sway over the society was great, and they believed that she could accomplish even impossibilities, for the faces of all cleared as if by magic. The look of dread, the expression of terror disappeared, and there only remained an uneasy feeling, as though none felt themselves quite safe until Queen Beelzebub performed her promise. For his part, Dan believed that the woman was lying, as he could not see how any could win free of the net which was even now being cast over the house. "You are a set of fools, as well as a pack of wolves," cried the young man, in a vehement manner; "the police know too much for you to escape them. My friend Laurance will lead them here; he knows this house; you are safely trapped, say what that woman will. Thieves, rogues, liars, murderers----"

"Lawyers, doctors, actors, soldiers," scoffed Queen Beelzebub; "they all belong to the Society of Flies and you can see them here, Mr. Halliday. Some of those ladies are in society; some are in shops; some are married, and others are not. But both men and women have acted for the good of the society, which I have founded, to give each and everyone what he or she desires."

"You are all devils," raged Dan, his wrath getting the better of his discretion; "red-handed criminals. The only decent one amongst you is Mrs. Jarsell."

"I am decent?" gasped Mrs. Jarsell, looking up, surprised. "Yes; because you were driven by that fiend," he pointed to the smiling Miss Armour, "to compulsory crimes. You feel remorse----"

"Does she?" cried Queen Beelzebub, gaily; "and what good does that do, my very dear Eliza, when you know what you have to do?" Mrs. Jarsell looked at her companion with a long and deadly look of hate, such as Dan had never thought a face was capable of expressing. "I loath and detest you," she said, slowly, "but for you I would have been a good woman. I have been driven to sin by you."

"And I shall still drive you," shouted Queen Beelzebub, furiously; "take that man away until we decide what tortures we will inflict on him. Then when he is dead and punished for his meddling, you will either do what I have commanded you to do, or you shall be tortured also!" The assembly, now quite certain that in some way their head would deliver them from the talons of the law, shouted joyfully, glad to think that two people would be done to death instead of one. Mrs. Jarsell smiled in a faint, bitter manner. "You shall be obeyed," she said, slowly; "come Mr. Halliday!"

"And say your prayers," cried Queen Beelzebub, as the door opened to let the pair out; "you'll need them"; and, as the door closed with Dan and Mrs. Jarsell on the outside, the young man heard again that cruel laughter. "They are all in there," whispered the woman, catching Dan's wrist and speaking hurriedly; "the men who captured you included. The house is quite empty outside that room. Come."

"Where will you take me?" inquired Dan, hanging back and wincing, for now his fate hung in the balance, indeed. "Outside; I am setting you free. Run away and probably you will meet your friend and the police. And pray for me; pray for me," she ended, vehemently. "Why not come also," said Dan, when he found himself at the entrance door of The Grange; "you are a good woman, and----"

"I am not good. I am wicked, and may God forgive me. But I am doing one decent thing, and that is to set you free, to marry Lillian Moon. When you leave this house, I shall do another decent deed."

"And that is?" Dan stepped outside, yet lingered to hear her answer. "You shall see. Tell the police not to come too near the house," and in a hurry she pushed him away and bolted the door. Halliday ran for all he was worth from that wicked dwelling. On the high road he saw a body of men approaching, and was certain that here were the police and Laurance coming to save him. Shouting with glee at his escape, he hastened towards them, when he heard a sullen heavy boom like distant thunder. He looked back at The Grange and saw a vast column of smoke towering into the sunlight. Then came a rain of debris. At last the Society of Flies was disbanded, for the house and its wicked inhabitants were shattered into infinitesimal fragments.

CHAPTER XXI

SUNSHINE

After the storm came the calm, and with the spring a realization of Mr. Halliday's hopes with regard to his future. Sir John Moon no longer objected to Dan as the husband of his niece, and was indeed profoundly thankful that she had escaped becoming Lady Curberry. The story of the Society of Flies and the wickedness of Queen Beelzebub and the blowing up of The Grange was a nine days wonder. The papers, for some weeks, were filled with little else, and *The Moment* almost doubled its circulation when the able pen of Mr. Frederick Laurance set forth the complete story. Halliday became quite a hero, as indeed he was, although he did not appreciate the rewards of his conduct. To be interviewed, to have his portrait, more or less unlike him, in dozens of illustrated papers, to receive offers from music-hall managers, and even proposals of marriage from various enthusiastic ladies, did not appeal to Dan. As soon as he could, he went out of London and took refuge in Sir John's country seat so as to escape publicity. Needless to say, Lillian was there, and Mrs. Bolstreath also. Laurance was due within seven days to be Dan's best man at the June wedding, and with him Mildred was coming at Lillian's special request. Once, twice, and again the owner of the house had heard the story of the late events, and also had read them more or less garbled in different newspapers. Yet he never wearied of the recital, and admired Halliday greatly for the part he had played. From objecting to Dan as a nephew-in-law, the baronet now urgently desired that he should make Lillian Mrs. Halliday. In fact, when he thought of what the young man had saved Lillian from, the uncle of the girl could not do enough for his estimable young friend. So Dan, having become famous, was about to become rich, but neither fame nor wealth appealed to him so much as the undoubted fact that he was on the eve of wedding the girl he adored. "And I think," said Lillian, holding on to Dan as if she feared to lose him, "that you and I would be as happy in a cottage as in a palace. Money is a nuisance, I think, dear."

"You say that because you have never experienced the want of it," said Dan, in a sententious manner. All the same he slipped his arm round the girl's slim waist, and kissed her for the pretty sentiment she had expressed relative to a poor but Arcadian existence. The happy pair, not yet joined in holy matrimony, but to be made one in seven days, were seated in the delightful garden of Sir John's house, which was situated in the pleasant county of Devon. They had strolled out after dinner, leaving Mrs. Bolstreath to chat with the baronet, who approved of the big, placid woman, and enjoyed her society. Lillian and Dan, however, liked to be in one another's company without any third person to spoil their pleasures and on this occasion--being humored as lovers--they were entirely alone. The garden sloped down to a yellow beach, which was the curve of a tiny bay, and under the orb of a brilliant May moon the waters of the vast sea murmured softly almost at their feet. There was a marble bench here, with a marble statue of Cupid near at hand, perched on a pedestal, so the spot was quite that which lovers would have chosen. Dan chose it because the screen of shrubs and trees quite shut off the nook they occupied from the many windows of the great house, and he could kiss Lillian when he wished, without any uneasy feeling that someone was looking on. It is quite unnecessary to say that he frequently availed himself of his privilege. The about-to-be bride fully approved of his ardor in this respect. "But you really must be serious," said Miss Moon, sedately, after the last embrace given out of compliment to her love-in-a-cottage sentiment. "I want to ask you a few questions."

"Ask what you will; I can deny you nothing."

"It's about the Society of Flies," hesitated the girl. "My dear," said Dan, patiently, and coaxing a loose leaf around his cigar, "I don't want to be disagreeable, but I am really tired of the Society of Flies."

"Only a few questions," said Lillian, nestling to his side, "and then we can forget all about the matter."

"That won't be easy for me to do," replied Mr. Halliday, rather grimly. "I can never forget what I suffered when I was expecting to be tortured by that fiend."

"Queen Beelzebub?"

"She could not have chosen a better name, my dear. I sometimes doubt if she was a human being at all."

"Poor, misguided woman," murmured Lillian, resting her head on Dan's shoulder. "Don't pity her, dear. She does not deserve your pity. Now, Mrs. Jarsell--I have always been sorry for her."

"So have I," said the girl, promptly; "she was very good to you, dear."

"Good is a weak way of expressing what I owe her," retorted Halliday; "think of what she saved me from."

"Perhaps Queen Beelzebub would not have tortured you, after all." Dan laughed incredulously. "I shouldn't have cared to have trusted to her mercy. I tell you, Lillian, as I have told you before, that already the implements of torture were being made ready. They would have crowned me with a red-hot circlet of steel, and pinched my flesh with red-hot pincers, and----"

"Don't, oh, don't." Lillian turned pale. "It is really too dreadful. And to think that I was with Bolly at Mrs. Pelgrin's, quite ignorant of the peril you were in. I wish I had been with you."

"I am glad you were not. My one feeling of thankfulness was that you had escaped being hurt in any way. I didn't mind dying so long as you were all right, my darling, although I much prefer being alive and here. Lillian, my dear, don't cry; it's all over, weeks ago."

"I--I--I can't--can't help it," sobbed the girl, clinging to him; "it is all so dreadful. When Mr. Laurance came that day with the police and said you were at The Grange, I thought I should have died."

"There, there," Dan soothed her, as he would have soothed a fretful child; "it is all over and done with. By the way, how was Freddy so certain that I was at The Grange? He never quite explained his certainty."

"Well, dear," said Miss Moon, drying her eyes with Dan's handkerchief, "when he did not hear from you in London, he went down to Blackheath with Inspector Tenson of Hampstead. They saw the local inspector and called at Lord Curberry's house, after what Mr. Laurance told. But already a policeman had been summoned by the servants. Lord Curberry was dead of poison, and they found his confession, saying how he had taken it because he believed that his connection with the Society of Flies was found out. Then the servants explained how Queen Beelzebub had come in an aeroplane----"

"They did not call her Queen Beelzebub--the servants I mean," said Dan, who had heard the explanation before but was glad to hear it again told in Lillian's soft voice. "No; they did not know who she was, as she was cloaked and veiled. But they told Mr. Laurance that you had declared this veiled lady had murdered Lord Curberry--that wasn't true, you know."

"True enough in one sense," interrupted Dan, quickly, "seeing that she drove him to suicide. Well?"

"Well, then, Mr. Laurance guessed that she was Queen Beelzebub and wondered where you were. He went to the shed where you kept your aeroplane and heard that you had followed her. Those at the shed thought that it was a race." "It was," said Dan, grimly, again, "and I won."

"Mr. Laurance guessed that you had followed her all the way to Sheepeak, although he fancied, and indeed hoped, that both aeroplanes had broken down. He dreaded lest you should get into trouble at Sheepeak."

"Which I certainly did, although not quite in the way Freddy expected." Lillian laughed at the memory of his escape, and rubbed her soft face on the sleeve of his coat. "Mr. Laurance told the police all about the matter, and they wished to telegraph to Thawley, so that the police there might go over to Sheepeak. But Mr. Laurance stopped them, as he fancied you might have been taken captive by Queen Beelzebub, and that if such a move was made, she might hurt you."

"She intended to hurt me very severely. And then Freddy heard from the police about those numerous telegrams all in the same words, calling thirty people to Sheepeak. It was the similarity of the messages that made the telegraph authorities suspicious and, when the police came to ask--knowing where Queen Beelzebub lived from Freddy--they were shown the telegrams."

"But by that time all those who got the telegrams had come north," said Lillian, quite excited; "they all went up by the early train."

"Yes, and the police, with Freddy, followed, delaying action until such time as they thought they could collar the whole gang. By jove, they just came in time. Freddy was a fool to tell you that I was in The Grange."

"He was not quite certain, and only thought so because the wrecked aeroplanes were found in the field near the house. Oh, Dan," Lillian put her arms round her lover's neck, "Mr. Laurance told me how thankful he was when he saw you running along the road and knew that you had escaped."

"He might have been thankful also that I caused him and the body of police to halt," said Dan, quickly; "if they had not, everyone would have been blown up. As it was, I very nearly got smashed by the falling sticks and stones and what not. There must have been tons of dynamite in the cellars of The Grange."

"Who do you think put it there, Dan?"

"Queen Beelzebub, of course. She said that she had made everything ready against possible discovery, and warned poor Mrs. Jarsell that she would have to commit a last crime. Crime, by Jove. Why the best day's work the woman ever did was to blow up that gang of devils." "I suppose Mrs. Jarsell did blow up the house, Dan?"

"Of course she did. Her heart softened for some reason, and she pushed me out of danger. Then she must have gone straight down to the cellar, and set a light to the stored dynamite. The explosion happened so quickly after I was free that I am sure she acted in that way. It was certainly efficacious, for not one of the blackguards, either men or women, remained alive to be hanged."

"Well, that was a good thing," said Miss Moon, with a shudder; "you know that their relatives would have been disgraced." Dan nodded. "Quite so, and the names have never become public. This person and that person and the other person disappeared from various neighborhoods and from various family circles. But, when the relatives read about the explosion in Hillshire and Freddy's brilliant account of that infernal society, they made a pretty good guess as to what had happened to the disappearing party. Very few people gave information to the police that their relatives or friends had disappeared. Tenson was rather annoyed, as he wanted to make a big fuss over the matter."

"I don't see what bigger fuss could have been made, Dan. Why, the papers were filled with nothing else for weeks."

"All the same, Tenson wanted the names of those who belonged to the gang, and people declined to gives names of those who had disappeared from their midst. We know that Curberry belonged to the gang, and Penn; also Mrs. Jarsell, Vincent, and Queen Beelzebub. But only one or two other names came to light in print."

"I think," said Lillian, thoughtfully, "that so many well-connected people were mixed up in the matter that everything was hushed up as much as was possible." "H'm," said Halliday, throwing away the butt end of his cigar; "it is not unlikely that a hint was given in high quarters that no more need be said than was absolutely necessary. Heigh ho!" He rose and stretched; "I am weary of the business. Come down and walk on the beach, dear, and let us talk about ourselves." Lillian was only too glad and the lovers descended the marble steps which led down gently to the sands. The moon glowed, pure silver in a sky of the darkest blue, with the old moon in her radiant arms. In dark ripples, fringed with creaming white, the wavelets murmured on the sands, and at either side of the bay great cliffs bulked, huge and densely black. It was a night of soft winds and glorious moonshine, fit for Romeo and Juliet to converse about love, yet Lillian still harped on the prosaic facts of the dangers she and Dan had escaped. Perhaps it was natural, for they had assuredly passed through a most trying time. "Why did Queen Beelzebub found such a wicked society?" asked Lillian. "She wanted power and perverted her talents to base ends in order to gain it, my dear. Well, well, she has gone to her account, so we need say no more about her. She was a clever woman, but a fiend incarnate."

"And Mrs. Jarsell?"

"Poor soul. She was but an example of the influence of a strong mind on a weak one. I think she loathed the whole business thoroughly, but she had gone too far to retreat."

"Do you think Mrs. Pelgrin or her nephew knew anything of the matter?"

"No, I don't," said Halliday, very decidedly, "although Tenson had his suspicions of George. Mrs. Jarsell, who was used as a blind by Miss Armour, in her turn used George as a blind to say, if necessary, how seldom she went to town. I forgot to tell you, Lillian, that the police discovered that both Mrs. Jarsell and the leader of the society used frequently to motor for miles and miles to different stations further down the line in order to reach London without remark being made. Mrs. Jarsell only used the Thawley Station so as to get George Pelgrin's evidence that she scarcely ever went to town. In that way, of course, it was next door to impossible to connect two harmless old ladies with these many dreadful murders."

"It was only your cleverness about that scent which formed the link," said Lillian, proud of Dan's characteristic sharpness, "and by using the biplane to travel to Blackheath, when Mr. Durwin was murdered, Mrs. Jarsell was able to get Mrs. Pelgrin to prove an alibi."

"Oh, it was chance that showed Mrs. Jarsell's complicity on that occasion, my dear," said Dan, modestly; "but that we went into that animated picture entertainment, we should never have known she was at Blackheath. I suppose Miss Armour did not feel equal to committing that particular crime, so sent Mrs. Jarsell to carry out the job."

"Miss Armour was never really paralyzed, I suppose?"

"No. She pretended to be when anyone paid a visit. Nor do I believe that either she or Mrs. Jarsell were so old as they pretended to be. What a queer thing human nature is," went on Dan, thoughtfully; "here was Miss Armour, who could have lived a very pleasant and comfortable life, plunging herself and that miserable woman into dangerous crime just for the love of power. One would have thought that she would have liked to show her power publicly, but she was quite content to be a secret despot. I suppose it gave her a certain amount of pleasure, though it is hard for a simple person like I am to see where it came in."

"But her power could not have been exercised amidst public applause, Dan, seeing what it meant."

"Quite so. The police would soon have ended her career had her infernal sway been known."

"Do you think," asked Lillian, after a pause, "that the members of the society expected that explosion?"

"No," answered Halliday, very promptly. "I do not, else, in spite of the danger, I believe the half, if not the whole, of them would have run out even into the arms of the police to be hanged in due course. But they seemed to have an enormous belief in Queen Beelzebub, who was undoubtedly as clever as her father the devil. The members expected that in some way she would manage to save them. But all the time--as I guessed, although I could not understand what she was aiming at--she was preparing some way of getting rid of the lot, herself included. She must have summoned them to a pretended conference so as to house all under one roof and then fire the mine. I expect she filled the cellars of *The Grange* ages ago with dynamite, and arranged with Mrs. Jarsell to explode the mine. Of course, where Mrs. Jarsell got the better of Queen Beelzebub was that she did not give her the pleasure of revenging herself on me, and fired the dynamite unexpectedly. While Miss Armour and her demons were thinking how to torture me, they all went--well, we won't say where they went. But there wasn't enough left of them to form a single human being."

"And there is an immense hole in the ground where The Grange stood," said Lillian, with awe; "Mr. Laurance told me, and Mildred also."

"I daresay that hole will form the basis of a legend in years to come," was Dan's reply, "and a very picturesque story can be made out of the material supplied by that infernal woman. She was as wicked and cruel and callous as that Ezzelin who played dice with the arch-fiend. By the way, Lillian, I suppose Mildred Vincent was very much cut up over the death of her uncle."

"No, she was not. Of course, she regretted his awful end, and that he should have been so wicked, but he was never kind to her and she had not much love for him. I don't know," ended Miss Moon, reflectively, "if we can be sure that he ever committed a crime."

"Yes, he did," declared Halliday, quickly; "every single member of that society had to commit a crime in order to belong to the gang. Vincent, I truly believe, was not a bad man, as his sole idea was a craze for inventing aeroplanes. But Queen Beelzebub, wanting him for her purpose, no doubt inveigled him into committing himself as a criminal, as she inveigled Mrs. Jarsell and Curberry."

"Poor Lord Curberry," sighed Lillian; "he is more to be pitied than blamed. I don't think the young man who holds the title now cared that he died."

"Can you expect him to?" asked Dan, sceptically, "seeing he has got a title and a lot of money. In a clean way, too, for Curberry consented to the murder of two relatives so as to secure what he wanted. No, Lillian, it is your kind heart that makes you pity Curberry, but he was not a good man. No decent fellow would have belonged to that association of demons. But I think we have discussed the subject threadbare. Let us talk of more pleasant matters."

"About Mr. Laurance and his marriage?" cried Lillian, gaily. "Well, yes, although being selfishly in love, I would much rather discuss our own. Freddy will be able to marry Mildred now since you have given him enough money to start a newspaper. It is very good of you."

"I don't think so," said Miss Moon, as they began to climb the steps again, and return to the house. "Mr. Laurance helped you to learn who killed my dear father, and deserved a reward, as you did. I gave him money and----"

"And you gave me yourself, so I have been rewarded very richly. Well, Freddy will make a very good proprietor and editor of a newspaper, and Mildred can help him to make it a success. All's well that ends well."

"And you are quite--quite happy, dear?"

"Quite, quite. Only I fear," Dan sighed, "that some people will call me a fortune hunter, seeing that I, without a penny, am marrying a rich woman." Lillian stopped in the path up to the house and took hold of the lapels of Dan's coat to shake him. "How can you talk such nonsense," she said reproachfully; "why, after your portrait and an account of all you have done appearing in the papers, you could have married half a dozen women."

"But none so sweet as you, dear," said Halliday, kissing her, for her lips were temptingly near his own; "well, I must not despise my good fortune. But what can I give you in return, Miss Crœsus?"

"A promise," said Lillian, earnestly, "that you will not go up any more in those horrid flying-machines. I shall always be afraid of losing you if you do; you know that quite well."

"Let me take a tiny little flight occasionally," coaxed Dan, gaily. "Well, yes, on condition that you take me. If there is an accident, we can be smashed up together. Don't argue;" she placed her hand on his mouth; "that is the only way in which I shall agree to your flying."

"Wilful woman will do what she wants," said Halliday, resignedly, and tucked Lillian's arm beneath his own; "hello, there is Sir John and Mrs. Bolstreath on the terrace. They seem to be very happy together."

"So happy," whispered Lillian in his ear, "that I believe----" She pursed up her lips and looked unutterable things. "Well," said Dan, laughing, "it would not be at all a bad thing for Sir John to make Mrs. Bolstreath Lady Moon. She can nurse him and amuse him and bury him in due course. What a heap of marriages; you and I; Freddy and Mildred; Sir John and Mrs. Bolstreath. See; she's waving her hand to us. Let us go inside, as it's growing a trifle chilly."

"Hark," said Lillian, raising her finger, and Dan listened to hear the wild, delicious strain of a nightingale singing from a distant thicket. "It sings of my love for you," he whispered, "and of your love for me. What other than such a song can express our feelings, darling."

"This," said Lillian, and kissed him fondly.

"Clever girl!"

THE END

Milton Keynes UK
Ingram Content Group UK Ltd.
UKHW010849010724
444982UK00005B/466